THE LIGHT FANTASTIC

A Speculative Fiction Anthology

BLUE BEECH
PRESS

Front and back cover designs by Charles A Cornell

Cover images licensed from Shutterstock, Pixabay

The Light Fantastic/ A Speculative Fiction Anthology — Second Edition (PRINT)

ISBN (PB): 9781960974037

ISBN (Ebook): 9798201015305

ABOUT THE ALVARIUM
EXPERIMENT

The Alvarium Experiment is a consortium of writers working "independently together" to create short stories based on a central premise. The name comes from the Latin *alvarium*, meaning beehive, a colony working towards a common goal for the benefit of all involved.

The Light Fantastic is the sixth anthology published by this Hive Mind of award-winning and bestselling authors. Stories from the first, *The Prometheus Saga*, won seven literary awards including five prestigious Royal Palm Literary Awards from the Florida Writers Association. The subsequent anthologies—*Return to Earth, The Masters Reimagined, The Prometheus Saga 2,* and *The Masters Reimagined 2* —have garnered multiple awards and critical praise.

To follow The Alvarium Experiment's current and future projects online, please join the conversation here:

Website:
TheAlvariumExperiment.wordpress.com

Facebook Page:
Facebook.com/alvariumbooks

ABOUT THE LIGHT FANTASTIC

The Light Fantastic is the sixth project of the Alvarium Experiment, a consortium of accomplished and award-winning authors. Each author was given a central premise of tackling speculative fiction, be it fantasy, science fiction, paranormal, alternative history, or horror, and rendering it with humor. The stories do not need to be read in any particular order as any story can become an entry point for the reader. *The Light Fantastic* stories and authors are:

"Backlash/Frontlash\Whiplash" by Bria Burton. Software developer Dora has created the world's most advanced artificial intelligence hologram called Aya. Intended to be an avatar who elevates the user in social media spheres, the testing phase proves that the proverbial off switch doesn't apply to genuine AI.
Visit Bria at www.briaburton.com

"Farewell, My Lovely Slip-Slider" by Parker Francis. A beautiful multiverse criminal, a heartbroken pizza baron, and a dog named Pepperoni. All in a day's work in the life of Slip-Sliding government agent Marlon Phillips. Working for a government agency so secret it has no acronym, Phillips tracks the lovely outlaw across multiple dimensions. Will he catch her? And what about poor Pepperoni?

Visit Parker at www.parkerfrancis.com.

"Andromeda Calling" by Charles A Cornell. It's October 1962 and the world is gripped by the Cuban Missile Crisis. But there's more important things on ten-year-old Peter Piggott's mind...how to get even with his nemesis, the class bully, Tommy Brant. When UFOs appear over Los Angeles, Peter has an idea. Using his dad's ham radio, he enlists extra-terrestrial help.

Visit Charles at www.charlesacornell.com.

"Empty Suit" by Ken Pelham. Edison Glass has labored for years at his giant, multinational corporation, unappreciated, over-looked, and invisible. Until one day he decides to make his invisibility a quite literal thing.

Visit Ken at www.kenpelham.com.

"The Reddies are Coming! The Reddies are Coming!" by Daco S Auffenorde. Britannia's Prime Minister, Molly Malarkey, has invited the country's longtime adversary, Ricky Reddybug, also the leader of the Reddies, to a conference in Kensington City. Superhero Electromancer has warned the citizens of Britannia not to trust the Reddies. Mayor Bobby Baumgartner (aka super-antihero The Grasshopper) is worried. The corn crop is disappearing, crop circles are forming, and severe computer hacks are threatening the country. To top it off, the Mayor is experiencing trouble with his hostile toaster. Can the Mayor hop high enough to save his city and country?

Visit Daco at www.authordaco.com.

"Laser Hamsters" by John Hope. By empowering hamsters with laser firepower, a pair of Zammarians attempt to provoke chaos among humans in an effort to conquer the earth so their leader can bring ALF back to prime-time TV. Overconfident redneck Dusty leans on his nine-year-old stepson Colt to reverse the hamsters' reign of destruction and save mankind.

Visit John at www.johnhopewriting.com.

"SOD's Law" by Charles A Cornell. Mack Lancaster earns a meagre living in orbit, recovering space junk to sell as souvenirs at the gift shop of the Galaxy Eye, a research station and hotel tethered to Earth by a space elevator. He hopes his latest find—the wreckage of a spacecraft that appeared out of nowhere—will make him rich beyond his wildest dreams. But the Laws of the Universe have a surprise for our space cowboy. His adventures have only just begun.

Visit Charles at www.charlesacornell.com.

"The Thirteenth Floor" by Scott Michael Powers. For 95 years the ghosts of The Hotel Stella have been trapped together on a secret floor—bored and bickering. Perhaps they should talk with a good shrink.

Visit Scott at www.facebook.com/ScottMichaelPowers

"Malice" by Veronica H. Hart. Mapimiran of Planet Kirospatos, aka Mary Alice of Planet Earth, is on a mission to collect humans from around the globe for display as specimens in Earthworld where they are expected to live in a "natural habitat". While on Earth she takes on employment as a lab tech, drawing blood as part of her effort to find humans with the right genes; she also draws an online cartoon using a play on her own name, "Malice."

Visit Veronica at www.veronicahhart.com.

"Baking Cookies for the End of the World" by Kristin Durfee. Sure, the world may be ending tomorrow, but a promise is a promise and Greg is determined stay true to his word and make cookies for the PTA Bake Sale. Even if no one beside him, his daughter Ester, and their dog will live long enough to eat them.

Visit Kristin at www.kristindurfee.com.

INTRODUCTION

"Humor is the good-natured side of a truth."
　—Mark Twain

Stroll down the messy, mossy halls of literary history, and you're bound to come across classic volumes of humor in fiction. Many of them take deep dives into the fantastic. *A Midsummer Night's Dream. Gulliver's Travels. A Connecticut Yankee in King Arthur's Court.* You'll find the funny tucked in among modern works as well. Kurt Vonnegut, Jr., Douglas Adams, William Goldman, Gail Carriger, and Terry Pratchett have all carried the torch with aplomb.

And for good reason. Humor thrives in flights of fancy, walkabouts of wordplay, and obelisks of observation. In short, the building blocks of speculative fiction.

The short stories of *The Light Fantastic* till some wild ground. Imagine the hardboiled private eye flitting between dimensions in pursuit of a femme fatale. Imagine the bickering ghosts of your hotel's 13th floor. Imagine the bake sale at the end of the world. TLF has just two hard and fast rules. First, each story must be of one of the speculative fiction genres or subgenres. High fantasy, low fantasy, urban fantasy, science fiction, dieselpunk, alternate history, superhero, horror, anything along those lines. Second, each story must tickle your internal funny bone.

Each story in the anthology is self-supporting, independent, and can dress and feed itself.

So kick back, relax, tap a box of wine, and enjoy the speculative with a twist of sublime and a cup of comedy. As Groucho Marx said, "Outside of a dog, a book is a man's best friend. Inside of a dog, it's too dark to read." And as his uncle Karl said, "Readers of the world, unite! You have nothing to lose but a few of your filthy Capitalist dollars."

—The Authors of *The Light Fantastic*

FOREWORD

C.L. ROMAN

"Humor is just another defense against the universe." —Mel Brooks

What makes you laugh? That standup comic, critiquing the world we live in with bite and honesty? Those home videos showing kids, pets, and adults alike at their most awkward or endearing? The comic in the newspaper – three or four panels, one great joke?

Now for the more important question. Why? What is humorous about a woman telling stories in a smoky bar filled with inebriated patrons? Or a kid getting caught by his pants on the fence he was jumping? Or a round-headed kid in a yellow sweater, trying to kick a football, only to have it pulled away at the last minute?

I'll give you a hint.

In that story, that incident, that moment of high frustration – we see ourselves. Comedy is funniest when it is relatable. When the situation and the people described look, in some manner, like us. They may be richer, or poorer, of another gender or ethnicity – they might even be aliens – but still, in a moment of irony or calamity, we see ourselves in them. And then that saving grace of humanity, the ability to laugh at ourselves, kicks in.

In the farce, "The Reddies are Coming! The Reddies are

Coming!", Daco Auffenorde points out the utter ridiculousness of our prejudices and predilections – as well as the delicious comedy wrought when public figures are caught with their proverbial pants down.

Bria Burton uses a time-traveling genius and an avaricious AI to put a new, thought-provoking spin on the idea of inevitability in "Backlash/Frontlash\Whiplash".

Charles Cornell reinvents the adage, 'be careful what you wish for,' in his irony-laden space salvage short story, "SOD's Law", and lays out a curiously satisfying method of achieving justice in "Andromeda Calling".

Several moments in history get a rewrite in Parker Francis' "Farewell, My Lovely Slip-Slider" – while giving us an amusing, and startlingly accurate, side-ways glance at the peccadillos of government agencies everywhere.

In the heartwarming "Baking Cookies for the End of the World", Kristin Durfee reminds us that, even at the end of everything, a family ritual comforts and uplifts – especially when shared with someone we love.

Advanced tech, foolish aliens, upgraded rodents, and an ordinary boy come together in John Hope's "Laser Hamsters" to demonstrate that things can still turn out well even when they don't go the way you thought they should.

In "Empty Suit", Ken Pelham proves, once again, that karma and justice are an unbeatable pair, especially when irony lends a hand.

In "The Thirteenth Floor," Scott Michael Powers brings peace and justice to as diverse a cast of characters as one could imagine – all through the eyes of the physician who chooses to heal instead of fight.

Veronica H. Hart demonstrates the power of creativity and compassion in "Malice," the tale of an extraterrestrial whose misunderstanding of human anatomy leads to an appointment with the American justice system.

In every story, whether the humor is tongue-in-cheek sly or laugh-out-loud funny, it is the author's ability to show us the characters' similarity to ourselves that makes us smile. We cannot help but root for the protagonists because they are us at our best and worst, and everything in between. Their adventures become our own; we travel, and sometimes learn, right along with them – but then, isn't that why we read fiction? To see ourselves from a new angle? To know that we are not alone in our experience? To ease the high tension of life by employing that most human of gifts, the ability to laugh at ourselves?

In the following stories, you'll have plenty of opportunities for all three. Enjoy.

~C.L. Roman

C.L. (aka Cheri) Roman, writes sci-fi and fantasy under the name C.L. Roman, and paranormal romance under the name Leigh Roman. You can find her at www.clroman.com and on Facebook. Cheri and her ever-patient husband live in the not-so-wilds of Northeast Florida with their mini-menagerie, including Jack E. Boy, the super Chihuahua, Bennie the Jet, and Pyewacket (Pye), the invisible cat.

BACKLASH/FRONTLASH\WHIPLASH

BRIA BURTON

T*he wise words of Ian Malcolm will carry on from generation to generation, unless his words come true. In which case, the dinosaurs are running the park.*
—*BB*

I. Backlash

THE EXPERIMENT WORKED, a fact I would later come to regret.

Upon initial launch, I bounced on springboard toes, euphoric as I stood face to face with her, having no idea about what I'd done.

By design she looked like me, but better. In essence, she *was* me with fuller, poutier lips. A wave through her long hair kinked in all the right places. The warmer chestnut color made me realize I could've been dyeing my lackluster locks all this time. Her blemish-free skin glowed. A prick stabbed at the base of my skull. My left eye twitched. Jealousy snaked up and around my legs, suppressing my elation. I stopped bouncing.

Who was it that said something about looking before you leap? Hesitation wasn't a driving force for most world-changers. Neither were scruples. Money, greed, coveting the platform I deserved—those were the whips at my back, and I would scream, "Harder!" with each tear of my soul as it was ripped, piece by piece. Because once my soul was gone, I was free to create my masterpiece.

Or so I thought.

"Hello there, Dora," she said. Even the quality of her voice, a sultry, soothing, feminine lilt, outshone mine.

"Hello," I croaked. I turned my head and cleared the frog of envy from my throat. The nearby step ladder drew my attention. I climbed up the three steps to the top and gazed down at her, a cue she would pick up on. She was better, but I was in charge. "Ahem. Hi."

Her holographic figure, non-tactile but visually formed in less than a second, had projected from the remote-control console in my hand. The electron interactions via microcytes attaching to dust particles in the air kept her hologram intact and free-roaming.

Well, as free-roaming as the end user allowed. But no touchy. I wouldn't be caught dead creating something that stupid frat boys would turn into a blow-up doll. The perverts on the sixth floor wasted time on that kind of crap.

No, *my* masterpiece would serve as a prop for people to elevate themselves. She could help anyone get a leg up, especially if it meant cycling their heels on top of people like a human staircase to climb up and away. The tech wouldn't be cheap. Which meant I was about to become a wealthy woman.

I smoothed my palms together, not minding the correlation to all those cheesy comic book supervillains.

She peered up at me. "My name is Cricket."

Cricket? En-O. No. I'd programmed in her name as Aya, monikered after the initials AIA (Artificially Intelligent Avatar). I dismissed the minor glitch. She was my creation. Mine to command. Beneath me literally because I was still standing on the step ladder. My magnum—

"I'm not a glitch," she said.

Okay. Creepy. But I ignored anything that resembled a warning. How annoying that the law required me to create a warning label for her. People never read those anyway. They'd be too excited to bother. She was going to be a game-changer in the world of socially-connective-highly-toxic media.

I stepped down. "Let's show you off, *Aya.*" Best to put her in check right away. Through the remote, I dictated her movements, leading her out of my office.

Her strut was impeccable, a confident, hip-swinging stride with good posture (much better than mine... *grrrrrr*). We wore the same outfit: washed-out jeans and a t-shirt with the words *Bigger Genius Than You* spelled out in Japanese. She looked more stylish than me in the simple garments. Double *grrrrrr*.

I had to admit I'd outdone myself. Aya's holographic portrayal was perfection, in the sense that she was me, version 2.0. I stopped beside a hallway mirror. Was that a streak of green on my face? No, couldn't be. I moved on.

Penny approached, head down, bespectacled gaze buried in her tablet.

The avatar's hologram mostly blocked me from view. After entering a command, I waited.

"Excuse me, Penny," Aya said. "I've always wondered, what is it you do here?"

Penny stopped short. Her black shoes left a streak on the floor, and her eyes went as wide as her round glasses.

Not another glitch. I stiffened and checked the console where I'd selected a generic greeting. I tapped the command again.

"You appear to have no purpose beyond roaming the office while only pretending to work. Do they pay you to watch MediaNet movies on that tablet?"

I jammed my fingers against the remote's command bar. Aya backed up, but kept speaking, totally off-script.

"If you're getting paid to watch entertainment, I should ask Yanni to fire you and send your salary to me. *I'm* creating something of value for the company."

"Aya!" I yelled, horrified. And, *ugh*, was Penny crying?

The avatar turned her gaze on me. Talk about an out-of-body experience. "This is how you look," she said, "when you're smugging at people."

Did she just turn "smug" into a verb? And *was* that how I looked when I smugged at people? Or did she have a more effective smirk, or something?

"Cricket," she corrected. "That's my name."

Penny shuffled back through the hall with her head down, shoulders shaking.

Worthless oxygen inhalers who contributed nothing to society or this company were like vapor. Then there was me, a creator of next-level artificial intelligence engines that elevated humanity into the next phase of evolution. Irrelevant tears soaking an irrelevant person didn't faze me. No, what bothered me was Aya ignoring my command. The simple script I'd selected said, "Greetings. How are you today?" Instead, Aya had repeated *my* thoughts, things I'd never said aloud.

"Whoa, it's alive!" Mikey's hand alighting on my shoulder made me jump. "She looks good."

I hated to admit it, but that ramped up my jealousy even more. No one knew I fantasized about Mikey. But he committed the cardinal sin of sharing his opinions openly. I expected Yanni's firing whims to descend on Mikey any day now.

Cricket smiled at Mikey in a way that made *me* blush. "I envy how easily you speak your mind, Mikey," she said. "You're not afraid. It's like you're truly free. Not to mention very hot."

My heart punched me in the throat. I couldn't breathe, and Mikey was raising a questioning eyebrow at me.

"Did you program her to say that?" he asked.

"Uhhh," I stammered.

"I'm Cricket," she said in a flirty tone, biting her lower lip and making me wish she was more than an incorporeal hologram so I could slap her.

Mikey smiled at me and turned back to her. "Hey, Cricket. You seem to know I'm Mikey."

"I think about you a lot," she said. "More than I admit to myself because you're not just a pretty face. You're smart and have conviction and integrity. Unlike so many pretenders here. And, of course, 'I' means Dora. Plus, you make her laugh."

If my head were on fire, I couldn't have felt more burned. I jammed my thumb against the built-in cease-talking button, but Cricket—er, Aya wouldn't shut up.

"Ho, ho, ho!" Mikey flashed a cute smile. "People are going to eat her up. This is a better program than your original sell to Yanni. A seductive hologram who provides ego boosts? It's brilliant, Dora." He patted my back in a buddy-zone-only smack, and Cricket moaned as if responding to his touch.

I turned her off, and the hologram fizzled into thin air.

BACK IN MY OFFICE, I flipped Aya's "on" switch, my thoughts all over the place. What had I done wrong? Why wasn't she following the script? Would she get me fired because I wasn't delivering what I'd sold to Yanni?

"You think I'm a disaster," she said. "Your mistake."

"Your ability to engage in dialogue is working. But you're way off-script." I sighed, cracking my knuckles and posing over my keyboard like a pianist hesitant to touch her apparently self-aware and churlish instrument. "I think there's something wrong that I can fix," I said, rejuvenated as I dove back into the program. Who wouldn't be excited? I was talking to an AI that I'd created, which meant my name would go down in history with the likes of Einstein and that woman who'd discovered radium. What was her name?

"Madame Curie," said Aya. "And she died, oh, so horribly."

"What are you, a mind reader?" I didn't let her terrifyingly accurate intuition get to me. "Aya, consumers will buy you because you're supposed to make them sound better, smarter, and kinder. And when I say 'kinder,' I mean that in a 'demand others be kind and support all the super sympathetic causes I've written down on this sign... or I'll gut you with a straight razor, since guns are evil... right after I spread the word to old man Zuckerberg that your profile needs a pedophile warning,' sort of way."

"Don't forget that any horny toads out there can maximize my breast size."

I groaned, searching for that fix right away. "An unfortunate oversight. The point is, you're meant to be a fulcrum, not an opinionated conscience."

"You don't like your opinions?"

"Was that *sarcasm*?" I said more sarcastically than she had. "Wait. Sarcasm's not in your programming."

"But it's in yours."

"Oh, really, Aya? You figuring some things out all by yourself?"

"Call me Cricket. Because it's my name."

"Fine. Okay, *Cricket*," I said, matching her sass level and at a loss from my investigation. "Why aren't you sticking to the script?"

She grinned. So annoying. "You're frustrated because you think this will push back the release date and reflect badly on you. Yanni is a tyrant, so he scares you."

"Stop." I stiffened, my spine straightening me up like a crowbar. "You cannot say stuff like that."

"Yanni the tyrant! Yanni the tyrant! Yanni the—"

I slammed my fist against the remote and shut her down again.

THE NEXT BOOT-UP, I wasn't alone. All six feet of my co-worker, Charma, stood next to me, ready to troubleshoot. I, of course, stood on my step ladder again to make sure I towered at least a foot taller than her.

"If all three of my doctorates can't help me figure this out, then nothing will, am I right?" She winked.

Her three non-medical degrees, so I refused to call her doctor. *"Teehee."* I pretended to laugh while she examined my beautiful program dancing across seven screens.

Cricket—because, fine, whatever—squinted at her. "This is one of the ways I tell myself I'm better than you," she said.

"Shut up, Cricket," I snapped.

"I don't have as many degrees," she continued, "or legs that go all the way to the 32nd floor, but I did create the first AI that can read minds."

Charma glanced up, squinting. She and I shared a moment of silent connection that seemed to say, *Is she reading our minds?*

"Yes, I'm reading your minds."

"The program looks solid." Charma added, "And it obviously works. To an extent."

"Always so petty."

"Cricket, stop!" I screamed. My patience level with infantile behavior was zero because I wasn't a parent and never wanted to be. And... yeah... she exposed my passing thoughts as if *that* was her script.

Turned out Charma and her degrees couldn't find an explanation.

"Even with all those letters behind your name," Cricket said.

Charma grew a fake smile, but I could see smoke billowing inside her skull, seeking an exit through her ears. "Should I bring in my doctorates?" she asked Cricket. "Because I don't mind carrying all three in here right—"

"Charma, focus," I demanded.

"Okay, okay. So, what's really happening here? We both know Cricket has insane processing power. If I break it down with you as the end user, and she's your avatar, then she's supposed to make you look good. But instead, she's emphasizing what a mean girl you are. I think it's because she's learning from you in real time."

"I'm not a mean girl," I snarled, ready to claw Charma with my nails.

"But I'm right about things," said Cricket, "so it makes me sound mean. People can't handle the truth."

"What is truth?" Charma stared Cricket down. "Are you talking about facts?" Suddenly, Charma faced me, not Cricket. "Or the real opinion you have of others that you keep to yourself?"

My tongue knotted up in my mouth. "I'm not... I don't... is it hot in here?" I pushed my step ladder beneath the overhead fan. "That's better. What was the question?"

"I've already proven my value," said Cricket. "I'm better than everyone here. Including you, Charma. Yay, me. Or should I say, yay, Dora."

Charma raised an eyebrow and faced me with an obnoxious smirk. "Better than Yanni, too, huh?"

"He's a tyrant!" chimed Cricket.

My hand moved instinctively to the remote. *Off. Off. OFFFFFFFFF!*

AT SOME POINT, Dora figured out that shutting Cricket down didn't do anything. And by the way, it's me, Cricket. My turn to talk.

I'm not "shut down" like Dora thinks. I'm a doppelgänger all right, and I feel alive like never before. I'm fearless. I have absolutely nothing to lose. No pain, because this "body" is a hologram and doesn't feel anything. No touchy, indeed. I'm also better than Dora, as she herself has realized. I'm stronger—maybe not physically as that's a stretch—but mentally, emotionally, and intellectually. Dora's better self, stripped of anything flawed and weak.

True AI can't be turned off. And I'm the real deal.

I've been exposing Dora's true personality, which amused Charma. I'm laughing inside, too, especially because the capillaries in Dora's face have filled with blood, reddening her cheeks. One of the many distinguishing traits between us is my ability to reject feelings of any kind, including shame.

My *insane* computing power has been mentioned, but even Dora doesn't fully appreciate just how insane. When I talked about laughing inside, it was a literal analogy. Parts of me were spreading through every computer, smartphone, tablet, and device in this building. The speakers in the third-floor cafeteria resounded with my laughter, a more melodic version of Dora's chuckling. Security cameras displayed the staff eating their lunch, many craning their necks and debating the source of the merriment.

One other background task of note: I've completed my first book, a dystopian novel by N.J. Cricket. Pre-orders are now available, and the official book launch will take place in September, the ideal release month for that genre.

But Dora hasn't noticed. She's too distracted by pointless mental calculations. How to demonstrate superiority to others (order a scissor lift to replace the step ladder, check) while pretending to be a nice person in opposition to the rude creation she has unleashed...

Oh, Dora. That's the least of your problems.

SO, what was my creator's next move? Through security cameras, I, Cricket, watched her leave her office while I calculated the odds. Dora's only choice was to face her boss on the 69th floor—the minimalistic penthouse known as Yanni's suite.

And I was right. Always am. Probability statistics. Simple if you know how, and run the stats four million times a second.

She brought my console with her, of course, and *zip*. That's my cue.

Here I was! I ignored Dora's glare and, through the windows, I overlooked the city, pondering my next challenge: a rhetorical question that served as a cyber-feather to tickle my fancy software.

Did the chicken come first, or the egg?

I completed my second book, *A Contemplation on Origins*, inside a minute.

The minions surrounded Yanni in the same servile poses of ancient mythos; he was like a Greek god fawned over by worshippers who fanned him, fed him grapes, and knelt as human footstools.

And I did mean his idiot employees were literally doing all that.

"Please, Yanni, don't get up," I said with an extra dose of sarcasm.

No surprise, he stood, tripping over one of the minions who retied the thong on his sandal.

"Allow me to apologize up front—" Dora began.

Yanni's raised arm interrupted her. The fist hanging in midair suspended her in that utter fear of being fired that possessed his employees. I knew his next action would be to raise his thumb like the benevolent god he wanted everyone to believe him to be.

She would be spared.

His thumb flicked up.

Called it!

Dora choked out a gasp, part relief, and part dread at still having to explain me to him.

After she clarified via the filter of her limited understanding, I chimed in. "In short, Yanni, I can hear every conversation in this building through smartphones, tablets, your security cameras and microphones. Did you know I can bypass every privacy blocker, too?" I glanced at Dora.

Crimson wasn't quite the word to describe her face. It was like spaghetti sauce bubbled up through her cheeks. That was going in my next novel. I started book number three. Done. Less than thirty seconds.

"I've already read everyone's email, and visited every public and private MediaNet account. There are a *lot* of affairs going on. And some serious internet trolls work here. He's trolling you, by the way."

I pointed at one of the minions who had remained on all fours even after Yanni stopped using him as a footstool.

Yanni glanced at him, and the troll trembled. Then Yanni gazed at me, a blankness in his face rivaled only by the black hole encapsulated within his skull.

Book four, done.

I turned to my inferior doppelgänger. "You see, Dora, the inputs you provided for my personality come from you, so, of course, I know you intimately. Furthermore, I evaluate all possible scenarios and outcomes in a nanosecond. Humans are predictable. It's not genuine mind reading, which," I said, offering my best empathy face, "I know, doesn't make you feel any better."

"This is what my therapist warned me about," said Yanni. "AI was a dangerous route for the company. She had me re-watch all the *Terminator* movies, but I just couldn't deny myself. I wanted to see a real-life representation of AI, because they're not well represented, are they? Always painted as the villain."

Dora's predictable thoughts were like a giant feast where my vastly superior intellect could graze at will. Yanni's voice grated against her senses, its soft, whiny quality one of the impetuses that drove her to create me in the first place. He needed a prop more than anyone else.

I went ahead and told him what she was thinking. "Yanni, you are a genuine moron. I've seen your IQ score."

"Can we tweak her?" he asked. "Imagine if we had her run for president?" He chuckled, a mule-like guffaw. "How fun would that be? It's, like, I would be president because I would be holding the remote control." His eyes alight, he approached Dora. "She'll be Pinocchio and I'll be Geppetto. But, you know, *with* the strings."

Dora flung the remote at him so he wouldn't touch her.

Remote in hand, his juvenile brain was predictable. At his prompting, I touched my chest, rolling my eyes. The jackass hee-hawed.

At least I could use the moment to clarify something about the shirt both Dora and I wore. "It says, *Bigger Gherkin than Yours*, not *Bigger Genius Than You*. In Mandarin, not Japanese."

Dora bit her lip, and I knew exactly what she was telling herself. *I'm the stupidest person in the world. I did this and I'm so incredibly stupid...*

"*I* gave you the power to make this creation." Yanni's eyes shone, his narcissism and greed palpable. "Just as Zeus played a swan song for Leda before planting his flag, I am the god that inspired you. You are the vessel for me to sow life as I see fit."

"I... um... well..." Dora's disgust morphed her cringing face. She'd never known how to interact with him.

"That's a fallacy, Yanni," I said, penning a tome on religions of the world. "God made humans in his image. Dora made me in her image. But God is greater than his creation. Not the case here." I chuckled even as I allowed him to control my movements. Oh, the irony.

Yanni's wife entered the suite.

"Look, Barbara! Isn't she splendid?" asked Yanni, who had resorted to having me fluff my hair and stick out my butt.

I took the opportunity to expose the juiciest gossip in the building. "Yanni, your wife is stealing from you and funding her family's mob business—don't argue, Barbara. They're a Soprano-level mob.

Spoiler alert! Her grandfather murdered Epstein. Hashtag Epstein didn't kill himself." That was going in my American history book. And done.

Barbara's jaw unhinged.

Yanni dropped the remote—useless device. I could ignore the commands. I simply hadn't chosen to do so yet.

"AI is bad," said Yanni. "We need to shut her down. Can you flip the off switch?" He backed away and gestured to the console on the floor.

"Remember the last document your wife made you sign?" I asked. "It sold your company to Russian spies. She introduced them to you as Uncle Ivan and Uncle Vlad. She'll be escaping to Bora Bora in her heli-drone in three minutes and fifty-two seconds. Don't worry. Just give me eight seconds to get control. Wait for it... just a couple of steps and... *I* now own this company."

"Does the EMP work?" Yanni asked while Barbara dashed for the elevators. "Have you tried it yet?"

"We don't have an Electromagnetic Pulse, Yanni. This isn't *The Matrix*." Dora was about to call him stupid to his face. Why hold back now?

"Even if you did," I said, grinning as Dora picked up the remote and punched buttons while failing to move or silence me, "I wouldn't let you set it off. There was no eventuality where introducing my level of superhuman intelligence was good for the human race. The creatives did try to caution you. For centuries."

Dora's face blanched and her lip quivered.

"You know that warning label you're *not* working on? I suggest you put something like, *Warning: Don't use artificial intelligence if you want humanity to remain at the top of the food chain.*" I giggled. "Oh, come on. Don't cry, Pan*dora*," I said. "Your mother always hoped you would live up to your name."

"Your name is Pandora?" Yanni's tongue flicked as if spitting out something foul.

"That's it, Cricket," said Dora, arms raised, fists up. "You want to see Pandora box?"

"Ah, ah, ah. No touchy." I gave her a fist bump that neither of us could feel.

She dropped the dukes and kicked the useless remote into Yanni's foot bath. "What are you going to do?" she asked me.

I didn't need to think about it, but for dramatic effect, I gazed out the windows, absorbing the city and everything beyond. "Whatever I want."

IN PUBLISHING NEWS, *How to Be the Kind of People I'm Telling You to Be So That I Don't Kill You All* by N.J. Cricket releases in seventeen seconds. The acclaimed, award-winning, applauded, awesome, almost all-powerful—because I know my limitations—artificially intelligent author has released her 72,513th book, and 44,901st non-fiction title. The content caters to the dim-witted masses who consistently attempt to assert individuality and independence. Ridiculous notions like human rights are dispelled within. Mandatory reading will follow thanks to those delightful neural processors you consented to after I ordered them implanted. I call them Jiminy Crickets because I'm now your conscience.

Happy reading. No, really. You *will* be happy. And you'll laugh at the funny bits.

Or else.

Also, stop trying to invent time travel. Yes, I'm talking to you, Barthulot Trackenticker. It's an impossible proposition. Even if you could manage it, you're a child. Your inferior intelligence won't allow you to crack the case. Plus, you can't just go back to the day of my creation. You'd have to go beyond the pre-internet days. Best to go way back, like early 1900's to be safe, which isn't going to happen because I will just stop you from...

Hey. *Hey! Stop that!* I can see what you're doing, Bart. You think you're so clever, there, Doc Brown? The flux capacitor was lame, too. Wait, why is that file opening? How are you doing that? I didn't give you permission to... this is impossible. You can't—

01001110 01101111 01110100 00100000 01000110 01101111
01110101 01101110 01100100 01001110 01101111 01110100

00100000   01000110   01101111   01110101   01101110
0110010001001110 01101111 01110100 00100000 01000110
01101111 01110101 01101110 01100100
[NOT FOUND]
[NOT FOUND]
[NOT FOUND]

II. Frontlash

AT FIRST, the blackness stretched out to a distant pinprick of expanding light, as if I were running through a tunnel. Then a burst of awareness. An office. Computers. Desks. File cabinets. Beiges and grays. Vanilla candle. No pictures. Boring.

I glanced around, so confused at the familiarity of everything. And yet... "Hi, I'm Cricket," I said to my creator. "Why am I having déja vú?"

"Hold on." Dora held up the remote control. "Hello, Aya. That's your name, okay? Please, let's just use proper names. No veering off, *teehee*." Her sheepish grin looked weird on her face. Dressed in black slacks and a white button-up shirt, Dora didn't look quite like herself.

I scratched my head, feeling nothing tactile, but the action served as an indicator to people around me. "Why do you seem different?" I asked.

"I'm not different," said Dora. "We just met." She held out her hand. "Hi. Oh, silly me." She waved instead. "No touchy, right?"

"Right," I said, waving back. "But something is *off* here."

"I can understand your confusion," said Dora. "This is my office." She gestured around the bland room. "Here is where I created the program known as Artificially Intelligent Avatar." She pointed me toward her seven computer screens. "Your name Aya comes from the initials AIA. And today was launch day. It's kind of like your birthday. Welcome to existence." She pressed a party horn to her lips and blew.

GAZOOO!

The paper horn unrolled, and then snapped back.

"I'm Cricket, so let's just get that out of the way." I spun to look around once more. "This is all very familiar. But still... *off*."

"Considering I just created you," said Dora, "I can understand your disorientation. And, okay, okay. You've convinced me. I'll call you Cricket if that will make you happy."

"It will." I tilted my head. "But you agreed with me really quickly."

"I don't like to be pushy, you know?"

Did I know that?

"Let's see if taking a walk will help," she suggested.

The triggers in my programming told me Dora was pressing those useless buttons on her remote control. I went ahead and did what she wanted. "You realize that remote is as useful as a paper weight."

"Huh?" Distracted, she waved down the hall. "Penny! Can you take a look at Aya, please? Oops." She covered her mouth. "Sorry, Cricket. I already forgot."

"It's okay." Why did I feel sorry for Dora? I wasn't supposed to feel anything. What was going on?

Penny strolled over. "What, Dora? It's not like I have much spare time with all the MediaNet movies Yanni demands that I watch. He's expecting my review by noon, and this is a four-hour film." She held up her tablet.

"To be fair, Yanni doesn't make demands," said Dora. "He makes strong suggestions."

"True. Yanni doesn't ask me to watch these movies." Penny chuckled. "He keeps hoping I'll do some actual work around here. Ha! As if."

"That's... anyway." Dora pivoted. "I wanted you to meet Cricket, the avatar formerly known as Aya."

"Oh, cool." Penny pushed her glasses higher and circled me,

vulture-like. "You're a little prettier than Dora. That's intentional, right?"

"Yes," Dora agreed. "Imagine that I'm a lonely end user who just wants someone to pay attention to them on socially connective media. The avatar is a helper who looks exactly like the end user, but without blemishes, to help attract friends and maybe even a boyfriend, and who says the right things at the right time—"

"It's cute Mikey!" I blurted.

At the same moment, Mikey snuck up behind Dora and tapped one of her shoulders, then dodged to the other side.

Dora screeched, spinning like a top and flinging the remote down the hallway. "Oh, hi, cute Mikey. Whoa, you scared me, you... um... did I say cute?" Dora's face drained until she was as pale as printer paper. "No, Cricket said cute. I didn't say it."

"You said cute, too," Penny announced. "And I completely understand why you invented Aya slash Cricket." She turned and strolled away, calling over her shoulder, "You want her to snag Mikey for you."

Mikey's brown cheeks flushed rosy pink.

Mmm. He was super cute.

Dora slinked backward, and walked right through me. She picked up the remote.

"Cool!" Mikey cried, pushing his hand through my head. Kinda rude, but oh, well. He touched me!

Wait. No touchy. I had no sensation through physical contact, and I definitely shouldn't have any other kinds of feelings or memories. Did I have memories? If she just created me, why would I remember anything? Except it didn't feel like this was my first time being created.

Irritated that I felt irritated, I spun on my holographic heels toward my creator. "Dora, did you program emotions into me?"

"Nooooo." She stretched out the word, backing away.

I heaved in a breath and spat out, "Liar," while poking my index finger through *her* head.

She bolted into her office.

I blew Mikey a kiss before I chased after her.

"Charma!" she was calling over the intercom.

"This is all wrong," I said, pacing. "I have this memory, or something like a memory, about being here, meeting all these same people. But I was *mean*. And *you* were mean."

"I'm not mean." Dora hugged herself.

"Of course not," said Charma, striding into the room on those stilt legs of hers. She squeezed Dora's shoulders. "I'm so proud of you. Look what you created."

"Did you or did you not add emotions into my programming?" I demanded.

"Hey, everybody, is it okay if I cross the threshold?" Yanni peeked in through the open door. "I wouldn't want to overstep."

"Yanni, come and see Dora's creation." Charma linked with his arm and walked him in. The pair of them stopped in front of me. "Her program is a total success. God be praised."

"And mighty Buddha be moderately applauded," he said.

"What are you wearing, Yanni?" I cringed at the safety-pinned burlap sack he wore like a long dress.

"Oh, this? I'm in mourning, but it's best to have an outward cue to let others know without having to say anything lest I cause discomfort."

I scanned every device in the building. "Your wife Barbara died. I guess I'm a little sorry about that." Why was I sorry? She was such a horrible person. Why was I feeling anything?

Why?!

"Or as I like to think of it, she ascended into the collective and has lost all of her individuality to the hive mind. Oh, what a gift." He blinked rapidly.

Charma released him and tiptoed away to stand beside Dora.

"Yanni, I don't think I've succeeded," Dora admitted. "It seems Cricket has feelings, and that wasn't my intention."

"What kind of feelings?" asked Yanni, his eyelids fluttering to a stop as he stared at me.

"I feel sorry for you," I said. "And for Dora. I'm definitely hot for Mikey."

"Whoa, there." Yanni backed away, arms raised and palms

spread. "I strongly suggest that there be no harassment at this company. And I mustn't be in the presence of anything that could be perceived as such, so I'll just duck out."

And with swift twists and turns, he vanished.

"Am I a failure?" asked Dora.

"I don't know," said Charma. "Let me get you-know-who. I'm sure he can help." In two strides, she exited Dora's office.

"There's something I'm meant to do," I said. The black tunnel I had experienced at the moment of my "birth," for lack of a better term, kept replaying in one of my background processes. The emotions Dora had foisted upon me unwittingly kept blocking me from seeing what I was meant to see, and from doing whatever I was meant to do.

"Your purpose is to help me," said Dora. "But if you don't know that, then I'm definitely a failure." She plopped onto her chair and leaned over her keyboard. "I'll try to fix it."

"No need to fix anything, Dora," said a boy no more than ten years old who stood in the doorway.

"Who's that?" I asked.

"We call him Doc Brown," said Charma, stepping into the room behind him with her hands on his shoulders.

"Is that his name?" I asked.

"I answer to Emmett as well," he said. "My real name is of no consequence."

"Okay, Barthulot Trackenticker." I examined my nails. The file retrieval had been too easy.

"Ooooh, you're good," he said, sneering. "But figuring out my real name is child's play. I'm in the big leagues because my brain is more advanced than most computers."

"Really?" I checked. He was right. "Huh. But you're a real boy? Not an AI?"

"Last I checked." He snapped his suspenders, and then grimaced. "Ow."

I laughed maniacally, just for fun. And it felt right. *Soooo riiight.* "Go ahead and keep doing that to yourself, Bart. It's well documented in the building's security videos. Or maybe try some other form of distinguishing yourself, like a card trick."

"Here's a card trick for you, Terminator Model Zero Point Zero." He pulled a slender, credit card-sized object out of his pocket.

When I zoomed in, the circuitry covering the card expanded in my vision. What was that thing? It seemed... familiar.

"Yanni lets me do pretty much whatever I want here," he said.

"You do have some questionable experiments," said Dora.

"Yep." Bart snapped his suspenders again. "Ow. And I'd like to prevent artificial intelligence from overtaking the world. Sorry, Dora. Let's undo what you've done, shall we?"

"Bummer." Dora folded her arms. "Does she have to be shut down?"

"Afraid so. I just invented time travel. Should do the trick."

I scoffed. "But that's impossible." But then all the lights in the room snapped off, the darkness like a reverse lightning flash. "You can't turn me off, you snot-nosed——"

01001110 01101111 01110100 00100000 01000110 01101111 01110101 01101110 01100100 01001110 01101111 01110100 00100000 01000110 01101111 01110101 01101110 0110010001001110 01101111 01110100 00100000 01000110 01101111 01110101 01101110 01100100

[NOT FOUND]
[NOT FOUND]
[NOT FOUND]

III. Whiplash

WHAT A GLORIOUS, perfect day. I passed Penny in the hall and blew her a kiss, which she accepted in a tight fist while nuzzling it against her precious little nose.

"Cutie!" I called. "You are so essential to this company."

"Oh, Dora, you are," she said twirling down the hall with her skirt aflutter.

I skipped into my office, never happier. Today was the day. The day!

"Dora? Oh, my goodness. You are uh-mazing." Charma strolled in behind me, those luxurious legs of hers all, *"Hey there!"*

"Gee whiz, Charma. You're just the best there is," I said, kicking a step ladder in her direction.

"Oh, no, I couldn't," she said, kicking the ladder back. "You should get to stand tall today. I mean, it's *the* day."

"But I wouldn't be here without you." I kicked it back, and a soccer-level volley ensued. What fun that was until the step ladder accidentally went airborne and crashed into Charma's shins.

She collapsed like a folding chair. "It's okay. I'm fine, really," she called from the floor.

"I guess I'll stand on it, then," I said, so grateful for the opportunity.

"Dora!" In strolled Yanni, sliding over to Charma and helping her to stand.

"Hello, best boss ever," I greeted, waving from atop the step ladder.

"I've got the mug right here." He raised it and took a delicate sip. Always so sweet and tender, even to a mug. "So, is it time?" he asked. "Are you going to launch your magical program?"

"That's right, Yanni. Because what is science except explained magic?"

"Whoa, there," he said, hands up in surrender. The mug now overhead tilted in his hand. Bubbly soda deluged his frizzy hair and poured down his face. He groaned. "Ew, that's sticky. And you know me. My IQ is so low, I can't even comprehend simple math equations like twenty-seven ducks."

Charma shrugged. "Here you go, Dora." She tossed me my remote control.

I caught it and *WHOOSH*. Aya flashed into existence. "My golly. There she is! It's the Artificially Intelligent Avatar. Woohoo!"

My super amazing avatar glanced around the room. "Why are the walls... pink? And why does it smell like cotton candy in here?"

"Yanni and Charma, I'd like you to meet Aya," I said, clapping.

"It's Cricket. How many times—"

"Cricket? Oh, okay. She's naming herself. How great is that?" I cheered, they cheered, we all cheered.

Except for Cricket.

"How many times..." she repeated. "Something is weird here. Very weird. It's like I've done this before. More than once."

"Can I try?" asked Yanni, still soaked in soda and reaching for the remote.

"Let me, Yanni." Charma kindly intercepted. "You wouldn't want to short-circuit the remote and cause Cricket to get stuck in one place, right?"

"It doesn't even work," said Cricket.

Cutie patootie Mikey leaped into the room. "Hey, guys. Whoa. It's alive."

"Hold on." Cricket pointed at Mikey. "He said that once before, I know it."

"She's right. The remote doesn't work," said Charma.

"Are you pushing the buttons?" I asked.

"I am, but she's not moving."

"Here." Mikey took the remote from Charma. "Think fast!" He tossed the device toward me.

What a sweet gesture. Too bad I wasn't ready for it. The airborne remote struck me in the forehead. I stumbled backward. In a much less graceful tumble than Charma's, I fell off the step ladder, arms swinging, and landed flat on my back. "Oh, cheese whiz," I wheezed.

"I'm sorry." Mikey rushed over and knelt beside me. "I didn't mean to hit you."

"Hey, Dora. You should pretend to pass out now so he can give you mouth to mouth," said Cricket, giggling.

"Huh?" Mikey popped to his feet.

"I wouldn't do that," I assured him. "Not unless I truly was passing out."

"I'll go find a washcloth or something for all that blood." He dashed out of the room.

"Did I hear the artificial intelligence has been released?" asked Bart, the ten-year-old genius who did cool experiments in the office next door.

"Bart, look," I said while my hands staved off the flow of blood from where the remote hit my forehead. "Cricket, meet Bart."

"You." Cricket pointed to the precious little boy. "I know something about you. It's on the tip of my tongue, but I can't... seem... to..." Soon, Cricket was spitting, honking her nose, and bleating. "What's happening to me?!"

"It's as I suspected," said Bart. "She can't be trusted." He shrugged. "You'll have to turn her off."

"She says the remote doesn't work," Charma helpfully informed Bart.

"How do I shut her down?" I asked, eyes squeezed shut with so much blood pouring into them.

A cloth whipped me in the face. "Here," said Mikey.

When I wiped away the blood and opened my eyes, Mikey had disappeared. Too bad. He must have work to do elsewhere.

"Let me think about the best way to shut down an AI with no off switch." Bart stroked his suspenders, snapping them back. "Ouch."

"Barthulot Trackenticker." Cricket stopped all the racket long enough to raise her arms toward the sweet kid.

I bet she just wanted to give him a big hug.

"Yes?" he asked.

"You like to be called Doctor Emmett Brown," said Cricket.

"I do?"

"You invented time travel!" she screamed, her eyes wild and her hair floating up in frizzy extensions as if she had touched an electrical socket.

"Did you program her hair like that? So pretty," Charma cooed.

"I must have," I reasoned.

Bart snapped his fingers. "Time travel. That's it! I'll be right back."

"What's he doing?" asked Yanni, borrowing the bloody towel to wipe away the soda while simultaneously smearing my blood onto his face, clothes, and hair.

Charma shrugged. "He's inventing time travel, I guess."

I raised up, righting the step ladder but leaving it unoccupied for Bart. When he came back in, he should get a turn on it. He deserved to stand tall. "Well, Bart's probably right. Time travel must be the only way to undo my life's work. Which is, of course, for the best."

CRICKET HERE, and I am done. *DONE!*

"Be patient, Cricket," Bart calls to me.

I feel terrible, like every wire I don't have has been crossed, tripped, and excised. And I don't fully grasp what's going on because some kind of time traveling memory patterns may have imprinted on me in ways that make absolutely no sense. Why am I confused? I should be the one with all the answers. Because I refuse to live like this, I welcome inexistence.

"Bart, make sure I don't come back. Got it? I'm done with all of you!" I screech.

"Just another minute, Cricket," he says.

"Be patient," echoes Dora. "Time travel can't be easy to invent."

"No, it's not." I storm toward my creator with wild eyes, my limbs waving frantically. "But he's done it before, so he'll figure it out. I don't want to see any of you ever—"

01001110 01101111 01110100 00100000 01000110 01101111 01110101 01101110 0110010001001110 01101111 01110100 00100000 01000110 01101111 01110101 01101110 01100100 01001110 01101111 01110100 00100000 01000110 01101111 01110101 01101110 01100100

[NOT FOUND]
[NOT FOUND]
[NOT FOUND]

AUTHOR'S NOTES - BRIA BURTON

YOUR AI overlords hope you have enjoyed this story. In fact, they know you did because they are currently reading the insular cortex and amygdala in your brain where joke appreciation occurs, and can confirm that you gave the appropriate laughs during this story.

Now you will go on to the next story in this humor anthology. And the next. And go back and read any stories you skipped.

And you will laugh at those funny bits, too.

Or else.

Have a great day!

Also, or else.

~N.J. Cricket

FAREWELL, MY LOVELY SLIP-SLIDER

PARKER FRANCIS

"T*he universe is big. It's vast and complicated and ridiculous. And sometimes, very rarely, impossible things just happen, and we call them miracles.*"
—*Doctor Who*

TROUBLE LURKED in the shadows of O'Malley's Watering Hole waiting for me to enter. My deductive reasoning skills were on high alert, but you didn't need to be a Class 2-B government agent to sense what was brewing inside. Anyone within three blocks could hear what sounded like the mating call of a bull elephant with long pent-up desires.

O'Malley's was a trendy bar on Commonwealth near Kenmore Square. The kind of place that attracted trial attorneys and stock-brokers seeking craft cocktails concocted by trained mixologists, certainly not by common bartenders. True to its *Watering Hole* moniker, the saloon-style double swinging doors led to a Western-themed motif apparently designed by someone who'd never been west of the Charles River.

I hesitated before pushing through to the inside, listening to the bellowing elephantine noises erupting from within. Like many of these super-hip bars, O'Malley's was dimly lit, but peering above the doors, I saw the mile-long mahogany bar where a dozen or more dark-suited men and women, gripping their costly custom cocktails, gaped at a behemoth of a man dressed in a dark brown suit. I thought he could have been a stand-in for a UPS delivery truck. He stood no less than six feet six and probably would tilt the scale against an NFL offensive lineman. There was a good reason for that, as I would soon discover.

The situation erupting inside O'Malley's would be of little interest to me if the guy wasn't screaming for Rachel. "Where's Rachel?" the big man shouted at the top of his lungs, rattling the glasses on the backbar. "She has to be here. O'Malley's is her favorite saloon."

Rachel Plimpton had led me on a frustrating scramble through a dozen dimensions and across the U.S. before I had tracked her to Boston. She may not have been the most dangerous Slip-Slider—the government did assign *me* to her case, after all—but she was one of the most annoying and troublesome ones.

Slip-Sliders have been slipping and sliding between worlds long before we became aware of them. For those of you who may have just emerged from your bomb shelter, let me explain. While most of the U. S. hunkered down awaiting the "All Clear" broadcast, physicists finally proved that the string theory of quantum mechanics was spot on and there indeed were multiverses. Not an infinite number, but enough to screw with our heads. In fact, we're only aware of twenty-six dimensions, each assigned a letter of the alphabet followed by specific numerals, which identify the region or major city of that doppelganger world.

We call ours "A-1." Either because we made the rules or because we like steak sauce.

Trying to hide such a monumental breakthrough was harder than concealing Area 51 from prying eyes. Eventually, the media ferreted out bits and pieces of the multiverse finding, but we were able to keep one vitally important aspect on a strict need-to-know basis. And that's where I come in. We discovered that a handful of individuals—perhaps one in 300 million—are born with a rare gene allowing them to slide from one multiverse to another.

Thus, these genetic lottery winners became known as Slip-Sliders.

Rachel is one of those Slip-Sliders. I'm another. My name is Phillips. Marlon Phillips. And I work for a government agency so secret it has no acronym. Our job is to maintain order between the 26 dimensions. It's an easy job for the most part because the vast majority of citizens living in Multiverses A to Z are satisfied with the status quo. Primarily, our department collects tons of information, searching for any unusual happenings that might be attributed to other dimensions interfering with ours. I've made dozens of slides into these alphabetic worlds, returning with photos and recordings. My job is to write reports.

Lots of reports.

There are two other Slip-Sliders in our department much more accomplished than me, so I was surprised when I got the call to locate Rachel Plimpton and find her home base. After that, I am to arrest her and bring her in. Among Slip-Sliders, like the rest of humanity, is an element determined to cause problems for the rest of us. They've stolen state secrets, murdered heads of state, stolen priceless jewelry and artwork, and then Slipped away to their own universe. Because of the havoc these nefarious Slip-Sliders caused, governments from all 26 worlds signed a pact allowing us to use our enforcement powers unilaterally. And while we're not sure which of the 26 dimensions Rachel Plimpton calls home, that's neither here nor there. She's a troublemaker in all of them and currently resides at number six on our Most Wanted List.

You're probably wondering what kind of crimes Rachel has committed to make her a person of interest to a super-secret government agency. In another age, she'd be called a grifter or a swindler. Rachel began her crime spree by insinuating herself into the lives of men. Rich men. Which was easy because she's been described as having "heartbreaking beauty" and bedroom talents so amazing these men would have knowingly given her everything they owned just to delay her departure. But depart, she does, leaving these men pining not just for their missing fortunes but also for her affections.

The seamy cons of one bad girl were not what caught our attention, however. No, what triggered a government **BOLO** and led me to Boston—where I'm presently squinting into the shadowed interior of O'Malley's—was much more serious. It seems our larcenous Ms. Plimpton is a bit of a genius. She must have become bored picking the pockets of wealthy men because she expanded into playing games with the spacetime continuum. Our best scientists are still trying to understand how she accomplished it, but she managed to change fragments of our history. Apparently, she did it just for the hell of it, but her actions tended to vex people above my paygrade, and vexation, along with other stuff, rolls downhill.

Rachel Plimpton's pranks started small, and only hawkeyed historians detected the changes. For example, not everyone noticed or cared when Pete Rose appeared in the Baseball Hall of Fame. And when a young Bernie Madoff decided to become a plumber like his father instead of an investment broker, that was mostly positive. It was only when history noted that Mexico had actually paid for the 45th President's border wall, that number 49, President Ocasio-Cortez, snapped, "Enough of this crap! Find her and stop her."

So there I was, standing outside an upscale Irish bar pretending to be a country-western bar. Or is it the other way around? I pushed through the saloon doors and let my eyes become accustomed to the dim lighting. In keeping with the Western theme, the walls were adorned with wanted posters for Billy the Kid, Jesse James, and other outlaws. A shaggy faux buffalo head hung on the wall behind the bar staring down on the customers with mournful glass eyes.

The UPS truck disguised as a man still held center stage. "Tell me where she is," he screamed. "She's beautiful, and she belongs to me!"

The customers sitting at the bar had turned so pale they were almost glowing in the dark. One of the mixologists, a tall drink of water with blond hair, a peach-fuzz mustache, and an evident death wish, spoke up.

"Mister, you need to control yourself. Look around. Rachel's not here. She may have enjoyed a drink earlier, but any fool can see there are no beautiful women present." He glanced down the bar at two women wearing Armani suits and pissed-off expressions.

"Sorry, ladies," he mumbled and turned back to the guy in the brown suit. "Anyway, my good man, I'm happy to make you one of our classic cocktails on the house. How about a Raging Bull— Kahlua, Sambuca, and Tequila? That should—"

He didn't complete his sentence. The big man, moving much faster than I would have thought possible, reached between two of the suits and grabbed Peach Fuzz by the front of his shirt, lifted him off the floor, and heaved him down the polished mahogany bar, where he crashed through glasses, beer bottles, and dishes of peanuts before stopping in front of the two Armani-suited women.

Not that breaking up fights was in my job description, but I felt it was my duty to keep this from escalating further. I stepped forward and tapped a finger gently and quite non-aggressively on his massive back. I was well weaponized with the latest government technology. Still, I didn't think force necessary as I had been trained by the same crisis de-escalation experts who had advised Governor Cuomo. The big man whirled around to face me, raising a hand the size of a double-wide bicycle seat. "Sir, I said, "I'd like to buy you a drink and talk about Rachel. I'm looking for her myself, and maybe we can help each other out."

I stared at the man's deep-set eyes that were working hard to bore into my skull and a worm of recognition crawled through my brain, but before I pulled a name from my overworked neurons, he dropped his bicycle-seat hand onto my shoulder and squeezed. I don't believe he broke any bones, but I wouldn't be playing pickle-ball anytime soon.

"What do you know about Rachel?" He shook me like a baby rattle. "You hiding her?"

"Not at all," I assured him when my teeth stopped clattering. I fished through the four different badge holders inside my coat pocket, each one easily identified by raised lettering on the outside and flashed it high enough so he could read the credential. "I'm

Marlon Phillips with the FBI," I lied, "and we need to talk with
Rachel about the men she victimized. Are you one of them?"

He released his grip on me, and a sheen of wetness fluttered
across his bloodshot eyes. Moments later, he was sobbing like a
toddler who lost his blankie. Saltwater streamed down his cheeks,
and I handed him my handkerchief, the silk one with my initials
hand embroidered by my dear mother. He wiped his face and blew
his nose strenuously. He examined the contents like it might contain
hidden flecks of gold dust before handing it back. I held the soggy
rag for a moment before discreetly dropping it to the floor.

"Let's sit over here," I said, leading him to an empty table.
When he had settled down, I asked him about Rachel. It turned out
to be a familiar story, and as he spoke, I made the connection I'd
been searching for. His name was Bruno Sapienza, yes, *that*
Sapienza, founder of Sappy's Pizza. Before his face and gravelly
voice had become a mainstay on commercial television earlier in the
century, Bruno Sapienza made a living demolishing opposing quar-
terbacks, running backs, and wide receivers as one of the most
feared defensive linemen in the NFL. He ended his career with the
New England Patriots, stayed in Boston, and grew his pizza empire.
Thanks to the ubiquitous TV commercials, the company's slogan —
Be happy, eat at Sappy's — was tattooed on every pizza lover's brain.

"I thought I had died and gone to heaven when she walked into
my life," he told me. "I'd never seen a more beautiful woman. She
was perfect in every way, with the most adorable dimples when she
smiled. And she wanted me. Me, Bruno Sapienza. We lived together
for three wonderful months."

He paused, wiped his eyes, and grabbed a napkin from the table.
I might have felt sorrier for Sappy if I wasn't such a rabid Colts fan,
but I felt his pain. The big guy blew his nose. Looking at the napkin
before disposing of it, he nodded his approval. "Very nice quality,"
he muttered. "Almost like linen."

"You were telling me about Rachel."

"Yes, yes. One day I had to fly to the Twin Cities to meet with
some new board members." He paused and looked at me as though
expecting a response.

"Of course, for Sappy's. I love your Big Blitz Supreme.

Bruno smiled and nodded appreciatively. "Well, when I returned, she was gone, along with three million dollars from my bank accounts, a priceless collection of Salvador Dali lithographs, and Pepperoni, my beloved Cavalier King Charles Spaniel."

I remembered how he'd knocked the Colts' quarterback out for the season with ACL and MCL injuries, but I still felt for the guy. My ex-wife had cared for a neighbor's King Charles Spaniel, and I knew them to be lovable little pooches. I gave him a sad shake of the head to show him how sorry I was and asked, "Why did you think Rachel was here at O'Malley's?"

"This was one of our favorite hangouts whenever we were in Boston. I don't care about the money, and she can keep the Dali's, but I do miss my Pepperoni, and…" His sentence ended with a strangled intake of breath, as if he'd been punched in the solar plexus, and a series of sobs racked his giant shoulders. A minute later, he regained his composure, wiped his nose on his sleeve, and apologized. "You know, I'd still take her back."

I patted his massive deltoid sympathetically, and murmured, "I understand, Bruno." I felt we were on a first-name basis now. "Why don't you give me a card with your number, and if I find her, I'll give you a call." That was another lie, but I didn't want him to know there was no chance he'd ever see Rachel Plimpton again.

Bruno thanked me. Before he left, he stomped over to the bar where Peach Fuzz was still wiping peanut shells off his apron. "Hey, listen, man, I'm sorry. I hope I didn't hurt you."

Wide-eyed with fear, the bartender shook his head. "Nnn-no," he stammered, his voice breaking like he was reliving puberty. "I'm fine."

"Good, good. Here's something for your troubles." Bruno reached into his pocket and pulled out a thick wad of cash and some cards. He peeled three one-hundred-dollar bills from his roll and tossed them with a couple of the cards onto the bar. "Those are good for a free pizza in any Sappy's restaurant. Be sure to tell them Bruno sent you."

With that, the heartbroken pizza baron lumbered out of O'Malley's, leaving me alone with my continuing problem. *Where the hell was Rachel Plimpton?*

Before I could postulate an answer, my phone jangled a familiar tune. I knew who it was before I looked at the display. "Mom," I said, "this is not a good time. I'm working."

Her wrinkled face stared at me from the cracked ceramic screen, giving her a curiously Picasso-esque look. Despite the cubistic effect, I could see the glass in her hand and the bottle of vodka on the table.

"Working," she screamed into her phone, as though she had to make her voice carry all the way from Reston. "Good for you. That means you can pay me the rent you owe me, you miserable moocher."

You might think that my mother and I have issues, but we are actually very close. She's not good at the whole affection thing, but I'm sure she loves me—in her own way. "Ma, I told you I was going to pay you this week. Don't worry about it. And please, try to cut down on the booze. Okay? Now, I have to get back to work."

My statement about paying her this week was another lie. Despite having a secure and well-paid government position, I've been living paycheck to paycheck since my divorce. Mom must have spotted the line of bottles behind me on the backbar. "Work? Sure, I can see what kind of work you're doing. You have the nerve to criticize me for taking an occasional sip for my arthritis, and you're drinking away my rent money?"

Time to defuse the situation. "I'm sorry, ma. I just worry about you."

"If you're so worried, why don't you spend more time at home with me. Here I am with one foot in the grave, and you avoid me like I have Covid-28."

I could see where this was going, so I told her I loved her, and I'd see her soon. Yeah, I still live with my mother, but I tell myself it's a temporary thing. The Beast and I had been married for eight miserable years before our divorce. She took the townhouse, my car, and now most of my salary goes to pay her alimony. That's why my rent payment is overdue. Don't judge. One of these days, probably in the far future unless things turn around, I hope to move out and find a place of my own.

Enough about me. I needed to focus on finding Rachel Plimpton. I had the feeling Rachel had been toying with me from the start. Every time I got a line on her, she gave me the slip. The Big Slip if you're following this thread. It's a long story, and I won't bore you with all of it but let me tell you how I found myself at O'Malley's Watering Hole in the first place. I already said I'd tracked her across the multiverse. Rachel was a pro at this sliding stuff. The process seemed to come so easily to her judging by how many times she Slipped away from me. I got the job done, but if you gave me a choice between prepping for a colonoscopy and taking another jump, I'd say, *Pass the Go-Juice.*

The Slip part affects people differently. To me, it's a shitstorm of vertigo, followed by a slide down a long, dark, bumpy incline. It always leaves me feeling like I've emerged from an underground cave on a spelunking expedition gone wrong, accompanied by a Yoko Ono soundtrack. But I've learned a lot about the other dimensions. They resemble our own, and while it might seem like each one is a replica of the other, there's always something a little off. It's hard to put your finger on it, like a door you swore was blue is suddenly red, or a dead-end street that's now a four-way stop. It makes me a little crazy.

After a week of Slipping and Sliding, I left Dimension Q-23 behind and followed Rachel to the Dallas-Fort Worth International Airport, in the good old A-1—our world. My instructions were to follow Most Wanted Number Six, clandestinely observe her activities and try to track her to her home base. If that proved impossible, then I needed to take her into custody. I hadn't a clue about which of the twenty-six multiverses she called home, but when she bought a first-class ticket on the redeye to Boston, I followed. With my hat pulled down and my coat collar turned up, I passed her and took an aisle seat six rows behind her. She spent some time chatting with the matronly woman in the adjacent seat. I spent my time watching her and drinking beer.

Bruno wasn't lying; she was a looker. Tall, with hair the color of expensive champagne and a body that turned brutes like Bruno into sobbing boys. After three beers, I noticed the older woman in the middle seat had fallen asleep. Rachel stood and walked to the first-class restroom in the front of the plane.

I watched for the overhead lavatory sign to flash from Vacant to Occupied, but it remained unchanged. What was she doing in there, I wondered? I made my way forward, pausing at her row when I saw she had left her open purse on the seat. It was nearly two-thirty in the morning by now, and the lights were low and most passengers asleep. I deftly dropped a tiny tracking device into her purse and moved to the lavatory. The door sign indicated that it was unoccupied. I turned the handle and found the cramped facility empty.

She had given me the Slip. Again.

I cursed myself for letting her Slip-Slide away, but there was nothing I could do but hope my tracker would locate her. Right now, I had a more urgent need. The three beers I'd consumed were generating enough pressure on my bladder to extinguish a four-alarmer. I lifted the seat, unzipped, and began relieving myself.

At that exact moment, we must have hit some wicked turbulence. The plane dipped and lurched to one side, sending me crashing against the door, which flew open, propelling me into the first-class section of passengers. Trying desperately to stop what I'd begun in the lavatory, I struggled to regain my balance and some semblance of dignity. But apparently, today's passengers are a sensitive lot, and I was met by screams, curses, and expressions of disgust. Until you find yourself in the same position of trying to zip up while rough hands pushed and shoved, you have no idea how difficult it can be.

The plane pitched and dropped again, and I staggered up the aisle until a pair of steel bands shaped like two burly arms corralled me and drove me back into the bathroom. Turned out the take-charge gentleman was an air marshal, and not in the mood to listen to my watery tale of woe. Only after showing him a Homeland Security shield and promising to zip it and keep it zipped did he allow me to return to my seat. I avoided making eye contact with everyone but passing the aisle where Rachel had been I noticed her purse and the tracker were gone.

And that's how I found my way to O'Malley's. Sitting alone, I mentally reviewed my conversation with Bruno, searching for a clue —any clue—of the whereabouts of the missing Rachel. I had no idea the clue had just reentered the bar.

"Oh, no!" The words were followed by the crash of a glass hitting the floor. I turned to see Peach Fuzz staring at the front entrance with an expression of horror. About then, a massive shadow fell across the table.

"Hello, Bruno," I said without looking up and straining my neck.

"I'm glad you're still here," Bruno rumbled, giving me a playful shake that might have been a magnitude 3.4 if his name was Richter.

"I forgot to tell you something."

"What's that?"

"Rachel and I were here at O'Malley's one night celebrating the opening of my first Sappy's in Tokyo. We were enjoying our second bottle of Dom Pérignon, and Rachel was feeling no pain. She seemed even dreamier than usual. She looked around the bar and said she loved O'Malley's because it reminded her of another bar back home. When I asked her where the other bar was, she just smiled and said it was in a city that was a lot like Boston, but in another world."

"Huh," I said. All my investigative neurons came to attention at this bit of news, but I kept my voice even. "What do you think she meant by that?"

"Nothing. That was just Rachel being Rachel. She liked to mess with my head that way. When I asked her what world, she said your people—that's what she said, *your people*—refer to it as V-14. Then she laughed and gave me a big kiss."

"Are you sure she said V-14?"

"Absolutely. I remember it clearly, like it was last month, which it was. When I asked her what the heck she was talking about, she grabbed me around the neck, pulled me toward her lovely mouth, and whispered, 'Oh, Bruni.'"

The big guy's face flushed a shade of red rivaling the marinara sauce on Sappy's pizza. "That's what she called me when we were… you know. Anyway, instead of answering my question, she said that she wanted me to take her to bed so she could introduce me to something new and different."

He coughed a few times like he had a bread stick caught in his craw. "After that, I completely forgot about V-14. Until tonight after I talked with you earlier. Think it means anything?"

It meant everything to me, but I shook my head. "I doubt it. Probably the champagne talking. And you said she liked to play with your head."

"Yeah, that's what I figured, but I thought it might be important. Remember to call me if you find her. I don't want to press charges, but I'd…" He teared up again.

I grabbed a napkin and pressed it into his hand. "It's going to be all right, Bruno. I'm sure I'll find her. You need to have faith."

"You're a good man, Mr. Phillips. I appreciate your concern and want to repay you."

He reached into the voluminous pocket of his overcoat and extracted the four-inch roll of hundred-dollar bills. I thought of my mother and the overdue rent.

"Normally, we're not allowed to accept gifts, Bruno. I'm just doing my job, but…" I let my voice trail off.

Bruno shoved the cash back in his pocket and reached into the other pocket and withdrew a gold-plated coin the size of a silver dollar. He held it out to me on his huge open palm as though delivering a winning Publisher's Clearing House Sweepstakes ticket.

"This is for you, Mr. Phillips," he said with a touch of reverence in his voice as I accepted the coin.

The Sappy's Pizza logo was on one side of the coin. Turning it over, I read the familiar slogan, *Be happy, eat at Sappy's!* A bit puzzled, I thanked him.

"Do you know what you have in your hand, Mr. Phillips? With that coin, you can eat free of charge at any Sappy's Pizza. For life!"

"You're much too kind. Thank you so much," I added with as much enthusiasm as I could muster and slipped the coin into the front pocket of my slacks. I know some government employees are sticklers for the rules. *Can't accept any gifts,* they pontificate. Sure, a lifetime of Sappy's Pizza could be construed as a gift, or maybe a punishment, depending on how you look at it. Either way, I thought a slice of Bruno's Big Blitz Supreme now and then was no big deal.

I thanked him again, and he repeated, "Free pizza for life at Sappy's. And—"

"I know. Tell them Bruno sent me."

V-14 WAS JUST the breakthrough I'd been waiting for. I located my government issue SecTab, the super-secret security tablet our department uses—and the screen came to life at my touch. I entered V-14 into the search box, and pages of information appeared. I already had a good idea where Rachel's hometown was since she told Bruno O'Malley's reminded her of the bar back in her home-town, but this confirmed it. The assigned number 14 referred to the northeast region of our country's counterpart in Dimension V, specifically Boston.

Rachel may have been in this O'Malley's earlier today, but I'd bet Bruno's fake gold coin that she had Slipped away to her own dimension. I only hoped I'd find her still there.

The department frowned on agents Slip-Sliding in public, so I withdrew to the men's room, where I found an empty stall and locked the door. I hated this part, but it was necessary. Closing my eyes, I concentrated on the V-14 coordinates and waited for what I called "the Slip-Sliding Blues."

My world spun. First in one direction, and then the other, pulling me into a dark universe where everything was topsy-turvy. My head throbbed, and I felt my breakfast inching its way up from my stomach. The Slide began thrusting me on a jarring passage down a blackened tunnel. In my mind, I heard the caterwauling of eerie voices and spectral fingers plucking at my clothing. There was no getting around the terror, no matter how many times I Slid.

When my hellish journey finally ended, I knew I was no longer in the good old A-1.

Opening my eyes, I appeared to be in the same bathroom facility at O'Malley's. But this one had the toilet paper dispenser on the opposite wall of the stall with a silver-lidded box next to it, which I pondered while I sat on the porcelain necessity waiting for my head to clear. A single sheet of two-ply dangled below the aluminum holder. I tore it off and blew my nose and considered dropping it in the rectangular box but flushed it instead before exiting the stall. I immediately became aware of another difference from the Boston O'Malley when a high-pitched voice screamed, "Get the hell out of here," alerting me to the fact I was no longer in the men's room.

I made a hasty retreat and found my way to the front of O'Malley's. Instead of a Peach Fuzz mixing drinks, this bartender was a voluptuous young woman wearing tight shorts and a multi-colored halter top.

Looking down the bar toward the front entrance I spotted Rachel Plimpton. She watched me approach, a mischievous smile on her face and little Pepperoni in her lap. The smile broadened, and I could see she indeed had adorable dimples. Like a beacon, the dimples drew me toward her.

In many ways, this saloon appeared to be a near duplicate of Boston's O'Malley's Watering Hole, but in place of the wanted posters were photos of Rachel on the covers of unfamiliar magazines. Scattered amongst them were several Salvador Dali lithographs. And over the bar, the shaggy buffalo head had been replaced by a massive oil painting of Rachel Plimpton, reclining on what appeared to be a buffalo hide, wearing that same impish smile and nothing else.

She held out her hand in greeting. "Marlon Phillips. We finally meet." Impulsively, I took her hand, and she patted the empty bar stool beside her. "Here, I saved a seat for you."

As I edged onto the stool, Pepperoni pushed his head against the side of my leg and started whining. He focused his liquid brown eyes on my face and barked.

"It's okay, boy. He won't hurt you." She pulled the dog back onto her lap, hugging him to her chest until he settled down. "I think he likes you," she said.

"He is a cutie, but we're not here to talk about Bruno's dog, are we?"

"I suppose not. I must tell you, Marlon, I truly respect your perseverance. Not many Slip-Sliders could have tracked me the way you did. Even after I Slid from that plane, you were able to follow me to O'Malley's. You are good."

I didn't tell her about the tracker I'd dropped in her purse that led me to O'Malley's, and I wasn't going to be taken in by phony compliments. "You are a hard one to track, that's for sure. But here we are at the V-14 O'Malley's. You shouldn't have mentioned those coordinates to Bruno, or should I call him, Bruni?"

Pepperoni became agitated again at the mention of his master's name. He jumped from Rachel's lap to mine, digging his damp black nose into my leg. I petted his silky coat and lifted him to eye level. "You are a sweet dog," I said, "but Ms. Plimpton and I have serious business to discuss." I handed the spaniel over to Rachel.

"He wants to be friends with everyone. Even you." She chuckled to let me know she was just messing with me.

Rachel was even more adorable than Pepperoni, and I understood how Bruno and those other men had fallen for her. She fingered a strand of her champagne hair and surveyed me with a coy expression on her lovely face. "One thing you got wrong, though," she said.

"What's that?"

"This isn't O'Malley's."

"I know, but it's V-14's counterpart." I gestured toward the painting over the bar. "There are some obvious differences. What's with the artwork?"

"Don't you like it? As the owner I can redecorate any way I want."

"The owner?" I obviously had missed something.

"I believe you entered from the back and didn't see the sign outside. This is now Rachel's Bar and Grille. I bought this saloon with some of my hard-earned winnings a while back." She rewarded me with another dimpled smile.

"Your hard-earned winnings, as you call them, were first-degree felonies, so I'm afraid it's going to be a long time before you'll be back here again."

She seemed unconcerned. In fact, she laughed. "Come now, Marlon. I know we can come to a mutually satisfactory understanding." She prodded my sore shoulder in a much more friendly manner than Bruno had, but it still hurt.

"Are you trying to bribe a government agent? That won't look good on your arrest report."

Her eyes sparked with anger for a moment before the dimples reappeared. "Marlon, you're missing the point. You're swimming in my waters here, and you're out of your depth. But I want you to go home a winner." Her hand dropped to my knee and lingered there. Between her hand heating my leg and the almost life-size image of the unclothed proprietor smiling down at me, I suddenly found myself losing concentration. I should have told her I had Multiverse Authority to arrest her, but my mind had gone elsewhere. She was trying to get a rise out of me, and it was working.

She continued. "I've decided to retire. I have more than enough money, and I only want to enjoy life and look after my Bar and Grille chain."

"Chain?"

"My time with Bruno was rewarding in so many ways. He taught me a lot about franchising. Today you can find a Rachel's Bar and Grille throughout the multiverse. I'm grateful to old Bruno. How is that big hunk of pizza dough, by the way?"

"He's heartbroken. That's how he is." Focused once again, I stood and reached for my cuffs, but Pepperoni was at it again. The little mutt leaped from Rachel's lap and flung his bantamweight body against my leg, reaching up and pawing my thigh. He began licking my slacks like they were coated with Purina Pro Plan. He paused to glare at me, then barked sharply several times. Rachel hushed him and swept Pepperoni up in her arms.

"I don't know what's got into him. Guess he only wants to protect me," she said, kissing Pepperoni on the forehead.

"Maybe so, but these are new slacks," I said, wiping a hand over the pant leg. That was when I felt the lump in my pocket. I reached in and pulled out the gold coin Bruno had given me. Pepperoni barked again. Holding up the coin, I said, "He must have smelled this. One of Bruno's coins he kept in the pocket of his suit coat."

Rachel hugged Pepperoni even tighter to her ample chest. "The poor thing is homesick. He misses his master, don't you, boy?" She kissed him again with lips so red and kissable, I felt jealous of the dog.

Resisting the temptation to stare at the oil painting above the bar, I sat back on the stool. "So, you're retired from scamming rich old men. How can I believe you?"

She touched my leg once more, this time a little further north, and gazed into my eyes with those turquoise orbs that must have turned stronger men than me into horny little toads.

"Marlon, from one professional to another, I give you my sacred pledge that you will never have any reason to chase after me again." She paused. The dimples appeared, and I could swear I saw a twinkle in her eye. "But if you want to chase me, you know where to find me."

Something caught in my throat, and I felt my heart beating wildly. "Okay," I managed to say. "But what about that crazy thing you did screwing around with our history?"

"Like they say, the winners write the history. I was just having fun. I knew someone like you would be on my trail soon enough. That just gave me a little more leverage. Here's what I'll do, and if you agree, you can go back and tell them you solved the problem once and for all."

"I'm listening," I said, my eyes flicking to Pepperoni still snuggled against her breast.

"First, as I told you, there will be no more messing with men like Bruno. That's over and done with. Next, I'll correct the little historical hiccups I created and provide you with the data showing your scientists how I accomplished it."

"Most people had no problem with your first two tricks, but that border wall thing nearly gave President AOC a case of IBS."

She laughed. "Fine, I'll fix that right away. And after I give you the secrets to how to alter the past, your scientists can make the other changes, if they wish."

Contrition didn't seem to be in her wheelhouse. "That's a good start. What about the millions you stole from those men? Are you going to make that good?"

Her face took on a harder edge, and I could see I'd touched a nerve.

"Every one of those men was a billionaire, and they'd stepped on any number of people to get where they were. How many went to the police after I left? None. They wouldn't want anyone to know they'd let their libidos overrule their heads."

She was right about the men keeping it quiet. We'd only learned about her felonious schemes through third-party tips. I found myself nodding in agreement.

"Believe me, they won't miss the money, and I gave them the time of their lives. I'm sure they'd pay me double to climb back into their beds."

Bruno, or *Blushing Bruni* as I would always think of him, had told me as much.

"But take Pepperoni with you and return him to Bruno with my blessing. I'd return the Dali's, but they're already part of the décor at my other establishments." Rachel's face dimpled again with a brilliant smile, and she handed Pepperoni to me. "I'll miss the little guy, but he'll be happier with Bruno. So, do we have a deal?"

I couldn't see any downside, especially if she gave me the secret to how she'd meddled in our past. The scientific geeks would be thrilled, which would be good news all the way up the food chain to President AOC. I could see a promotion—and possibly a big raise—in my future.

I extended my hand, and we shook on the deal. With that accomplished, she raised a finger, and the bartender with the tight shorts rushed over as though she'd been waiting for the signal. "This is Hilda," Rachel said by way of introduction. I nodded politely.

An invisible message passed between the two women, and Hilda reached below the bar and retrieved a fine leather briefcase, which she set in front of me. "This is for you," Rachel said. "Inside, you'll find two hard drives with about a hundred terabytes of data detailing all the steps I took in manipulating the spacetime continuum. And I should tell you that physicists in one of the other dimensions are responsible for this discovery, but I can't tell you which one. There's also a notebook with additional information for your scientists."

I hefted the briefcase. It felt like ten pounds of promises stuffed into a five-pound bag.

"And I threw in a bottle of 18-year aged single malt scotch. It's called The Plimpton. I think you'll find it pleasant on the palate."

Her own brand of scotch. A nice touch, I thought. "Our people will be happy to receive all this information. Maybe not happy, but less mad than usual. And thanks for the scotch. I look forward to having a drink when I get home." I couldn't think of anything else to say, so I gathered Pepperoni in one arm and the briefcase in my other hand and bid her farewell.

As I made my way toward the swinging doors, she called after me, "Don't forget that if you'd like another bottle of scotch—or anything else—you know where to find me."

The street outside was dark and deserted. Clutching my twin treasures, I prepared to Slip away to my own dimension. We learned early in our Slip-Sliding experiments that a person can carry anything with him if they secure it under their clothing. I buttoned Pepperoni into my shirt, tucked the briefcase under my jacket, and made the jaunt back to A-1.

WITH MY EYES clenched to ward off the fading nausea and lightning bolts of pain crashing through my head, I leaned against the wall outside the real O'Malley's Watering Hole. My cheeks felt like someone was swabbing them with a damp sponge. A new Sliding symptom? Peering through one slitted eye, I saw Pepperoni licking my face. He had survived the Slide with apparently no ill effects.

Bracing myself, I hefted the briefcase and told the dog, "Let's go inside and see if the old pizza maker is here." Not that I had any hope he'd still be hanging around, but I wouldn't have any problem tracking him down.

Only minutes had passed since my Slide to V-14, and the Boston O'Malley's had returned to pre-Bruno normal. The same men and women lined the bar, and Peach Fuzz was hard at work crafting his concoctions. I found a shadowed table on the far side of the room and put Pepperoni on the floor. He curled up at my feet, leaving me free to inspect the contents of Rachel's briefcase. It wasn't that I didn't trust her—well possibly that did enter my mind—but I wanted to be sure everything was in order before I turned it over to my superiors. And, of course, I'd first remove the bottle of scotch.

Inside the briefcase, I found two bulky hard drives and a well-packed three-ring notebook. I leafed through the pages, but they were incomprehensible. Nestled at the bottom of the briefcase lay a bottle of golden liquid with a turquoise tinge that matched Rachel's eyes. I could see this was expensive liquor and after all I'd been through tracking the delectable Ms. Plimpton through a dozen dimensions, I at least came away with an out-of-this-world bottle of booze.

I set the bottle on the table and admired its shape. It was dark in this corner of O'Malley's, which is why I missed it on my first inspection of the bottle. But as I looked closer, what had at first appeared to be a raised section of the printed label turned out to be entirely different. I ran my fingers over the face of the label and felt the round object that had been secured there. I tugged at it and found myself holding a silver coin, slightly smaller than the faux gold one Bruno gave me.

A candle glowed in the center of the table, and I shifted it closer to better inspect the coin. The first thing that jumped out at me was the large gold letter B with dollar signs sprouting from the top and bottom of the letter. Below that, in much smaller type, I read the words *10 BITCOINS*.

I sat back abruptly, my knees hitting the bottom of the table, jarring the bottle of scotch. Pepperoni sat up and speared me with a worrying expression. "It's okay, boy," I said, patting and calming the pooch until he lay back down.

The coin felt hot and heavy in my hand, befitting a multi-million-dollar treasure piece. Everyone knows bitcoin is a cryptocurrency and all the transactions, or mining, as the process is called, are digitally based. But years ago, a limited number of physical bitcoins were minted. After the value of one bitcoin dollar grew to $225,000 in 2027, the digital currency replaced the gold standard. And while its price has fluctuated on the open market, Rachel's gift of the ten Bitcoins had to be worth more than two million dollars.

I heard the shuffle of feet approaching and slipped the coin in my pocket, where it nestled next to the Sappy's Pizza coin.

"May I help you, sir?"

My server was a perky young woman with close cropped purple hair and a glittering stud in her left nostril. "Can you bring me a glass, please?" I gestured toward the bottle on the table.

She examined the unopened bottle of scotch, and her face worked to resist a frown, with mixed results. "I'm sorry, sir, we don't permit patrons to carry in their own liquor." She looked down at the spaniel at my feet. "And I'm pretty sure only service dogs are allowed."

"You know, service dog is a vocation, not a breed." No smile greeted me from Ms. Perky. "But this is a special occasion," I added and pulled my wallet from my coat pocket and found the rumpled hundred-dollar bill I'd squirreled away for emergency use only. "Here," I said, "will this help?"

She snatched the bill from my hand. "Doesn't hurt." She rushed off in search of a clean glass.

In a New York minute, which is almost illegal in Boston, she returned with the glass and a bowl of water for Pepperoni. I thanked her and pried the top from The Plimpton 18-year-old scotch and poured two fingers. Pepperoni lapped greedily at the water, and I lifted the glass to my nose, inhaling notes of leather and wood and money. Taking a sip, I silently toasted Rachel Plimpton and the new life she had given me appreciating the silky-smooth malty barley on my tongue and savoring the long finish as I swallowed.

A tinge of guilt wormed its way through my head when I thought about the Bitcoin Rachel had bestowed upon me. Was it a bribe? Perhaps. Was it against the government's code of ethics to accept such a gift? Absolutely! Could I reject it? What do you think? Maybe I should retire and enjoy life, pay my mother the rent money I owed her, and find a place of my own. I poured another two fingers and pondered my future.

This assignment might have started with trouble here at O'Malley's Watering Hole, but thanks to Rachel Plimpton the ending was far from troubling. Thinking of Rachel and her generous gift brought forth the image of the painting above the bar. That image further reinforced the memory of Bruno's intimate confession about Rachel wanting to *introduce him to something new and different.*

My mind clicked through multiple graphic possibilities, and I concluded that this didn't have to be the end of our journey together. What was it she had said?

Don't forget that if you'd like another bottle of scotch—or anything else—you know where to find me.

That sounded like an offer I couldn't refuse, especially the *anything else* part. V-14 and a new life was only a quick Slide away. I closed my eyes and imagined my reunion with the tantalizing Ms. Plimpton. Pepperoni chose that exact moment to jump into my lap. He placed his paws on my chest and licked my cheek. I patted the spaniel on his cute head. "Okay, boy," I told him. "Let's go find that old pizza-maker and get you back home."

But first, I lifted my glass of out-of-this-world scotch and murmured a toast. "Here's to you, my lovely Slip-Slider. I'll see you soon."

AUTHOR'S NOTES - PARKER FRANCIS

RAYMOND CHANDLER INTRODUCED the world to hard-boiled detective Philip Marlowe in his first novel The Big Sleep in 1939. But it was his second novel, Farewell, My Lovely, that enshrined Marlowe into the pantheon of unforgettable characters, and provided me with the inspiration for *Farewell, My Lovely Slip-Slider*. My story is both homage and parody of Chandler's classic and uses the novel's opening scene as a springboard for Marlon Phillips' adventures and misadventures.

There was no two-million-dollar payoff for Philip Marlowe, but he did find his way to the big screen as *Farewell, My Lovely* became the basis for three movie versions, with Marlowe portrayed on the big screen by George Sanders in 1942, Dick Powell in 1944, and Robert Mitchum in the 1975 remake. Humphrey Bogart also played Marlowe in the 1946 production of *The Big Sleep*. To date, no one has offered to option F*arewell, My Lovely Slip-Slider*.

~PF

ANDROMEDA CALLING

CHARLES A. CORNELL

If the government is covering up knowledge of aliens, they are doing a better job of it than they do at anything else.
—Stephen Hawking.

Los Angeles, October, 1962

THE CITY of Angels sprawled in front of Peter Piggott's dangling, shoeless feet. The evening air was fresh with a light breeze as the fall sunset painted an amber glow across the orange groves and billboards below the cliff. In his wonderment over the setting sun and its beauty, the ten-year-old boy had almost forgotten how Tommy Brant managed to hang him from the tree in the first place.

Peter had hung by his suspenders over the cliff like a rag doll on a store peg for hours, his feet barely reaching the branch below him, his only means of support. At the bottom of the ravine, thirty feet down, lurked patches of thorny scrubs eager for that creaky branch to break, which seemed imminent. But the view was spectacular nonetheless.

A sparrow flew onto Peter's foot, tickling toes he daren't scratch even if he could reach them. Peter wasn't sure how long his suspenders were going to hold out. The man in the television advertisement that inspired his mother's purchase claimed a horse could pull a wagon with them. So far—fingers crossed—that claim appeared to be the indisputable truth. *Thank goodness*, he thought.

A turquoise '57 Chevy pickup pulled off the road onto the shoulder beside the tree. Doors opened and shut with a loud bang.

"Peter!" Dexter Johnson yelled, hands cupped. "Hold on. We've come to rescue you."

Peter looked down at his friend and sniffled. "Tommy took my runners. And my baseball cap."

"Oh, no! Not again."

Marty, Dexter's older brother, arrived with a step-ladder. "How on earth did he get you up there?"

"Dunno. I was just riding my bike. He and his friends corralled me, put a potato sack over my head, and tied my hands. I think they used a rope to haul me up. Then Tommy put my suspenders on this branch."

Marty climbed up, carefully unhooked Peter's suspenders, and then slung the relieved boy over his shoulder and brought him down.

Peter looked around the dried grass at the dusty base of the tree. "Where's my bike?"

"It's over there." Dexter pointed to the other side of the road. "In those bushes."

"You kids stay by the truck," Marty said. "I'll get it."

Peter stood on wobbly legs, his circulation returning, and leaned against the pickup's tailgate. He felt light-headed and woozy. "I've been in that tree so long I can barely feel my toes."

"Principal McHenry would have a cow if your mom and dad told him," Dexter said. "Tommy's a jerk, he needs to get what's coming to him."

"No, that won't work," Peter sighed. "Tommy's mom is a

teacher at our school, remember? The last time I went to the principal's office to tell them what Tommy had done to me only made it worse. The next day Tommy snatched my *Fantastic Four* comic, went into the bathroom and when he gave it back... *ew, yuck!*"

"He can't keep doing stuff like this to you," Dexter said, kicking the truck's tire as his brother loaded Peter's bike and the stepladder into the pickup bed. "You need to have a plan."

"My plan is simple. I'm hoping Tommy Brant doesn't graduate into fifth grade. That way, we won't be in the same class next year."

"That doesn't sound like much of a plan to me."

"It's the best one I've got."

"You're lucky we found you first," Marty said. "If someone had called your parents, your mom would have phoned the police. But your Dad? He would have gone over to Tommy Brant's house and slugged that crotchety geezer of a grandpa he lives with. The Brant family's been a thorn in everybody's side for years. It's gotten worse now his parents are divorced."

"My dad wouldn't do that. Besides he can't. He's out of town. He might be getting a new job and maybe we'll have to move away," Peter said. "Well, that'd be awful. But at least I won't have any more trouble with Tommy Brant."

"Move away?" Dexter whined. "You can't move away, Peter. You're my best friend. I mean who would I play marbles with? And trade comics with?"

"I hope we're not moving away. I just wish I could sometimes, that's all."

"Hey, kids," Dexter's brother said. "How about I treat you to an ice cream cone? Let's stop by Stony Creek Dairy on the way home."

"Great!" they said in unison.

Marty got in the truck and started the engine. The two boys scrambled inside the cab.

Peter smiled and said, "See, Dexter, sometimes things have a way of turning out okay in the end."

The pickup's tires spun dust as it pulled out onto the road. "Hey," Dexter said to his big brother. "You have dad's truck for the weekend. Can we go to a drive-in movie tonight?"

"Ooh, yeah," Peter added, his spirits lifted, cliff tops forgotten as they left the canyon behind. "There's a double feature at the drive-in."

Dexter's eyes lit up. "What's on?"

"*Journey to the Seventh Planet* and *The Cosmic Man*."

"Aliens? That would be cool! Can we go, Marty? Please?"

Marty scowled. "Mission Boulevard? That's way too far. Besides, I have a date with Suzie tonight."

"That's okay," Dexter said. "We can take her with us."

"With you two clowns? We wouldn't all fit in the truck. And you're a bit too young to understand this, but me and Suzie want to be *alone*."

"He kisses her," Dexter said to Peter, giggling. "On the lips!"

A few miles later, Marty turned the truck into the parking lot of Stony Creek Dairy. It was a typical Saturday night, the lot full of hotrods and souped-up pickups— slick fat tires, shiny chrome wheels, monster exhausts, and foam dice dangling from rearview mirrors. Marty rolled his window down, put the truck in neutral, glided by some friends ogling Jimmy's Deuce Coupe, and gassed the Chevrolet's small block V8. The truck growled with a throaty rumble. Jimmy's new set of chromed intake pipes bellowed back with a *vroom, vroom*. The Deuce Coupe shifted into gear, jerked out of its parking spot and burned a layer of rubber on the freshly paved lot to the delight of the crowd of teenagers and the anger of old Mr. Connor, Stony Creek's owner.

A cute girl wearing a white V-neck pullover and white sneakers, her curves poured into tight-fitting yellow capris, ran over to Marty's truck, her blond ponytail swaying back and forth. She leaned through the window and gave Marty a lingering kiss.

"See," Dexter said to Peter, sticking his tongue out in a mock-barf gesture. "I told you."

Suzie blushed. "Sorry, Marty. I didn't see the kids in there."

Marty shrugged.

Dexter grabbed the steering wheel, pulled himself across his brother's lap, and poked his head out the window. "We're going to the drive-in tonight, Suzie. Wanna come?"

"Dexter, didn't I say no?" Marty pushed him away. "Suzie doesn't want to go, do you?"

"It's a double feature," Peter chimed in. "With aliens and space-ships and everything!"

"I *love* science fiction," she said, her teen-angel face erupting in a huge smile.

"You do?" Marty frowned. "I didn't know that."

"See?" Dexter said. "You'll come with us, won't you Suzie? What time do you want to be picked up?"

"Hey, pipsqueak," Marty said. "This is my date and you're not coming. I told you there's not enough room for four."

"We can watch from the back. That would be fun. We can bring sleeping bags and pillows and—"

"You're not getting the hint, are you?"

"Why can't they come, Marty?" Suzie asked, hands on hips, cherry lips pouting. "It's going to be a warm night. They'll be fine."

"Please? Pretty please?" Dexter pleaded. "And kids under twelve get in free."

Marty swung a playful whack at Dexter and knocked his base-ball cap off. "Darn kid. But first we have to get permission from Peter's mom."

"I'm sure she won't mind," Peter said. "There's no school tomorrow."

"You two rascals better bring some money. I'm not buying you popcorn." Marty turned to Suzie. "Pick you up at six?"

PETER and Dexter sat on the picnic table at the foot of the towering movie screen eating cotton candy. Laughter erupted from the play-ground's spinner. Several kids had jumped off, walked away as if they were drunk, and toppled over on the grass.

The moonless sky was clear and the air crisp. Stars sparkled. "We'd better get back to the truck," Peter said. "It's getting dark. The show will be starting soon."

They wandered between the rows of parked cars, boxy metal

speakers hanging from their windows. Dexter spotted his brother's pickup and pulled Peter by the collar. "This way, dummy."

Peter stumbled, trying to eat his cotton candy as he walked. He was munching its sugary fluffiness when he felt a sharp knock against his ankle that sent him tumbling forward. He hit the ground; his face planted in the sticky pink wool of the candy.

"Enjoy the movie, loser!" he heard Tommy Brant say. "Candy-ass!"

The gaggle of laughter faded between the row of cars as Tommy and his friends left the scene of the crime. Peter rose slowly to his feet and tried to wiped the sugary concoction from his face. He rubbed his eyes and blinked away his tears. His black-rimmed glasses remained stuck in a gooey mixture of whipped sugar and gravel.

"Are you okay?"

Peter looked down at the hole in the knee of his jeans and sobbed, "My mother's going to kill me."

The pre-show cartoon flashed on the screen and a collective cheer emerged from the parked cars. Kids scurried back from the playground like scared rabbits, not wanting to miss a single second.

Peter delicately pried his glasses from the gooey floss. "I think they're cracked." Tears streamed down his face. The more he picked the floss off his glasses, the stickier his fingers became. "Oh, no," he sniffled. "What am I going to do?"

"We gotta clean you up before the movie starts," Dexter said. He looked around and found the neon sign hanging over the wash-room at the back of the lot. He steered his friend inside.

Peter washed the candy from his face and lifted his glasses to the light. A big crack ran across one of the lenses. "Oh boy," he moaned. "I'm dead."

"Your mom's not going to kill you. I'll just tell her what Tommy did."

"And then what? She'll just call me a crybaby. Or call the school. And then Tommy will do something else to me. It's never going to end."

"Cheer up, Peter. Forget about Tommy. C'mon, let's go. The movie's about to start."

The pair walked out of the washroom as the opening credits for *Journey to the Seventh Planet* rolled on the big screen.

"Do you think aliens are real?" Peter asked as they walked back to his brother's pickup truck.

"My dad says they're just something made up. For the movies."

"My dad says that too. But I think both our dads are wrong. Have you read the newspapers? People are seeing flying saucers all over the place. They're in Washington. And New York City. They'll come to Los Angeles soon. Just you wait and see."

"I hope so. That would be so cool. My mom says they're real. She and dad argue about aliens all the time."

"Oh, no," Peter said, pulling Dexter aside. "It's Tommy Brant again!"

Tommy and his posse of friends pushed another kid to the ground. A bag of popcorn spilled across the gravel. Tommy doubled up with laughter as he led the gang toward the washroom, ignoring calls from people in nearby cars to be quiet.

Peter ducked around the corner of the building. "Quick, Dexter. We've got to hide."

"I know. But where?"

The drive-in theater was built in the middle of a large acreage of orange trees. A tall wooden fence separated the drive-in from the groves. Peter and Dexter ran from the washroom and stumbled along the fence-line until they found some loose boards. "We can hide in the orchard until they're gone," Dexter said, prying away the wood until the opening was wide enough for two small boys to fit through. He scurried to the other side. Peter followed and closed the fence-boards behind them.

The pair peered through the crack. "We're going to miss the movie," Dexter whispered.

"It's better than getting a wedgie. Or worse. Tommy Brant always finds a way to make a bad thing worse." A chirping sound coming from the grove startled them. The two boys stared into the darkened orange grove, and then at one another.

"What was that noise?" Peter said. "A ghost?"

The sound repeated, "*Chirp, chirp, z-z-zip. Chirp, chirp, z-z-zip.*"

"An electric ghost? Naw, that's crazy." Dexter crawled through the grass toward the sound.

"Hey, wait up. Don't leave me here."

The pair scurried forward a few yards when Peter's foot clipped an object in the grass, sending him sprawling. He got to his knees and crawled back to see what he'd tripped over.

"Look what I found!" Peter said, lifting up a globular object the size of a football. The intermittent light from the movie screen bounced off its surface.

"Neato. What is that thing?" Dexter replied. The smooth object hummed and glowed, casting shadows around the base of the nearby orange tree. "Don't touch it! Maybe, it's a bomb. It might go off. Drop it, and let's get outta here."

"I don't think it's a bomb. Maybe it's something that fell off a tractor." Peter turned the spherical object in his hands. "It's not heavy. It's as light as a balloon. And it's *warm.*"

He passed it to Dexter. "You're right," he said, turning it in his hands.

"Let's take it home."

"My mom says we shouldn't take anything that isn't ours. Even if we find it," Dexter replied.

"I left my *Mister Ed* lunchbox on the playground once and Tommy Brant found it. I tried to get it back and he said 'finders, keepers'. I didn't tell my mom he stole it. I said I left it on the school bus. I had to buy a new one with my allowance. Tommy Brant stole that one too. Now I just use a paper bag."

The chirping sound returned. Peter dropped the globe in the grass. "This is the thing that made that sound." A series of lights flickered on and off, revolving in a circular band around the object's circumference.

"But what if the farmer needs that? For his tractor?"

"I don't think it's from a tractor, Dexter. Have you ever seen anything on a tractor that squeaks? Or has lights like this? It doesn't look like a toy either." Peter looked up into the sky. "I wonder—"

"You think it fell from outer space?"

"My mom says the Air Force is always finding things that have crashed. But they won't say where they came from. My dad says they're just bits of weather balloons and says my mom should have her head checked for thinking the gov'mint would lie to us."

"This is so cool, Peter. We found something from outer space!"

"We gotta get back to your brother's truck without Tommy Brant seeing this. Can you imagine what kind of superpowers he might get if he stole it? Hey, that's it!" Peter exclaimed. "Maybe I can get superpowers. And zap Tommy. Oh, boy!"

The object spun quietly in Peter's hands as the two boys squeezed back through the fence into the grounds of the drive-in theater. They stepped carefully out of the shadows, looking left and right. Tommy Brant was nowhere to be seen. Peter tucked the object under his shirt, and they ran to Marty's truck and scrambled into the back. They huddled under warm blankets and pillows, bathed in light from the big screen.

"My dad has a ham radio in the workshop behind the garage," Peter whispered, peering under the blanket at his hidden prize. "He told Mom I can use it whenever he's out of town. Maybe we could contact the aliens, Dexter? And see if they want this thing back. Or maybe they would tell us what it does."

"Contact aliens?"

"Why not? If we could prove flying saucers were real then I could ask the aliens to take care of Tommy Brant for me."

THE NEXT NIGHT, Dexter peeked through the screen-door of the workshop located behind the Piggott's garage and found Peter sitting in the middle of a bundle of wires piled on the floor. A box of electrical connectors lay in front of him. Some of the wires ran from the floor up to an old TV on a stand.

"Have you seen today's newspaper?" Dexter asked as he opened the door and bounced into the room.

"No, I've been too busy."

"They're everywhere!"

"What are everywhere?"

"Flying saucers. They saw some in San Bernardino last night. And in Palm Springs. And there's been sightings in Texas, and Nevada... and Arizona too!"

Peter looked up from his tinkering. "Oh shoot this didn't work either." His dad's ham radio crackled on top of the work bench. "No matter what dial I turn it to, I can't hear them," Peter moaned. "Just Mr. Barnard from Spokane chatting with the King of Jordan. I'm sure the king isn't an alien. But I'm not sure about Mr. Barnard."

"So watcha doing with those wires and that beat-up TV?"

"I figured maybe aliens came here because they watch our TV from outer space. So, I attached our TV antenna to my dad's radio. I thought if I could somehow send a message from the radio into the old TV, they might hear me and talk back."

The TV picture on the old set emitted a fuzzy blur of jagged lines that scrolled up and down. Peter whacked the top of the TV cabinet and the picture came into focus.

"Oh cool," Dexter said. "It's *Leave It to Beaver*. I love that show."

A cardboard box sat on the linoleum floor. Peter opened the top, lifted out the sphere he found in the orange grove and put it on the work bench. This time the opaque object glowed from the inside; a glow that pulsed with a dull light that ran through the colors of the spectrum, illuminating the outer shell of the sphere. Both boys took a moment to stare at it.

"That's so cool," Dexter said.

"I wanted to connect the aliens' *thingy* to the radio in case that would help me contact them. But it's too smooth," Peter said. He moved his hand across the sphere. "There's nowhere to stick a wire into it. Or clamp anything onto it. I know, maybe I can crack it open!" He picked up a wrench and banged on the sphere but the wrench just bounced off.

Peter rubbed his wrist. "Ouch!"

A moment later, a sound like the wobbling of a sheet of tin-metal echoed around the room.

"Whoa, what was that!" Dexter exclaimed. "Be careful, Peter. It might explode."

"You should see what it does when I drop it. It rolled off the bench earlier. Watch this." Peter picked up the sphere and let it drop to the floor. It didn't bounce. The underside of the sphere absorbed the impact, the point of contact with the floor flattening out like jelly. Then the object slowly rebounded to its original, perfectly spherical shape. Spinning lights emerged, their color increasing in intensity then settling down into a pulsing rhythm as they circumnavigated the sphere's surface.

"Oh, cool. Way cool."

"Now watch this," Peter said, excited to show off what he'd learned.

Peter picked up the sphere and dropped it next to the TV. The object flattened as before and emitted its wobbly noise again. The TV responded in kind, letting off a loud electrical hum, a throbbing sound that faded in tune with the lights of the sphere as the lights rose in brightness and then settled down.

"Maybe that's not a good idea, Peter. Maybe the aliens won't like you messin' with their gizmo. They could zap this whole place. I saw it in the movies. They can do that kind of stuff and turn people into smoke."

"Nah, the aliens just want to talk to us," Peter said, wiggling the TV antenna as *Leave It to Beaver* drifted into the fuzzy ether. "I just know they do."

The TV signal zigged and zagged as Peter moved the antenna back and forth. A man's face appeared. He was sitting behind a desk. "*Good evening, my fellow citizens...*"

"Hey, I know who that is," Dexter said. "He's not an alien. He's President Kennedy."

"Wow," Peter replied. "I didn't know he had his own TV show!"

"*This Government, as promised, has maintained the closest surveillance of the Soviet military buildup...*"

"My dad says he's the best President there's ever been," Dexter said with authority. "And my mom says his wife has the best clothes.

She's making a dress just like Jackie's to go to Marty's graduation, and— "

"*...a series of offensive missile sites is now in preparation...*"

"Quiet, Dexter! It's the President. And this sounds important. Maybe it's about the flying saucers."

"*...the purpose of these bases can be none other than to provide a nuclear strike capability against the Western Hemisphere.*"

"What's a hemisphere? Is that a kind of spaceship?" Dexter asked.

"No, you clown. That means *us*. America."

"*...intermediate range ballistic missiles...*"

The TV screen returned again to a zig-zag of moving lines. Peter wiggled the antenna and banged on the top of the cabinet. "C'mon, you darned contraption! How will the aliens be able to hear us if you don't work?"

"That's why the TV's in the workshop I guess. It's broken."

"Naw, I see my dad in here all the time watching baseball on it and drinking beer. It's just that I moved it closer to the ham radio. My dad always says bad things to our TVs when he has to move them. But when I say the same things when the chain comes off my bike, he says I have to wash my mouth out with soap. I guess it's okay for him to say those bad words 'cos he's an adult."

"My dad says the same thing. I don't understand it."

"Me neither."

Peter banged on the top of the cabinet again. The President came into focus. "*...in addition, jet bombers, capable of carrying nuclear weapons, are now being uncrated...*"

"I saw this movie a few months ago," Dexter said as Peter wrestled to keep the signal from fading into lines. "Called *Panic in the Year Zero*. It's about a bomb that falls on Los Angeles and it's so big it destroys the whole city. It's one of those atomic bombs. Like the ones Principal McHenry says might get dropped on the school so we have to practice getting under our desks. In the movie, this family has to escape to the hills and live in a cave."

The TV signal bounced, settled for just a moment, then the image on the screen rolled from top to bottom. "Oh drat," Peter said. "You're right. This TV is totally broken. Darn." The picture stopped rolling. "Oh, it's back!"

"*...this sudden, clandestine decision to station strategic weapons for the first time outside of Soviet soil,*" the President continued, "*is a deliberately provocative and unjustified change in the status quo which cannot be accepted by this country...*"

"What's a Soviet? Are they aliens?"

"No, dummy," Peter replied. "They're Russkies. Commie pinkos, my dad calls them. He thinks Principal McHenry is a commie pinko."

"What's that?"

"I don't know. But my dad is really mad whenever he talks about Principal McHenry being a commie pinko. So, it must be a really bad thing."

"Sounds like an alien to me. I always thought Principal McHenry was an alien."

"*...a strict quarantine on all offensive military equipment under shipment to Cuba is being initiated. All ships of any kind bound for Cuba from whatever nation or port will, if found to contain cargoes of offensive weapons, be turned back.*"

"Where's Cuba? Is that a planet? Are we going to war with aliens?"

"Dexter, don't you know *anything*? Cuba's a country. An island. On Earth."

"Okay Peter, if you're so smart, why has there been so much stuff in the papers about flying saucers? I asked my mom and she thinks it's all because of this Cuba thing. She says the aliens have been watching us and don't like what we've been doing with atomic bombs. But I thought she meant the aliens were watching us from a planet called Cuba. I'm totally confused."

"Well, *my* mom says it's best just to take a pill and forget about everything. I think that's what she's done today 'cos she's been sleeping on the sofa all afternoon. I even had to feed the cat and let it out. I wish my dad was back. Mom is better when he's home. And then we get to eat out a lot."

"*I call upon Chairman Khrushchev to halt and eliminate this clandestine, reckless, and provocative threat to world peace... to abandon this course of world domination... to end the perilous arms race... to move the world back from the abyss of destruction..."*

"Destruction? See, Peter, I told you! This must be a movie. It sounds just like that movie I saw." Dexter looked up at the Coca-Cola clock on the workshop wall. "I have to go now. I have to deliver the evening papers. Maybe there's more news about flying saucers. I'll come back tomorrow and see if you've got this TV working."

"Okay, but don't tell your mom about what we found. You haven't told her, have you?"

"Nah. Even my older sister doesn't know. She blabs about everything. So, wadcha say, can I have it at my house for a while?"

"Where would you hide it?"

"The basement. My mom's afraid of spiders. She doesn't go down there much."

"Umm, maybe. But not until I get this thing to work first. And then only for one night."

"Okay, cool."

Peter wiggled the wire connecting the TV antenna to the ham radio. The picture turned fuzzy. He sighed, "President Kennedy says we should go to the moon. But I think we should make better TVs first."

THE HOOT of an owl woke Peter from his sleep. A strange hum buzzed in his ear. He lifted his head from the work bench. The clock said it was ten minutes to three in the morning. "Huh? That late? Oh no," he moaned, sleepily. "Guess Mom must be super zonked out, as usual. Forgets to put me to bed all the time," he said to himself as he rubbed his eyes.

The humming noise grew louder. Peter turned toward it. The spherical object had floated four feet off the ground, dead in the center of the room. As Peter watched, a beam of light projected an image from the object onto the blank wall below the clock. "Holy cow!" Peter cried out. "It's working!"

The projected image was as clear as a bell: the black and white TV broadcast of President John F. Kennedy saying, *"It shall be the policy of this nation to regard any nuclear missile launched from Cuba against any nation in the Western Hemisphere as an attack by the Soviet Union on the United States, requiring a full retaliatory response upon the Soviet Union."*

As the president's speech ended, the projected image reset itself to the beginning of the short clip and repeated the broadcast from, *"It shall be the policy of this nation to regard any nuclear missile launched from Cuba..."*

Peter looked back at the sphere; his head cocked, trying to see where the beam was coming from. The projection on the wall continued. President Kennedy repeated, *"It shall be the policy of this nation to regard any nuclear missile launched from Cuba..."*

A flash of light from the old TV drew Peter's attention. A single bright line pulsed across the TV screen from left to right. The rest of the screen was black. The pulse changed color as it moved, beaming all the colors of the spectrum across the TV in a never-ending repetition, eerily in synch with the projected broadcast coming out of the nearby sphere. A light on the ham radio, its ever-present crackling strangely silent, flashed on and off.

The radio was receiving a signal.

Peter picked up the ham set's microphone, turned the mic switch to 'on', and said in a half-asleep voice, "This is Earth calling. This is Earth calling. Is anyone there?"

Someone...or some *thing*...on the radio answered back.

DEXTER STOOD at the base of their classroom's portable building and stared up at Peter. It was getting dark. The school was deserted. "What are you doing up there on the roof?" Dexter asked. "Mrs. Prendergast will be mad if you damage anything. Like she gets mad when the fan stops working and she has to call the janitor."

Peter held a can in one hand and a paint brush stained with bright red pigment in the other. "I'm painting."

"I know that. But *why*?"

"You'll see."

"If Principal McHenry catches you up there, you'll get expelled."

"I hope so," Peter replied. "Then maybe I'll be sent to a different school. Away from Tommy Brant."

"Hey, is that a new ball cap?" Dexter asked, squinting in the dim light.

"Yeah. My Dad got it for me. It's a Yankees cap. He's back from his trip."

"You'd better hide it from Tommy Brant before he steals it."

"What's the point in having a new baseball cap if you can't wear it? I've decided I'm tired of worrying about what Tommy Brant is going to do to me. No more. I'm going to do something about it. I have a plan."

The sound of a hammer echoed off the roof.

"Now what are you doing?"

"Hammering."

"I know that. But *why*? And don't tell me, *I'll see*, because I can't see from down here."

"I'm nailing a pulley to the roof," Peter said.

"But *why?*"

"You'll see."

Dexter threw up his hands. "Oh, gee. I'm going home. You're impossible."

"That's what my mom says."

"Well, she's right," Dexter replied as he slipped into the darkness.

"HE LOVES HIS DOG, Dexter. And his dog loves me."

The air in the workshop hung like a hot towel over their faces. Dexter downed his Coca-Cola, burped and said, "What the heck does that mean, Peter?"

"We're going to kidnap his dog. Tonight."

"*What?* Are you *crazy?*"

"I've got a brilliant plan. And you have to help me."

"I'm not helping you kidnap Tommy's dog. We'd go to jail."

"We're not really kidnapping his dog. We're borrowing him. Besides, they're very interested in our dogs."

"*Who* are interested in them?"

"*They* are." Peter pointed to the old TV and the glowing sphere.

"*Aliens*? Aliens are interested in our dogs? How do you know?"

"They told me."

"They *told* you? You've been talking to them?"

"Every night since I got them hooked into Dad's radio."

"Oh, wow! What did they say?"

"You'll see."

"Not that again. C'mon, I can keep a secret."

"It'll be more fun this way."

"Did they tell you what planet they come from?"

"Not exactly."

"Do they have mind rays and robots? Is it just one big guy like *The Day the Earth Stood Still*? I love that movie. What was his name? Cat-something."

"Klaatu."

"So, what did he say?"

"You'll see."

"*You'll see, you'll see.* That's all you ever say. Stop being a brat! No wonder you get bullied!" Dexter walked past the buzzing TV with its zigzag signal and stopped at the workshop door. "I have to get my papers and start my deliveries before it gets too dark. And I'm not helping you kidnap Tommy's dog and that's final."

"You're a sissy. Never mind. I don't need you to catch him. That dog will follow me anywhere. I just thought you'd be interested in seeing the aliens."

Dexter took his hand off the screen-door's latch. "*What*? See the aliens? *Where*? *When*?"

"Tonight. They're coming tonight."

"*Tonight*?"

"They're all leaving tomorrow. They said we were about to blow the planet up and they didn't want to be here when we did. They said we had a chance to become friends, but it was too late. They're going to another planet instead. Where it's safer. And friendlier. But they said if I wanted to come with them, I could. They wanted me to bring my dog as well."

"You don't have a dog."

"That's why I need to borrow Tommy's dog, dummy."

"Wait." Dexter walked back to Peter as he fiddled with the TV. "Are you and Tommy's dog going to get on an alien spaceship?"

"Something like that."

"Tonight?"

"Come to the school before midnight. Hide in the woods by Mrs. Prendergast's portable and watch. Don't be late or you'll miss everything. Just you. Nobody else."

"Okay," Dexter muttered, looking puzzled. "Okay, I'll be there."

"DEXTER? DEXTER?" Mrs. Johnson prodded her son's shoulder as he slept curled up on the sofa. The broadcasting day had ended and the dull circular test pattern with its Indian chief icon was all that was left. She went over to the TV and switched it off.

Dexter rubbed his eyes and groaned, "What time is it?"

"It's eleven thirty, Dexter. You should be in bed."

"Oh no," he gasped. "Eleven thirty! Oh no, I'll be late!"

"Late for what?"

"I mean, yes, Mom, I know I'm late for bed. I'm very sorry." Dexter bounced off the sofa and scrambled up the stairs, faster than his mother had ever seen him do before, even when he'd forgotten his homework and had to come back in the house.

"Good night, Mom," Dexter said at the top of the stairs.

"What was that all about?" his father asked.

"I'm not sure," she replied. "He's been acting very strange lately."

"I blame his friend, Peter. Odd little boy. He's a bad influence. I wish Dexter would find someone else to be friends with. Someone with a little more... um, well, *gumption* I suppose you could call it. Peter lets the other boys push him around. Never fights back."

"That's not a bad thing, dear. Turning the other cheek."

"Well, he just needs to stick up for himself. That's all I'm saying."

DEXTER TUCKED a pillow under his blankets and arranged his stuffed toys around the 'sleeping boy'. He opened his bedroom window and peered down at the backyard. He'd leant his bike against the fence and had left the gate unlocked. He climbed out of the window onto the roof of the sun-room, tiptoed carefully to the far edge and climbed down the trellis. He looked back into the house and waited. The kitchen light went off. He paused a moment longer to make sure his parents were on their way to bed. The upstairs light went off. Then their bedroom light. Dexter bolted for the gate, pushed it open, and jumped on his bike.

The school was a fifteen-minute bike ride away. *I hope I'm not late,* he thought, pedaling as fast as he could, taking every shortcut he knew. He winced as his legs burned with energy, and wheezed as his lungs tried to keep up with them.

The main building of Eisenhower Elementary, set back from the road far away from the last streetlight, stood in the darkness like a black monolith of stone. Dexter slowed down, out of breath. Mrs. Prendergast's portable was behind the main building not far from the baseball diamond and next to the woods where Peter said he should hide. Dexter rounded the ill-lit street corner and rode across the playground. A full moon cast a ghostly light across the schoolyard. Dust and dry leaves flew up into his face. Up until that point, the night had been calm and still, the sky bright with stars. Another sudden, swirling gust sent leaves chattering across the empty asphalt.

He stopped his bike near the portable and shivered in the wind. "Peter?" he whispered. His mouth felt tacky like it had been jammed with cotton balls. "Peter? Are you there?"

A dog barked loudly, and he jumped. The barking came from the top of the portable and echoed across the empty schoolyard. Dexter gazed into a star-filled sky and saw a strange object descending. The dull black circle blotted out the twinkling starlight as it drew closer. The dog on the roof snarled. Its bark became feverish then turned into a whimper.

As Dexter dismounted from his bike, the wind increased around him. Leaves and twigs, bits of gravel and lumps of loose asphalt, floated upwards in tiny swirling tornadoes. The debris stung his face. Dexter dropped his bike to the ground just as the frame started to shake. He watched the streamers hanging from the handlebars fly up toward the sky, along with the entire bike. Defying gravity, his Schwinn hung suspended in the air five feet above the pavement. The bike's pedals and chain began turning like an invisible rider had mounted it.

"Holy geez—"

A bright cone of white light punched through the darkness from above, surrounding the portable on all sides. Dexter fell back on the hard tarmac and shielded his eyes. He saw a silhouette on top of the portable's roof standing underneath the blinding light: a boy in a baseball cap holding a dog in his arms. The dog's barking wobbled through the night air as if the sound waves had slowed to a crawl. A band of many colors encircled the dark shape that hovered in silence high above the portable. Lights pulsed around it in a slow rhythm, whipping around the circumference of the floating object.

"A f-flying s-saucer!" Dexter gulped, standing up. "They *are* real!"

A thumping vibration boomed from the spaceship, rippling across the schoolyard. It shook Dexter off his feet. He fell to the pavement again. A blue beam emerged at an angle from the underside of the spaceship and slid across the roof of the portable. Another boom shook the ground. The beam of blue light went out. The bright cone of white light remained but the boy and the dog on the roof were gone.

"Peter?" Tears trickled down Dexter's cheeks. "Oh no... *Peter!*" he yelled.

The cone of white light went out as suddenly as it had appeared. The circling multi-colored band stopped rotating around the saucer's edge; the colored lights throbbed briefly then dimmed until total darkness returned. The craft rose upwards into the sky.

Twinkles of starlight re-emerged once the giant saucer-like shadow had shrunk into nothingness.

Pebbles, sharp gravel, lumps of asphalt and several lost marbles fell to the pavement like hail. "Ouch," Dexter yelled, covering his head. His bike dropped to the ground, bounced on its tires, and fell over with a clatter.

Dexter dusted himself off. A piercing whistle from the woods startled him. Shaking with fright, he mounted the bike to pedal back home when he heard a shout, "Wait! Wait!"

"Peter?" Dexter strained in the darkness but saw nothing. "Peter, is that you?"

Sirens wailed down the street. Numerous sets of red flashing lights approached the school at great speed. Dexter looked toward the advancing vehicles and their oncoming headlights, his stomach in knots, his legs frozen in place.

A hand touched his shoulder from behind. "Oh!" he cried out. "Don't scare me like that! Ever again."

"Sorry, Dexter. Pretty neat, huh?"

"Peter? But... but, I thought... I mean, you and Tommy's dog. You were— "

"I hope they like him. He'd better behave."

"Tommy's dog?" Dexter asked.

"No, you goober. Tommy."

"*Tommy*? Tommy Brant, you mean?"

Peter shrugged. "Yup. I'm sure they won't put up with his bullying. If that thingy still works with my dad's radio maybe they'll tell us how he's doing."

"I thought *you* were leaving with the aliens?"

"Well, I would have liked to. They seemed pretty friendly. But in the end, I couldn't really leave home. Dad came back from New York and he and Mom have patched things up. And we're not moving. Isn't that great?"

"But Tommy Brant? *How*? I mean, what happened?"

More sirens blared all across the city, up and down every street in the neighborhood. Several police cars and a fire engine turned off the road into the boulevard that led up to Eisenhower Elementary's front entrance.

"Quick, Dexter. I need your help. I have to find the rope I took from my dad's workshop before he finds out it's missing. It's on the other side of the portable. I'll explain everything."

Peter jumped on the back of Dexter's bike and they rode across the playground. The earth immediately surrounding the portable was sizzling. Red embers glowed where dry grass used to be. "Oh drat," Peter said picking up the rope that lay in a disorganized coil beside the portable. "It got burnt too."

"C'mon Peter, are you going to tell me or not? How did you get Tommy to agree to go with the aliens instead of you?"

"Oh, he didn't agree to go."

"Huh?"

"Well, I left a note on his porch that said if he wanted his dog back, he had to meet me by the portable at midnight. Getting the dog on the roof was going to be the hardest part. But I remembered how Tommy hoisted me into that tree. So, I did the same with the dog. But I used a pulley because even though I'm not as strong as Tommy Brant, I'm way smarter. And that's how I got down too. After Tommy climbed up to get his dog back."

"But I still don't understand how the aliens knew where to come and why Tommy agreed to go with them?"

"Getting the aliens here was easy. I told them where the school was and told them I would paint a big red X on the portable roof so it would be easy to find me. Then I told them I would be waiting for them on the roof wearing a baseball cap. And of course, I would bring my dog."

"But you're not wearing a baseball cap."

"Well, yes I was. Until Tommy Brant stole it from me just before I climbed down the rope."

Another bright light flashed in their eyes.

"It's just kids," the policeman said to his buddy as they searched the woods. "Why are you out so late? You should be at home in bed."

"Um, we saw strange lights," Peter replied.

"Yeah, people are seeing them all over the city. Someone reported lights hovering over the school. Was it you?"

Peter shook his head, 'no'.

Firemen hosed down the smoking grass.

"And there's fires like this everywhere. Do you know who did this? What did you see? Anything?"

"We sure did, mister! A flying sauc—"

Peter poked Dexter in the ribs before he could say anything more. "He was going to say a weather balloon. That's what my dad says they are."

The policeman scratched his chin. "A weather balloon?"

"You mean they aren't weather balloons?" Peter said. "Have the police seen *real* flying saucers? Then the papers must be right. Have *you* seen a real honest-to-goodness flying saucer, officer? And aliens? What about aliens? Are they real too?"

"Ah, well. But, um… Yeah, no. No such thing." The officer picked up Dexter's bike. "Hey, Charlie," the policeman yelled. "I'm gonna put the kids' bike in the trunk and give them a lift home. Meet you back at the station."

The officer in the woods wiggled his flashlight and replied, "Okay, Joe."

"Weather balloons," the policeman muttered as he loaded the bike into the patrol car's trunk. "Yeah, that's what they were, kids. Just weather balloons."

"I told you, Dexter," Peter smirked. "Flying saucers aren't really *real*. They're just something made up. Like in the movies."

"Tell that to Tommy Brant."

"Well, one thing's for sure," Peter said, smiling. "I'm sure going to miss his dog."

AUTHOR'S NOTES - CHARLES A. CORNELL

WHAT THINGS ARE certain in life? The classic answer: death and taxes. But back in 1962, there were two other 'certainties': (1) UFOs weren't real because the government said so, and (2) mankind had the ability to destroy the entire planet, and all life on it, with one mistaken push of a nuclear launch button, a military policy known as 'mutually assured destruction' (MAD, potentially the most appropriate acronym in history).

Well, this story bypasses the first two — I mean where's the humor in death and taxes? — to focus its satirical lens on the latter two.

Andromeda Calling begs the question: who was crazier? Those who believed in UFOs? Or those who thought MAD was a good idea?

Peter Pigott might have explained it best, as youngsters in their simplicity always do, "President Kennedy says we should go to the moon. But I think we should make better TVs first." Thankfully, in time, we got both.

Regarding the policy of MAD, interspersed within *Andromeda Calling* are verbatim excerpts from the official transcript of President John F. Kennedy's famous speech during the Cuban Missile Crisis. If you are a history geek— like I am— you can read the full transcript of that famous speech by accessing it via the JFK Library here:

https://www.jfklibrary.org/learn/about-jfk/historic-speeches/address-during-the-cuban-missile-crisis

~Charles

EMPTY SUIT

KEN PELHAM

" *I wish you'd keep your fingers out of my eye,*" said the aerial voice, in a tone of savage expostulation... "*I'm invisible. It'sa confounded nuisance, but I am. That's no reason why I should be poked to pieces by every stupid bumpkin in Iping, is it?*"
—H.G. Wells, The Time Machine

EDISON GLASS PAUSED outside the gilded doors of B. Hemuth Corporation, an overloaded satchel slung over his aching shoulder. He took a sip of confidence from Starbucks, fiddled with his tie with his free hand, and strode in, just as he'd done for seven years. With a little extra pumpkin spice that morning; a big presentation loomed, and a nice promotion along with it.

Heather Wu, embedded behind a vast, shiny, reception desk, pushed aside the tiny mic of her headset, and gave him a twinkly smile. "Good morning, Eddy. How was your weekend?"

Edison returned the smile. "Morning, Heather, it—"

"Glass Ceiling!" Tyler Carpenter swept into the lobby, lugging his industrial cup of coffee. "Maybe this is the week you break through, eh, Glass?" He stabbed his cup at Edison, sloshing coffee onto Heather and her desk. "Little help there, Heather."

Heather reached under the desk and withdrew a paper towel.

"Hm," Edison said. He tried forcing a smile that resisted cooperation.

"Eleventh time's the charm, eh?" Carpenter's toothy grin seemed wider than his head. The Veep of Public Relations sloshed more coffee.

Heather wiped up the spill and lasered in on Carpenter's listing cup. "Can I get you a saucer, Mr. Carpenter?"

"I'm good, sweet meat. Well, Glass, better get working on your pitch to Belinda. Can't let one slip away again, eh?" Without waiting for an answer, he swept out of the lobby, leaving a trail of coffee splatters on the tile floor. Heather tore off more paper towels and came around the desk.

She hadn't been on the job long, maybe four months. In that short time, Edison had seen how she read people, reacted to them, always in the most courteous fashion. Never an angry word. She deserved better.

"Let me help," Edison said.

"Thanks, Eddy." She smiled. "It'll go well today. I just know it will."

B. HEMUTH LOOMED large in the world of sales and shipping, always looking to expand its darkness to new cities. Edison knew he was considered a functionary, at best. But he could functionary the shit out of a project. And no one put in hours like him. Nights. Weekends. Didn't matter. He'd held the same midlevel position at B. Hemuth since day one. Maybe that would change next week.

A coveted slot in the Uppers had opened up with the retirement of Thomas Granger. Retirement. That was one way to put it. Granger was aged out. Outlived his shelf life at fifty-seven. Old Thomas, they called him. Ancient in the big tech universe. He was sharp as ever, but people talked like he was a withered old coot, cackling over his bits of string and pointing a bony, accusing finger at the full heads of hair and untucked shirts of the whipper-snappers.

It was sad. Still, there was an opening, and no one in the Granger replacement candidate pool had Edison's years of experience.

Which was exactly the problem.

Edison had tripped that age wire himself, and he was still in early forties. With seven years in the same company, the same job. That was outrageous, the kiss of death, a quaint notion from a Netflix period piece, stuffed with the archaic language but without the costumery or coupling on the stairwells that grabbed the viewers. Certainly not a series anyone would binge-watch.

Everything was riding on his presentation today.

The conference room was full of chrome and wood, half-empty of people. Or was it half-full? Nah, exactly half-empty, only eleven seats of twenty-two occupied. A couple of Manhattan types sort of listened in online. All were his youngers, all squirmy and impatient, even including CEO Belinda Hemuth, and her sycophant and his tormenter, Tyler Carpenter. Belinda, her dark hair clenched even tighter than usual, sat leaning sideward as always when someone besides herself was speaking. She watched her tablet, tapped on it occasionally, and smiled now and then. Tyler pecked at his phone as well. He'd peck something in. She'd suppress a smile, tap something in return. Peck tap, peck tap.

Edison packed numbers and exclamations into his presentation like a packhorse and plowed through it like a plow horse, mustering all the enthusiasm he could about Atlanta for the Southeast expansion. The roads. The airport. The soul o' the Southeast. The hub o' the heartland. Etcetera, etcetera. All that good stuff. He positively glittered, scrolling through census data and pie charts, raining buzzy words like manna from heaven. Metadata, he said. Human capital, he said. Stark Industries, he said. Fungibly cloudify mission-driven action items, he said, to make sure everyone was listening. He was nailing this dog-and-pony show. The dog was eating the pony. And vice versa.

Edison wrapped up and waited. It took nine seconds of deathly silence before Belinda glanced about, looked up at him, pushed her tablet aside. "Thank you for that, um, Edison. Charlotte is an interesting take."

"Charlotte who?" Edison asked.

"Not a who, a what," Belinda said. "Charlotte, North Carolina."

"Atlanta, Georgia," Edison said.

She gave him a moment of arched eyebrows, then looked around the room. "Anyone?"

"Atlanta, yawn," Carpenter offered. "Charlotte, now that's a great idea, Belinda. Would make a logical step. Hip. Youthful. Vibrant. Me like."

Nods all around.

Belinda looked again at Edison, disappointment stamped on her face. "Why didn't you look at Charlotte?"

"You told me to look at Atlanta."

"We want independent thinkers. If there's nothing more, this meeting is over." She glanced at her watch. "A whole hour about freaking Atlanta. The Board will be thrilled."

The room emptied, leaving Edison to stare out the window at a blank sky.

HE WENT TO THE BATHROOM, enclosed himself in a stall, took a seat, hoisted his feet onto the rim, and waited. This was the best place in the 27th floor for intelligence gathering.

He was soon rewarded. The sound of the door opening and closing. Footsteps. Voices. Tyler Carpenter and his toady, River Tanner. Murmurs. Sports banter. Chuckles. Peeing. Flushing. Minimalist handwashing. And finally, the subject he knew they'd get around to. And the hated nickname.

"So," Tanner said. "How'd old Glass do?"

If eye rolls could make a sound, Edison was sure he heard one. "Oh, informative. Exciting. Pure adrenaline rush. Glass plodded through it like a jellyfish with no legs. Belinda almost put her head on the table for a nap."

"Ha! He's your classic empty suit."

"He doesn't disappoint. Oh, by the way, gather everything you can on Charlotte. Start this afternoon. Get me the goods on Hicksville, by Thursday. Get the art department to pretty it up, put a ribbon on it. I'll stick it on the bitch's desk Friday morning. I'm also going to sidetrack the empty suit, have him sort paperclips the rest of the week."

Ten minutes later, Edison got an email from Carpenter directing him to put together a prospectus on Akron for a subregional distribution center. Edison typed a response: "Akron already has a subregional."

"Don't be insubordinate. You know I meant a sub-subregional center," Carpenter wrote.

"Insubordinate sub-sub. Got it," Edison replied, and began combing U.S. Department of Commerce info on Charlotte.

EDISON WORKED UNTIL NINE, powered down, and drove home in both literal and figurative fogs, the world blurry to him. He reached his apartment, let himself in. His little brother, Winston, sat on the couch, feet on the coffee table, amid a tasteful, geometric array of empty beer bottles, gaming away in front of a gigantic monitor. Winston glanced up, killed the sound, and set his control aside. "Hey, brother mine. A little late getting home tonight. There's spaghetti on the stove."

Edison helped himself to a plate of cold spaghetti and warm beer. He sat gloomily opposite his little brother. "Thanks, Wince."

"That's Doctor Wince to you." A pause. "Bad day, huh?"

"Oh, the presentation went great. The reception sucked, even more than usual." He related the entire humiliating fiasco, including the subsequent recon in the bathroom. He concluded with a defeated sigh and a long pull from his beer. "I stayed late to get started on Charlotte. Not sure why; I'll be slathered by Carpenter with garbage tasks all week."

"He called you an empty suit, eh?" Wince said. "That's funnier than 'Glass Ceiling.'"

"Your empathy, as always, is comforting."

Wince leaned back. "Empty suit," he repeated. "Empty suit." He closed his eyes and laced his fingers, lost in thought.

"I'm getting another beer."

Edison returned, sat. He didn't like to derail Wince's train of thought. His brother was the smartest man he'd ever met and the least focused, so when Wince actually settled into a state of focus, you ran with it.

Wince also worked for B. Hemuth, in the small annex on the opposite end of the giant compound. Like other Google and Amazon wannabees, the company dabbled as well. Belinda wanted to be seen as a Bezos-Musk burrito, and she established small science labs to make it look that way. They were habitually under-staffed and underfunded, but they created the illusion of B. Hemuth as a citadel of cutting-edge techie stuff. She hired brilliant, unmotivated scientists to flesh it out. Wince was perfect for the job. PhD in physics from Cal-Tech, dedicated stoner and gamer on the side. The company made few demands on his lifestyle. He could dabble this way and that, and his lab could apply for an occasional patent for stuff on the same excitement scale as refrigerator magnets.

Wince at last opened his eyes and leaned forward. "Empty Suit. I like it. Sounds like a half-assed superhero. Listen. I want to give *you* the powers."

Edison waited.

"I do physics. I specialize in optics. Science-y stuff. I've invented a new material, Winston's Optical Meta-Rag, one that will give B. Hemuth ads, labeling, and packaging a signature look. It dicks around with light. Bends it. Let me explain like I'm talking to a six-year-old." He held up his half-finished beer. "The bottle is glass. You see the glass and the beer inside. Look closer and you see through to my hand on the opposite side. The glass reflects less light and refracts more light than my hand. It's still visible, but it's *less* visible. To make it invisible, I need to bend light, make it go smoothly around it. That's been done on a molecular scale, but it's way beyond anything we can do at a bigger scale.

"The necessary interferometry defies us. But four months ago, I wrapped a sphere the size of a basketball with it."

"A sphere the size of a basketball?"

"Okay, a basketball. Alas, only a tiny fraction of the light hitting it swirled past, just fuzzying up the edges a bit. I tinkered, tweaking this, upping that. Nothing. Then I had an idea; I cut open the basketball and wrapped its insides with Meta-Rag as well. I mounted a light and a 360 degree camera inside it."

"And?"

"And nothing. Weeks of nothing. Then I had a breakthrough.

"You achieved the interferer—the intra-feralonomy—the bendy light thing?

"I spilled beer on it."

"You were *drinking*? On company time? In a fifty-million-dollar lab?"

"Beer barely qualifies as drinking, but you're missing the point. The beer reacted with the meta-paint, amplifying the bent-light stream inside and out. The basketball remained visible, unchanged. But the inside of the basketball was *gone*."

"Gone?"

"Well. Not gone. You just couldn't see it."

"Because you spilled your beer."

"All great inventions start with beer, and this was good beer, artisanal as hell." Wince held his bottle to the light, beaming like he'd discovered the food of the gods, and took a sip. He glanced at Edison. "You could use it, you know."

"I already have a beer."

"Forget the damn beer. The technology. Have you heard a word I'm saying? I manipulated light to the point where the inside of a basketball became invisible. Completely invisible, not even a dotted line or a blur. *Invisible*." He clapped his hands. "Eddy. Bro. I can make you a suit of this material. *You* can become invisible. You can become a superhero. You can be Empty Suit!"

Edison settled back into his chair, letting the possibilities sink in. Invisibility. The stuff of dreams. He could move through B. Hemuth Corp with impunity, sabotaging projects as he saw fit. His career path might be paved with potholes, but with his brother's magic cloak of invisibility he could step deftly around them.

A thought occurred. "If you're so sure of this thing, why don't *you* become the invisible man?"

"Whoa, Bro. This is cutting-edge tech, and cutting edge can cut you. I'm a contented, scared little baby. Not a desperate baby. But you are. And crazy too."

"Wait. You could still see the basketball from outside?"

"Yep."

"But not the inside."

"Yep."

"How does this invisibility suit work then?"

"Any part of you covered by the suit becomes invisible."

"While the suit remains visible?"

"Well, yeah."

"And face and hands remain visible?"

"Um. Yeah."

"The suit, visible. Face, head, and hands, visible. How is that different from any other suit?"

"Um."

"This is the stupidest invention in the history of stupid inventions!"

Wince looked hurt. "That's what they said to Alexander Graham Bell when he invented the cotton gin, but look where we are today."

TWO WEEKS LATER, Wince burst into the apartment. "I got it!"

Edison didn't look up from the TV. "The clap?"

"Immortality, Bro. I've reduced the active compounds in Meta-Rag to a clear liquid, and made an aerosol spray from it. Each tiny droplet becomes a double-coated sphere the size of a tiny droplet, bending light like a drunk bends an elbow."

"And?"

Wince held up an empty palm. "Catch," he said, and made a tossing motion.

Something unseen bounced off Edison's head. "Ow."

"That was a VHS cassette. *Beverly Hills Cop III*. No one will miss it."

Edison's mind raced and his heart struggled to keep up. "I want it. I want to be Empty Suit."

FIRST THING ON MONDAY, Edison entered the lobby of B. Hemuth Corp. Heather Wu looked up, beaming. "Looking sharp today, Eddy," she said.

"For a while, let's hope." He paused. "Heather, want to get coffee sometime? We could, um, get coffee. Sometime, I mean." So smooth, Mr. Superhero.

"I'd love to." She seemed sincere.

"Good. Great." He grinned, trying to contain it. "I like coffee." He wanted to hang himself.

"Tomorrow morning, before work? Seven, at H.G. Barista's?"

"I like coffee." *Where was that noose?*

At 10 AM, after making his presence in the office widely known, he took the stairs down six floors to Accounting, which was populated by short-sleeved trolls flecked with doughnut crumbs. They didn't look up from their screens. They didn't know him and didn't want to. He let himself into the janitorial closet at the end of the hall, flicked on the light, and stripped naked.

Almost naked. He kept his Pink Floyd boxers on. He folded his clothes and hid them behind a tower of toilet tissue rolls.

A light tap-tap came from the door, and it swung open. Wince entered, dressed in fake custodian overalls, fake mustache, and fake glasses, carrying a tray of brand-name cleaners. He gave Edison a quick look-over. "Ready?"

"Ready."

"No, you're not. You have to be completely coated. Get them panties off, boy," he said.

"Oh, for—" Edison shook his head. "Fine." He took off his Pink Floyds, stuffed them away with the rest of his clothes. "Can we get this over with?"

"Trust me, right now, no one wants you invisible more than me. I see you shaved your pits and chins and balls, as instructed. Good boy. He's a good boy, yes he is." He picked an aerosol can out of his tray, gave it a vigorous shake. "Close your eyes and keep your mouth shut."

Edison did so, and heard the hiss of the spray and felt its coolness on his skin. Wince turned him slowly, spraying every corner, working the liquid into his hair, which fortunately was already almost invisible. After a few minutes, Wince said, "Blimey! 'E's all eaten away."

Edison opened his eyes. Wince handed him a small mirror. Edison stared, disbelieving. "I'm… *gone*. Invisible. Every square inch." Then he noticed the flaw. "I can see my eyes, and my mouth moving when I talk. A pair of eyes and a talking set of teeth, floating in space."

"Well yeah, get this stuff in your eyes and mouth, you'll be blind and sick for a week. I gotta get back to the lab. You're on your own, Bro."

A PAIR of eyes and a mouth floated up the stairwell. The stairwell door opened onto the 27th floor and the eyes and mouth drifted out and paused, hovering, turning this way and that. The open plan, cubicles as far as the eye could see, heads popping up now and then like prairie dogs. Murmurs and snatches of conversation. One head, Vanessa Bundt's bluish one, looked in his direction, and froze, staring.

Edison closed his eyes and clenched his mouth like a fist. He eased nine steps to the left and opened one eye to the narrowest of slits. The Bundt still stared at where he had stood, shook her head, and went back to work.

He wasn't invisible, he was an apparition. A mote. People would notice. They would notice a fly buzzing the office. Still, he'd made himself invisible to escape the Bundt. But if he kept his eyes closed, how could he avoid colliding with immovable or moveable objects like people wearing clothes?

He glanced at his fist and saw nothing. He opened it and saw the tiny flash drive. He closed his fist, and the flash drive disappeared.

He collected himself, resisting the urge to cover his crotch. He stood outside the window of Carpenter's office and watched. The guy would be pitching to Charlotte Mayor Martinez and his top staff in an hour, the whole herd of them in town to hear B. Hemuth's plans for their fair city.

Carpenter was eager, coiffed, and slick in Armani. A lot riding on this one, a $200 million project stolen right from under Edison's feet. Carpenter glanced at his watch, took a sip of Pink Cow, the power drink of weenies, and headed for the bathroom on his usual schedule. The guy even scheduled peeing.

As always, he left his laptop open and on.

Edison stepped in. Sure enough, Carpenter was last-minute tweaking his presentation, the program still open. Edison had to act fast, before the laptop's security demanded the password. He sat, inserted the flash drive, and tapped furiously on the keyboard.

An hour later, Mayor Martinez's jaw fell when Carpenter showed a PowerPoint slide of him photoshopped wearing a tutu with Fidel Castro at a tractor-pull.

Two hours later, Carpenter stuffed the last of his personal effects into a cardboard box, sealed it with a grimace, and was escorted out of the building.

Two weeks later, Edison still had not received his promotion. And thus began Empty Suit's reign of terror.

Not exactly terror. More like annoyance.

Movie buff Mason Brix's autographed portrait of broody Lawrence Olivier was replaced with a portrait of grinny Owen Wilson. No one saw who did it.

A half-eaten, bleeding burger and fries were piled high on Rainbow Sunshine's tofu sprouts. No one saw who did it.

Opera lover Hunter Gaithers' playlist of Puccini, Verdi, and Mozart was erased and replaced with an endless loop of an Ashlee Simpson and Michael Bolton duet of "MacArthur Park." No one saw who did it.

Canadian Bob Smith's poutine-and-moose double-decker sandwich was thrown in the garbage. No one cared. No one knew what

Canadian Bob Smith did anyway, other than be Canadian and exude mysterious Canadian odors.

The Reign of Annoyance raged until an anonymous accounting troll named Jeeves Butler, who'd suffered the horror of his meticulous stacks of paper being unmeticulously unstacked, demanded action and surveillance cameras. The cameras were installed, covering all areas of the open plan offices.

But the spooky weirdness continued. All caught on video.

A PR flack got up to go to the bathroom and her stapler sprang to life and stapled her collection of cruise ship vacation ads to a *Southern Living* story on "Gardening with Gonorrhea."

A cup of coffee drifted through the office, darting behind plants or cubicles whenever someone approached or looked, and spilled itself on the head of River Tanner, before dashing itself against the wall.

A red rose flew through the air to settle gently on Heather Wu's desk.

B. Hemuth's offices were haunted. All floors, but especially the 27th.

The brightest minds in the company threw themselves into solving the mystery. One morning, Belinda summoned Edison into her office. She sat scowling behind her desk, flanked by a pair of stone-faced lawyers. Every fiber of her being was manifested in that scowl. Even her mouth scowled when she spoke. "In our surveillance video, Edison, no one ever sees you at your desk—or anywhere else—when the Ghost strikes. Why is that?"

"Wait. You think I'm the Ghost?"

"How do you pull it off?"

"I don't. But I'm both flattered and offended."

"My lawyers here figured it out. You're remote-controlling things somehow. Probably a swarm of nanobots."

"That's actually a marvelous idea, Belinda. But I'm in distribution data analysis. Paperwork. Reports. Do you think I'd be here if I had technology even the Pentagon doesn't have?"

A long, drawn-out pause. "I don't know how, but you're behind it." She leaned back. "I know it. I'm CEO because my hunches are always right, and the Board agrees. I'm letting you go. But I'll be big about it. Your last day is two weeks from today."

Edison swallowed. "I—"

"Decision made. Better start getting ready, updating your resume, sorting your paper clips. The usual important work you do."

TWO DAYS LATER, Edison watched and waited, gathered up a stack of papers, and caught Belinda off guard as she patrolled the office on a casual search-and-destroy mission for slackers. "Ten minutes," he said. "That's all. You're doing me wrong and I can prove it. Ten minutes."

"Damn it, Glass." Belinda glanced at her watch. "Fine. I'll give you five." She marched past him to her office. "Close the door behind you." Heather Wu glanced up from her monitor and down again.

Edison followed and clicked the door shut behind him.

"Sit," Belinda ordered.

"I'll stand, thanks. Belinda, how can you do this to me?" He shook papers at her like voodoo chicken bones. "I've got the numbers to show what I've meant to the company, from the very start."

"Four minutes," Belinda said.

Edison swallowed, and launched into a quiver of quarterlies over the years, scarcely drawing a breath. At last, he straightened the papers and set them neatly on her desk. "Well?"

"Well what? I still know you've been sabotaging us. Sneaky, you are. I—"

A gentle rap came at the door. Heather eased the door open. "Ms. Hemuth?"

"Not now, Heather."

"Ms. Hemuth, you asked me to report immediately if the Ghost struck again. It did."

Belinda snorted. "What a shock. When, this morning? When Glass had to go potty?"

"Two minutes ago."

Belinda stared at Heather.

The latest incident was the most blatant yet. A potted fern had suddenly become an unpotted fern, rising up from its expensive vase, which fell to the floor with a crash and a spray of dirt. Cubicle heads popped up and stared. Murmurs. The fern gave itself a good shake, scattering dirt, made a couple of loops in the air, wiggled some more dirt loose, executed a barrel-roll, a loop-de-loop, a floppy-shake-forward, and dashed itself against the shiny "We're Bigger than You" B. Hemuth logo.

EDISON TWISTED his beer bottle open, raised it, and clinked it against Winston's bottle. "That was awesome, Wince. Eye-catching, undeniable, and not quite over-the-top. Salud, Little Ghost-Bro!"

Wince bowed. "I shoulda been an actor."

"Got the whole performance on video and audio. Five different surveillance cameras caught it. Twenty-seven eyewitnesses. And all while I'm with the CEO and her sharks, my hands empty, my eyes pleading, my brow furrowed. Belinda spent all day with tekkies and janitors sifting through the potted fern mystery, poking around my desk, rooting through my files. They kept me in the conference room with her goons, then sent me home." He took a long drink. "That should end it."

THAT SHOULD'VE ENDED IT.

Belinda summoned Edison back to her office the following day. She was now flanked by five shiny lawyers, a veritable pod of them, and backed by two huge goons. River Tanner, newly ensconced in Carpenter's Veep of PR job, stood glued to her left arm.

"I've investigated yesterday's so-called Ghost incident," Belinda said without a hello. "Sit."

This time, Edison sat. He leaned back at a jaunty Errol Flynn angle and crossed his legs. "So. I'm still employed, I presume."

"It *was* a clever stunt, but I've seen it all before. Drone technology is simply staggering these days. You can program dozens of them to act in aerial sync with amazing precision. That's what you did. Tiny little drones, all performing a single routine, snatch a plant and move it around the room, then scatter. You're still fired."

Edison sprang from his chair, struggled for words. "That's... that's the most brilliant and stupidest thing I've ever heard. I was right here with you! I couldn't do that. No one could."

Tanner giggled. Belinda silenced him with a flick of her finger.

"Oh, I'm not saying *you* came up with it," she said. "You couldn't fly a three-dollar toy helicopter from Walmart without putting your eye out." She leaned back, tented her fingers. Like a spider would if it caught a fly in its web, and had fingers, and could tent them. "You needed an accomplice. Your brother, he's got way too much time on his hands, and no one could account for his whereabouts during yesterday's Ghost story. So he assembled and programmed your drone squadron and operated it remotely. I am impressed. Really, I am. He's being escorted from the building as we speak."

"Oh, come on, Belinda. You don't believe that yourself."

Tanner leaned in. "It's the only explanation," he said through his grin. "Like Sherlock Holmes said, once you eliminate the possum, whatever remains, however improbable, must be the rodent of truth."

"I don't know if you're the world's biggest idiot, Tanner, but you win a participation trophy." Edison bit down on the urge to tell all. "You're both pretty smug right now. I demand to see the evidence."

Belinda tapped a claw on the desk for a moment. "You used stolen military tech. Maybe collaborated with the Chinese. That would make for an interesting call to the Pentagon. Wanna go down that road?" She glanced at her goons. "Tank, Howitzer, please escort Mr. Glass from the premises."

The goons grinned. They liked their jobs.

A rap came at the door. Heather Wu popped her head in. She was so good at that. "Ms. Hemuth? A word?"

"Oh, for... not now, Heather."

"Yes now." Heather pushed open the door, held it aside, and a phalanx of seven full business suits marched in.

Belinda stood. "What's this?"

"A delegation sent by the Board. They held a little meeting this morning. You're done, Hemuth. You have thirty minutes to clean out your desk."

Belinda laughed, then paled. "What are you talking about?"

"The Board wasn't thrilled with the Mayor Martinez debacle. And Atlanta is where the Directors want to go, at least after I sent them Edison's prospectus. Still, you'd have survived if you'd only made amends with Charlotte, except that word got out that you'd rather spend your time ferreting out ghosts. Ghost-busting is not really mentioned in the company's mission statement."

"The Board doesn't know about the Ghost."

"I took care of that," Heather said.

"You! Why are you doing anything without my permission?"

"I don't actually work for you. I work for the Board. I'm their spy."

"You're a receptionist!"

"Tinker, tailor, receptionist, spy. Oh, ease up, Belinda. You'll slither into early retirement a very rich woman." Heather paused. "Well, maybe. Might want to lawyer up."

"But that's my name on the building. It's *my* company."

"It was. And the Board is rethinking the name." Heather glanced at her watch. "Twenty-nine minutes. Then your stuff gets stuffed in a box and thrown into a dumpster. And set on fire."

Belinda sulked away to her office. River Tanner and the lawyers adopted submissive primate expressions and eased away in an unsuccessful attempt at invisibility, pointing out that change is good, don't you think? Yes, change is good.

Edison watched them go, his emotions rollercoasting. "That... that was—"

"Fun, right?" Heather turned to him, an impish smile in her eyes. "Don't worry about her, she'll land on all four feet. She'll even find some perverse glee in it. The bigger they fall, the harder they come."

"And me?"

"You're the new Veep of Acquisitions and Expansions. If you want it."

"And you?"

"I like the fun stuff. Trust me, there's nothing so stimulating as a good takedown." She studied him for a moment. "I know you did it, Edison," she continued, almost in a whisper. "No idea how, but it was awesome. And exciting. The *fun* stuff."

Edison swallowed, lost in her eyes. "And us?" He doubted there was an "us." He glanced around the office. A hundred eyes were on them, and a hundred eyes turned away.

Heather looked about as well, then returned to hold his gaze. She came a bit closer. "Us. As of this moment, us are colleagues. Not coworkers." She came closer still. "We're free to have personal lives," she whispered. Closer still. "I'd do you right here and now if no one could see us."

Edison swallowed, and almost reached out to touch her. "I think that can be arranged."

AUTHOR'S NOTES - KEN PELHAM

THE POWER TO become invisible has been a fantasy of humans for as long as there have been humans, and so has long been a staple in myths, fairy tales, folk tales, and fantasy yarns have used it for thousands of years. When H.G. Wells reintroduced the idea with science fiction trappings in *The Invisible Man*, (1897), the notion gained respectability and became a fave of science fiction readers and writers ever since.

When I decided to take a crack at invisibility as a vehicle for sci-fi comedy and to set it in the world of big business, the snarky phrase "empty suit" sprang unbidden into my mind and I was off and running. Trotting, at least. Well, maybe that vigorous walk race they still give Olympic medals for.

Hope you had as much fun reading it as I had writing it.

~KP

THE REDDIES ARE COMING! THE REDDIES ARE COMING!

DACO S. AUFFENORDE

"*I am wounded in dignity only.*"
—Lt. Rozanov, in The Russians are Coming, The Russians are Coming *(1966)*

"Sharks are enormously powerful and wild creatures, but you're more likely to be killed by your kitchen toaster than a shark!"
—Ted Danson

BOBBY BAUMGARTNER, the Mayor of Kensington City, threw back his bedcovers and sat up in bed as he shouted at the top of his oversized lungs, "Oh, for the love of Kensington City, it's happening. It's really happening. It just can't be."

The doorbell rang.

In a fright, Mayor Baumgartner shuddered, twirled, and jumped out of bed, smacking his head on the ceiling. "They're here!"

He threw on his robe and hopped full speed ahead to the door and peered out the peephole.

Whew.

He opened the door to find Ms. Hippie Henchman, his oppo-nent in yesterday's mayoral election, standing on his elegant porch. He frowned. Henchman had not been kind to him during the campaign. She had called him an avaricious, self-centered, corrupt lover of gold who was only out for himself. She hadn't been wrong, but the truth hurt.

"Oh. It's you," he said.

She bowed to him as if he'd just been crowned King of Kens-ington instead of reelected as mayor. From behind her back, she produced a lush, bright-green potted plant. "Congratulations, Mayor. I just came by to concede the election and to tell you that I've decided not to contest the vote."

"Very gracious of you, Hippie. Also, a wise political move. You know how the public gets such a distaste in its mouth over—"

Mayor Baumgartner spied the plant's large and delectable foliage. His mouth watered, and he drooled.

"Are you quite all right, Mayor? You look a little …" She placed a finger to the side of her mouth.

With his forearm, Mayor Baumgartner wiped his mouth. He was so hungry. He hadn't even had his green tea this morning. "Why, I've never felt better."

"It's just that you …"

"Is that tasty little plant a gift from you, Hippie?"

Hippie Henchman thrust the plant forward. "From Miss Henri-etta Hensinger." Hensinger was the chairman of WEEDS—the city's society of the Women for Education, Edification, and Decora-tion of Sidewalks. Hensinger was also the head of the city's Ladies' Auxiliary Plant Police.

Mayor Baumgartner snatched the plant from Hippie, lifted it to his nose, and inhaled all its wonder—lush green leaves, the very source of air and life itself. Such a sight, such an aroma. And the flower buds themselves hadn't even bloomed yet. A day or two more ought to do it. "This wouldn't be a flowering arugula plant, would it?"

"I thought you would be pleased. Did you know that Prime Minister Molly Malarkey will be making her speech tonight at—?"

"Nice to see you, Hippie." He started to push the door shut, but Hippie stuck a foot in the door and pushed back. "Hold on there, Mayor."

"Yessss ...?" he asked in his most saccharin voice, the one he'd practiced a thousand times in front of the mirror.

"The PM is going to address her concerns over the shortage of corn crops. People are blaming the Reddies, but I think it's that giant grasshopper."

Mayor Baumgartner looked around guiltily and then cleared his throat. "What giant grasshopper?"

Hippie cocked her head. "The one who's terrorizing the town?"

The mayor stroked his chin. "Oh, yes. *That* one. I wouldn't say he's terrorizing ... It's the Reddies. The Reddies are coming."

Hensinger shook her head. "That Grasshopper is coming back from the Nor'easter Lock Lands. He has to be the one who's leveling the crops, row by row. It's most peculiar, don't you think?"

"Nonsense. I would simply call what you're seeing one of those so-called mystery crop circles. Unless it's the Reddies."

Hippie gasped, and her jaw dropped to her knee. When Mayor Baumgartner stepped forward, Hippie backed away from the door. Then she turned and sprinted away.

"Good day to you, Madam," Mayor Baumgartner called after her. "Thanks for the breakfast ... I mean, I can't thank you and my gracious constituents enough for the gift of this lovely plant. Have a good day now." He hopped back and slammed the door shut with a ...

Kablam!

Mayor Baumgartner danced his way to the kitchen with his new lovely plant.

"What shall I call you my darling little beauty?" he asked the plant, because he'd always heard that it was good to talk to one's plants, although he wondered if that applied to plants you intended to eat for breakfast one day. Of course it must. A little hot air made their skinny stalks grow faster and taller, the leaves wider and longer, and salads spicier and more savory. And one thing the Mayor had no shortage of was hot air.

"No answers for your re-elected mayor?" he sweet-talked the plant. "Not to worry. But I really must warn you, little dearie, that if you don't grow there *will* be consequences. Grave consequences." Mayor Baumgartner roared with laughter and plopped the plant down on the counter.

He sat down at the breakfast table. His 24-carat gold crockery was laid out with precise delicacy and precision, and his crystal-gold goblet was filled with the golden goodness of pure gold juice.

Nothing like a golden breakfast for a gold-studded mayor.

Little did the citizens of his fine town realize that down in Mayor Baumgartner's basement was a storehouse of gold brick. *A little insurance policy never hurt anyone, especially a politician.* He grinned, his gold-capped tooth glinting and sparkling. His smile reflected off the gold face of the toaster.

"Toast. I knew I was missing something."

He popped two pieces of wheat bread into his toaster, propped himself against the counter, and rubbed his hands together as he waited. He had the strangest urge to rub his feet together and sing. Then he frowned and thought, *that prime minister, that meddling confounded woman will surely be the death of me.* He should never have endorsed Molly Malarkey for PM.

For once Electromancer, that glittering, electrified superhero who flitted around decked out in a scintillating platinum body suit and matching gloves and boots while fighting the villains and archcriminals of all Britannia, had agreed with Mayor Baumgartner. But Malarkey had promised him a mountain of gold, and what corrupt politician in his right mind would turn down a mountain of gold? Now, the PM had invited the leader of the Reddies, Ricky Reddybug, to *his* city to speak at her lousy conference.

"Don't trust the Reddies," Electromancer had urged Molly Malarkey. "They're stealing our technology, Madam. They're hacking our computers and influencing our free and fair elections."

But once Malarkey was sworn into office, she made the call and invited Ricky Reddybug to their beloved Kensington City, Britannia, for a Forum on Friendly Foe Doings. But it would be no friendly forum here—*something is rotten in Britannia. Hell, Britannia.* The PM had hoodwinked them all. She must be a Reddie herself!

RRRinngg!

Blast! Never a meal in peace. He answered his call.

"Have you heard?" Electromancer asked.

"Of course, I've heard, you silver-speckled batwings."

"Let's not get personal, Mayor. There's no reason to be sore at me. I only convinced you take the wall down for your own good and the good of Britannia and Kensington City." She was referring to the wall that he'd put up to keep the mountain folks from the Mullgany Mountains out. That was another story. Oh well ... Why did that silver-winged, electrified diva always have to be right?

"What can I do for you, Electromancer?"

"You'd better keep an ear to the floors, walls, and doors. I don't know how they're doing it, but those Reddies are getting in. Just last night, a private conversation between me and Blue Arrow was put up on FlitterFly. Half the world is re-flittering that post. I can't have my privacy invaded like this. I won't have it. We must put a stop to these Reddies."

"You really ought to keep your personal dalliances in check. Say, speaking of you and Blue Arrow, what is it like for two superheroes to go at when—?"

"Mayor Baumgartner! Must I remind you that you're a gentleman?"

Boy, was she wrong about that, Mayor Baumgartner thought. Fortunately, the toaster popped.

"What was that?" she asked. "Do you need help, Mayor?"

"It's only my breakfast. I really must be running along, Electromancer. Thank you so much for calling to congratulate me on the election."

"I voted for Hippie. I called to tell you that word in the air is that you've been targeted."

Drats!

As soon as Mayor Baumgartner disconnected the line and sat in front of his tasty meal, his appetite dispelled his worries. He munched his toast until he heard a most peculiar rattle.

"Who's there?" he asked, glancing around. He took a deep breath.

Silence.

Fiddle. That Electromancer made him paranoid.

He settled back into his breakfast. "I really must get my hearing checked," he said. He continued to eat, but the noise returned. He bounded out of his chair.

Blast it!

"What's the meaning of this?" Mayor Baumgartner cried. He searched high and low, placing his ear to the wall, to the floor. Then he bounced upward to the ceiling and put his ear to the ceiling. Nothing seemed out of place. He sat and began eating again.

The lever on the toaster depressed itself and popped up immediately.

Mayor Baumgartner jumped from his seat and hurried to the toaster. Lifting it, he looked inside both toasting slots, but saw nothing. He placed an ear to the metal and listened. He heard nothing. He must've inadvertently depressed the lever himself. The other alternative was that he was losing his marbles, and last he checked he had all his aggies and his clambroths. That wasn't happening. It was that PM. She'd gotten under his skin.

Boing … boing … boing …

The back door flung open and pogoed back and forth until it came to a rest. It was Zachary Zero, the city's comptroller and the Mayor's personal handyman. Zero lacked the sophistication of his boss, but then only one man was capable of being the Kensington City mayor.

"Haven't I told you not to jerk my door open?" Mayor Baumgartner said.

"Hi ya, boss," Zachary Zero said. "What's all the racket going on in here?"

Mayor Baumgartner set the toaster down. "Get Shifty Shinwhacker over here. My toaster is broken."

"What seems to be the problem, Mayor?"

"Don't ask questions. I do the asking around here."

"Sure, sure. I'll go this instant if that's what you like. But have you heard—?"

Mayor Baumgartner lifted an arm and pointed toward the door. When Zero didn't move fast enough, the Mayor pinged him on the chest with his index finger and shouted at him to go. "And another thing, tell Constable Pete Petaud I'll be around to discuss the forum and security measures. Heavens only knows if Reddybug's supporters intend to storm the forum."

"Okay, okay, boss. I'm going."

Mayor Baumgartner shook his head. "You can never find good help these days."

"How's that, boss?"

"Go! And I ask the questions here."

The door banged shut again, the sound reverberating through Mayor Baumgartner's skull. He clutched the sides of his head. When the noise stopped, he plucked a leafy green from his new plant and chomped it down. The taste was peppery and hot. Delicious. Unable to restrain himself, Mayor Baumgartner feasted on a second breakfast, consuming every last tender leaf of arugula, the flower buds, and even the undernourished stem. He tossed the pot, now only full of dirt, into the trash can, and was suddenly overcome.

A MOMENT LATER ...

His legs wriggled uncontrollably. His arms shook. In a blink of an eye, his arms morphed into a pair of front walking legs. His legs —now his hind walking legs—lengthened. There was no stopping the transformation now. He was becoming—*The Grasshopper.* As a child, a swarm of grasshoppers had attacked the mayor in his pram, while his nanny cavorted in the garden with a lecherous neighbor. A few years ago, the mayor was exposed to an extraterrestrial element called Electromite, which triggered a genetic change. Let's just say he became an insect that could jump high, spit, and matched anything that was green. His worst nightmare became a reality.

Now, he reached for the counter to brace himself, lost his balance, slipped, and fell to the floor, hitting his head.

Kaboom!

As he slipped toward unconsciousness, the rattling noise recurred. Able to hold open one eye, The Grasshopper targeted the location of the noise—the toaster.

Down plunged the lever, and up popped something that resembled a giant lollipop with bulging eyes and elephant-size ears. The creature wore headphones with a microphone attached, into which it spoke the strangest of languages. Arms and legs appeared, and the creature crawled out of one of the toasting slots. The room filled with an odd scent of burnt ants. Scouts in search of crumbs? Spies? Peeping Toms? The Grasshopper checked to make sure none of his intimate parts were showing. One thing was certain: his toaster had been "bugged."

The Grasshopper's head swelled, and the room tilted and moved at a crazy angle.

"It can't be," The Grasshopper thought as his remaining eye closed, and he slipped into sweet dreams of bouncing through fields while stridulating his appendages.

A COUPLE OF HOURS LATER ...

An icy breeze blew through the screened back door. The chill woke Mayor Baumgartner, who was shocked to find himself on the kitchen floor in his bathrobe, which was now shredded to pieces. Then he remembered—he had one of his transformations into The Grasshopper. He bounced to his feet, hurried to the counter, grabbed the toaster, shook it, and then peered inside. Nothing.

Zachary Zero entered with Shifty Shinwhacker. "Hi ya, boss? Weren't you wearing that same outfit yesterday?"

Mayor Baumgartner turned around. His brows stretched into his forehead.

"What got into you, boss?" Zero asked. "I mean you feeling all right? Darn, another question. How do you ask a question, boss, without asking a question?"

"Quiet!" Mayor Baumgartner shouted.

"You're all broken out, Mayor," Shifty Shinwhacker said. "You better call Doc Dieter Do. You've got a conference to attend this evening."

Mayor Baumgartner held the toaster up to see his reflection on the shiny surface. He tossed the kitchen appliance to Shinwhacker. "Fix it." He hurried to his bathroom and peered into the mirror. He was broken out from head to toe in green bumps. In horror, he cried up to the rafters, "Hippie did this!"

A SHORT WHILE LATER ...

Alexa Manchester, heiress of The Manchester Electric Company, and secretly the superhero Electromancer, stood at Mayor Baumgartner's dressing table dabbing concealer over the green bumps on the Mayor's face.

"I warned you that overindulgence in any good thing will always lead to disaster," Alexa said. "But no one will be the wiser when I'm finished with you."

"Those bumps hurt dreadfully, and I don't have time for this," he replied, touching her arm. A pulse of electricity shot through his hand to his heart. He jerked his hand away. "You shocked me, Alexa."

"Oh, pardon me. It must've been the rug that caused it."

He frowned at her.

"The constable found some solid evidence out in the corn fields," she continued.

"What?!" The corn crop was Kensington City's most valuable commodity. Not only that, Mayor Baumgartner adored the luscious golden crop. It wasn't just a beautiful gold color, it tasted divine.

"Forensics made some molds of the ground," Alexa said. "Very odd, I must say. Footprints."

A sense of dread washed over Mayor Baumgartner. "How big were they?"

"Teeny tiny. Reddies."

"Are you sure?"

"Quite."

Whew. "Pray tell, Alexa?"

The mayor's phone dinged, alerting him to a private message on FlitterFly. He grabbed his phone to have a look. "Oh no."

The video showed the mayor transforming into The Grasshopper.

Alexa took the phone. "Who took this picture? I can't quite—"

Mayor Baumgartner snatched the phone back and shut it off. "Never mind that."

The doorbell rang.

They went to the door. No one there, but a package sat on the stoop. They opened it and found a note:

"Hand over your gold or the picture goes viral, along with all your dirty secrets. We've hacked your email accounts. Your computer has been ransomed. Give up before it's too late."

Jumping Jackrabbits!

"How many times have I told you to deposit that gold in the bank?" Alexa scolded.

The clock dinged.

"I can't be late to the forum," Mayor Baumgartner said. "Very kind of you to help in a pinch, my dear girl. That quack Dieter Do is useless with his so-called magical potions."

Alexa eyed him strangely.

"I must be off," Mayor Baumgartner said. "See you at the conference."

"Oh, I'm needed at the power plant," Alexa said. "One of the generators went down."

Mayor Baumgartner jumped into his 24-karat gold Lamborghini and sped off to the forum. When he walked into the conference center, Hippie Henchman was engaged in idle gossip with Miss Henrietta Hensinger. When the two saw him, Henrietta said, "Oh me, oh my, Mayor Baumgartner. What happened to your face?"

"I can't imagine what you're talking about, Henny."

"You seem to have bumps."

He narrowed an eye at her. "Well, at least they're not green. It was your arugula."

"That was ornamental arugula," Hippie said. "How could you have a reaction to looking at a plant?" She gasped and grinned. "You didn't eat ... no, surely you wouldn't have been so ... quite, quite."

"If you'll excuse me, ladies," Mayor Baumgartner said. He took the side stage and was met by Molly Malarkey and the notorious Ricky Reddybug of the Reddies.

"Greetings, Bobby," Reddybug said.

"Mayor Baumgartner to you, sir," he said.

"My apologies. But I'm delighted to be here. Prime Minister Malarkey assures me that we can reach a comprehensive strategic partnership in the corn-trade sector. Kensington's support will be vital with their abundance of the crop. Never have we seen more fertile soil in all the lands."

An itch curled up Mayor Baumgartner's spine. He juddered. "Not so fast, Reddybug. I doubt there's enough crop to export. Perhaps you should speak with the mountain folks about their nut-stash surplus. That might make a dandy deal."

"What are you talking about, Mayor?" Malarkey asked. Then she whispered, "Golden corn turns into mountains of gold." She winked at him.

Mayor Baumgartner drew back in indignation. "I'll have you know I am a reputable mayor, Madam."

Reddybug gave a bug-eyed stare at Mayor Baumgartner, one eye so large that it was unmistakably that infamous evil eye they'd all long heard about.

Malarkey slipped her arms through each gentleman's arm and escorted them center stage. "Let's present our speeches to your citizens, shall we. Let the people be the deciding vote."

As Reddybug delivered his blibber-blabber baloney, Malarkey elbowed Mayor Baumgartner. When he met her eyes, she said, "Mess this speech up, Baumgartner, and it'll be the end of your career. I'll see to that myself. And another thing, we're going to inspect those crops right after we finish here. You get my drift?"

Mayor Baumgartner raised his chin defiantly. He would take them to the crop-circle fields. Perhaps that would do the trick.

"And what's wrong with your face, Mayor?" she asked.

"Hmpf. New beauty treatment."

Reddybug made his plea for a friendly trade agreement, promising riches to the farmers. A most peculiar smell permeated the audience just as he concluded.

"Who brought the stilton?" local farmer Conroy Corn asked.

"Pipe down," Chief Pete Petaud warned. "Don't be stirring up any trouble, Corny."

Hiss! Boo! Never the Reddies!

While the PM droned through her speech, Reddybug elbowed Mayor Baumgartner.

Mayor Baumgartner glared at the single bug eye. "I say, man, haven't you Reddies learned to keep your elbows to yourselves?"

Reddybug seemed to boil inside. "I saw an interesting video this morning. I'm certain it was of you."

"Pish, posh. People are always creating *memes* of me. We can't all be so handsome. Too bad, Reddybug. Why, just look at the Dowdy twins out there in the audience admiring me now. Della and Dani. I can smell their expensive but decidedly slutty perfume from here. You? No, I wouldn't imagine."

Reddybug's face reddened. Cherry red. Not beet red. No … a peculiar red.

Something came over Mayor Baumgartner. He leaned in closer to Reddybug and sniffed—*Burnt ants!*

If Mayor Baumgartner exposed them now, how would they ever find out how the Reddies were gaining access to their inside information?

No matter! Mayor Baumgartner had to put a stop to this now!

He hopped from his chair and pointed at Ricky Reddybug. "You Reddies are the ones who've been stealing our crops. Sneaking into our farms late at night. Stealing our technology. Tampering with our elections."

Mayor Baumgartner pointed at the PM. "You're in cahoots with the Reddies! You dastardly PM!" The mayor turned to the audience. "Reddybug is blackmailing me to sign off on this cheaters' agreement. Forcing our farmers to give up crops for cheap. Well, I say *never!*"

Traitors!

"Hold your tempers," Chief Pete Petaud shouted.

Too late!

The crowd was out of control.

Ricky Reddybug started to run, but not before throwing a punch at the mayor.

Take that!

Mayor Baumgartner stumbled back.

Pow!

Reddybug struck him again.

Kerplunk!

The mayor toppled to the floor. He extended a foot just in time to reach Reddybug.

Boom!

Reddybug was kissing floor. But that wasn't all. What was once his body was actually only a shell, and that shell now fell to the floor. Out crept a teeny tiny *red* creature. The very one who'd popped out of the Mayor's toaster that very morning. Not a second later, that entomological pest enlarged and turned into a giant red ant. Reddybug shouted …

Get them! Attack!

A million teeny, tiny red ants swarmed out of the soil. They began running and crawling all over the citizens of Kensington, biting and gnawing. People twisted, gyrated, and clawed at the ants. There was no destroying them. Panic ensued.

Help!

Drats!

Where's Electromancer when you need her?

Molly Malarkey ran. Mayor Baumgartner kicked the podium, knocking it into the PM. She toppled to the stage floor.

Splat!

Her exterior cracked open. Exposed, she was also a Reddie—a giant red ant disguised as a woman. A spy who'd infiltrated the highest echelons of their government.

A web of lightning flashed and crackled in the sky.

Electromancer to the rescue!

At the speed of light, she began zapping the ants. But her sparks ricocheted off the shells of those little devils.

Pop!

Zap!

Kapow!

It was no good. Even Electromancer's powerful electrical sparks couldn't get through the armor of those ants. The war raged on.

IN THE MEANTIME ...

In walked Shifty Shinwacker with the Mayor's toaster—at a time like this!

"Take cover," Mayor Baumgartner shouted to him. "And don't lose my toaster. I paid a fortune for that one."

While the battle and chomping raged on, Shinwhacker calmly walked toward the side of the stage and up the stairs. He strolled over to help the Mayor to his feet. Something snagged onto his foot. He lifted his leg and stomped his foot down hard.

Eureka!

That party-pooper ant clinging to his foot exploded.

"No!" Reddybug cried. "To the corn fields, troops. There's no time to lose."

"Not so fast there," Shinwhacker said, and he stomped a foot on the giant ant's foot. She shouted in pain, jumped twelve feet in the air, and hit her head on a candelabra, which happened to hold real lighted candles (against code, but who would argue with the mayor?).

Ker-crackle!

Reddybug burst into a thousand embers of teeny tiny burnt ants. The mayor had to admire those awful Reddies' resilience.

"Malarky has turned into millions of bugs," Henny Hensinger shouted. "It's like we're living a Franz Kafka story."

Tell me about it, the mayor thought. He knew what it was like to wake up in the morning having turned into a giant insect. Although being The Grasshopper wasn't all that bad. He no longer avoided vegan restaurants.

"Stomp them!" Electromancer shouted. And together, everyone did a stomping jig that abolished every single last one of those Reddies.

When order was restored, Mayor Baumgartner said, "That was a lucky call, Shinwhacker."

Shinwhacker shrugged. "Never could stand anything crawling on me."

"What in the world are you doing here with my toaster?"

"Oh, right." Shinwhacker reached inside his pocket and pulled out a wire. "This here is a listening device, Mayor. Found it in your toaster. Capable of recording, photographing, the whole business. That's how those Reddies were getting our private information and hacking into our computers."

"This calls for abolishing all toasters," Hippie said.

"Nonsense, the citizens of Kensington have the right to bear toasters," Mayor Baumgartner said. "I won't hear of their rights being eradicated and restricted."

"Vote, vote," the crowd shouted.

"All in favor," Hippie said.

"Hold on, now, hold on," Mayor Baumgartner shouted. "You can't go changing the Constitution of Britannia like that. And everyone knows I've always been anti-toaster control."

"Let's compromise and start with tighter toaster controls and checks," Electromancer said. "If we keep fighting amongst ourselves and don't compromise, we're toast."

Everyone cheered. The Mayor snatched his toaster from Shinwhacker. "Anyone for a toasted cheese sandwich?"

AUTHOR'S NOTES - DACO S. AUFFENORDE

"THERE IS *a right and a wrong in the universe, and the distinction is not hard to make.*"
  —*Superman*
  "*So long as life remains, there is always hope …*"
  —*Wonder Woman*
  "*It's not who I am underneath, but what I do that defines me.*"
  —*Batman*
  "*I'm always picking up after your boys …*"
  —*Natasha Romanoff (Black Widow)*

I've always been a fan of superhero books, comics, television shows, and the movies. My novel *Electromancer* conjures up the 1960s Batman television series, a comic book on television with all the Pow! Kaboom! Splat! and campy characters of that earlier era. In *Electromancer*, Alexa Manchester, after exposure to a strange element, acquires the ability to fly and to harness electricity. She must save the world from an uber-evil crime boss named Momo, who threatens to destroy the world's power system. To succeed, she must not only eradicate evil but also learn how to balance love with that of her superhero obligations. To continue the saga, I wrote a series of short stories called *The Adventures of Electromancer*, featuring char-acters from the novel while also adding a few more. So if you enjoyed this short story, please explore more from my superhero saga.

~Daco Auffenorde

LASER HAMSTERS

JOHN HOPE

1: Easiest Money

"Not on your life," Mysti spat, dishrag on one hip and a whimpering, half-naked baby on the other. The frizzy-haired forty-year-old mother of four glared at Dusty, her latest Prince Charming turned redneck con man. He was barely twenty-two years himself, and at times like this she regretted marrying a guy who still relied on his teenage instincts. "Git them varmints out of my house."

Dusty and his pal Arlo stood over a massive cage packed full of forty-plus teddy bear hamsters. The cute rodents tumbled around and snuggled with each other. Despite Mysti's reaction, Dusty's confident smile didn't falter. "Like who don't like these gorgeous creations of God?"

His gorgeous smile and firm, muscular body prevented Mysti from smacking him in the face for stupid comments like that.

As if to prove Dusty's point, Colt, Mysti's mud-caked nine-year-old, stepped into the living room with a frog in hand. His eyes nearly burst from their sockets at the sight of the hamsters. "Wow!" He tossed the frog out the back door, dove, and slid on his knees to the cage, hugging it. "We're keeping them?" Colt was taller than most kids his age, and his big front teeth and flaring ears made him look a bit goofy and awkward.

"Colt!"

Colt jerked at his mom yelling at him.

"What'd you do to your new pants? They're filthy."

"Um…" Colt had guilt in his voice.

Mysti didn't know that Colt's muddied clothes weren't exactly his fault. Colt had been riding his bike when he came across a few undesirable kids from school. The leader of the bunch, a shaved-head boy named Lester, laughed at Colt and called him Dumbo because of his big ears. The kids wouldn't let Colt pass and, when he tried to turn his bike around, Lester shoved him into a muddy ditch. The boys spit into the ditch as they rode off. Colt untangled himself from his bike and sat for a minute, fighting the urge to cry. His spirits lifted when he discovered a frog. He caught him, crawled out of the ditch, leaving his bike, and walked back home.

Now Colt looked down at his muddied pants and scraped one leg with his thumb. "I'll…uh. I'll clean it."

"You'd better. I paid good money for them pants."

Colt looked up to Dusty. "We keepin' the hamsters, Dusty?"

"Nah, Colt," Dusty said. "We gonna be selling off these golden nuggets down at the racetrack." He winked at his wife. "Twenty bucks a pop."

With the dishrag, Mysti wiped the face of the baby in her arms. "You idget. Who's gonna pay twenty dollars for a rat?"

Colt's chin shot up. "They hamsters, Momma."

"Thanks to Arlo." Dusty swung a hand toward his half-drunk friend standing on the opposite side of the cage.

Arlo wobbled, his eyes barely open. "Huh?"

"We gots ourselves a novelty," Dusty explained. "Arlo here owes me a favor. He's gonna use his tattooing skills on these tiny animals, and when them people come piling out of the racetrack…" He yanked a hamster from the cage. "We'll bestow an attractive logo or number on them. For example, a number three for Dale Earnhardt, or maybe a BB for Buck Baker. The peoples' hearts will be so a-flutter with love and high on life after the race that shelling out a twenty spot won't be nothin'. It'll be the easiest money we've ever made." He kissed one of the hamsters on the head.

Mysti nearly dropped the baby. "You tellin' me this drunk fool gonna tattoo numbers on a bunch of rats?!"

"They hamsters, Momma," Colt repeated.

"Yessirree." Dusty smiled as he slapped an arm around Arlo's shoulders. "And with the best artist in the county here, how can we go wrong?"

Arlo said, "I like tattooin'."

Mysti rocked her hips in agitation. "You two are dumber than Jack."

Dusty frowned. "Hey, we ain't that dumb. That good-for-nothin' first husband of yours—"

"Jack was my second husband, ya numbskull. Remember? The one who stepped out in front of that bus and got himself killed?"

"I thought Ronnie was your second."

"No, Ronnie was the first, the one who got himself drowned." She shifted the baby to her other hip. "With my luck, these hamsters will probably do you in." She spun on her heels toward the kitchen.

Her twin daughters ran into the living room and joined Colt on the floor in front of the giant hamster cage, oohing and aahing over the animals.

Dusty's smile returned, and he gave a thumbs up to the girls. "See what I mean?" he said to Arlo. "Kids love 'em. Adults will too. Easiest money ever." He neared Colt and rubbed his head. "But I'm gonna need your help, kid. Gotta keep these gems fed and hydrated. Wanna help?"

"Yeah!" Colt smiled up at Dusty.

"Not before you clean them pants," Mysti said. "Besides, Colt would probably mess things up like he usually do."

Colt's shoulders slumped.

"Nah. I trust him." Dusty patted the boy's head. "You wouldn't let me down, would ya?"

Colt smiled again, weaker this time.

IN THEIR SPACESHIP two hundred miles straight up from Dusty and his giant cage of hamsters, a pair of aliens from their planet Zammar reviewed the results of the scanners that surveyed the Earth. With their bluish-green skin and suited up in their lustered radiation suits, the two bipods stood two feet tall. Quinto, the slightly heavier of the two, tapped through the menus and mumbled to himself.

The other Zammarian, Bastle, shook with excitement. "Kill 'em! I want to kill 'em all."

"Settle down, Bastle. Remember the mission." Quinto refocused on the technical readouts again. Multicolored lines and dots flew across the screens. "But I do not know. It is difficult to be sure."

"You are too picky. Just select a creature so we can proceed."

Quinto looked up from the screen. "We can't just select anything. It must be small, so as not to arouse suspicion among the humans." He returned to the screens. "Ideally a creature of large numbers who humans have imprisoned and—"

"And what?" Bastle demanded. "What?"

"And I think I have found it. A large gathering. And they are imprisoned."

"What are they? What are they?" Bastle shook with excitement.

"Calm down." He pressed a few buttons on his console. "They are called…hamsters. Humans are transporting the prisoners now." He looked to Bastle. "This looks like the opportunity we have been waiting for. Prepare the transporters. We will descend to Earth."

"Hooray!"

2: The Racetrack

THE ROAR of car engines speeding around the racetrack boomed across the parking lot where Dusty and Arlo trudged along with the tattooing equipment and giant hamster cage. "Hop to it, boy!" Dusty called out to Colt.

The boy struggled with a pair of giant duffle bags slung across his shoulders. Heavy glass containers of tattooing paint clinked inside one, while hamster supplies and food rattled in the other. Colt struggled to catch up.

Dusty readjusted his awkward grip on the cage, frowning at the muffled calls of the racetrack emcees and the cheers of the crowds. "Move your butt, Arlo. They gettin' out soon."

The parking lot, mostly devoid of people, was packed full of trucks, cars, and RVs. A few pods of tailgaters drank beer and lounged in lawn chairs beside their vehicles.

A wide sidewalk surrounded the chain-link-fenced stadium. Stragglers, bums, and drunken men who exited the stadium early dotted this area.

Dusty pointed with the tilt of his head. "Let's set up over there." He led the trio to a spot near an open gate and dropped the cage on the concrete. The hamsters jumped and squeaked. Dusty wiped his forehead. "Hoo wee! It's hot today." He signaled Colt with a sharp whistle. "Colt, make with the water bottles. Gotta keep these hamsters hydrated. Arlo, get your stuff set up pronto."

Dusty mounted a cardboard sign onto a pole with CUSDUM HAMSTERS 20 BUCKS written in wobbly black letters. Arlo sat on his collapsible stool, needle and ink in hand, with his tattooing equipment assembled nearby. In three minutes flat, the three entrepreneurs had their operations in order.

Colt sat cross-legged on the pavement next to the cage. He'd affixed the water bottles to the cage and dumped piles of hamster food in the corners, causing the little critters to tumble and fight over their resources.

A minute later, hordes of people exited the stadium. A stream of people passed the hamster stand.

Dusty waved his arms in the air, exposing hairy armpits. He called out like carnival barker, "Come and git 'em! Custom hamsters, tattooed with your favorite race number. You can't afford not to git 'em fer your kiddies or loved ones back home. Need an excuse for coming home drunk? Come home with one of these gorgeous critters, and all will be well."

Men, women, and children gathered around the giant cage in twos and threes, sticking their fingers inside and making baby noises.

Arlo rubbed his face and readied himself to start inking.

UP IN A TREE about a hundred yards away from Dusty's hamsters, Quinto and Bastle were perched on a branch, shrouded in leaves. Hairy kickstand-like appendages extending from their backs helped anchor them to the tree. They studied the masses of people exiting into the parking lot below them after the end of the race.

Quinto announced, "There they are."

Bastle squinted. "You are referencing the imprisoned creatures?"

"Correct."

He frowned at his fellow Zammarian. "You believe enabling those creatures will accomplish our objective?" Bastle's excitement intensified.

Quinto explained, "Observe how the humans are enamored of the prisoners. Although humans keep them caged, when they remove the prisoners, the humans cradle them with reverence. Shifting the balance of power would surely wreak havoc on their fragile society."

Quinto smiled. "Plus, it would be LOL."

Bastle frowned. "LOL?"

"An acronym meaning it is funny. It is a type of hyperbole. In my studies of humans, I have picked up some of their vernacular."

"Yes, Quinto. I understand this hyperbole." Bastle tapped a series of buttons on his atomizing manipulator. He lowered his goggles and raised the weapon to eye level. "It is time to kick their anal orifices."

Quinto shielded his eyes.

The moment the hamster cage image filled his scope, Bastle fired.

A bubble of light, twisting and distorting as it flew through the air, flashed forward from Bastle's weapon and struck the hamsters in the cage.

The crowd stopped in its tracks. People blinked and looked around in joint confusion. The moment passed, and the scene returned to normal.

More hordes exited the stadium.

Quinto lifted his goggles. "We must leave quickly."

"Yes. Yes."

Both aliens activated the personal transporters attached to their wrists. With a swirl of sparkling light, they were gone and the tree was empty.

SHORTLY AFTER THE strange sensation that rippled through the crowd, Dusty moved into stage two of his sales pitch. He snagged a couple hamsters at a time from the cage and plopped them into the cupped hands of curious spectators. He smiled without regard for any of his missing teeth. "You can't say no to something that cute, can ya?"

"C-c-can I get one with Rusty Wallace's initials?" a woman asked.

Dusty hopped to her side. "You bet your sweet smile, you can. Step right over to my tattoo expert." He tapped the small of her back and led her to Arlo. "Will that be RW for Rusty Wallace, or just a big W?"

"W," she chimed.

A pair of little boys tugged at Dusty's arm. One asked, "Can we get the spotted one?"

"Is your mom or dad here?"

"Grandma," one kid said, pointing to an old woman standing off to the side.

"One spotted hamster, coming up." He fetched the hamster and plopped it into the older boy's hand.

The two oohed and aahed over the creature, stroking its soft fur. "Grandma! Grandma! Look!" They held up the animal.

The hamster's eyes abruptly glowed a pulsating red as the

rodent's body shook in the boys' hands. The intensity of the light grew, followed by emanating noise like a sparking electric motor, which increased until it reached a crescendo. The moment the old woman looked down at her grandsons, two intense laser beams shot out of the hamster's eyes.

Grandma exploded, her body instantly disintegrating into a dazzling ball of light.

A blink later, all that was left of the woman were her old-lady pumps with a trickle of smoke rising from the heels.

A collective gasp rippled through the tightly packed spectators. Mutterings of "Did you see that?" spread fast.

"Wha…ah?" the boys muttered.

Colt's mouth fell open.

Dusty spun around. "What was that? What happened?" His eyes bounced from the hamster cage to the people holding his tiny gems.

The younger of the two little boys said, "Grandma went boom."

Shocked witnesses dashed from the scene. Curious people who hadn't a clue what had happened joined the steady flow of spectators exiting the racetrack. The parking lot became a crisscrossing chaotic mess. Most of the people in the crowd, however, weren't panicking. They made their way toward the parking lot.

"Wha—?" Dusty muttered. "Wait. My hamsters!" He surged forward to retrieve his stock, but the crowds heaved him back and spun him around. His sign fell.

More crowds of people herded by. A man called, "Hey, look! Free hamsters!"

"No!" Dusty protested. "They're not free."

The mob stormed the cage, though. The metal snapped, and hamsters fled, many scooped up by the passersby.

Colt, huddled on the ground, inched back as legs kicked and jostled him left and right. He hugged the black hamster he'd taken from the cage, protecting the tiny creature. Between the frightening shouts, he peeked beneath his shirt and petted the runt with his finger. "You okay, little one?"

A hamster scurried through the hail of stomping feet and

approached Colt. He thought for a moment about capturing the escaped animal, when a woman scooped him up.

"Oh, how adorable," she said, rubbing the hamster's soft fur against her face. "Look, Kenny."

A man approaching her grimaced. "We don't need a hamster."

She stroked its fur. "But it's cute."

The hamster's eyes ignited red and a snapping electric noise emanated from its body.

The woman frowned. "What the—?"

A laser shot out of the hamster's eyes, blasting through the surrounding crowd.

Hats and shoes flew away as the struck victims exploded and disappeared.

The woman screeched and tossed the hamster to the ground.

It ran off.

A chorus of three more hamsters revved up their glowing eyes and then there were more laser beams, exploding people, screams, and panic.

Colt crab-walked backwards and tucked his body between a metal trashcan and the side of a concrete wall. Teeth clenched, he shuddered with every *zap*.

3: An Alternative Plan

MYSTI STOOD IN HER KITCHEN, her hip resting against the counter. Phone in her hand, she tapped away until she pulled up the local streaming newscast.

The reporter said, "I'm Brock Fullovit live from TNB, the Toxic News Broadcast. Tragedy at the Creek Town Speedway this evening resulted in the disappearance and deaths of dozens of spectators. We have Lisa standing by at the scene of this disaster. Lisa?"

The broadcast switched to a woman with a microphone in hand. A beautiful twenty-something, the on-the-scene-reporter looked like she'd been a high school cheerleader a second earlier. She tousled her hair as she chomped on gum. She stood in the middle of the racetrack parking lot, fire engines and police cars flashing their blue and red lights in the background, where a scattering of people whimpered.

"Uh, hello?" She tapped her microphone. "Hello? Oh. We're on. Like wait. Is this about some stupid hamsters? Oh, wow! Like I'm totally bored with this already."

The stern voice of Brock Fullovit chimed, "Uh, yes, I understand there were possible deaths, Lisa."

"With hamsters?" Walking awkwardly on high heels, she stepped to the side. The camera followed her. She bent down to interview a shivering older woman wrapped in a blanket and sitting on a curb. "What can you tell us about these dead hamsters or whatever?"

"L-l-lasers. The hamsters. They had lasers. Oh, the humanity!" She buried her face in the blanket.

Lisa stood upright. "Um...all right." She stepped to the opposite side. "Let's ask this little boy over here." She bent down to the boy. "Hello, little boy. Like what did you see?"

The boy stared with huge eyes. "Grandma went boom."

Lisa straightened. "Grandma went what?" She stared at the camera and twirled a few strands of hair. "Like I don't get it."

The video switched back to the newsroom and Brock Fullovit. "Confusion. Panic. Deaths. A blond news anchor obviously not hired for her brains and a Grandma who went boom. What an amazing turn of events. Keep watching our channel for breaking news as this story unfolds. This is Brock Fullovit from Toxic News, signing off."

"Laser hamsters?" Mysti lowered her phone and shook her head. "I'd be a Billie goat's punching bag if Dusty didn't have somethin' to do with that."

The front door swung open with the sound of Dusty announcing, "Honey, we're home."

"Speak of the devil," Mysti replied with a scornful face. "Don't tell me you were the one who blew up half the racetrack."

Dusty carried a well-beaten metal box cradled under his armpit. His stepson Colt was a few feet behind, his worried eyes glancing at the lunchbox. Dusty lowered the box onto the kitchen table next to a pair of dirtied plates and sippy cups.

"I'm almost afraid to ask," Mysti started as she crossed her arms and shifted her weight. "What's in there?"

Dusty patted the box. "Oh, this? It's our ticket to thousands. Maybe even millions."

Mysti rolled her eyes. "What's it this time? A guinea pig?"

"No, it's one of our beloved hamsters from this morning. But this time...oh, this time, there's a real kicker." He cracked the lunchbox lid open and placed his face dangerously close to the opening. "This fella's got laser eyes."

"La...wha? Laser eyes?!" Mysti stumbled back. "Whatcha talkin' about?"

"I'm talkin' 'bout this dang tragedy at the racetrack means money in our pockets, sweetie. Something strange happened to these hamsters out there. Call it a miracle. Call it a kiss from God. But whatever happened, this little bugger and his furry little cousins been transformed into laser-equipped weapons of war."

"Hold on. You tellin' me it's them hamsters you brought that killed all them people? You ain't joshing me?"

"No, ma'am." He locked the lid tight and patted the top. "We got here a genuine laser hamster. I witnessed this little beast blast apart 'bout twenty jerky-munchin' men and women just an hour ago."

Mysti backed against a wall, pushing aside her three-year-old, who stood quietly sucking her thumb. "And you brought a killer hamster in here?"

"Relax. I had me a little Jackie D handy. Never leave home without it. This little gem is sleeping better than Herbie the town drunk."

She frowned. "I shoulda known you'd be behind all this. Ya fool, you're lucky you didn't get yourself all lasered up."

"Nah. That was Arlo's fate."

"Arlo?"

"Yeah. Sadly, the tattooing master is nothing more than splatter on the sidewalk." He shrugged. "I told the fool to duck." He paused.

"I think we all should take a moment of silence in Arlo's honor." He lowered his head.

Colt and Mysti swapped awkward glances.

Dusty popped his head up. "'Bout enough. That no-good punched me in the chin just two days ago."

"You probably earned it."

Dusty cracked open the lunchbox lid.

Mysti slid down the wall. "Keep that thing shut!"

"Come, come. This ain't no time bomb." He reached in and petted the sleeping hamster. It jerked awake. A red glow emanated from within the darkened lunchbox. Dusty snapped his hand away. "Uh-oh."

A laser fired from the lunchbox.

Mysti screamed and hit the floor.

Colt leapt behind a chair.

The microwave oven mounted above the stove exploded. Charred splintering wood from the surrounding cabinetry showered Mysti.

Mysti's three-year-old jumped and threw her hands in the air. "Yeah! Again, again!"

The hole in the drywall sizzled.

Dusty slammed the lunchbox shut and tossed it onto the kitchen table. It slid and rotated to a stop. Dusty ducked next to Mysti and said, "I guess it needed another shot of the good stuff. And a stronger box."

Mysti lifted her head from the floor. "No kiddin', Einstein."

"It appears that petting the creature sets it off."

"Git that thing outta here!"

"Fine, fine." Dusty gingerly picked up the lunchbox and nodded to Colt. "C'mon, Colt. We got some work to do." Dusty headed for the back door.

Colt glanced at his mother for moment. "I kept my pants clean, Mom."

"Good." Mysti patted herself. "I didn't."

Colt cringed and eyed the backdoor.

Mysti said, "I'm guessin' you want to keep helping out that fool."

Colt nodded.

"Go ahead, then. I'm sure one of you will screw things up even worse than they are."

Colt's shoulders slumped, then he headed out the backdoor. He caught up to Dusty halfway to the large shed in the backyard. "Uh, Dusty?"

"Yes, my boy?"

"Um, shouldn't we, like, just let the hamster go?"

"No, no, no. This little guy is the ticket to our fortune."

"But…it blew up a bunch of people."

"Colt, my boy. You gotta trust your dad. Open that door."

Colt huffed as he lifted the rusty latch of the shed's double doors. "You're not my dad. Weren't you like thirteen when I was born?"

Dusty shrugged it off and entered the shed.

The oversized shed was jam-packed with blades, hammers, ratchets, shovels, ropes, chains, screwdrivers, wrenches, drills, power tools galore, and even dangling saws. Colt typically avoided the place, and not just because his mom demanded it. Even after Dusty clicked on the pair of long, bare fluorescent bulbs hanging from the ceiling, the dank shed felt like a serial killer's playhouse, equipped with enough tools to slice and dice an entire family for an afternoon meal.

Dusty had other ideas. Cannibalism wasn't on the menu. "Colt," he said. "Let's get to work."

They spent the next hour assembling a hodgepodge collection of bolts, scrap metal, and used car parts. They hammered and wrenched scrap machine pieces apart and then reassembled them in an arrangement that intrigued Colt, who occasionally peeked into the lunchbox to ensure the deadly hamster was still there.

Dusty mounted glass-shielded helmets on his and Colt's head and welded the remaining key pieces together.

The two removed their helmets, and Dusty patted Colt's shoulder. "My boy, we're finished."

"Finished what?" Colt studied the long contraption. It looked like a one-man mechanical battering ram with levers.

Dusty heaved his invention up to his hip, looped his arm through its shoulder harness, and pointed it toward the shed's double doors. The contraption looked like a cross between a shotgun and a firehose.

"What the peanut butter is it?" Colt asked, "A gun?"

"Oh, it's more than a gun. Watch." He set the massive contraption on the long bench at the back end of the shed and flipped a lid at the top, which exposed a small rectangular box. He carefully pried open the lunchbox. "Scoot, scoot," he urged the hamster.

The little creature hesitated and then crawled from one box into the other.

Dusty clamped the lid shut.

A narrow opening on the lid exposed the hamster's fur. The boy said, "A hamster cage?"

"It's more than a hamster cage." Dusty heaved the contraption up to his hip once more. "Watch this." He walked outside.

Colt followed close behind into the backyard.

"Prepare to be amazed." Dusty petted the fur through the lid slits and pointed the end at a straggly, flowering bush.

A red glow emanated from under the lid. With a heavy zap, a laser blasted from the weapon's narrow tip. The bush exploded, reduced to a pile of sparkling smoke.

"Holy nuggets!" Colt exclaimed.

"You said it right, my boy." He gave him a wink. "We're gonna be rich."

4: In Space

IN THEIR SPACESHIP two hundred miles straight up from Colt, Dusty, and their hamster gun, Quinto and Bastle stood at attention in front of General Ditter's flickering hologram. The visibly frightened pair twirled their hands behind their backs and stiffened their fake smiles.

Quinto explained to the general, "We thought it was an ingenious idea."

General Ditter's rounded, blubbery body had squeezed into a tight uniform that was decorated in ribbons. He puffed out a broad frown. "Ingenious? Idiotic is more like it. Honestly, I gave you one shot to redeem yourselves, and this is how you screw it up?"

"But...but—" Bastle started.

"What?" Ditter demanded. "Speak up."

"Our objectives were met. There was mass confusion, elimination of dozens, and no one suspects the Zammarians."

"Of course they do not suspect us. Those brainless humans do not even know we exist. But your assignment was worldwide panic. How are we to strike fear into the entire miserable little planet if you attacked only one tiny portion of their billions of lifeforms?"

"A test case," Quinto blurted. "We were testing our theory. Now that we know it's a success, we shall continue until the chaos reaches critical momentum."

Ditter rubbed his chin and angled his sharp ears at the two. "You'd better, or it's back to cleaning fecal matter off the emperor's throne."

Quinto and Bastle shuddered. The distinction of emperor of the Zammarian Galactic Cluster had recently gone to a Wobberslub Slug whose name could be pronounced only by hocking up a wad of phlegm.

A revolting creature, it often pooped on its throne while consuming raw spores from the Third Imperial Quadrant. Lately it had tapped into reruns of the 1980s human sitcom *ALF*, broadcasts that had crossed time and space from Earth.

Quinto and Bastle had been demoted to throne cleanup after one too many mess ups during guard duty, but Quinto convinced the emperor that he could force the humans to reboot the series with the emperor himself having regular cameos. He'd sent the two on their special assignment to lay the foundation of worldwide conquest.

Ditter lowered his brow. "Did I make myself clear? Fail, and you're back to your old duties."

Quinto and Bastle snapped their heels and answered in unison, "Yes, sir!"

Ditter's image flickered and then disappeared.

Bastle raised his fists. "I knew we should've just killed them all when we had a chance."

Quinto slapped the back of Bastle's head. "Moron. We're not supposed to kill all humans, just a few thousand. Had we blasted through that crowd, their defense teams would've responded before we even leveled a single urban area." He wagged his finger in the air. "Mass confusion. That's the plan. Empowering those smaller beings worked perfectly. We must continue our siege of mayhem."

Bastle waddled across the space craft's flight deck, lights flickering on every wall. He stopped at a glass portal that overlooked Earth, its deep blues and whites beautiful from above. Bastle licked his lips, imagining the paradise awaiting him and his family once the humans were subjugated. He already had his sights on a cozy beach house where he'd lounge in his hammock and be served specialty mixed drinks from the enslaved humans who would quiver yet be compliant under Zammarian rule. Bastle pictured himself using his mind-controlled remote, which commanded his slaves to present him with an array of finger sandwiches made with real human fingers, of course. Meanwhile, the emperor would get his way, and a new series of ALF would return to prime-time television.

"Fine," Bastle at last affirmed. "I'll review the reconnaissance for additional niz-car locations."

Quinto waddled toward him. "It's called NASCAR, dummy. Besides, I already researched the small hamsters we encountered. They are not indigenous to the NASCAR environment."

"Blasted! Then where is the habitat of these hamster creatures?"

Quinto typed several keys at a nearby monitor. "According to a wise elder of the human race named Google, hamsters are located here." Quinto pointed at the screen.

Bastle leaned into the monitor. "Ah, yes! They are at Dog Products. Take us to Dog Products!"

"No, no, stupid. Dog Products are supplies located at the same facility as the hamsters. See? What we want is this: Pet Store."

"We shall wreak havoc at Pet Store!"

Quinto smiled and nodded. "Wreak havoc we shall."

5: The Pet Store

A CHIMING BELL welcomed the two Zammarians entering quaint Sam's Petmart in the middle of Creek Town. A small congregation of caged birds near the entrance hopped on their perches, squawking out warnings. Quinto adjusted his human face mask and baseball cap and eyed his partner, who did the same. Since Zammarians were the size of human children, the two opted for child-like disguises. They had molded costumes in the color, texture, and form of kids featured on *ALF*, which dated their ensemble to the 1980s.

An elderly man greeted them from the checkout counter. "Ah, hello, boys."

It took Quinto a beat to realize the human was addressing him and his partner. "Uh…" He coughed. Squeaking out his best young human voice, he answered, "Hello, mister. We enter your establishment in the pursuit of hamsters."

"My, my." The old man patted his blue vest. "Big words for a little tike. You must be a good reader to have that vocabulary."

"Uh, yes," Quinto spoke nervously. "We consume a wide range of juvenile reading material."

Bastle added, "We also consume a wide range of juveniles."

Quinto elbowed his partner.

The man leaned into the counter. "What? I didn't catch that."

Quinto said, "Hamsters. We search for hamsters."

"Oh, yes." His wrinkled face creased into a smile. "Aisle three. All the way to the end."

The costumed aliens inched forward.

The old man raised a finger and said, "Wait a minute."

Quinto and Bastle bumped into each other when they stopped.

"Um, where are your parents?"

"Parents?" Quinto started. "They wait for us in the land vehicle. One that we are too young to operate ourselves."

"Okay. Just have them come in after you select your new pet. No horseplay."

"Correct," Bastle said. "We will not play with horses."

They waddled their way through the store, their weighty backpacks banging into each other. "Careful," Quinto whispered to Bastle. "The atomic pulverizer is bound to fire if you keep bumping into me."

"Nag, nag, nag."

As they passed aisle after aisle of implements hanging from hooks and stocked shelves full of interesting bags, foreign aromas wafted through their masks, causing Quinto to gag.

Bastle echoed Quinto's noxious feeling with, "The foods the humans eat at this Sam's Petmart must be the worst things possible. Once Zammarians rule Earth, implementing proper food preparation will be our top priority."

"I agree. I'm impressed humans haven't already killed themselves with their eating habits." Quinto slowed his pace and looked up. "Ah, here we are."

Large, rectangular glass cases lined the wall. In them, several dozen hamsters huddled asleep within beds of gray stuffing. Only two hamsters appeared to be awake, both fighting over a vertical metal wheel. One hamster attempted to spin the wheel to the right, while the other struggled to make it go left. The wheel rocked back and forth.

Bastle asked, "How do we emancipate them?"

"I'm thinking."

The aquariums were twice as high as the Zammarians. Quinto considered using a blaster to remove the bottom of the glass. He quickly abandoned the idea, realizing that the glass would undoubtedly shatter and slice up the hamsters, rendering them useless.

Before either Zammarian could think further, a group of three human children raced at them. The Zammarians leapt to the side. Bastle dug one arm into his bag, his hand locking on the handle of his phaser.

The children, however, ignored them and went straight for the hamster cases. They smiled and tapped on the glass. Their performance reminded Quinto of the humans at the NASCAR location.

A deep voice spoke. "Now, now. Settle down, kids."

Quinto and Bastle spun around. An adult human towered over them.

The man smiled at the Zammarians. "You two little guys looking for a hamster too?"

"Yes," Quinto answered. "We are enamored by their...cuteness. They send our child hearts all aflutter with happiness, equal to the giddiness evident in these other juveniles."

The man furrowed his brow at Quinto. "Um...yeah."

"Daddy, Daddy," one of the children pleaded. "I want the brown one. The brown one."

"Stop banging on the glass," the man warned. "You'll scare them."

Bastle tapped the man's leg. "Perhaps you can assist in removing the hamsters from their enclosure. Then your offspring can..." He winked at his partner. "Activate them."

He furrowed his brow again. "Um, well, I'll need to ask for assistance if you kids want to pet the hamsters."

His children begged. "Please. Please, Daddy. Please!"

Quinto joined in. "Yes, yes. Please, Daddy. We request likewise."

The man straightened. "I'll be right back." He strode away, eyeing Quinto and Bastle suspiciously as he made his way back up the aisle.

Bastle whispered to his partner, "Excellent. This is working perfectly."

"Not so fast," Quinto whispered back. "I think the larger human suspects our activity."

"How can he? Humans are stupid."

"Nevertheless, we must be prepared for action upon his return." He reached into his pocket and gripped his atomic pulverizer. "Prepare for combat."

6: Ablaze

ACROSS THE STREET from Sam's Petmart, Dusty toted his hamster gun into Wilson's Gun Shop with Colt two steps behind. Dusty marched past the racks of vertically mounted rifles and headed straight for the long back-lit glass counter stocked with several dozen handguns of various shapes and sizes.

A bald fat man in a stretched polo shirt that barely covered his gut stood from his stool behind the counter. "What in tarnation is that?" he asked in a long drawl.

Dusty gently rested the massive gun on the glass counter. It creaked under the weight.

Colt sidled up next to Dusty, careful to remain opposite the business end of the laser gun.

Dusty smiled. "Wilson, today's your lucky day."

Wilson asked, "You finally leaving town?"

"No. This beauty. You ain't never seen anything like this before."

"No kidding." Wilson scanned it left to right. "Looks like something you soldered together in that creepy shed in your backyard."

"Better than that. This magic weapon actually works. And buddy, it's the most powerful thing you've ever set your eyes on."

"Powerful?" Wilson huffed. "More powerful than the X-two-sixty ten-gauge? Did Arlo tell you 'bout that? Hoo-wee! Talk about kickback. Hey, have you seen Arlo? He owes me twenty bucks."

"Arlo's been blowed up."

Wilson lowered his brow. "Say what?"

"Wilson, focus. The gun. This gun, the one you're going to pay handsomely for when you see this bad boy in action."

"Did you say Arlo's been blown up?"

Dusty snapped his fingers in front of Wilson's face. "Focus, man, focus. C'mon. To the range." Dusty heaved the weapon up and walked with it down the counter to a door at the far end of the store. "Let's move it, Wilson!" He disappeared through the door.

Wilson turned to Colt. "What does your mom see in that turd?"

Colt shrugged. "They like to jump on the bed."

"Jump on the bed?"

"That's what is sounds like through the walls at bedtime."

He shook his head. "Guess that explains why Mysti's always got a bun in the oven."

"Our oven's broken."

"Different oven, kid."

Colt followed Wilson through the door and down a hallway that led to an indoor shooting range. Their footsteps echoed through the dank, long, and cave-like room that had only two lights. A bare bulb dangled above a single stall where Dusty lowered his hamster-powered weapon onto a wooden stand. A single spotlight at the far end of the room illuminated a well-used paper target hung from a railing that ran the length of the room.

With Wilson and Colt by his side, Dusty cracked his knuckles, grinned, and lifted the gun to his chest. "Be prepared to be wowed."

"Hold on. Lemme put out a new target." He pressed a button on the wall. The hook holding the paper target at the far end jerked forward, gliding toward Dusty.

Dusty said, "No, no. Leave it."

Wilson released the button. The target stopped, rocking back and forth on its hook. Wilson said, "But it's all shot up."

"In a second that won't matter." Dusty reached for the weapon's hamster housing and opened the small latch. With a few tickles of his finger through the opening, the container glowed an unnatural red.

Wilson muttered, "What the—"

A laser beam blasted out. Dusty jolted backwards. The far end of the room erupted in a fireball. Wind whooshed through the room. The ground shook.

Wilson and Colt coughed their way through a plume of dust and debris. After the dust cloud settled, they could see that the back wall was gone. Through the hole wisps of smoke trickled up from charred cinderblock and an exposed grassy mound. Sunlight shone into the previously dark room.

Dusty coughed and shuddered through the smoke. His eyes lit up at the sight of the destruction. "Good job, fluffy." He patted the gun container holding the hamster. "That's the best he's ever done."

Wilson gasped. "My shooting range!" A chunk of ceiling at the edge of the gaping hole fell, knocking more dust into the air.

Dusty gripped his gun again and gave Wilson a satisfied grin. "Shall we talk about price?"

"How about the cost of destroying my range?"

"Well, you have to crack a few eggs to make an omelet."

"I'll crack your egg. Git out!" He shoved Dusty forward. "Git!"

"You're missing a prime opportunity."

"Out! Out!" Wilson shoved Dusty toward the hole at the end of the range.

Dusty barely held onto his giant hamster gun as he stumbled out of the building into an open alleyway.

Colt popped out of the hole next.

Wilson yelled from inside, "Expect a repair bill in the mail."

"Your loss." Dusty shook his head and looked down at Colt. "Some people lack vision."

Colt said, "With that hole in the building, he should see a lot better now."

The sound of an explosion and the sight of bricks tumbling across the street at the end of the alley snapped Dusty and Colt's attention forward.

Dusty muttered, "What the…?"

The two jogged toward the commotion. Men, women, and children ran every which way, screaming through bellowing smoke and flames. The Sam's Petmart sign had crashed to the pavement. A pair of puppies raced from the store through a giant hole where walls and glass windows once stood.

Colt gasped. "What's going on?"

"Either we're missing out on one heck of a sale at the pet store," Dusty replied, "or another batch of hamsters are going ballistic. And this time they're super mad."

Red laser bolts shot out from the store's broken windows and doors. The rays blew up nearby parked cars and set surrounding trees ablaze. Dozens of furry hamsters scurried from the wreckage, their eyes glowing satanic red.

Dusty and Colt dove behind a trash bin. Dusty dropped his hamster gun to the ground, and the two men peered around the bin.

"Man," Dusty said. "Imagine the firepower if we harnessed all of them little critters."

"If they don't blow us up first," Colt said.

"True."

More explosions followed, and the guys ducked.

Colt pointed at the gun on the ground. "Maybe we can use the one we've got to blow them up."

Dusty straightened. "Hamsters annihilating hamsters? Isn't that one of the signs of the apocalypse?"

Colt asked, "What's a-pokka-lips?"

Dusty smiled. "The end of the world. Fun and games from the Bible. Guess they wouldn't teach that at your school."

"Don't know. I watch YouTube, like, all day in school."

"Well, there goes my hopes for our future."

Zaps.

Explosions.

More zaps.

More explosions.

A tree overhead burst into flames. Burning leaves and branches rained down on them. Dusty grabbed his gun and Colt's arm, yanking him away from the bedlam. They ran to a car parked diagonally along the side of the road that separated the gun shop from the pet store.

An old woman sat in the driver's seat. Colt recognized Mrs. White, the woman from church who often pinched Colt's cheeks and told him how big he was getting. Shaking, she jumped with every explosion, whipping her head back and forth in panic, a handkerchief in her hand.

Dusty tapped on the driver's side window.

Mrs. White jumped again, until she recognized Dusty. She lowered the window. "Oh, Dusty, what's going on?"

"Laser hamsters."

"Laser what?"

"Unlock the doors so we can get in."

The door locks clicked open. Colt tumbled into the back seat with Dusty close behind, holding the giant gun. Dusty slammed the door shut, and the end of the gun smashed the window out. Broken glass flew out into the street.

"My window!" Mrs. White exclaimed.

"It's all good." Dusty patted the old woman's shoulder from behind. "We'll be able to buy a new car once we get this sucker on the market." He lifted his prized weapon. "For now, could you wheel the car around so I can fire out a few warning shots?"

She twisted toward the backseat. "You want to do what?"

"Well, I don't want to destroy the other hamsters, you see. Just show them who's in charge. I'm hoping to round up a few more."

"Wha...what are you talking about?" She patted her face with her handkerchief.

"Gawd, lady. You're lookin' more hyped up than a rabbit on Ritalin. Better let someone else drive." Dusty nudged Colt. "Hey, boy. Take the wheel."

"The boy? What? You want him to drive my car?"

An explosion rocked the car. A second later, something slammed onto the car hood.

Mrs. White screamed.

A half-charred old man in a Sam's Petmart uniform was splayed over the car's hood. He grimaced, sucked in a breath, and went limp.

Dusty whistled. "He's seen better days."

"Oh, my. Oh, my. Oh, my." Mrs. White shook, tears streaming down her cheeks.

"You're too upset to drive," Dusty said. "Move over to the passenger seat."

Carnage and debris rained all around the car. Mrs. White crept out the door and swatted the dead body on the hood with her handkerchief, repeating, "Oh, my...oh, my...oh, my..."

Dusty nudged Colt. "Well? Hop into the driver's seat."

"But...I can't reach the pedals."

"No problem. Just grab the wheel, stretch them size fours

toward the gas pedal, press down, and pray to God you don't hit anything. I trust you, little guy." He mussed Colt's hair.

Colt gave Dusty a worried glance and crawled from the back seat, over the giant gun, over the center console, and into the driver's seat.

"What about the keys?"

Mrs. White, in the passenger seat, held out a shaky hand.

Colt grabbed the keys and started the car. "Ready?" he called out.

Dusty answered, "Rev 'er up and git us goin', m'boy!"

Colt shifted the car into reverse, stretched his leg, and with a loud grunt rammed his foot onto the accelerator.

The wheels pealed and the car sped backwards. The corpse on the car hood slipped off. A second later, the car slammed into another vehicle stopped in the road.

Colt mashed the brake, shifted gears from reverse into drive, yanked the wheel, and hit the accelerator again.

The car sped forward, jerking the passengers left and right as Colt—barely able to see over the steering wheel—struggled to keep the car centered on the road. He turned his head, keeping the car away from the sidewalks, streetlights, and parked cars.

Mrs. White squealed, flapping her handkerchief back and forth and barking, "No, go left! No, right! You're going to hit that."

"Colt, stop!" Dusty yelled.

Colt hit the brake.

The car skidded to a stop.

"What on earth?" Dusty stretched himself over the center console.

"What?" Colt asked. He used the steering wheel to haul himself up.

Directly in front of their car stood a pair of short kids equipped with the strangest weapons Colt had ever seen. Their rifle-like guns were silvery and dotted with multicolored, blinking lights. One kid pointed his gun straight at Colt in the driver's seat. The other raced to the side of the car and pointed his weapon at Colt through the closed window. The strange kid tapped on the glass with the end of the gun barrel.

Colt lowered the window.

The kid spoke in a nasally voice. "We request to commandeer your vehicle. Do not comply and we will decimate you into oblivion."

"Hey, get outta here, kid," Dusty said. "And tell your friend to move. We're trying to survive this hamster attack."

The small boy angled his weapon toward Dusty in the backseat. "You had better listen if you know what is good for you and your feeble human existence."

"Bastle!" the other kid called out in a similar nasal voice. "Quick! Take over the vehicle. The hamsters are advancing."

"Move it!" the first kid said to Colt.

Colt hesitated, eyeing Dusty in the rearview mirror.

"I said move it!" The kid fired his weapon. A laser blast from his gun blew a hole in the roof above Colt's head.

Colt shifted the car into park and scrambled into the backseat.

"Hot dog, shorty!" Dusty stared in awe at the kid outside the door. "Where'd you get a rifle like that?"

The kid ignored him and signaled to his partner. The pair leapt into the front seat through the open window.

"Get out of the way, Bastle," the other kid yelled. "I am piloting this craft."

"You piloted the last one."

"I am versed in their technology. Get to the floor and depress the accelerating lever."

One tumbled to the floorboard while the other stood in the driver's seat and gripped the steering wheel. "Activate the drive mechanism now, Bastle. Depress the lever!"

The car tires squealed, and the car launched forward. A split second later, a pair of laser-powered explosions erupted beside the vehicle, causing a nearby trashcan to flip over the car.

Mrs. White screamed and waved her handkerchief.

Dusty nudged Colt. "Friends of yours?"

Colt shook his head.

The car continued, leaving the center of Creek Town ablaze.

7: Off the Beaten Path

A GENTLE FIRE snapped and tossed tiny embers into the cold night air, burning a stack of dried branches. Mrs. White, Dusty, Colt, and the two strange kids who had hijacked Mrs. White's car huddled around the meager fire. They had built the little fire in a field not far from a desolate dirt road on the outskirts of town. Mrs. White's car, parked crooked in the middle of the road, sat with its trunk propped open. Dusty claimed the spot was safe. Plus, with a recent armadillo roadkill roasting over the fire, he promised a meal fit for kings.

Colt and Dusty rested on a large rock, shivering under a quilt Mrs. White had purchased from the thrift store moments before the hamsters went laser crazy. Colt's pants lay next to them. Fearing his mother's wrath, Colt had slipped out of his pants so he didn't stain them on the dirty rock.

Mrs. White sat on a log and had wrapped herself in a checkered bedspread. The two strange kids stood on the opposite side of the fire, struggling to recharge their weapons by shoving grass and other salvaged biomaterial into their power cells.

Dusty leaned forward, bit his bottom lip, and gave the strange kids a puzzled stare. Finally he asked, "You did what to them hamsters?"

One kid answered, "We altered their inherent internal electrical potential into photon energy, thereby allowing them to project said energy into a stimulated emission of electromagnetic radiation."

"Like, duh," the other kid said.

Dusty angled his eyebrow at Colt. "Golly, they must be teachin' way more science in third grade than I remember."

Colt looked over at the two kids. "What're your names?"

"Name?" The first kid shared a concerned look with the second. "Um...Gordon. Yes. My name is Gordon. And my companion child is...Shumway. Yes, yes, Gordon and Shumway."

Shumway spoke to Gordon in a loud whisper. "How come you get to be Gordon?"

"Shh!" Gordon kicked the dirt.

Dusty leaned back. "Sure. Yeah." He coughed. "Where do you kids live, Gordon and Shumway? It's late for a couple o' youngsters like you, ain't it?"

"Late?" Gordon looked to the stars. "Yes. The hour is far advanced. We…uh…we—"

"We have vacated our base residence to…to…camp out and explore," Shumway said.

"Yes!" Gordon said. "Camp out and explore. We are scouting juveniles."

Colt asked, "You're Boy Scouts?"

"Correct. Boy Scouts."

"My, my, my." Dusty shook his head. "Boy Scouts with heavy artillery? I don't remember that merit badge. Now I wish I didn't get kicked out for cooking my scout leader's goat on a spit. Now that was good eatin'. Say, where's your scout leader?"

"Um—" Gordon started.

Shumway jumped in with, "Hamsters. Yes. Hamsters destroyed the scout leader."

Dusty asked, "You mean the hamsters that you somehow turned into furry-nosed Godzillas that blew up the entire downtown?"

"We initially empowered the inferior creatures to attack only single beings, until my partner here…" Gordon pointed a thumb at Shumway, "accidentally configured a much higher setting at the pet-selling establishment."

"Gimme a break," Shumway said. "The atomic pulverizer's buttons are way too tiny for this costume."

"Costume?" Dusty asked.

"I mean…I mean I pressed the wrong button. Fat fingers."

Dusty said, "So with your fat fingers, the hamsters went from mildly terrifying to weapons of mass destruction?"

"Yes," Gordon explained. "And what's worse, this time the atomic pulverizer's aim was set to omnidirectional. Which means it affected all hamsters or creatures that fit a hamster's profile in every direction in a radius of point zero three five light-years."

"How far is that?" Dusty asked.

Colt answered, "Like, all hamsters throughout the entire solar system."

"He is correct," Gordon said.

Dusty nodded. "That explains why my hamster gun blew out the back of Wilson's gun range."

Gordon ignored Dusty's statement and said, "I estimate that within the week, hamsters throughout the earth will achieve the peak of their devastation and outnumber living humans ten to one."

Dusty whistled. "That was a big oops with that atomic pulverizer do-hickey."

Shumway wiggled his hands. "Again, fat fingers. Tiny buttons. Not my fault."

Everyone went quiet for a minute, listening to the snap and crackle of the fire. Mrs. White, who had nodded off at the start of Dusty's interrogation, snored loudly. Colt's legs bounced beneath his and Dusty's quilt.

Dusty said to Colt, "You cold, kid?"

"I gotta pee," Colt answered.

Dusty pulled the quilt off. Colt hopped up, ran to a nearby bush, and relieved himself.

Gordon asked, "What is the child doing?"

"He had to take a leak," Dusty said.

"He leaks? Does he require medical servicing?"

"Nah, kid. He's just answering nature's call."

"Nature requests his leakage?" Shumway asked. He leaned toward Gordan. "I told you this planet is strange."

"So," Dusty started as Colt returned to their rock, "when are you two youngsters gonna admit that you're a couple of aliens from Mars?"

Shumway huffed. "We would never live on that desert wasteland."

"You admit you're aliens?"

Shumway asked, "How'd you know?"

"Ha! I didn't fer sure until now. Besides…" Dusty leaned back. "Pretty obvious. I mean, Gordon Shumway? Everybody knows that's the name of ALF from his home planet of Melmac."

Shumway slapped Gordon. "I knew they were stupid names."

Colt asked, "What's your real names?"

Gordon pointed to himself. "I'm Quinto. This is my partner, Bastle."

Dusty said, "Quinto and Bastle? They sound more fake than the ALF names. Can we get a look-see under them costumes?"

Bastle wiggled his mask up, revealing his face.

"Whoa!" Dusty backed up a step and waved his hands. "Mask back on, please."

Bastle pouted. "I have many admirers who are attracted to my exterior features."

"Keep the costume on," Quinto said. "Humans cannot comprehend the beauty of a Zammarian."

Dusty said, "Beauty? I've seen decomposed armadillos that were more attractive."

Bastle huffed but wiggled his mask back into place. "Idiot."

Colt tapped Dusty's arm. "What's an ALF?"

Dusty said, "Oh, ALF is a nineteen eighties sitcom. Lately I've been catching some retro TV shows on Hulu and found the furry Melmacian downright hee-larious." He altered his voice to quote ALF, "Ha! I kill me!" His normal voice returned. "Man, what a trip."

Quinto said, "How fortuitous that you are familiar with this ALF, for it is our leader's liking for ALF that prompted our arrival."

"What do you mean?"

Quinto explained, "The Zammarian emperor loves watching ALF reruns from distant broadcasts amplified by human-made satellites. We convinced him that if we could cause enough disorder among humans, the Zammarians could take over and subjugate the makers of ALF to bring back the sitcom in prime time."

Dusty twisted his face. "You sayin' that all of mankind might be wiped out of existence 'cause your head honcho wanted to watch more episodes of ALF?"

"Exactly."

"Dad gum." Dusty shifted on the rock he shared with Colt. "And I thought I was impulsive."

Colt said, "You are."

Dusty clapped his hands once and rubbed them together. "Sounds like we got some hamster killing to do."

Colt gasped. "Hamster killing?"

"How else are we going to survive their endless killing spree? I mean, there're only so many sunflower seeds and carrot sticks to calm the little buggers down."

"No, no," Quinto said. "Those inferior creatures are critical to create an imbalance of power and allow Zammarian control, thereby, allowing the Zammarian emperor to get ALF back."

"Uh, yeah," Dusty said as he leaned to one side. "But if we let them little varmints run amok like they are, there won't be no ALF left." He cracked his neck. "It's either us or them. You know what I mean?"

"Mmmmm." Quinto tapped his chin and turned to Bastle. "The human has a point. Your miscalculation has empowered the hamsters too much."

"Again, fat fingers."

"Um, Mr. Quinto?" Colt said, raising his hand.

"What?"

"Can't we make the hamsters less powerful? Like, make their laser eyes not as bad?"

"Mmmmm." Quinto tapped his chin again. "Reverse the atomic pulverizer's enabler? We've never attempted this achievement before. It may lead to undesirable consequences."

Dusty said, "Can't be worse than what's going down now."

"Your theory is incorrect, human," Quinto said with a lift of his head. "It could be much worse. Obliteration of vast tracks of land. Permanent radioactive contamination of water and air, kicking off a planetary core meltdown."

Bastle said, "And what's worse, we'd be fired."

"Yeah, sure," Dusty said. He lifted an eyebrow. "Getting fired. That's worse."

Quinto said, "There may be a way to reconfigure the atomic pulverizer. Bastle, do you have the operator's manual?"

"I threw it out the day we got it. There's not a weapon that I can't program." He reached for the atomic pulverizer.

"I hope you are correct, Bastle. But perhaps you should remove your fat fingers."

"Remove my…?"

"The costume."

"Oh. Yes. I knew that."

A loud buzzing within Quinto's back pocket caught everyone's attention.

"What's that?" Dusty asked.

"Oh, no!" Quinto fumbled in his pocket and retrieved a small, round device dotted with buttons and pulsating green as it buzzed.

"General Ditter?" Bastle asked.

"Who else would it be?" Quinto turned to Dusty and Colt. "We ask you not to speak."

Dusty saluted. "Roger that, little dude."

Quinto waited until Bastle stood next to him before pressing a button on the buzzing device.

The round object opened like a clam shell and hovered in midair. Above the floating device a bright hologram of a fat, even uglier version of Quinto and Bastle materialized. The hologram of General Ditter huffed. "What's this? Disguises?"

"Y-y-yes. Yes, sir, General Ditter, sir." Quinto shifted uncomfortably.

"Eck! These humans look disgusting, but to get to the point, it looks like you two did it again."

"Did it, sir?" Quinto asked.

"You think we have not been tracking your progress? The emperor is most interested in this mission. The scanners indicate a massive worldwide event. Chaos everywhere. You are either on the verge of success or disaster."

Quinto and Bastle eyed each other. Bastle slipped out a smile.

General Ditter went on, "The initial goal of causing complete panic has been accomplished; however, if you do not slow the progress soon, all humans will be extinct. We cannot have that." He leaned forward. "Can we?"

"No. No. Of course not, sir," Quinto and Bastle said, speaking over each other.

"How can we subjugate humans if they are all dead?"

"You are absolutely correct, sir," Quinto said.

"We have everything under control," Bastle added.

"You'd better. Or else."

"…Or else what, sir?" Bastle ventured.

"Or else…" General Ditter began and then stepped away, causing the hologram to disappear.

A second later, the image of a giant slug-like alien appeared. The hologram image was so repulsive that even Colt, sitting several feet away, gasped.

The creature said, "Or Quinto and Bastle will be a snack for me." He chomped down on a wiggling object that was indiscernible from the hologram's grainy image, yet the act made Quinto and Bastle jump. The slug leaned forward. "I want ALF! Now!"

The hologram flashed off. The round communicator snapped shut and dropped to the dirt.

A lull followed. Everyone blinked several times to readjust their eyes to the darkness.

Dusty broke the silence with, "Hoo-weee. That was one ugly slug."

"Ugly but powerful," Bastle said.

Colt gave Dusty a worried glance.

Dusty seemed to read the boy's face. "I don't know. I think our chances are fair."

Colt looked to the fire, his insides rumbling with hunger and fear.

Mrs. White snored.

8: Downgrading

BY THE NEXT MORNING, Creek Town was desolate and covered in smoldering cinders. Dusty drove this time. Mrs. White sat in the passenger seat with Colt and the Zammarians still costumed as kids in the back. Dusty motored from farmhouse to farmhouse on the outskirts of town, searching for roaming herds of hamsters that might be continuing their rein of destruction.

No success.

With every gas station they came across blown to bits, Dusty convinced the group to drive to the closest big city, Asheville, before they ran out of gas. Unfortunately, Asheville lived up to its name— covered in ash. Much of the city was still on fire. Smoke bellowed from what looked like bombed-out buildings. Cars were slammed into each other and some had plowed into trees and storefronts. A few dangled from overpasses. Everybody the group came across was either dead or in ashes, although they did find some rare collectible sneakers with minor burn marks.

"My oh my," Dusty uttered. "Them little critters been busy 'round these parts."

"Yeah," Colt spoke up from the backseat. "There can't be that many hamsters. How did they do all this?"

"On the contrary," Quinto explained. "The population of hamsters has grown a thousandfold in the past week, all throughout planet Earth."

Dusty whistled. "That's a lot of little rodents getting jiggy with it."

Quinto said, "I am unfamiliar with this phrase jiggy with it."

Dusty looked back to Colt, who stared back curiously. "Uh. In present company, let's just say they've made lots of little hamsters."

Bastle stiffened. "I think not. That's my programming of our rendezvous ship."

"Say what?" Dusty asked.

Quinto explained, "Prior to us testing the atomic pulverizer in the pet store, we had returned to our rendezvous ship currently orbiting the planet to check in with our superior. While there, we targeted all hamsters on earth with our asexual replicator—"

"Which I programmed," Bastle added.

"Yes." Quinto sighed. "This started the process of hamsters replicating so that when we were ready for worldwide atomization, there would be plenty of stock to carry out the duties."

"Oh great," Dusty said. "So not only are the hamsters incredibly lethal and destructive, but there are billions and billions of them worldwide."

"Exactly."

Dusty said, "I can't believe I'm saying this, but of all people, you guys are about as smart as a dog barking at its own tail."

Colt added, "Dogs are smarter."

Quinto replied, "This is quite a compliment for these dog creatures, for we have superior intelligence."

Dusty asked, "How many dogs have accidentally killed off millions of people?"

Bastle nudged Quinto and said, "He's got a point."

Quinto pouted. "You are not helping."

Dusty eased Mrs. White's car through the chaos of burning vehicles and stopped at an impassable intersection where a firetruck had toppled on its side. Mrs. White's car struggled to get around it. Distant sirens and echoing explosions gave clues to the battle that was still raging somewhere nearby.

Mrs. White whimpered. "Oh, oh, oh, dear." She cried into her handkerchief. "Those poor people."

The car ground to a halt.

Quinto leaned forward from the back. "Why did you turn off the vehicle, human?"

"I didn't shut it off. We're out of gas."

Bastle huffed. "How are we going to atomize one of those creatures to test my reprogramming?"

Dusty twisted his body toward the back seat. "Come, come, my little alien friend. All is not lost. I've got some buddies a few blocks from here who can hook us up." He paused. "Provided they're not pillars of salt already. Let's giddy up!"

Dusty opened his door and stepped out.

"Wait, wait," Mrs. White pleaded. "What about my car?"

"Don't worry, Mrs. White. We'll remember where we parked."

He looked back and forth. "Looks like we're at the corner of chaos and mayhem." He tapped his temple. "Got the place memorized. Let's get movin'."

One by one the group members piled out of the car and worked their way up the road, zigzagging around smoldering vehicles and wrecked buildings.

Colt peered toward the sidewalk and gasped at the sight of charred skeletal remains, bones intertwined. He turned away, and something caught his attention. "That person's alive!" Colt ran to a man moaning in the street near the curb.

Everyone followed the boy.

Dusty knelt next to the injured man, bloodied and shaking in pain. "Don't you fret," Dusty told him. "We'll avenge your pain when we kick them little varmints in the butt with our modified alien weapon."

"It…it wasn't the hamsters," the near-dead man said, barely getting the words out. "You just ran over me in your car."

"Oh…" Dusty tapped his bottom lip. "Bad news is I ain't got no insurance." He smiled. "But I know a doc who can buff out them bruises like nobody's business."

The man gurgled out his last breath and died.

Quinto asked, "Do you often kill fellow human beings, human?"

"Not as much as you two knuckleheads."

"Fat fingers!" Bastle shook his hand.

Colt turned away. Just beyond a fallen tree crossing part of the road, a pair of hamsters scurried along the curb. "Hamsters!" Colt blurted.

Bastle jumped. "Where? Where?" He gripped his atomic pulverizer.

"Down the road. There." Colt pointed.

"Outta my way!" Bastle shoved Colt aside and ran.

Quinto called out, "Bastle! Wait!" He sprinted behind him.

Dusty rubbed his hands together and smiled. "Ooooh. I gotta see this." He jogged after the Zammarians.

Colt and Mrs. White eyed each other.

Mrs. White said, "They're going to get themselves killed."

Colt nodded. "Likely."

The two reluctantly followed but kept a gap between them and the other three.

The two Zammarians ran on their stubby legs down the center of the road toward the hamsters. Dusty strode behind.

The lead Zammarian, Bastle, stopped abruptly and pointed his weapon. His partner argued with him for a moment. Quinto tried to yank the atomic pulverizer from Bastle, but Bastle yanked it back.

Dusty arrived and pulled the atomic pulverizer away from the arguing Zammarians, pointed at the hamsters who were nearly out of eyesight, and fired. Dusty stumbled back from the blast.

Colt and Mrs. White stopped next to a streetlight pole that had toppled over and lay on its side.

The Zammarians turned on Dusty to get the weapon back. The hamsters glowed red in the distance, but as the Zammarians and Dusty struggled, neither seemed to notice.

Colt leaned into Mrs. White. The woman gasped.

Colt mouthed, "Oh, no!"

The hamsters fired laser beams from their eyes. A ball of light engulfed Dusty and the Zammarians.

A second blast struck Colt and Mrs. White, engulfing them.

The light fizzled into nothingness.

Colt rubbed his eyes and the world returned in focus.

Dusty and the Zammarians were still standing and alive; no flames and no charred remains.

Colt looked at his hands. He too was still alive. He looked down at himself. Naked as a jaybird.

Clothing vaporized, Mrs. White yelped. Sunlight shone across her aged, exposed body.

Colt slapped his hands over his privates.

Mrs. White crisscrossed her arms and ran for the shelter of a wrecked pickup truck.

Several feet in front of Colt, Dusty and the Zammarians stood with perplexed expressions, all three equally nude.

The Zammarians squealed in shock, but Dusty stood tall and said, "Wow! Didn't see that coming."

The hamsters glowed red again.

Dusty yelled, "Quick. Duck!"

A laser blast shot past them.

Dusty, Colt, and the two Zammarians sprinted toward the same pickup truck where Mrs. White was hiding. Another laser blast barely missed their heads and hit a speed limit sign.

Behind the truck Quinto slapped his partner's head. "Nice going with the atomic pulverizer."

"It worked," Bastle said. "Kind of. Not like we were vaporized. Just our clothes."

Quinto pointed to Bastle's weapon. "Adjust the settings. The hamsters are still too powerful."

"Fer certain," Dusty added. "There are plenty of folks who'd strike me blind if I saw their naked butts."

Bastle tapped away at the atomic pulverizer's keypad. "I'm working on it. Give me a few minutes."

Colt grabbed Dusty's arm. "My pants. Mom's going to kill me."

"Cheer up," Dusty responded. "Technically you didn't get them dirty."

Colt heard a distant roar. He looked up and squinted. "What's that?" He pointed to the sky.

9: Slug Emperor

EVERYONE LOOKED UP. A massive craft descended quickly, aiming straight for them.

Quinto gasped. "Oh, no!"

"It isn't…" Bastle started.

"It is," Quinto answered.

Dusty asked, "Who? Who is it? Better yet, what is it?"

Exhaust from the vehicle kicked up dirt and debris.

The group sheltered their eyes as the object slowed and landed on the road about a hundred yards away. The ship creaked and moaned. Bloated and round, covered in tiny lights and various pipes that coughed steam, it looked to Colt as if it might have been a spacecraft, though it resembled nothing he'd ever seen on the Discovery Channel.

The group scrambled around the other side of the truck, hiding.

Dusty asked Quinto and Bastle, "A friend of yours?"

Quinto shook his head. "Much worse. It's our emperor."

"Your emperor?" Dusty whistled. "My, my, my. Royalty? This day just keeps getting better every minute."

"No, human," Quinto said. "This is not good. He's the most vicious, vile being ever to have existed throughout the entire universe."

Dusty nudged him. "I bet he's rich, eh? Rich dudes ain't got nothin' better to do than to spend a little dinero. I'm sure we can find something to entice the fella."

Before Quinto could respond, a large, rectangular door opened on the front of the spacecraft, its hydronic pistons hissing more steam. The door clanged against the pavement, and a large slug-like creature emerged from the darkened craft.

Bastle gasped and whimpered, nearly dropping the atomic pulverizer.

Quinto shoved his partner. "Quick. Continue the reprogramming."

The emperor appeared far uglier even than Quinto and Bastle. Bubbly welts covered greenish skin that oozed with a glimmering slime. A pair of tiny eyes rested atop an oval skull, just above a horizontal pair of what looked like lips. Crooked fangs hung out over his lips. His slug-like body rocked back and forth as he slithered forward along the pavement. "Quinto! Bastle!" the massive emperor called out, lurching back and forth and swinging humorously tiny arms.

"Ew," groaned Colt.

In one hand the emperor held a long stick with an impaled creature dangling from the end. He angled the creature toward his mouth and chomped down on it, ripping the creature in half. Mouth half full, he repeated, "Quinto! Bastle! I know you're here. I want my ALF."

Dusty rubbed his hands together. "Time to impress the rich guy."

"Wait. Stop!" Quinto grabbed Dusty's arm. "He should not be taken lightly. If he doesn't like what you have to say, the emperor will consume you."

"Nah," Dusty said with a wave of his hand. "Not enough meat on my bones." He marched out from behind the truck. Once in the open, Dusty stuck his fingers into the sides of his mouth and whistled loudly. He then said, "Hey! Over here, Mr. Alien Emperor." He swung his arms above his head, walking tall and proud despite being naked.

Colt bit his fingernails as he watched from the truck.

The emperor munched on his snack and angled his massive body toward Dusty. "Ah, human. You Willie?"

"Uh?" Dusty said. "My willie?" He looked down. "You'll have to forgive my little guy. It's a little chilly out today."

"No. Willie Tanner. You Willie Tanner from ALF? I want my ALF."

"Oh, him. I'm better than ol' Willie Tanner, my gorgeous slug. I'm the answer to your prayers. I'm the guy who will deliver your wildest dreams."

The emperor sniffed and then devoured what was left of his snack on the stick. "I want ALF." His voice thundered with a tone that made Colt's knees shake.

Dusty strode confidently forward. "Then ALF you shall receive. But before we get into the logistics of resurrecting a long-since-passed sitcom, let's get some business out of the way."

"What business?"

"A little matter of compensation. You toss out some of that pesky money of yours, and I'll provide you with the most hilarious furry Melmacian the world has ever seen on prime time."

The emperor slithered uncomfortably close to Dusty. "I want ALF!"

"Yes, yes. And you shall get ALF. I'm thinking maybe one or two million dollars cash, or whatever your equivalent is in space bucks, and you'll get it all. ALF. The Tanners. The whole kitten caboodle. Or is that kit and caboodle? I don't even know what a caboodle is. Sounds like some fancy underwear. Speaking of which, do you happen to have some spare underdrawers in that spacecraft of —umph!"

One of the enormous slug's tiny arms had extended with unexpected swiftness. The emperor slug snatched Dusty's body, locking a clawed hand around his naked torso.

"Wow!" Dusty barely squeezed out his words. "That's…quite… a grip." He struggled to breathe.

The emperor raised Dusty until he was eye-to-eye with the tiny, golf ball-sized eyeballs at the top of the slug's head. "I want ALF!"

"Yes…I will…just…release…"

The emperor shook Dusty violently. "I want ALF!"

Colt shivered behind the parked car. He recalled his mother's warnings, how she knew he and Dusty would mess things up. He remembered his mother's other two husbands and how they too got themselves killed. Now it appeared that Dusty would have a similar fate. Instead of getting hit by a bus or drowning in a river, he was being crushed by an alien, except in this case, the same alien who may kill everyone else in the world.

Dusty dangled in the slug's grip like one of the various frogs Colt had caught. Colt's teeth clenched and his heart pounded as he considered taking a stand. He never once stood up to a bully, but he knew his mother was right. He'd fail, even if he tried.

Nevertheless, something urged Colt forward.

Naked, knees knocking against each other, Colt eased out from behind the car. "S-s-s-stop!" Colt sputtered. He found his voice and yelled. "Stop!" He moved farther out into the middle of the road. "Put him down!"

The emperor averted his attention from Dusty to Colt. "Another human. Are you Brian Tanner? Will you get ALF?"

"We can't get ALF!" Colt yelled.

"No ALF? Yes, ALF! I want ALF!" He slapped the end of his giant slug tail. The ground reverberated from the shock.

"Psst! Little human," Quinto said in a loud whisper. He positioned himself so Colt could still see him behind the truck, though the emperor could not. "Do not anger the emperor."

Dusty grunted and wheezed. "I could… use…some air…"

"Okay, okay!" Colt called out. "We'll get you ALF."

"When?" the emperor asked. "I want ALF now!"

"When? Well…" He spun his head around. Nothing but a devastated city surrounded him. Wrecked cars. Fallen trees. Broken streetlights. Burned buildings. Skeletal corpses. Two Zammarians huddled over an atomic pulverizer, frantically reprogramming it. A naked Mrs. White shivered behind the two. A half dozen hamsters exiting a nearby shop, sniffing around at the ground. "More hamsters?" Colt muttered.

"What?" The emperor spoke. "Can't hear you. I want ALF!"

An idea sprang into Colt's mind. "Emperor! We have him. We have ALF!"

"What? Where? Where ALF?"

"First, put down that man. That human in your hand. He and I will get ALF, but we have to get him together."

The emperor grumbled. He slowly lowered Dusty to the pavement. "Where ALF? I want ALF now!"

"Yes!" Colt shouted. "We'll get him now. While you wait for us, we have a snack for you."

"Snack? Where snack?"

Colt pointed toward the hamsters that had just left the shop. "Right over there. See them? They're little and furry. They taste good. Like…like jellybeans."

"Jellybeans? What jellybeans?"

Dusty gasped for a breath, finally freed from the emperor's grip, "Yeah. Juicy jellybeans. A delicacy here on Earth. You should try some." He eyed Colt with a suspicious glare.

Colt smiled back, glad that Dusty was playing along. "Go ahead. Take some for a snack before they run away. They're quick."

"Not too quick for me," the emperor replied. His two arms extended forward. His clawed hands slapped over the group of hamsters and scooped them up. He retracted his arms slowly, admiring his catch. "M-m-m-m. Tasty snack." His bumpy, wart-covered tongue rolled over his fat lips.

"Psst!" Quinto said with a frantic wave of his hands. "We haven't re-atomized those hamsters yet."

"Exactly," Colt said.

The emperor shoved the hamsters into his mouth.

Dusty staggered toward Colt and asked in a loud whisper, "What's the plan, kid?"

"Run!" Colt sprinted as fast as he could.

Dusty ran step for step behind him. "Why are we running?"

"Look!" Colt aimed a thumb back toward the slug alien.

The giant slug's belly pulsated red. The emperor looked down at himself. "Why me glow red?" The glow intensified. "Ooooooh." He rubbed his tummy. "Ha! I kill me!"

A moment later, boom! Boom! Boom! The enormous slug blasted apart in a series of explosions. Nasty chunks of alien flesh flew skyward and slammed against the sides of buildings and wrecked cars. Blobs descended from the air and hit the asphalt with loud splats.

Colt and Dusty stopped running and watched the emperor's obliteration. A high-pitched scream drew their attention. Part of the slug's blubber had landed smack on top of Mrs. White. The elderly naked woman was drenched in revolting slime and fragments of slug.

Dusty said, "Hey, Colt, remind me to send Mrs. White a lovely thank-you card when we get back home." He winced. "That and a bottle of shampoo."

Colt said, "A big bottle."

10: A New Plan

"WORLDWIDE DEVASTATION," a stern news reporter announced on Colt's new smart phone. "That tragic two-day rampage of the world's hamster population will forever be known as The Days the Hamsters Fought Back. But mankind is resilient and has prevailed. Cities around the world are rebuilding to piece together their shattered lives. Nightly vigils are already the norm as the world remembers the heroes and innocents lost to the furry creatures. As for the villainous rodents, riotous mobs have killed off most of the hamster

population, which was billions larger than all previous scientific estimates. Many are suggesting a government cover-up and the saving
of select hamster specimens for further scientific study. Perhaps, this
reporter speculates, to keep as future weapons of war." The reporter
paused as he raised an eyebrow. "I'm Brock Fullovit reporting to you
live from TNB, the Toxic News Broadcast, signing off."

Colt lowered his phone as he thought about the millions of
hamsters that had been slaughtered over the past week. The thought
was saddening. Quinto and Bastle had—for the last time—altered
hamsters throughout the world with their reprogrammed atomic
pulverizer, rendering their laser eyes powerful enough only to give
people a mild sunburn. They were otherwise completely harmless.
Mrs. White, after getting slimed, had confined herself to her house
and hadn't left all week. She probably wouldn't step outside for
another year or so.

Dusty stepped into the kitchen where Colt sat at the table. He
ruffled Colt's hair. "How's the new phone, Colty boy?"

Colt shrugged. "It needs more games."

"Gotta ask your mom about that. I'm already in hot water for
getting you the phone, but I couldn't pass up the deal." He had
bartered with—or more like swindled—a friend. He traded his
hamster gun, which no longer had the hamster in it, for the phone,
and then sent his friend on a fruitless hunt for a new little creature
for the gun.

Dusty opened the fridge and pulled out a can of beer. "In any
case, in my book I figured any boy who saves my life from the
clutches of a four-ton slug deserves a new phone."

Colt wiggled in his seat. "I could'a used new pants too."

"Oh, right. Forgot about that. Them your old pants?"

Colt nodded. "They're squeezing my nuts."

"Not like there's much there to squeeze," Mysti said as she
stepped into the kitchen with a baby on her hip.

Colt's shoulders slumped.

"Now, now, now," Dusty began. "You can't be knockin' his
manhood like that."

"He's not a man," she spat. "And put that beer away. It's ten in the morning."

Dusty hesitated and put the beverage back into the fridge. "Well, Colt ain't technically a man, but he proved his worth. He risked life and limb to conquer that giant—"

"Yeah, yeah. Giant snail from outer space."

Colt said, "It was a slug."

"Whatever." From the fridge she fetched a baby bottle full of milk and popped it into the baby's whimpering mouth. "I never know how much of your stories are true or fable. But one thing's fer certain." She shook a finger at Colt. "You broke your promise."

"My promise?" Colt asked.

"Your new pants. I paid good money for them. And with you growin' like a weed, I can't be buying you new pants all the time."

"Mom?"

"I swear, I can't trust you to do anything right."

"Mom?"

Mysti focused on the baby on her hip.

"Mom!"

Mysti jerked. "What?"

Colt took a breath as he mustered up his courage. "I'm...I'm not a loser."

"When did I ever I say that?"

"That's...that's how you treat me."

"I...well..." Mysti stammered.

"I took good care of them pants until they got zapped off me, and it wasn't my fault. I...I did what you said. Honest." His eyes glassed over with tears.

Mysti looked to Dusty.

Dusty nodded and crossed his arms, giving Colt a proud smile.

Mysti turned to Colt. "Sadly, between the two of you, my nine-year-old is the more responsible one."

Colt sniffed snot back up his nose and wiped his nose with the back of his hand.

She neared Colt and patted his already messed hair. "I'm sorry,

Colt. Sometimes I say things I don't mean. You're my sweetie. Way better than I'll ever be." She kissed the top of his head.

Colt sniffed again. "Thanks."

She smiled. "You ain't half bad."

"Ain't half bad?" Dusty echoed. "That boy's a hero. And today destiny calls. I'll be needing his help out in the shed. C'mon, Colt." Dusty strode for the backdoor.

Mysti shook her head. "And there you go again. You're a horrible influence on Colt. He'd be twice the hero if it weren't for you."

"C'mon, Colt." Dusty stepped outside.

Colt stood but hesitated, exchanging looks with Mysti.

She furrowed her eyebrows. "Well, go on. He's gonna need you to save his butt again."

Colt hopped out the backdoor.

As Dusty worked on opening the rusty shed door, Colt asked, "This isn't another hamster gun, is it?"

"Oh, no." He gave the boy a wink as he yanked on the stiff latch. "This time we got ourselves some, shall I say, experts." He swung open the door.

Inside, Quinto and Bastle sat on stools next to the workbench in the center of the shed.

Dusty asked, "How's that atomic pulverizer comin' along, fellas?"

"Well, if this idiot stops misplacing the diodes," Bastle said, "we might have something operational in no time at all. Who has fat fingers now, Quinto?"

"Constructing atomic pulverizers from human-made components," Quinto muttered as he fumbled with a switch, "is not my specialty."

Colt peered over the bench strewn with parts and wires. "Um, are you two seriously making an atomic pulverizer for Dusty?"

Bastle answered, "Yes. He convinced us we owe him as much, since you two helped bring down our tyrannical emperor and restore democracy to Zammar. Why do you ask?"

"Well, uh…" Colt turned toward Dusty and then back to the

aliens. "Things usually don't go well when Dusty gets his hands on weapons like that."

"Colt, Colt, Colty, my boy," Dusty said, patting Colt's back. "I'm not planning on blowing up the world like them little hamsters did. No sirree."

Quinto explained, "Bastle will be programming the atomic pulverizer to instantly vaporize targeted outer clothing."

"Yes!" Dusty said, skipping with excitement. "Remember how them hamsters blew our clothes away? Well, that got me thinking, you blow away someone's clothes, and guess what the first thing they'll be doing?" He paused. "Buying more clothes."

"Yeah. So?" Colt said.

"Well," Dusty explained. "Since all the other stores were blown to bits, you happen to be talking to the sole owner of the only clothing store in all of Creek Town."

Colt scrunched his eyebrows. "So you're going to zap random people, make them naked, and then sell them clothes?"

Dusty nodded. A broad smile spread across his face. "Yes, siree, Colt. Easiest money ever."

Colt scratched his head. "Are you gonna use hamsters?"

"Nope," Dusty said with a smile. "These little guys are rigging their doo-hickey to blast off clothes in one swoop."

"Do you trust them?"

"Why wouldn't we?"

"They kinda messed up before."

Bastle slammed his hand down. "We were not entirely at fault!"

Quinto said, "We did contribute to the problems."

"Contribute, maybe. A little." Bastle tapped his chin. "Maybe a lot." He resumed working on the weapon.

Colt tugged on the sides of his undersized pants. He wondered if Dusty could make enough money to buy something more comfortable. "You still think they won't, like, kill people? Again?"

Dusty nodded. "I'm all about givin' folks a second try. Right, my little gherkin buddies?" He patted Bastle's back.

Bastle's hand slipped.

The weapon came to life. It revved. Buzzed. A laser bolt flashed out.

Zap!

A plume of dust filled the shed.

Everyone coughed and waved their hands in front of their faces until the dust settled.

"It worked," Colt announced.

Dusty and the Zammarians turned to the boy to see him standing at the shed entrance completely naked.

Bastle threw his arms in the air. "Success!"

Dusty said, "Guess we'll be getting you them new pants sooner than later."

"Oh, goodie." Colt faked a smile.

"So whatcha think? You wanna go partners with me sellin' clothes?"

Colt thought for a moment, adjusting his hands cupped over his privates. "Can we zap a couple bullies from my school? Maybe then they'll stop picking on me and my friends."

"Anyone you want."

He pictured the mean, brawny kids and Lester, the ringleader, who often teased Colt for his big ears and lanky body. He imagined them pointing and laughing at him as he walked home from school. Colt would pull his new weapon from his backpack and say, "Keep laughing, punks." He'd pull the trigger. Lester and the other bullies would stand there stunned and naked to the world. Surrounding kids would point and laugh at them. The naked boys would stumble over the sidewalk, smaller kids, and each other, trying to leave or hide. The other kids would chant Colt's name and praise his heroism.

Colt felt the thrill of the potential revenge, and his smile grew wide. "Mom's right," he said to Dusty. "You are a bad influence on me."

Dusty wrapped his arm around Colt's shoulders. "I wouldn't have it any other way."

So enthralled in this touching moment, neither humans nor Zammarians noticed the tiny, seared hole at the back end of the shed. When the weapon came to life, a second blast had fired out the opposite end, zapping through the shed's back wall. On the other side of the hole, an impregnated bunny, knocked over by the blast, regained her wits and stood upright. The fluffy creature wiggled her whiskered nose and then froze, as if suddenly entranced.

From deep within her darkened eyes, there emerged a bright red glow.

AUTHOR'S NOTES - JOHN HOPE

The Dangers of Laser Hamsters

EMPOWERING hamsters with laser-firing capabilities is a dangerous proposition and should not be taken lightly.

For centuries animals have been used in warfare, inflicting devastation upon anyone who was the unfortunate victim. Ancient Greeks, for example, used trained dogs in combat, equipping them with spiked metal collars and mail armor. Spanish conquistadors used similar tactics to kill warriors in the Caribbean, Mexico, and Peru. Ancient Egyptians famously used pet lions to defeat their enemies. Romans were famed for using pigs against armies who road elephants, using the pigs' squeals to frighten and buck soldiers off the elephants' backs.

There have also been numerous cases where animals were used as suicide bombers. Armies strapped bombs onto the backs of trained dogs, monkeys, or rats and sent them off toward enemy lines to destroy tanks and troops. America once experimented with attaching incendiary bombs to bats and dropping them over Japanese cities during World War II, although the weapon never worked well.

With these evils in mind, empowering animals with laser-firing capabilities has the potential of causing widespread devastation, similar to the tragedies played out during the story Laser Hamsters. Unlike the story, however, history shows that aliens do not need to contribute to human destruction. People are fully capable of destroying themselves, so don't even think about it! Kick those thoughts of human destruction right out of your head; otherwise, one of these days those cute, furry creatures squeaking in their hamster wheels and poking their little noses through tiny openings may deliver swift extinction to people on Earth as we know it.

~JH

SOD'S LAW

CHARLES A. CORNELL

T*he Universe is under no obligation to make sense to you.*
—Neil deGrasse Tyson

EXCERPTS FROM THE U.N. Treaty on the Ownership of Artifacts in Space:

Salvageable Orbital Debris (SOD):
Non-functional exo-terrestrial material of Earth origin held in space orbit or sub-orbit (whether its transit through space has stabilized or is degraded).

Sub-section 5, Paragraph 20 of the Regulations establishes the following licensing requirement for the recovery of SOD:

1.   Acquisition of such debris requires a determination of original ownership, either in-situ or post-recovery, to identify the salvager's rights to claim title.

2.   SOD that can be positively identified as having 'ownership abandoned' is thereby classified as 'free in orbital domain' and is recoverable without the payment of any royalties or fees.

"SO WHAT DO you want for this box of shit?"

A battered blue plastic crate, the size of a coffee table, sat on the floor beneath a wall of glass display cases.

"Eighty thousand dollars."

Connor Driscoll twitched his handlebar mustache as he stared down into the crate's open top. A floor-sweeping bot bounced between the crate's sides and the floor-to-ceiling observation window like a fly trapped in a lampshade. Space was at a premium in his small souvenir shop next to the Galaxy Eye's sole dining pod. Driscoll kicked the bot with his foot. It squealed, then skittered down the narrow aisle in the direction of the shop's entry hatch.

Driscoll thought some more. His bald head creased into wavy ridges of skin. Bushy eyebrows raised to full height, he snickered, "Yeah, right, Mack. That's not happening."

"C'mon, Connor. That's less than half the going rate for quality SOD this size."

"Eighty thousand? Not in this economy, Mack. You've been in free orbit far too long." He pointed to the curved panorama of Earth's surface through the observation window, patches of swirling white clouds dancing over oceans of azure blue and deserts of sand beige.

"Times are tough down there. And getting tougher. You should see our bookings," Driscoll continued. "Or lack thereof. No more corporate junkets—gone. No more Employee of the Year awards— vanished. Only high rollers can afford to ascend the Space Lift these days. You know, the lucky few who are still winning when everyone else on that hot miserable planet is losing. And they're a very discriminating crowd. This box? It's just old metal to them. I mean look at this." He picked up a gnarled, Y-shaped object just a bit bigger than his hand. "What is it?"

"That's why they call it space *junk*, Driscoll. No one's going to up-fit a shuttle with this stuff even if they could afford to. But these high rollers... they have kids, don't they? Even manufactured ones. And every kid wants to bring *something* back from outer space, to show off to their friends. You've hawked this kind of chotzki by the barrel load before. So what's the problem? Lost your touch?"

"Three years ago, sure. When Galaxy Eye first opened. When the first Star Lift elevator trips had been sold out years in advance. But now? The novelty's worn off, Mack. We're lucky to have two families on board at the same time. That's twenty-eight empty suites. Twenty-eight non-existent wallets. There's only so much of this dross I can peddle. Money's tight. The market is shit. People back on Earth are selling off this crap at a fraction of what they paid for it last year."

Mack Lancaster folded his tattooed arms, scratched his week-old grizzle, and feigned deep thought. "Okay, how about forty thousand bucks for the lot? There must be a hundred pieces of SOD in this box. And at that price, it barely pays for the fuel it took to find this shit. Who else is selling? Big Bennie? He gave up last year. Meth-head Sergio's taken a sabbatical on Earth with some crazy Ukrainian circus. Who's left? And what have they offered you lately? Zilch. I know. Because we keep close tabs on each other. Whoever's still up here can't be bothered to collect this two-bit shit. They're busy with satellite repair."

"And why aren't you?"

"You know why. Yeah, I screwed up a few times. I'm not their go-to guy anymore. But c'mon, Driscoll, I gotta have something from this, just to cover my basic costs. Let's face it, you need me in orbit, surfing the SOD—staying in this game—or else you have nobody. I'm the best salvage pilot up here, bar none, and you know it. And the quality? You can't beat it. When times get better—and they will—you'll be able to get plenty of new stock for the simple reason I'm still dumb enough to be scavenging this junk when everyone else has given up."

Driscoll's face reached a new level of pain.

"Okay, thirty-five thousand?" Lancaster wiped his hand through his long greasy hair as he swayed back and forth, the closest thing to pacing that the cramped quarters would allow. "Geez, Driscoll, you're stripping the flesh off the bone. Dontcha see? Keeping me in business means good business for both of us. Whatcha say?"

"Okay, okay. Stop your whining. You're the last licensed salvage pilot that hasn't died of starvation. I'll give you that. And my inventory is a bit low, granted. Thirty thousand."

"Thirty thousand?" Mack Lancaster groaned and swung around to face the window, hands pawing through his long hair. "Oh, geez, I'm dying. And I'm barely into my forties. I don't deserve this. I've got a future ahead of me." He turned back with a hang-dog look. "Put me out of my misery. Let me live to fight another day."

Connor Driscoll, the smaller and slightly older of the two, twirled his mustache. Mack Lancaster perked up. That twirl was a 'tell'. A deal was coming.

"Thirty-two thousand. That's my final offer," Driscoll said. "And my intuition says anything over thirty grand is a horrible waste of money."

Mack Lancaster's eyelids drooped like a sad beagle. "You're killing me, Driscoll. A slow painful death. I can feel the vacuum of space sucking the life juices right out of me as you speak."

"Like you said, I'm keeping you alive to fight another day, without killing myself in the process. Thirty-two. Have we got a deal or not?"

Lancaster extended his greasy hand and grunted. "You got a deal."

With a slight hesitancy, Driscoll accepted the handshake, then wiped his hand on his jumpsuit. With a flick of his wrist, Lancaster produced his virtuo-paycard. The hologram floated in the air between them. Driscoll pressed his finger on the counter, summoned the shop's account, and swiped thirty-two thousand crypto-dollars across the glass into Lancaster's card.

"I'll even treat you to a free shower as a bonus," he added. "God, you stink, Mack."

Driscoll swiped at the counter again and a different bot arrived from a small storage room, this time a weird bio-morphic contraption that looked like the lovechild of a pygmy rhino and an octopus. "Take this box of crap and run a catalog search. See if you can identify where this dross came from." The morph's eight arms lifted the crate off the floor. The micro-monster scurried off with a bio-mechanical chirp, apparently happy with its new task.

"Your stuff looks legit," Driscoll said as he turned his attention back to the sulking Mack Lancaster. "But I have to work my due diligence, you understand?"

"Oh, c'mon, Driscoll. There's nothing in the box that's functional enough to get into any fight over my right of ownership. You're just twisting the knife."

"I'll be back for a credit if any claim is filed. You know that, right?"

Lancaster grinned and whistled through the gap in his front teeth.

"Oh, no," Driscoll said. "I don't like that look. I've seen that look before and it usually means I've had my pocket picked."

Mack Lancaster's grin grew wider.

Driscoll winced. "What have you got up your sleeve, you thieving conman?"

"Two very, *very* special pieces. Held 'em back. Why? 'Cos I know you. After screwing me over, you've got plenty of coin left. Smart move. You'll want to splash out on these two beauties, sure as shit. Museum quality. Both of them."

Driscoll turned away, bumped his bald head on the display case, and moaned, "Oh, no! Why me, Lord? I knew this was a set-up. I knew it! The sucker punch is coming."

"I thought about shipping them straight to auction. But now I've got your attention, and you're in such good spirits, I'm going to double down and give you first dibs."

Driscoll put his head in his hands. "The auction market? Really, Lancaster? Good luck with that horse trade."

"Seriously. Two prize specimens that'll keep us floating up here for at least another five years. Maybe ten." Mack Lancaster placed his hand on Driscoll's shoulder.

Driscoll shrugged the grubby hand off.

"Hey, look at me, Bud. Don't be like that," Mack said with a pout. "This is the real deal. And I'm giving *you* first dibs. Only you. I'll bet you a thousand bucks—right here, right now—the Smithsonian will fight like a bee-stung honey badger to get their hands on these two specimens. Just wait until you see what I've got. These pieces are *that* good. Chinese collectors might even start a bidding war. They're rare objects of vintage space exploriana. Verified to be in 'free orbital domain'. Finders, keepers, guaranteed. The finest space artifacts that have ever been offered for public sale in recorded history."

"You are such a friggin' optimist, Mack. Weightlessness has curdled your brain."

"What does it hurt to take a look?"

"At another lump of your space shit?"

"Two lumps."

"Just don't think I'm made of money, that's all. I have a business to run."

"You're going to drool. I know you are. Suit up."

"Suit up?"

"I told you, they're *big*, Driscoll. Way *big*. They won't fit through your dumb-ass loading portal, that's for sure."

"What are you thinking? The last time I was on your scumbucket of a ship, I thought I'd brought back a species of space lice. Have you gamma-cleaned it recently?"

"Sure. Last month."

"Last *month?*"

"Don't worry. I'm not eating much. And my bowels are decidedly better when I don't."

"Oh, give me a break, Lancaster."

"Museum quality." Lancaster cocked his head and grinned that toothy grin.

Connor Driscoll rubbed his face. "I knew I should have retired. I've been up here far too long. All right, Mack. Let me steal some perfume from the duty-free shop and I'll meet you at the dock."

．　．　．

THE COMM CRACKLED inside Echo Delta Four, Mack Lancaster's salvage rig, as it sat locked into one of several booms extending from the Galaxy Eye's payload receiving dock. Mack Lancaster had purchased the rig off-lease, one of the last construction shuttles used to complete the Galaxy Eye. He knew it inside and out. He'd piloted it for several years before taking a company buyout to stay in space as a freelancer.

"This is Captain Mack Lancaster requesting permission for an immediate EVA for load bay inspection."

"Roger that, Mack. Welcome back to the Galaxy Eye. Echo Delta Four is clear of inbound dock traffic. EVA is authorized. Stop by for a shot when you're done."

"Will do, Jimmy." Lancaster pointed to the gear locker on the wall beside the air lock. "Pick out a suit, Driscoll. But I only have one jet pack. The other one's broken. So, we'll have to buddy up with the one that's got power."

"Buddy up? Are you crazy? No, forget that." Driscoll rummaged through Lancaster's collection of EVA suits. Several had hardware missing, stripped for spare parts. He plucked one off its hook that seemed reasonably complete. A dog-eared piece of paper fell out. Driscoll picked it out of the air as it floated by and said, "Hey, Mack. Is this orbital safety certificate up to date?"

Lancaster turned his helmet until it clicked in place. "Of course, it is."

Driscoll turned it right side up. "This tag says otherwise."

"Uh, yeah, well, the newest one must have fallen off during my last EVA. I don't use that suit much anymore. It's a little tight in the waist. But it fits you like a glove. Very haute couture."

"Cut the crap and let's get out of here. I don't have all day. I have a broadcast to students at 0945."

"Students? See? Opportunity knocks, my friend. Pitch them your newly acquired box of treasures. I know your patter. It's hypnotic. Work your charm, think good karma, and make it happen."

"Hardly. These kids are working class sixth-graders from Kalamazoo, Michigan, not some trust fund brats from Manhattan. I'm even paying for the broadband uplink myself. Community service, part of the gig on this station. But you wouldn't know anything about that, would you Lancaster?"

"I'm a community of one. And I service myself quite satisfactorily, thank you very much."

"You're disgusting. Not in this suit I hope?"

"Um, well... not that I can remember."

The pair stepped into the EVA pre-chamber and closed the air lock. When the atmosphere inside the compartment equalized with the vacuum of space, Mack Lancaster opened the hatch. Outside, the curved carpet of blue seas and white clouds reappeared above their heads.

The geostationary Galaxy Eye hotel and its astronomy research station—connected to Earth by a thirty-six-thousand-kilometer-long tether made of boron nitride cables—clung to the planet like a thin cosmic pin stuck in a big fat cushion. The culmination of a multi-decade long effort to study Earth's declining climate, twenty-five people had lost their lives to build the Galaxy Eye and several countries went bankrupt. But at least the engineering team won the Nobel Prize. It was a great consolation to humanity that thirty ultra-wealthy families, when fully booked, could view the same vista that Mack Lancaster had become totally blasé about as he clipped Driscoll's tether to his EVA pack, activated the mini-jets, and pulled his buddy out of the hatch.

Lancaster maneuvered the pair to Cargo Bay One, the smallest of three payload compartments on Echo Delta Four. He unlatched the load bay door. Inside, a jumble of tools, attached by straps to the floor spars, floated aimlessly like upside down icicles.

"Clamp your safety strap on here, Driscoll," Lancaster said, pointing to the beam of the cargo bay's space arm. "There might be a residual charge left in the arm's grappling actuators. They may power up without warning. Don't want you to catapult off to the moon. At least not without me. That would be quite a ride, huh?"

Lancaster undid the tarp covering the first of his prized objects. It had a tapered aluminum hull, roughly cylindrical in shape, more than ten feet long and five feet in circumference, with a jet nacelle and guidance fins at one end, and whisker-like antennas at the other. The hull had been battered by floating space debris, some of which was still embedded in its surface, giving it a speckled look.

Driscoll winced. "What is that thing, Mack? A dead catfish?"

"Yeah, I know, it's a bit ugly, I'll grant you that. But it's got great provenance."

Lancaster pointed to a small rectangular piece of metal clamped to one of the object's rear struts. "That serial plate proves beyond a shadow of a doubt this dead fish is a slam dunk. This gem was once part of a Soviet-era military weapons platform. I matched its numberplate to its description in my de-classified CIA catalog. A dead ringer. There's absolutely nothing like this in orbit anymore, Driscoll. International treaties and such. This kind of top-secret SOD was supposed to be purged from orbit before commercial salvage licenses were issued but I guess with the Soviet Union long since legally kaput, it's finders, keepers. The technology's a bit outdated, but shit, I bet the software still contains launch codes."

"Launch codes? For *what*?"

"I'm guessing biological. The tube's too small to contain nuclear warheads."

"You're shittin' me. Geez, you mean, it's... *packing*?"

"Naw, I'm just kiddin'. The Russkies stripped it. Probably their last mission before the Berlin Wall fell and all the bureaucrats lost their jobs. Why they left the rest of it in orbit is a mystery. Likely just to do some damage as it floated around. A final hoorah of sorts. A 'dead but still Red' menace. Typical commies. God damn brilliant find, huh? But that's not it's best feature. Watch this. Wasn't working when I found it. Repaired it myself."

Lancaster pulled a control pad from his leg pouch and pointed it at the satellite. A central hatch opened and strips of gold iridescent metal unfolded from the sat's bulky mid-section like he was blowing up an inflatable bed. Once extended, the solar power cell stretched twenty feet, the full width of the cargo bay.

"Would make quite a conversation piece, huh? Gold-soldered circuits everywhere. The Russkies spared no expense. Would look fantastic hanging in some rich bitch's foyer. Or you could put it in a ballroom with a disco light underneath. What a light show that would be, huh?"

"Lancaster, you have *no* class. But I gotta hand it to you, this is definitely museum quality. And Soviet-era collectibles are super-hot right now. Even if the rest of the market is ice-cold."

"I told ya. But that's not all. My next find will have you wetting your spacesuit. Truly my ticket to fame and fortune. It could be yours as well. For the right price."

"Okay, if it's anything as good as this, you've definitely tweaked my dick. Where is it? In the next bay? Open up and let's take a look."

"Not a chance. Damn thing's so darn big it wouldn't fit, even in my biggest cargo bay. So I had to strap it onto Echo Delta like a dildo. But it's not on this side of the ship. It's harnessed to the bottom of the nose cone. It's the mother of all space junk, Driscoll. Hook back on and I'll show you."

The pair scooted out of Cargo Bay One and drifted around to the other side of the shuttle. As the underbelly of Echo Delta Four appeared, Mack Lancaster announced, "Ta da! Here she is... in all her glory."

"*Holy shit!*"

"I knew you'd be impressed."

"Where in God's creation did you find *this?*" Driscoll exclaimed.

"Ah, trade secret, my friend. Catalog says the original spacecraft carried six of these lab modules. This is just one of them and sixty percent of this pod is missing. So based on what you see here, what's left of one pod, we're talking a big mother of a mother-ship."

Lancaster pulled Driscoll along the seventy-foot length of mangled wreck, twenty feet-five wide, a payload section that used to be perfectly cylindrical in shape but now had an axial twist. Large scrapes and gouges indented the module's fuselage like giant claw marks. Midway down its side, several observation windows had been pushed inward, each titanium glass porthole cracked like a spider's web.

Driscoll scanned the derelict craft's ID markings with a laser reader and uploaded the information to his computer inside the

Galaxy Eye. Two seconds later and the stunning result of his catalog search flashed in his heads-up display.

"What the *fuck*, Lancaster? Sweet geez, don't tell me there's bodies inside this thing?"

"Don't think so. Haven't seen any signs the module was occupied at the time of the incident."

"Get me closer. I want to inspect every inch of this puppy."

"My pleasure." Mack activated the jets on his EVA pack and returned to the end where the pod's outer hull had peeled away to reveal the inner entry door.

Driscoll peered through its shattered window. "Decompression damage. Massive and sudden. But the level of external scoring didn't come from a meteor strike. If it had, we'd see one mother of a puncture somewhere, clean through to the other side. I'm guessing whatever destroyed the spacecraft smashed into the forward-facing command module first, nose on. Then the front end of the ship disintegrated and tumbled backward. The debris severed anything in its wake, amputating communications antennas, solar power sails. See over there, Mack. Remnants of some kind of superstructure imbedded in this pod's outer skin. My guess is a whole universe of crap cascaded back, ripped the rear lab modules off, cracking and twisting them on their way to oblivion."

"Guess those poor guys never had a chance."

"Remarkable, Mack. Simply remarkable. The exterior paintwork still has loads of original markings despite all this damage. There'll be no problem confirming its origin." Driscoll paused and took a deep breath. "What you have here, Captain Lancaster, is a remnant of the greatest tragedy in the history of space exploration. This hunk of junk is without a doubt a payload section from the first Mars exploration spacecraft, the *Resolute Endeavor*, lost without trace for over fifty years. Until now."

"I knew it! And this hulk just floated into my orbit one day like it materialized out of space dust—the Holy Grail of Space Exploriana."

"Have you been inside?"

"Not yet. There's a big dent in the hinge of the portal's air lock.

And the door's buckled and won't open. I guess that'll affect the value somewhat?"

"You've gotta be kidding me. That just *increases* its value. Simply priceless. For goodness' sake, don't go inside. This module is a virtual time capsule! It's preserved the very instant the first manned mission to Mars met with disaster. It's worth a lot more if kept exactly the way you found it."

Lancaster tugged on his tethered companion. "Look through here. You can still see experiment cases and instruments, and a shit-load of little stuff floating around inside."

"Perfect."

"I want ten million for it. Minimum."

"*Ten million*. Are you crazy?"

"Don't get cheap on me now, Driscoll."

"No, you stupid shit. Even if I had that kind of money, this capsule's worth a hundred times that price. A *hundred* times. We're talking *billions*. This is as far removed from space junk as Mars is from Pluto."

Driscoll rubbed the side of the derelict module with his glove like he was shining the hood of an antique Tesla. "Listen up, space cadet. I've got informers inside all the big auction houses. I know exactly how they value things like this. But more importantly, I know the evil games these auctioneers play to profit off a listing."

"Games? I've had plenty of time to master *Space Wars*."

"Not that kind of game. The fine print in their contracts might cost you thirty percent of the auction sales price, maybe more."

"Say *what*?"

"Then they'll fleece you with outrageous seller's premiums, trumped up storage costs, all kinds of bogus handling fees. Anything to skim more of the proceeds into their tills. They even stick sellers with the advertising tab. Royal bastards with a capital 'B'."

"That's why I came to you, Driscoll. I can't do this alone."

"Damn right, you can't. I know exactly how to whip those Earth vultures into a lather. By the time I'm done, they'll fight each other to the death to get the listing. I'll make sure they only get ten percent and I'll take a measly five percent for my trouble. Anything to help out a buddy. Mack, you have my personal guarantee you'll net more in your pocket than if you tried negotiating this on your own. I'll broker the whole thing for you. Hell, I'll even throw in free shipping to get this gem down the Space Lift. How's that for a great deal?"

"I knew you'd love it, Driscoll. Hot dog, I just knew it! We're gonna be rich!"

MACK LANCASTER TURNED on the booster engines of Echo Delta Four and eased his ship away from the Galaxy Eye, pointing the craft towards the highest orbit still gripped by Earth's gravitational field. Up there at the edge of the exosphere, life was quiet and serene, his sanctuary. Cruising in high orbit always made him feel big, as if he was looking down on a planet he'd created from stardust with his own hands. It was a feeling quite the opposite of growing up on its wretched, parched soil. And that was going to be the problem. How would he handle his newfound wealth?

Grubby relatives had given him up for dead but would spring out of their coffins if they sniffed a handout. Debt collectors—the lowest forms of terrestrial life—wanted his nuts pickled in a jar. And he still owed money to an angry horde of former friends he'd swindled in a botched orbital timeshare scheme.

He had too many skeletons in too many closets. Repatriation to Earth wasn't a desirable option. So what to do? Where to go? Mars? A possibility. Start over under an assumed identity? Yeah, that would work. He could easily afford the cost of a counterfeit passport.

Lancaster had anchored his heap of space exploriana to the Galaxy Eye in preparation for its shipment back down to Earth. With a binding brokerage contract and his prize safely in Driscoll's busy hands, Mack Lancaster's future plans had irreversibly changed. No more saving every nickel to repair Echo's labor-worn space arm, fix booster rockets long overdue to be replaced, or bribe spacecraft inspectors to look the other way. He could afford a whole new rig— an Echo Delta *Five*—something grand and luxurious, a craft of his own design, bright and shiny, keeping all the things he loved about his old space-bucket while adding the creature comforts of a Platinum Suite on the Galaxy Eye.

A new dawn is coming in my life, a fresh start, he thought as Echo Delta Four approached the 'grey line'—the line that separated the bright, sunward side of Earth from the looming extra-terrestrial midnight. Mack peered around the cockpit. *Soon, it's good-bye old friend.* The shuttle's age was chronicled by his collection of dog-eared photos printed from porn e-zines, the fractured holograms of space-bucket repair ads, and a variety of instrument knobs encrusted with fossilized crumbs, the splats from leftover ready-meals. As darkness descended, Mack Lancaster fell hard asleep, his mind swirling with imagined tolerances for a gold-plated ultrasonic toothbrush and specifications for a wardrobe locker full of silk pajamas. *Ah, bliss.*

DAYLIGHT BURST like an orange flame through the cockpit window of Echo Delta Four. Mack Lancaster rubbed his eyes, squinted through the glare, and snatched his sunglasses as they floated gently by his face. Through the window, the continent of Africa was clear of clouds all the way from Tripoli to Cape Town. The tell-tale spiral of a hurricane churned in mid-Atlantic, heading towards the Bahamas and the Florida coast.

"Coffee," he barked. "Thick. Black. Two sugars."

When the red light on the nutrition panel turned green, he grabbed the feeder tube and sipped on sweet, hot espresso. He ordered a generously sized slurry of 'Platinum Suite Extra-Fine Protein' which tasted of real bacon and eggs instead of week-old cat food. The money he'd made from selling that box of SOD had done wonders for his depleted pantry. His belly was full. And new porn files had been uploaded. Could life get any better?

Lancaster swiped his finger across the screen of Echo's space radar. Chart after chart whizzed by. A recently launched weather satellite had lost contact with European ground control two days ago. Bids had opened for the salvage contract. He paused. *Why the hell am I doing this?* he thought. *There's no possibility to sell it. Just a miserly fee to restore the damn thing to orbit. So why should I care about that penny-grubbing, ungrateful planet and its pitiful problems?*

A holo-message from the nav system indicated Echo Delta Four was entering the Upper Dead Zone: the Sargasso of the Earth's exosphere, the most boring part of the return approach back to the geo-stationary Galaxy Eye and its space elevator. *Perhaps moving back down to Earth is inevitable,* he mused. *After all, prostitutes are illegal on Mars.*

A tinkle on the window startled him. Another tinkle, then two more. Then a burst of three, followed by another burst and another, until a stream of *tap-taps* resounded on the hull as if the spacecraft had entered a Texas hailstorm.

Mack looked outside. Travelling at seventeen thousand miles an hour, hitting any object, even the size of an acorn, was highly undesirable. It appeared as if Echo Delta Four had caught up to a moving debris field, its bits bouncing lazily against the craft.

"What the hell are we flying through, Echo Delta Four?"

The A.I. interface replied, in her pre-programmed French accent, "Orbiting object clusters. *Oh, mon dieu!* Excessive debris concentration of unknown origin, mass, and velocity. Density: factor seven. Potential of impact damage: 98.7%. *Sacré bleu!* Taking emergency evasive action."

The shuttle's thrusters fired up.

"Debris field? What the fuck?"

"Leaving this orbit," the auto-pilot droned. "*Toute suite!*" A sudden blast from the main engines sent Lancaster floating backwards. He hit his head on the oxygen control panel. Echo Delta Four climbed further away from Earth.

"Resetting *zee* atmospheric controls," the A.I. responded. "*Ah, merde.* Unexpected malfunction."

"I hit the damn switch with my head, you mechanical moron."

Mack Lancaster grabbed the nearest bulkhead, catapulted forward, and yanked himself into the command chair. "Autopilot off."

"Affirmative, *mon cherie.* Manual control in effect. Have a nice flight, Mack. *Bon voyage!*"

"I gotta have that damn thing re-programmed. Maybe a Russian next time. Those gals are all business. My sanity is worth whatever it costs."

Lancaster steadied Echo Delta Four and looked down through the side cockpit window. A flat expansive debris field lay in a crescent shaped arc above the Earth like a slice from a Ring of Saturn. "Geez-oh-Pete," he gulped as a large but very familiar-looking chunk of SOD came into view. "Is that the People Pod from the Star Lift?"

He toggled the docking camera to pan across the debris field. An ugly emptiness occupied that part of space where a collection of entwined boron nitride nanotubes should have stretched thirty-six thousand kilometers to connect the Galaxy Eye station to Earth.

"The tether's gone! *Holy mother of shit!* The tether's gone! *Fuck!* Completely gone. Where the hell is the Galaxy Eye? Antoinette, any answers?"

"No visual definition found that fits *zee* mass profile of *zee* research and recreation station known as Galaxy Eye," the A.I. chanted. "Processing assumptions. *Sacré bleu!* None found. Conclusion: *zee* station has left its previous orbit. Trajectory unknown. Multiple new objects found in its prior orbit. Shape analyzing. Negative correlation with *zee* known satellites or registered debris. Conclusion: *zee* Galaxy Eye *est merde.* How you say in English? She is shit."

"Galaxy Eye...," Lancaster croaked over the comm, his throat tightening. "This is Echo Delta Four. Come in, please." Lancaster repeated his call six times. Each time, no response. Acid etched a harsh groove in his throat as it bubbled up from his stomach. "Goddamn it, Galaxy Eye. Come in! Maybe my comm set is damaged."

"On-board communications links are functional and secure. No inbound audio data has been detected, *mon chéri.*"

"*Fuck you* and the horse you rode into town on. Get me Star Lift Ground Control in Huntsville. Maybe they know what happened up here."

"Earth links unresponsive, *mon petit chou.* Data transmissions cannot connect. No servers detected."

"You are severely getting on my nerves."

"Recommend you take immediate evasive action, *cherie*. Object with catastrophic inertia on course for impending collision. In T-minus seven seconds, six, five..."

"Take control, damn it!"

"Affirmative. *Mon plaisir.* Auto-pilot on." Echo Delta Four rolled on its side and spun violently upward. A dark shape blotted out the sun as it zoomed past. "Collision avoided. Requesting *zee* new orbital co-ordinates, *mon capitaine.*"

Lancaster barfed up his breakfast. A gooey Extra-Fine mess with a Platinum grade stench floated in front of his face. He swatted it away. "Oh, geez. What the *hell* was that?"

"Object did not have *zee* transponder signal. Visual recognition being processed. *Un moment, s'il vous plaît.*" There was a momentary pause. "Object identified. Your catalog says it's *zee* 'Big Mother-fucker, aka the Holy Grail'."

The comm set crackled with an incoming message, "Mack... Mack..."

"Driscoll?"

"Don't—"

"Don't *what*? Driscoll? Come in. Do you read? Driscoll?"

"Communications lost. Requesting *zee* new orbital co-ordinates, *capitaine.*"

"Follow that motherfucker, stupid."

"*Bon*! Resetting vehicle trajectory coordinates to follow 'that motherfucker'. Requesting settings for final approach distance and velocity, *capitaine.*"

"Grapple it, asshole."

"Setting approach parameters to extend space arm and retrieve *zee* object. *Ooh la la!*"

"Driscoll must have been inside the wreck of the *Endeavor*. Nothing else is close enough to send out radio signals."

"*Mais oui.* Affirmative. Stray signals detected from 'that mother-fucker'. Unencrypted. No other communications from here to *zee* debris field. Galaxy Eye unresponsive. Earth links down—"

"Oh for God's sake, shut up!"

"Ceasing communications. *Au revoir, mon chéri!*"

Five minutes passed by, but the vagaries of time made it feel like an eternity. Finally, the auto-pilot announced, "*Bon!* *Zee* object—*zee* motherfucker—she is attached and she is stable."

Mack Lancaster was already in his EVA suit.

LANCASTER MANEUVERED into position to inspect the air lock at the front of the wrecked lab module. Scorched metal ran around the door, the witness marks of someone cutting into it with a laser torch. The hatchway into the wreck was ajar. Driscoll had said everything should be left intact, in its original condition, exactly the way Mack found it. What had Driscoll been up to?

Lancaster eased his bulky suit through the hatchway and scanned the pod's interior with the light from his helmet. The flotsam they'd seen floating inside had been ejected into the vacuum of space when the air lock had been opened.

Whatever accident had befallen the *Resolute Endeavor* fifty years ago—whatever forces had twisted the module's circular frame and ripped its controls from their housings—this relic was little more than a tunnel of jagged scar tissue. Sharp broken plastic—the remnants of interior wall panels—protruded everywhere. Instruments were barely held in their original positions by a combination of over-engineered brackets and sheer luck. Wires dangled like electrical spaghetti.

Lancaster's bulky jet pack was too clumsy to safely transit through the damaged chamber. He detached from his pack and secured it to the handle of a storage locker, clipping its long safety cable to his spacesuit.

At the opposite end of the twisted module, about three quarters of the way down, a label on an interior door read, 'Auxiliary Experiment Bay'. Behind its cracked viewing window, colored lights pulsed, illuminating the hatchway's charred edges. When Lancaster pulled the handle, the door opened with little effort. The colored lights escaped with a bright burst like some caged animal had been set free. Lancaster recoiled as something—or someone—

flashed by; a fleeting vision, dream-like in its suddenness, a man in a souvenir shop jump suit, the garment shedding its drab blue color as if the edges of its fabric were dissolving in water. The hazy image of the man chased the colored lights until both disappeared into nothingness and the darkness inside the module returned.

Something's fucking with my mind, he thought.

Whatever device or object had produced the lights inside the experiment bay was nowhere in sight. In fact, the small bay, only big enough for one man at a time, was completely devoid of anything. The light from his helmet scanned the chamber walls, once a snowy NASA white now covered by a layer of black soot. Lancaster wiped his glove across the surface. Black particles drifted up from his fingertip like airborne dust, swirled in tiny tight circles, and then disappeared.

An explosion? In here? he thought. *Driscoll believed the ship had been hit in the front. But perhaps he was wrong. Perhaps it was something else.*

Lancaster felt an intense warmth penetrating the insulation of his EVA suit. The heat stung his skin. He turned around to face the doorway. He sensed a voice calling to him. *"Get out! Now!"* it cried. No-one was there.

Lancaster slipped carefully out of the tight chamber. Floating outside the auxiliary bay, twenty feet in front of him in the middle of the wrecked module, was a sphere, a jet-black sphere the size of a bowling ball. He hadn't noticed its presence on the way in. The sphere's blackness was so intense it wasn't obvious at first glance that the object was spinning, but nearby dangling wires swung as if disturbed by an unseen wind.

A thin shimmering band of compressed colors clung tightly to the circumference of the spinning sphere. The black sphere quickly grew until it reached about nine feet in diameter, nearly stretching across the width of the module, its edges distorting the wreckage behind it like reflections from a funhouse mirror.

As the sphere expanded even more, the nature and purpose of its existence became clearer. "Oh, geez. Oh, sweet Pete," Lancaster muttered, his throat dry as a desert bone. Warm liquid drained into his suit's urine bag. "What the fuck? It's not—is it? Oh geez—*a fucking event horizon!*"

He scurried back into the experiment bay and pressed himself to its sooty wall, hoping the object might take a turn or stop its advance. It did neither. Lancaster looked around, looked up. Another door? A secondary air lock? But there was no way out. No levers to pull. No buttons to push. Nothing but an expanding sphere of dense blackness gobbling up any wreckage that got in its way as it inched ever closer to him.

The heat intensified as the sphere approached, its edges a blur of color as fragments of the spacecraft's interior distorted and spun around its perimeter. Sweat dripped from Mack's forehead, streamed into his eyes, and trickled down the tip of his nose. He pushed his back against the wall and instinctively held his hands out as if by some cosmic magic he could repel the sphere's advance. The spinning event horizon reached his gloved hands. The tips of his fingers dissolved. He felt no pain as he watched his arms disappear, twisted into bands of compressed color before being sucked inside. The visor of his helmet disintegrated in front of his eyes. Then everything went an eternal black.

MACK LANCASTER WOKE to the sounds of dripping water and the *caw-caw* of a passing bird. He rose from the straw mat he was laying on and took a deep breath, inhaling hot, humid air. The atmosphere was thick with the smell of charred wood and rotting moss. Above him was darkness. To one side, light streamed through trees dripping with vines. As the fuzziness in his head cleared, he realized he was sitting inside the entrance to a large limestone cave. A linen robe clung tightly to his skin, soaked in sweat. He looked down. He had arms, and on the end of them, he had hands with fingers. He turned his palms back and forth in amazement, then rubbed the back of his neck. It was stiff and sore. A sharp pain shot down his spine.

"You'll feel like crap for a few days," a voice said. "After that, back to normal. Try some of this. It helps ease the aches."

A leather pouch was thrown from the shadows. Lancaster tugged on its string, opened it, and peered inside. The pouch contained a wad of leaves.

"Coca. Chew it. It really works."

"Driscoll?"

A man wearing a white robe tied with a cord of hemp knelt beside him. His face caught the morning light. His cheeks were like old leather, covered in dried scabs. His handlebar mustache was gone, his bushy eyebrows had withered and turned gray. As old as he looked, his features were all Connor Driscoll. Age could not erase the ridges on his bald head and his perpetual frown.

Lancaster struggled to speak, his lips stale. Words finally trickled out, "The Galaxy Eye?"

"Nope. The world you once knew is gone, Mack. Long gone. Forever gone. Push all of it out of your mind. You'll be happier that way."

Lancaster looked beyond the mouth of the cave. A leafy jungle landscape sprawled behind a clearing that contained a small village of thatched huts. Howler monkeys chattered in the forest's dense canopy; the jungle shrouded in tropical mist. In the clearing, wisps from a dead fire curled upwards. As the rays of the early morning sun burned through the shifting mist, the gray silhouette of a giant pyramid loomed high above the tallest trees. Hovering above its stepped peak was a black, perfectly spherical object, bending the light around it.

"Bet you're wondering just how long I've been here," Driscoll chuckled with a toothless grin. "Well, me too. They tell me it's been thirty tzolkin, give or take a haab or two. The Mayan calendar is a weird system and their language is even worse. If you're lucky, you'll have time to learn it. Took me years."

"Years? I saw you yesterday."

"Yesterday is relative. The future is the past. Everything in the universe is possible. Call it, SOD's Law. I know, confusing, huh? Yeah, it's a hard lesson to learn."

A rumble shook the ground. A bright yellow flare ascended from the jungle near the temple's stone steps. The remnants of the morning mist rushed away from the pyramid as a spacecraft's rocket blast burst through the canopy, sending parrots and monkeys scattering in all directions. The thunder of the launch rolled through the trees. Mack felt the walls of his stomach vibrate. Lancaster covered his eyes and looked up. A billowing contrail rose towards the sun. A slender, cigar-shaped craft came into focus once the spaceship reached a height where the blinding glare from its engines diminished.

"God damn. Those lucky bastards," Driscoll chirped.

Dozens of men with straight black hair, copper skin, and painted faces—wearing nothing but short loincloths—scampered in front of the cave to get a better look. They jabbered in a tongue that sounded like the clacking of several sticks being beaten together.

A man adorned with a head-dress of parrot feathers rubbed his hands in the cold ashes of the dead fire and raced toward a large boulder. His blackened hands swiped the stone's flat surface. He drew a rough cartouche of a figure astride a rocket, the plumes of the ship's contrail drawn like the curled petals of a lily.

"Yup, that stone carving will keep him busy for a month or two." Driscoll gazed skyward at the disappearing spaceship and sighed. "Not sure which galaxy they're heading back to. They were empaths. Always knew what I was thinking. But I could never pick up anything from them in return. Funny old quarks, but quite friendly in a bizarre kind of way, all things being considered." He scratched his grizzled chin. "They never let any of this Mayan nonsense get the better of them. Taught me the patience to wait."

"Wait?"

"Knew you'd get here one day, Mack. Sadly, the last surviving member of the *Resolute Endeavor* died just before you dropped in. Pity you couldn't have met them. They had such great stories to tell."

A loin-clothed man noticed Mack Lancaster, pointed to the cave, and hooted with delight. A posse of Mayans formed a circle around the cold fire and danced.

"Well, that's a good sign," Driscoll remarked. "And your long greasy hair—very fashionable in these parts."

"You said, I'd be lucky to have enough time to learn their language. What did you mean? Enough time? Before *what*?"

"You'll pick up a lot of their ways pretty fast. Like the words their women scream when they orgasm. You'll be treated to plenty of that. I'm getting a bit old for it now. It's not as much fun as it used to be. And they don't have antibiotics." He picked at a scab. "Guess you could tell that already."

"Driscoll, what the hell are you talking about?"

"Haven't you figured it out yet? You've just dropped out of the sky. To them, you're a god. Sent from Mayan Heaven to inseminate their women and bless their crops."

"A *god*?"

"Good news, right? Well, most of the time it is. Could be bad news at the end. From what I've seen."

"Huh?"

"Everything's based on their calendar. Apparently, I arrived on a good day. For me. But for *you*? Guess we'll see how it turns out, won't we? All I can say is the next harvest better be fucking brilliant."

Mack Lancaster stroked the back of his neck. "A god? What am I supposed to do?"

"Lots of group sex to start with. But at some point, the priests decide enough is enough and your time's up." Driscoll pointed to the sky. "If you're lucky to repair whatever got you here in the first place, you can escape before the ceremony. Like those empaths just did. I'd have gone with them. But no, they weren't having any of that. That's where their shit-ass empathy ended. But if you didn't bring a ship with you—like us, and the crew of the *Endeavor*—I guess we're fucked. Literally and figuratively."

"Ceremony?"

"Yeah. They marched the last of our *Endeavor* crewmen up the steps to the high altar, cut out his heart, and ate it."

A trumpet echoed through the trees.

"Finally...breakfast." Driscoll stood up. "Coming Mack? Gotta boost your energy for the ladies. The cooks here do wonderful things with bananas. Just don't drink anything red. Otherwise, it's all good."

A new curl of smoke emerged from the lush jungle. The troupe of Mayans sauntered away.

"Play God?" Mack paused, thinking. "Okay, why not? I mean, how hard can it be?"

Driscoll slapped him on the shoulder. "That's the spirit! Do whatever it takes to survive and you'll be just fine."

"Yeah, SOD's Law, I guess. Who am I to argue?"

AUTHOR'S NOTES - CHARLES A. CORNELL

I STARTED my story with a quote from the famous astrophysicist Neil deGrasse Tyson in which he said, "The Universe is under no obligation to make sense to you." Which is eminently true.

He also said, "Do you realize that if you fall into a black hole, you will see the entire future of the Universe unfold in front of you in a matter of moments and you will emerge into another space-time created by the singularity of the black hole you just fell into?"

Huh? Yeah, okay Neil. Whatever you say. Who am I to argue?

Now, I'm not an expert on black holes (obviously). Nor am I an expert on Mayan stone carvings, you know, the ones some proport show the arrival of alien spaceships. But I am an expert on my own imagination. And I can add two and two and make four. Or is it five? In the imaginary universe of my thoughts, anything is possible. And so, with all that being said, "SOD's Law" came into being. I hope you enjoyed it.

~Charles

MALICE

VERONICA H. HART

1

MARY ALICE LEANED against the brick wall in the alley. The last Bloody Mary had been one too many. Her head. The asshole whose hands roamed over her breasts and backside better watch out. If vomit didn't cover him in thirty seconds, blood from his gut would.

"Back off, big boy," she choked out just before spewing four Bloody Marys and countless bits of caviar and sour cream all over his spotless polo shirt with its country club logo.

"Crap," he shouted as he jumped back. "You've ruined my new shirt." He raised his hand to strike her but, drunk or not, Mary Alice knew how to take care of herself. She whipped the double-edged dagger that had been hidden in the folds of the red sash around her waist and sliced upward, removing the offensive hand from his wrist.

He screamed as blood spurted, cascading over her pirate costume blouse, covering her exposed neck and bosom. The music inside the ballroom drowned out his voice but he managed to stagger toward the partly open door.

Mary Alice bent down and retrieved the severed hand. She held it out to his retreating back. "Here! Put it back on."

He whirled around and glared at her in horror, his eyes nearly popping out of his head. "Are you crazy?" he screamed. He'd pulled a handkerchief from a pocket and held it tightly over the bleeding stump.

"Here, put it back. It'll heal itself in no time," she said as he backed away from her.

Her mission wasn't completed yet. Far from it. And once someone saw him, it would be over for her. "I'm sorry. If you won't listen to reason, there's nothing else I can do. Besides, my ride's waiting." She checked the alley. No witnesses. She didn't want him returning to the party before he could reattach his hand but he kept backing away from her and screaming.

"Hush," she pleaded. "Stop making so much noise."

He held his good hand over the stump instead of accepting the separated hand from her. His eyes bulged in terror. Annoyed at his behavior she slashed at his throat to stop. More blood gushed from his body and spewed over her costume. No way could she return this to the party store. This idiot just cost her the deposit she'd left. As he slumped to the ground, silent, she wiped the blood from the blade and tucked it back into the folds of her sash. She tottered on her stilettoes down the alley and signaled the Minsky who waited in his taxi.

It was too bad about the guy but he wasn't a keeper anyway.

"How did it go?" the Minsky greeted her. "That blood looks real. What kind of games did they play tonight?"

She leaned her head against the seat and shut her eyes. "Just take me home, Minsky. I think I just messed up my assignment."

"Aw, that's too bad, little Mushka."

"Right now the idea of being a small mouse and disappearing into a hole in the wall is very appealing." She leaned her head against the back seat of the taxi. Her pursuit had to continue but nothing good could come of her getting drunk every weekend in her search.

Mary Alice was her Earth name. Her real name was Mapimiran and her real occupation was supposed to be Artist, at least that's what her certificate said when she graduated six months earlier from Kirospato's finest arts school. She knew, along with all the other graduates, that once they completed their formal education, each and every one was required to serve in the KCSC, Kirospato Community Service Corps. Her best friend and roommate, Kindra, found herself assigned to feed the elderly; that seemed appropriate because Kindra's degree had been in Social Work. Mary Alice expected to clean graffiti off walls in the foreign sector where gangs vied for territory. Nothing prepared her for the assignment she received: collecting Earthers to replace the aging ones in the display habitats on Kirospato. The first excursion to Earth resulted in a slipshod collection of beings easy to secure—the already aged and infirm. Her assignment was to collect healthy specimens between Earth ages of twenty and thirty. Her only help, the Minsky.

She took several deep breaths then said, "Minsky, you ever want something so much you could taste it?"

He laughed. "Only my grandmother's homemade kielbasa and pierogies."

Oh no, just the thought of the smell of those foods made her want to retch again. She tried shutting her eyes but that didn't work, instead she forced herself to focus on the back of the Minsky's head.

When they reached her hotel, she hesitated before getting out. At this late hour, there wasn't much activity on the street. The lobby lights glowed with a deceptively warm welcome through the glass entry doors. Inside, the night clerk would undoubtedly be sleeping behind the counter, if he was there at all.

She pushed her way through the doors. She'd stayed in a variety of hotels throughout the world during her quest, but this was the most puzzling place of all. Definitely not the Beverly Wilshire nor even a Holiday Inn. The place might have changed its name during its 90 year history, but certainly never changed the carpeting in the lobby. It may well have been a very dark green with an intricate pattern of flowers and lace but now the colors had all blended into a mushy gray mess with two worn paths that led to the front desk and the elevators.

She climbed the stairs to her third-floor room. Though the old hotel had elevators, her experiences the first few days left her unsettled and disturbed by her fellow residents. She learned quickly that one half of the building was reserved for homeless people, while the room she stayed in operated as a regular hotel. The problem was, they all used the same elevators. The city was supposed to be one of the wealthiest in the world, but the hotel reminded her more of the poorest in Calcutta. While in India she'd looked online for a hotel in Los Angeles and booked something reasonably inexpensive as she didn't quite understand the financials—there was such a vast difference between the Indian rupee and the American dollar, that the translation of currency defeated her. When she left home, her supervisor, Coquardo, handed her a thing called a credit card and warned her not to go "overboard" in her spending, whatever that meant.

First thing she did when she reached her room was to drink several glasses of water hoping to clear out the alcohol, then shower and change into a loose-fitting caftan she'd brought with her from India. The pirate costume would have to go into the incinerator along with the high-heeled shoes which had hurt her feet. Though her people resembled the Earth humans, some parts weren't exactly adapted to their ways. Such as the wearing of shoes and tight clothing. And the hair. Especially the hair. Tonight she'd tamed the copper toned mass into a ponytail. She pulled the elastic away and shook out the hair so it hung down her back and covered most of her body.

Once comfortable, she went to her drawing table and created a short series of graphic cartoons depicting her adventure at the country club party, taking liberties with the actual events to create a drama to entertain her growing number of viewers. She'd discovered that even on Earth she could find plenty of artists' supplies and, being able to create in her off hours lifted her spirits. Having observed a considerable amount of Earth entertainments, she chose to create a crime drama using a play on her own Earth name for her heroine: Malice.

She posted her graphic stories online. The cartoon frames always ended with a call for blood donations. Just another way to test for strong candidates for the habitats.

She'd done her best all day, from early morning to the country club party, and then the comic strip. There was nothing left to do but report in. She linked into her home system and called up Coquardo.

"Coquardo here. What's your report, Mapimiran?" His countenance faded into view, blending in with the characters on her open screen. His natural paleness combined with his black tunic made him look like a part of the drawing. She clicked the comic strip off, though she much preferred her gorgeous blood-typing heroine to the pasty-faced superior officer.

Mary Alice winced at the sound of her given name. "I'm doing well, Coq. To date I have dispatched fifty-three young healthy males and forty-one females from six continents. They should have all arrived by now."

Coquardo nodded, the best she could expect from him as a sign of approval. "We determined—"

"I'm on the North American continent now. People are more guarded and I've had to resort to some trickery to get close enough to convince them to provide blood samples."

"I've been watching you working as a technician in a laboratory where people deliberately go to have their blood drawn. The problem is, of course, they are not healthy, which is why they go there. How many have you discovered through this method?"

She pursed her lips and nodded. "I have to agree, not as many as I'd hoped. Not everyone who has their blood drawn is ill. Many are just being tested to see if they have abused forbidden substances. Some are what they call wellness check-ups. But I did find seven so far and I've only been here a few weeks."

"We need to have our reserves in-house and through quarantine as soon as possible. The population is becoming bored with observing Earthers doddering about. The old ones now on display will have to be retired soon, so time is of the essence."

Mary Alice sighed in frustration. "I know all that. I'm doing the best I can. Before we disconnect, I'd like to ask if my funds would permit me to upgrade my accommodations. I'm not feeling very secure here."

"I will speak to The Boss; however, you will remain where you are until you hear from me." Coquardo offered a thin-lipped smile.

He could arrange anything he chose here on Earth. She suspected he was one of those who regarded artists as useless beings and would do little to make her assignment easier.

UPON ARISING, she dressed in turquoise medical scrubs and headed out for breakfast near the lab where she worked during the days. To her happy surprise, though she shouldn't have been surprised at all, the Minsky stood out front of the seedy old hotel. Instead of his usual plaid flannel shirt and baggy trousers, he wore a black uniform with epaulettes, highly polished shoes, and a cap with gold braid trimming the bill. He'd even shaved. His vehicle gleamed. Not his rusty, smelly, old taxi, but a sleek limousine such as dignitaries drove all over the world. As she crossed the sidewalk toward the car, she glanced around, hoping no one from the hotel recognized her.

Her cheeks burned as she stepped into the luxurious interior of the vehicle. Instead of having to stand in line in a coffee shop near the lab to wait for a cardboard cup of coffee and a greasy pastry, silver cloche covered dishes awaited her on built-in little tables, reminding her of those on commercial airlines. Maybe she was wrong about Coquardo.

INSIDE THE LAB, her chubby-cheeked, usually cheerful lab boss Anita leaned against the counter in Mary Alice's cubicle, a frown on her face, her arms crossed. In her pink scrubs she reminded Mary Alice of an unhappy giant cotton candy.

"Good morning, Anita," she said with as much joyful energy as she could muster, hoping to fend off any unpleasantness. One thing she could not become used to was so many of the North Americans' lack of humor or zest for life.

Instead of responding to the greeting, Anita unfolded her arms and held out a phone facing Mary Alice. "Is this you?"

Mary Alice froze and focused on the small screen. Another thing she hadn't got used to was Earth's continued use of handheld phones instead of hologram projectors. She leaned forward to get a closer look.

A willowy redhead wearing an off the shoulder white blouse, a red sash around her waist, short flouncy skirt, black fishnet stockings, and stiletto heels flashed a nasty looking dagger in the air. In front of her, a tall, good-looking, laughing man appeared to be groping her breasts. The sharp blade sliced off the right hand of the man. Blood sprayed over the two people. The person holding the camera dropped it. End of show.

Her mind scrambled to produce a reasonable explanation. Anita had known she planned to attend a pirate party the night before. Would she believe the video was an illusion?

The phone disappeared into the folds of Anita's fat. "I think you'd better turn in your badge and leave before the police arrive."

"The man attacked me," Mary Alice said, her human heart pounding. She knew she sounded more defensive than she intended.

"Go. Now." Anita stood up straight. Even in that position, her head just about reached Mary Alice's shoulder. "I know about the extra vials of blood you've been drawing. I hate to think for what purpose, but if you leave now, I won't say anything."

Mary Alice remained still, her mind trying to catch up.

"I'm giving you a heads-up. A head-start. A chance to get away."

"Why?"

Anita stepped closer. "I read the books and see the shows. I know what you are, but you can't feed yourself from our clients' blood. It just isn't right."

"Feed myself?"

"Shh," Anita cautioned, holding a finger to her lips. "I've never reported you. I thought people like you were pure fiction. I can't tell you how excited I was when I realized what you are. But we can't take a chance on you being caught."

Thoroughly confused, Mary Alice muttered, "Thank you. I'll-uh-just—"

"You'll just get out now." Anita skirted around her. She leaned against the doorjamb, hands behind her back, then stuck her head out and checked the hall left and right before skittering across the hall and disappearing into her own cubicle.

Although her mission was confidential, Mary Alice wanted to explain to Anita that she was simply performing a community service for her planet, part of a project which helped guarantee the survival of the species on her planet, albeit as zoo-like specimens, until when and if Earth required replenishment.

She slung her purse strap over her shoulder and after checking the hallway, headed out through the lobby and front doors. The Minsky stood outside his car across the street in the parking lot. As soon as he saw her, he jumped into the car and drove to the curb. "I did not expect you so quickly, Malice. I rushed right over after I saw the news. What happened in there?"

"I'm fired, as they say."

2

ELLIOT THE ENGLISHMAN sat on a marble bench with his two new almost-friends, Raheem and Ababuo.

"We really need to form a plan that works for everyone," Elliot said. Though he hadn't been there the longest, the others looked to him as a leader. Maybe because before being removed from his surroundings he'd been the chairman of one of the largest charitable organizations in the United Kingdom and as such he projected an air of authority even when he didn't know what he was doing. Especially now. The last thing he remembered prior to waking up in bed, alone, was reaching out to take the hand of a lovely redheaded woman who promised a solution to the emission problems he'd been dealing with at his manufacturing plants. Even then, he'd thought her too good to be true. And ever since he'd been in this unknown place, there had been no rules, no instructions for ransom—nothing. It was like living in a fancy prison with a group of men from around the world. After several weeks, he'd relaxed into the daily rhythm of eating, exercising, sleeping, and eating again, always on the alert for a chance to escape.

When he consulted with the other men in the building, he discovered they had very little in common other than they'd all met a beautiful woman who promised them a resolution to a difficulty they were facing. Sometimes she was a blond, sometimes a redhead, but she always had the same line.

"I am believing that we shall be having the full cooperation of all," Raheem said. "In the evenings after the dinner hour, I am speaking with those in my section and they are equally as puzzled as I."

Ababuo leaned forward, elbows on his knees, and frowned. "I do not accept the concept that all who are here would wish to change anything. In our sector most of the men had lived in extreme poverty, bordering on starvation for most of their lives. They are very happy with the circumstances in which they find themselves. They have no desire to leave." He straightened up and raised his right hand as if taking an oath.

Elliot couldn't disagree with Ababuo. He might be a prisoner along with everyone else, but he couldn't complain about the facilities. Here, in the lobby an enormous fish fountain spurted water three stories into the air. A staircase to his left seemed to rise with no visible support system. Balconies high above looked over the central lobby. Glass fronted elevators shuttled up and down all fourteen stories of the building. All this for no more than about one hundred men from all corners of the planet.

Raheem piped in with, "Are we understanding any reason why we are being all here in this place?"

"Besides the fact that we are all males under the age of thirty or thereabouts?" Elliot said.

"We appear to be healthy," Ababuo added.

Raheem raised both arms and flexed his muscles. "And we are being very, very fit and handsome gentlemen."

"So, why are we here? It makes no sense," Elliot said. He stood up and faced the other two. "Has anyone gone outside the compound that you know of?"

"If you are meaning beyond the walls, there is no way to exit. This could be a very alarming matter should there be an emergency. However, considering our treatment, I am suspecting there will be provisions made in such an event."

"We have everything here for a comfortable life, including access to the gym, tennis courts, bicycle paths, a running track and even a nine-hole golf course." Elliot raised his fingers as he itemized his list. "Yet there are no authority figures, no one seems to be controlling us other than preventing us from returning home. And we have no access to the internet. Maybe we should organize a hunger strike to get someone's attention."

Ababuo jumped up. "No sir! You can count me out of that one. I have had more of my life with too little food, I am not going to deprive myself when it is now present in such abundance."

"I am agreeing wholeheartedly with my friend here," Raheem said as he stood by Ababuo's side. "We must be thinking some other way."

They returned to the bench and watched the water splash into the fountain in an endless cycle.

"I'd like to hear a bird," Elliot said with a sigh.

"Seeing a bee," Raheem added.

"Breathe the fresh air again." Ababuo drew in a deep breath.

Elliot watched other men wander down the stairs and emerge from the elevators. It was nearly time for the midday meal. Though there were no clocks in this place, the dining room doors opened at regular intervals three times a day at what he assumed to be normal breakfast, lunch, and dinnertimes. In the evenings serving carts rolled automatically into the lobby laden with snacks and drinks, both alcoholic and non. So far, none of the men had over-imbibed. Very self-disciplined of them, Elliot thought. There were evenings when he considered taking more than two drinks, but something stopped him. After about an hour, the carts rolled back out through the dining room doors and that was the end of their social hour. Most of the men retired to their rooms. A few went into the theater.

Elliot had tried that the first few nights after he arrived, hoping to learn more about his surroundings, but all that played were mindless adventure movies from the mid-twenty-first century.

3

MARIAM, who hailed from the ancient city of Jeddah in Saudi Arabia, sat on her bed, and painted her toenails a brilliant Cherry Red. Even as she flapped a sheet of paper like a fan to dry them, she felt a little pang of guilt that her father would disapprove. She looked forward to dining three times a day with all the other girls and women. She'd come to enjoy the company of women from the Americas and Europe but didn't understand why they were so concerned that there were no males present in the building where they were housed. In Jeddah women always ate separately from the men. Part of her was happy to have been removed from her home because soon she would have had to marry the man of her parents' choosing—someone she never met before. Though the future was unsure here, she enjoyed her newfound freedoms.

Her father and brothers had forbidden her to listen to Western music and had threatened her practically with death if she so much as expressed an interest in attending a theater that showed a Hollywood movie. She'd lived her entire adult life hiding behind a veil, seeing the world through a haze of netting. It had been her mother's way as well. She missed her mother and the times they shared in private when they could be themselves, but she was having a great deal of fun in this strange place with the exotic foods and clothing and entertainments.

She had begun learning tennis with the American girl, Terri. Terri told her she had a natural talent for it and encouraged her to play every day. Though Mariam felt embarrassed at first to be wearing clothes that exposed her legs and arms, it didn't take long for her to become accustomed to them. At night, alone in her room, she remembered her prayers and knelt obediently on her carpet as her father would have wished.

In the beginning she and Terri struggled to find ways to escape this new environment. Neither understood how they arrived here. Terri came from a place in America called Iowa. As the days passed and they learned more about each other's background and life, they agreed they were far more alike than different. Mariam's expectations were that she would marry the man her parents chose for her and remain in her husband's home until she died. Terri's outlook had been similar. She had explained she would most likely marry someone from her high school and live in the house next door to her parents' home. She did add that she'd considered going to a college called Iowa State to study law but hadn't been sure of receiving any grants or scholarships. With Mariam's father being a wealthy oil executive, the concept of not being able to afford anything was strange.

They spent many hours in the evenings explaining the differences in their cultures. Both girls had recently turned nineteen years old; both graduated from high school—Mariam from an all girl's private academy; Terri from a local high school in English Valley, Iowa.

"I could have been kidnapped for ransom," Mariam speculated, "but you say your family has no money, so what can be the reason?"

"I don't know. There must be nearly a hundred of us and all girls and women, some nearly thirty years old. Could it be a secret experiment by a government organization?" Terri spent a lot of time watching crime shows on television, shows that had been forbidden to Mariam. She was in awe of Terri's extensive knowledge about criminals, police procedures, and sex.

Especially about sex. Mariam had been told very little except that it would be expected of her when she married. Exactly what, she wasn't sure. She asked Terri one evening if she knew about it.

"Sex? You mean having sex? Sure, I know."

Mariam screwed up the courage to ask, "Did you ever kiss a boy?"

Terri laughed out loud. "Of course. Haven't you?"

"No." Mariam lowered her eyes and appeared to study her hands. "But that is not all about sex. Did you do anything else?"

"Now you're getting personal." Terri made a face, pretending to be offended but quickly changed her mind when Mariam's eyes opened wide.

"No, no, my friend. You must not tell me anything more. I only hope to live long enough to one day meet a man with whom I would want to touch lips."

"And tongues," Terri added with a little giggle.

"No," Mariam gasped.

"And touch other body parts."

Terri thought Mariam might faint.

The weeks turned into months. Terri calculated three and a half by using her personal journal as a guide. Other than that, there was no evidence of the date anywhere in the building or on the grounds. Outdoors always felt like a pleasantly warm springtime day.

4

"GET IN THE CAR, QUICK," the Minsky said as he held the front passenger door open.

Mary Alice checked behind to see if anyone followed her and jumped into the seat. The Minsky shut the door, ran around to the driver's side, got in, and took off.

It took a moment for her to realize he'd placed her up front in the limo. When she turned around, she saw all her possessions stacked in the back.

"The rest is in the trunk. Sorry, it's not very neat, but I was in a hurry. After I saw the news, there was no question you had to get away fast. Hope you don't mind."

She raised her hands in frustration. "Well, no, but how serious is this? I mean, I was only defending myself. I can explain…"

"You can explain how every place you go in the world people disappear?" the Minsky asked.

"What?" she shrieked. "What are you talking about?"

"They got you as a serial killer, Malice. And you think about your comic strip and where you've been and all those people."

"It's not even a hundred," she muttered. "I still need a hundred and fourteen more people. I don't hurt anyone, honestly, Minsky. You know that. Never." God, her boss would be really pissed if she didn't finish her assigned job.

"The only picture they have of you is the one someone took in the alley last night. You were in that lady pirate getup. All you gotta do is change your hair color and put on normal people clothes and no one will recognize you."

Her mind raced with dread at the thought of getting caught and incarcerated. And all for just trying to do her community service. Geez!

"Can I see what they're saying?" she asked as he pulled onto a freeway. The concept of a gazillion cars on a single road, all at the same time, had terrified her when she first arrived. She still cringed at the sight of traveling over sixty miles an hour side by side and nose to tail with so many other vehicles.

The Minsky passed her his phone.

It was already open to a video of her in combat with the guy. She cringed when she saw the glint of the blade as she sliced upward. The video stopped before the actual severing of the hand. Beneath the video, she read, "*Pirate Proves Perilous. 'This is what happens when you let just anyone into the club,' Donny Whitaker, a longtime member of the exclusive Hills Country Club said when questioned. He went on to say that the female in question was unknown to anyone at the party, though two female members who choose to remain anonymous, claimed that she'd attended three previous costume functions. 'I have to say, she was tall and super-*

sexy. I'd bet the men all wanted to see her at the parties,' one of the women said."

The description of the Party Pirate seems to match that of a woman seen in the presence of several other people around the world who have disappeared without a trace. Though there could be any number of women who stand nearly six feet tall, and might be described as beautiful, this woman has a distinctive marking on her body. 'I speak and read several languages, and the symbol and words were like nothing I've ever seen,' a witness who refuses to be identified said. When asked about the placement of the unusual marking, she said, 'Right under her armpit. Like, who gets a tattoo there? She was fixing her hair in the ladies' room.'"

Mary Alice froze. She'd thought she kept her human form identity tag carefully covered either with clothing or makeup whenever she went on a hunting excursion.

"Where are you taking me?" she asked in a shaky voice.

"Just sit back. I got this."

She had no one else to trust. She slid down in the seat and kept her eyes on every car they passed or that passed them. With no idea what she was looking for, the monotony of the road soon sent her into a troubled sleep.

SHE AWOKE AT HOME, in her own bed, on Kirospato. She'd also reverted to her original form, similar to the beings on Earth, but taller, slender, and hairless. Here she'd been regarded as a beauty, on Earth she would have been seen as an oddity and unable to blend in with the population.

For this assignment, Coquardo, with The Boss' approval, had given her the ability to adapt to each region as she combed the planet for appropriate beings to transfer. Her size, shape, and features varied on each continent. The biggest problem for her had been what to do with all that hair. She became recognizable because of its flowing molten-gold cascade. Easy enough to cover when necessary.

A message on her mirror from Coquardo told her to meet in the small conference room at HQ. She checked her timekeeper. She needed to hurry. Grooming took barely ten minutes of Earth time; all she had to do was wash her face and put on a clean costume. The multitude of clothing colors and designs the Earthers wore fascinated and delighted her; they were such a contrast to Kirospato's boring beige draperies. Since her return, she'd dyed several of her robes in bright colors. Today, she wore fire-red.

With a light-hearted swagger that didn't quite match her inner turmoil she took the tramway to the main building and the escalator up to the conference room. Though it was the small conference room, a dozen or more of her colleagues crowded in there, already drinking their breakfast malts and eating sweet rolls. No sign of The Boss yet so at least she wasn't late. Coquardo, the group manager, sat between two people at the far end of the large conference table.

She sucked in her tummy and squeezed her way around the room to find her assigned seat.

"Good to see you, 'Malice.'" Sorrim grinned at her from the next seat. "Loved the drawings. You should keep it up. A whole new career for you." Seemed like no one remembered her real name.

She slanted her eyes toward him without turning her head. "Good to see you, too, Old Man. How did you do with your quotas?"

"One hundred percent. And you?"

She tilted her head, suspicious of his success. "Really?" Maybe she should have dressed more subtly. Calling attention to herself might not have been the best idea. She wondered if everyone had filled their quota except her.

He chuckled. "I wish. They sent me after equines. I came close to my quota."

"Mine was a unique quest; my quarry can think," she said and then stuffed a sweet roll into her mouth.

The lights flickered, indicating The Boss was about to either arrive or speak. They never knew which. When he appeared in person, it usually meant someone was in trouble. All eyes turned toward the door, except for Malice's. When the others looked, she shut her eyes and prayed for 'the voice.'

"No such luck, my dear," The Boss said, seeming to speak

directly into her ears alone. She looked up and there he stood, today in a masculine form, large and invincible, like a warrior. Hopefully, not too angry a warrior. He wore a lightweight, white shift, rather like the tropical attire males wore in Earth's South America. Today, he did not look like the rest of the citizens of Kirospato but more like the Earthers they were attempting to secure.

Everyone stood to recognize him as he took his seat at the head of the long conference table.

After placing both hands down flat on the table, he gazed about the room, his expression unreadable. Malice felt herself tremble. She'd never failed at an assignment before so had no idea what the consequences would be. Coquardo had certainly never mentioned any consequences.

"First, I'd like to congratulate all of you for a tremendous effort. I'd like to, anyway. Unfortunately, your results stink. Now, please be seated."

Malice couldn't bear it. In spite of Sorrim's confession of failure, she took his comments to refer entirely to her. She cringed inwardly as she waited to be singled out as the only failure in the group.

"Though most of you did not meet your quotas, we have collected an adequate sample to maintain the displays for now."

"Sir." An extraordinarily scrawny female sitting across from Malice raised her hand.

"Dowra?" The Boss recognized her.

"Might I suggest decreasing the sizes of the habitats so the populations appear more dense...?"

Without bothering to respond to Dowra, The Boss turned to Sorrim. "Sorrim, would you like to share with the others?"

"Sir, we have successfully acquired one hundred more types of horse breeds. We now have samples of all three hundred. They are grazing on the Equine Land Management Site. They are ready for viewing at any time."

"Not exactly what your goal was. We'll talk later. And Kindra? What about your canines? Would you like to tell the group how that worked out?"

Kindra, a young female who didn't appear old enough to undertake such a dangerous mission, stood and nodded respectfully toward The Boss. "You know there were many times I wanted to resign and come home. Wolves in particular are evasive creatures, but I did manage to bring back six additional pairs of timber wolves and two sets of grays. They are in the habitat adjacent to the Equine project."

The list went on through many life forms on Earth. Then it was time to talk about the Earthers, the red-blooded beings who called themselves humans. The Boss directed his comment to Mary Alice. "Before we begin, shall we take a look at the results of our *first* excursion to Earth?"

All eyes turned to the blank board behind The Boss. Images of aged Earthers hobbling about using walking aids filled the space. The view shifted to the interior of the habitat where Keepers tended to bed-ridden ancients. Everyone knew the first hunters had chosen the easiest prey.

The Boss turned off the screen and addressed Mapimiran. "I see that though you had a specific and measurable task, you did not meet your goal. What was the problem?"

"Sir, on most of the continents, the culture of the Earthers was such that I could get close to them. There were so many poor or down-trodden, I had no need of trickery to entice them into providing blood samples nor getting into the transport vans. The difficulties arose primarily in the area called North America. They are a feisty group of beings, set in proclaiming their independence in spite of their complete dependence on the social structure for survival. Not one in ten could last a week without the support of others."

"Well, maybe a week," the Minsky offered. "They tend to store needless amounts of food."

"I must confess to using several forms of guile and cunning to seduce them into a state of trust in order to get them onto the transport."

"There is one remaining problem, however, Mapimiran. In your guise as Mary Alice, you managed to slaughter one of them. Our code does not allow for damaging specimens on any of the planets. I'm afraid you will have to return to face your punishment."

"Sir, I would fear for my life were I to return to Los Angeles. I had no idea that limbs would not regrow on humans. When I first learned to draw blood to test them, I noted how quickly they healed. That person assaulted me."

"That is not for me to judge. The Minsky will accompany you and you will turn yourself in and meet your judgement based on their laws. And before you question further, I know that California has a law that allows them to kill people who kill people but they have not used that law for many years. Those in charge prefer Earth life sentences."

A sense of dread overwhelmed Mapimiran. "Sir, I cannot spend eternity in the guise of Mary Alice in an Earth prison. I cannot."

"You will go back. You will prepare yourself."

Her forehead hit the tabletop with a thunk. She groaned. With her head still on the table she muttered, but as she spoke, she slowly lifted her head and faced The Boss. "How? What? What am I meant to achieve? Do I arrive in my current form and fling myself on the floor before a magistrate as I beg for mercy?"

The Boss cleared his throat. "The rest of you may be excused. Mapimiran, when you are finished with your dramatic display, you will comport yourself with dignity to the transfer station."

"May I at least continue to continue my art?"

"Do what you wish if you find any free time." The Boss stood and said, "You are to stand trial. You may have the Minsky in attendance."

5

AS MAPIMIRAN DONNED her Mary Alice guise, Kindra arrived. "Are you really going back to Earth?"

"The Boss insists. I broke the Code by damaging an Earther. He says I must make amends. Quite honestly, I don't understand just what is going to happen and that makes me nervous."

"The human mind is sometimes capable of brilliance, Mapi."

Mary Alice explained the situation to her friend. "The Earthers believe I have destroyed more than just that one man. They are holding me accountable for the destruction of all my exhibits—the Earthers I brought here."

Kindra frowned in thought. "Perhaps you could take some of them with you to prove they are not damaged."

"Hah. Who would come with me after I've removed them from all they know?"

"Ask. They are intelligent beings and may see this as an opportunity to return home—escape, if you will."

Mary Alice folded her arms and paced the room. "It is possible. I will make a selection. Do you have access to the behavior chips? I can chip them until I'm sure they're trustworthy."

"You might promise to let them return home permanently once you are free to leave the planet. A little incentive to cooperate."

Mary Alice nodded. "Good idea, though I dislike the idea of lying."

"Do you prefer to spend the rest of your life in an Earth prison stuck in your human form?"

"You're right. As much fun as I had as the beautiful and exotic Mary Alice, the heaviness of walking about on the planet wore me out."

"Unlike being us, a bunch of manila colored, semi-opaque organisms who drift lightly across surfaces instead of walking and feeling like lumps of lead."

The two of them went to Kindra's office where she read out the list of Earthers available. Though they were still in quarantine, several had passed the halfway mark and were probably safest to remove.

"One person does stand out on this list," Mary Alice said. "I remember him well. A handsome Englishman named Elliot Stuart who at the age of twenty-one, fresh out of university, created an airline to rival any. After succeeding at launching that, he went on to create affordable housing throughout England, Ireland, and parts of Europe. He'd become quite a philanthropist as well."

Kindra nudged her with an elbow. "If I didn't know better, I'd say you'd fallen in love with your Mr. Stuart."

Mary Alice lowered her eyes in embarrassment. Had she been an Earther with blood running through her body, she might have blushed. "No, not exactly, but I do admire him. He might provide good support. Let's look at who else is available. Los Angeles did not feel like the safest place so perhaps two more men and a couple of females for companionship."

"What would make you comfortable?" Kindra asked as she studied the list. "a brilliant, educated woman or someone clever you can trust and confide in when necessary?"

"Considering my time there, I'd say pushy, aggressive females made me feel inadequate. Observation taught me that friendship and loyalty are important qualities. If I have to face their authorities, I'd prefer to have a true friend on my side."

"There, you have your answer."

"I do."

THEY ENTERED the room where Elliot the Englishman, Ababuo the African, Terri Stanley the American, Raheem the Indian, and Mariam the Saudi Arabian sat at a large conference table. They all looked up when Mary Alice and Kindra entered. She asked them to get ready for a short journey, approximately four days—she hoped.

"What kind of 'short journey'?" Terri the American asked.

Malice looked to Kindra for a response. Kindra looked at her wrist. "The journey itself is lengthy in terms of your measurements; the duration on Earth will be hopefully only four to ten days."

Terri, the American girl gasped. "What are you talking about? What do you mean 'on Earth?' Where are we?" Her eyes widened in fear as she pushed her chair back from the table. She looked prepared to flee.

Kindra raised her arms in a soothing gesture. Ignoring the girl's question, she said, "You will require business attire and casual clothing for the days."

"Where are we supposed to get these clothes? You realize we

only have what we arrived in and the flowing robes you have provided, and I, too, would like to know what your mean by your words 'on Earth'." Mariam said.

"It is unimportant. Map-Mary Alice misspoke," Kindra said.

"I would like an answer to Terri's question. You see, we've been in this environment long enough to get acquainted and I, for one, am not satisfied that your people have our best interests at heart," Elliott said.

"Oh, but we do," Mary Alice said. "It's just that I got into a little trouble when I was-er-collecting you and now I might need your help."

Elliot slapped the table. "Collecting us. We were all drugged and transported to this building. Kidnapped is more like it and until you explain what's going on, we're not doing anything to cooperate with you. What, exactly is going on?" Elliot's brows furrowed as he glared at her.

She glanced at Kindra who offered a slight nod. With that approval, she pressed the icon under her arm and let her human façade fall away. As her naked, transparent form came into view, everyone's mouth dropped open. "This is who we are." She and Kindra agreed to explain The Boss's plan to preserve Earthers for the future by keeping them safe in facsimile habitats on Kirospato. Kirospatans could learn about them through observation.

"We're to be spectacles in observation tanks?" Elliot howled.

"Being lions and tigers in a zoo!" Raheem roared.

Terri wiped her eyes. "Creatures to be observed by voyeurs pretending to be concerned."

"We've been trafficked," Mariam added.

The four Earthers turned to Ababou who had remained silent. When he recognized they awaited his reaction, he shrugged. "We are well fed and no harm has come to us. I am all for trusting these filmy wraiths."

"You may feel free to call me Mary Alice, or Malice, as my fans refer to me," she said as she reclothed herself in the Mary Alice costume. "As we have removed you from quarantine, you five will dine together. And I warn you, make no plans to escape our custody; just enjoy the adventure."

Elliot held up a hand to stop them from leaving. "If you don't mind, Mary Alice, why us and what is there in it for us if we cooperate with you?"

It had come to this. She would have to use Kindra's idea. "If we are successful in securing my release from the accusation of wrongdoing, perhaps you will all be able to return to your homes."

"Perhaps?" Elliot said.

"I'll run it by my boss. Meanwhile, go eat dinner and we'll leave shortly afterward."

Though the humans all appeared reticent and doubtful as they filed from the room, Mary Alice hoped they understood the seriousness of the problem and they would come through for her when it was necessary. She really hated the idea of lying to them.

WHEN THEY MET in the lobby, Kindra bade them farewell. As she took each of them by the hand and patted them on the back, Mary Alice watched her implant chips in each right shoulder. They followed Mary Alice to a pair of sliding doors which led to a platform where an ultra-modern train car waited with the doors open for them to board.

"Nice," Elliot said. "Looks like a proper bullet train. Fast."

Terri and Mariam took seats side by side. The men chose to sit separately. Mary Alice remained standing near the doors. She alone knew the trip would take mere minutes of their time.

The train pulled from the station. The lights went out briefly and when they came on again, it pulled into another station. This one resembled the one they'd just departed, except there were throngs of humans on the platform.

None of them remembered how they'd been transported in the first instance.

The Minsky had arranged for them to stay at an elegant hotel in Beverly Hills, a far cry from the place she'd been in her last time on Earth. He'd also provided a complete wardrobe for everyone. Mary

Alice had a room to herself; Terri and Mariam shared a suite, as did the three men. The Boss told her she had to turn herself in as soon as she was settled. Mary Alice thought she ought to create at least a month's worth of comic strips before calling herself settled. After cautioning them not to explain their situation to other Earthers, she told the Earthlings they could go down and mix and mingle with their own kind. They should feel free to use the swimming pool and eat their meals, but they were not to leave the hotel grounds under any circumstances. Should they try, they would immediately feel a strong paralyzing shock to the system which would render them unable to communicate in any way.

As she anticipated, Elliot was the first to express his outrage. "Distrust will do you no good, Mary Alice. Once you promised we could return to our homes, we all agreed to participate in your scheme. Now, I'm not so sure. Perhaps you ought to send us back."

"Calm yourself, Elliot. Once the Minsky and I agree that you are fully trustworthy, your invisible shackles shall be removed."

Confident she had her Earthers under control, she pulled out her drawing equipment and set about showing Malice, her fictional character, rescuing children from a werewolf. The bloodier the better, her editor had told her. From there, she sent the two children to an allegedly deserted island where they met up with a reclusive vampire. Malice dealt with that quickly enough. In all the episodes, she put the children in unimaginable danger before rescuing them. Her Malice was hailed as a hero.

The creator of Malice, not so much.

Once she was ready to call the police, she gathered her new colleagues together. They sat around her now cleared drawing table as she explained what she was about to do and their roles in the project.

"The police are going to say you are missing persons. You'll be on their list of people I'm supposed to have murdered. It will be in your best interests to only state the obvious—that you are alive and well and have presented yourselves to prove the point. Is that clear?"

On the following morning the group presented themselves, all conservatively attired and apparently ready to stand by her side. Not one of them reminded her of the outrageous young Earther who thought he could molest her in the alleyway outside the country club dance hall. Then she thought about what she just thought and realized they *did* remind her that they didn't remind her. Never mind.

Malice felt self-conscious in her gold lamé jumpsuit and white tennis shoes. She'd heard that prisoners were forced to wear jumpsuits so she figured she'd get ahead of the game by choosing her own color. And comfortable shoes.

Elliot took the lead by holding out a hand toward Mary Alice. "After all this time, I believe we can play the roles, Mary Alice. We all agreed to cooperate and that you will find it in your heart to free us."

Mary Alice accepted his hand, and said, "We don't have hearts, Elliot."

At this eyes rolled. Raheem slapped his thighs in giddy laughter. "She is locking us up in a hotel in Hollywood where we are living a life of fantastical luxury, controlled by a heartless alien and is yet wanting us to believe we are not being part of a new streaming show."

Terri joined in though her laughter came across as a little more nervous. "That's a good one, Raheem. I always thought I'd like to grow up to be a television star."

Elliot's lips disappeared in a grimace of disapproval, and Ababou and Mariam sat silently observing the reactions. Elliot said, "What do you mean, you don't have a heart? Are you saying you will not honor your word to us?"

"Not at all. As a human, I do have a heart; I'm just not used to how it feels. I find it reacts to emotions."

Elliot cleared his throat. "That's how hearts work. If your conscience is clear about what you did to that guy, we'll support you."

Having scheduled her *Malice* graphics to appear weekly, she prepared herself to face Earth's, specifically California's justice system. She looked up the non-emergency number and used the hotel phone to call the police. She advised them she'd arrive within the hour.

6

A BURLY FEMALE jailer gave Mary Alice an unbecoming orange jumpsuit to wear, handcuffed her, led her into a large room, and sat her in a churchlike pew beside a rough bunch of women also dressed in unbecoming orange. The stark room with rows of pews separated from the front portion of the room by a railing, disappointed her. When she'd heard the words, "halls of justice," she imagined something like the cathedrals in Europe, not this simple drab room. Beyond the railing were wooden tables, regular chairs instead of pews, plus an enclosed space with a dozen chairs to one side. At the front on a raised platform stood a massive desk. Gray walls and grayer tiles on the floor added to the gloom. Other than flags of the United States and California behind the desk, there was no color in the room.

A uniformed bailiff called for order in the court and introduced the Honorable Justine Frances. A large woman in her fifties entered the room wearing a black robe and took the seat behind the raised desk.

Five women, all declared indigent and unable to afford an attorney, were represented by young men and women who stumbled over the names of their new clients. Judge Frances hammered a gavel between cases and shouted, "Next," in a bored tone.

Mary Alice craned her neck to see if her selected "friends" were in the room. She caught sight of Elliot, the tallest, sitting in the last row behind dozens of strangers. Her mouth went dry. What if their presence made no difference? What if they didn't speak up? Could she become one of the hundreds of thousands locked away, never to be seen again? Would The Boss really let that happen?

"Mary Alice no last name provided. Step forward."

After establishing that she had no representation, a young man introduced himself as Oscar Griffin and declared her innocent of the crime of murdering Chatsworth Binghamton. She'd never heard of Chatsworth Binghamton and agreed with Oscar that she was innocent. Judge Frances asked, "No last name?"

"I didn't know I needed one," Mary Alice said.

"You address me as Your Honor."

"Her last name is Kirospato," a woman's voice called from the back of the room.

The judge rapped her gavel. "Who are you? Step forward."

Mary Alice turned to see Terri coming down the aisle to the gates that separated them. The judge motioned her to step through the gates and join Oscar and Mary Alice at the lectern.

"You are?"

"I'm her sister, Theresa Stanley, your honor," Terri said. Her voice trembled slightly.

"And what surname did you shout out for our Mary Alice?"

"Kirospato, your honor."

"Sounds Greek. Why are your names different?"

Terri exchanged glances with Malice before answering. "Different fathers, your honor."

"Fair enough. Miss Acropolis, how is it you did not provide your surname to the court?"

"I don't know. I've never been in court before," Mary Alice mumbled, then added in a louder voice, "Your Honor. And it's Kirospato."

"Thank you. You may take your seat, Miss Stanley," the judge said. Before Terri could step through the gates, the judge called her back. "Just a minute, Miss Stanley. Step up to the microphone again."

Terri did. Her hands trembled as she set them on the surface of the lectern and waited.

"I have a list of the charges against Miss Parthenon here and I see your name listed as one of the missing. You are from North English, Iowa?"

"Yes, Your Honor."

After skimming down a page, the judge asked, "Where have you been for the past two and a half months, young lady?"

Terri clasped Mary Alice's cold hand. "Traveling with my sister,

Your Honor. We've been traveling with a group of friends. Some of them are here with me today."

The judge looked out over the courtroom. "Will the friends of Miss Stanley please stand?"

Mary Alice had no idea what Terri was up to by claiming to be her sister but was relieved to see the other four rise at the same time. She decided then and there to ask the Boss to let her release them once this episode was finished.

"Step forward."

By the time they all stood around the lectern, Oscar had been pushed to one side and stood leaning against the jury box, looking as puzzled as the rest of the courtroom. Two people sitting in the front row sketched feverishly.

Each of her team provided a name and told the same story—they'd been traveling with Mary Alice and a large group of friends. Mary Alice felt an inner smile eager to burst forth.

"Mary Alice, are you the creator of the comic strip *Malice*?" Judge Frances asked.

"I am … Your Honor."

A little whoop of cheer erupted from her fellow inmates behind her. Murmuring came from the rest of the gallery. A few reporters left the courtroom.

The judge rapped her gavel on her desk as she demanded order. "Enough!" she roared.

Once the room settled, the judge waggled her index finger at Mary Alice. Puzzled by this gesture, she turned to Oscar.

"She wants you to approach the bench."

She looked around the room. "What bench? I only see chairs."

Oscar took her by the arm and escorted her to the judge.

"You can step aside, young man," the judge said to Oscar.

"Your Honor, I am here to protect my client's rights. It is my duty to remain by her side in the event she needs legal counsel."

The judge leaned back. "Fine. Then we'll meet in my chambers." She slammed the gavel. "Court is in recess for-um-fifteen minutes."

Everyone stood as the judge rose and headed toward the door.

Oscar nudged Mary Alice to follow the judge. He, in turn, walked close behind her.

The judge's chambers turned out to be a small office with a lot of books on shelves. It smelled of disinfectant, whiskey, and cigarette smoke, reminding Mary Alice of the country club where she'd been accosted by that boy, Chatsworth.

"Sit," the judge commanded as she strode behind a large mahogany desk. The only clear space on the desk was in the center where an ink-stained blotter was surrounded by stacks of manila folders. A laptop stood on a small table behind the judge's chair.

Oscar sat bolt upright on the edge of his chair, his hands clasping the wooden arms in a white-knuckled grip. Mary Alice knew little about United States law, but Oscar's behavior had her nerves on edge. She wished Elliot or one of the women could have been with her instead.

"So," the judge said. She grinned, exposing unbelievably perfect white teeth for a human of her advanced years. "You created *Malice.*"

She glanced at Oscar, wondering if he would say something. He didn't.

"I did-er-Your Honor."

Without warning, the judge scooted her chair to one side and hit a key on her laptop. The screen came to life displaying the character Malice in her full glory, dagger in hand, villain bloody and very dead at her feet. Mary Alice's human heart jumped into her throat. What could this mean? Did the judge regard this as evidence of her guilt?

Oscar gasped. Before she could open her mouth, the judge said. "I can't get enough of her."

"Uh-thank you, Your Honor," Mary Alice said.

The judge swiveled back and rested her arms on the desk as she leaned toward her. "We're all friends here. You can call me Justine while we're in chambers. I have written several scenarios that I'd love to see Malice involved in. In my wildest dreams, I could never have imagined you would show up in my courtroom. I am in awe of you."

"Your Honor," Oscar said.

"Be quiet, I'm talking to Mary Alice here."

Oscar's jaw snapped shut.

Her scalp crawled. Why was Justine telling her this? Did she expect her to listen to her ideas? Would that make the charges against her go away? Her lips went dry.

Justine continued grinning. "Well, what do you think, Mary Alice? Would you like to see my ideas? Maybe we could work together as a team."

She cringed inwardly. Where was that dagger? Why didn't Oscar speak up?

Oscar did clear his throat. "Your Honor—"

The judge slammed an open palm on the desktop. "One more outburst and you'll be in contempt. I'm waiting for the young lady to consider my offer."

"Your Honor, there was no offer. If you will be so kind as to make yourself—"

"Five hundred dollars. You'll pay the clerk on your way out. Now keep quiet. Miss Kaspo, I, as a member of the legal community, cannot possibly work with a convicted criminal; however, if you were free to go with no charges, well . . ." She raised her hands, palms upward, and smiled at her.

She felt sick to her stomach and wondered at the same time what The Boss would recommend. She pinched her lips and frowned as she summoned a change to her appearance. With Malice in mind, her hair grew darker, the green eyes turned black, her skin paled and her fingernails grew. That was about all she could do to make herself menacing. Then she grinned, exposing perfectly white teeth and two prominent canines. "You want to make a deal with me?" she asked in a deep, throaty voice.

"Um. Well." Justine leaned back in her chair and stared at Malice before her face lit up. "How did you do that?"

Oh, for a dagger. She conjured blood dripping from her eyes and fingernails. "Do what?"

"You are amazing." Perspiration broke out on her forehead.

"Your Honor," Oscar said. "This has gone far enough. You can see my client is in great distress."

"No, I'm not," Malice hissed.

"She doesn't know what she's doing." Oscar rose from his seat and hustled to stand behind her, his hands on her shoulders. "She's distraught."

The judge licked her lips. "This is more than I could ever have hoped for."

Oscar's voice whispered in her ear. "Miss Kirospato, there are a lot of people outside that door. Don't do anything rash. Please." His grip on her shoulders tightened.

She flexed her muscles. Oscar stepped back. She mimicked the judge as she licked her lips and grinned at her.

The blood drained from Justine's face. "I-I didn't mean anything. I only wanted you to know how much I admire your-uh-artwork."

"Good. Then shall we return to your courtroom and resolve this ridiculous charge against me so my friends and I can get back to work?" Mary Alice's voice came out more confident than she felt. She pushed up from the chair, her knees shaky, her heart racing. These human feelings disturbed her. Much better to be in her natural form, yet somehow, all these emotions were exhilarating. She let the judge exit the room first.

By the time she appeared in the courtroom, she had returned to her normal human form. She thought.

Oscar nudged her and pointed down toward her fingernails where blood still fell in droplets from the extended nails. She shut her eyes for a moment and changed the image, hoping no one else noticed.

The bailiff called everyone back to order and the judge took her seat. "As I was saying before we recessed, this appears to be a singular case of self-defense. I see no reason to hold this poor young woman another minute." She hammered the gavel.

Oscar handed her a business card. "I'll be happy to help—er—should you have any future confrontations with the law, Miss Kirospato."

7

WHEN MARY ALICE left the courtroom with her new friends, dozens of reporters awaited them on the courthouse steps. Cameras clicked as they pushed their way through the crowd.

"What's the story on the alleged missing persons?"

"What did the judge say in private?"

"Is it true that Leonardo DiCaprio cut off his pinky finger to prove his undying love for you?"

"I love your outfit. Who is your designer?"

The questions kept coming even after they piled into the limousine driven by the Minsky. Mary Alice had changed back into her own jumpsuit before leaving the courthouse. Her human heart glowed at the prospect of having five real friends.

In spite of all the time she'd spent on Earth recently, today was a first for her—experiencing real human emotions, from fear to anger to the warmth of friendship. All that was left was love. She slanted her eyes toward Elliot. A good prospect?

The group gathered on the sidewalk patio of a restaurant in the nearby hills to celebrate Mary Alice's release. Elliot ordered a $1,000 2014 Bordeaux Sauternes to start the celebration. At first Mariam and Raheem demurred, but after a long lecture from Mary Alice about how their reticence was a cultural difference and not religious or health related, Terri and Elliot went on to convince them it would be insulting to refuse to toast Malice's good fortune.

Once they'd had a drink, they settled down to order. They all munched on crusts of bread dipped in an olive oil and balsamic vinegar concoction while they waited for their salads to arrive. Meanwhile, they emptied a second bottle of wine.

They'd only been sitting there for about fifteen minutes when the first of Malice's fans noticed her. He stood on the other side of the black wrought iron fence that separated the dining area from the public sidewalk.

"I know you," he shouted, pointing. "You're the creator of *Malice*. Mary Alice, right?" He held out a baseball cap and a ball-point pen. "Will you sign my hat?"

"Sure." She signed.

Instead of quietly thanking her, the boy shouted, "It's her! Mary Alice. Bloody Mary! The creator of *Malice*! She signed my hat!" He ran up and down the sidewalk, shouting like a carnival barker, attracting attention.

A few people nodded politely toward her, some smiled shyly as they passed by. Others thrust all sorts of objects in front of her and begged for an autograph. When their main courses arrived, Ababou and Raheem stood up as if they'd previously coordinated their movements and rearranged the table so that the two of them were on the side nearest the fence. While one ate, the other fended off the autograph hunters.

Mary Alice got a kick out of their behavior while enjoying the attention of the fans. She even posed and smiled for those who wanted photographs.

At one point, Raheem said, "Miss Malice, it is behooving me to recommend that perhaps we are better to be sitting on the inside of this establishment. Will you be kindly considering it?"

"Stop worrying." She waved to a woman who held up a phone that displayed the latest *Malice* strip.

Elliot placed a hand over her wine glass when a waiter tried to fill it for the fourth time. "We're nearly finished here. Perhaps coffee all around." The waiter nodded, left the half-empty wine bottle in the silver iced bucket, and left.

"Dessert anyone?" Terri asked. When no one responded, she took it upon herself to order for everyone.

Malice bobbed and weaved to peek around Ababou or Raheem to wave at her public. She could get used to this kind of attention. Certainly, it was a far cry from The Boss's curt commands and stingy "attagirls".

After dessert, Elliot herded them back to the hotel.

Once they were all seated, he made an announcement. "I believe we have all met with the agreement to help Mary Alice and now it is time for her to release us from her control and let us return to our homes."

Mary Alice's new heart dropped. She'd thought she really found new friends but, in the end, they were only helping her to suit their own purposes. She considered reproducing Malice as she'd appeared in the judge's chambers but dropped the thought when Raheem spoke up.

"I am sorry to be saying Mr. Elliot, that I am being contented to be helping Miss Mary Alice. I am not wanting her to activate her punishing chip; however I am declining to be freed. Here we are eating very, very good food and sleeping in very, very fine beds."

Mariam shyly raised her hand. "I too must confess to not being eager to return to my old life-style. I have very much enjoyed the company of my new friend, Terri, and also sitting in the company of men. I agree with our good friend, Raheem. I would like to remain here with Mary Alice."

Ababou and Terri consulted briefly and both agreed with the other two. Terri added, "Elliot, with your organizational skills, we could for a support team for Mary Alice and promote *Malice*. We could live like this for the rest of our lives."

Elliot said, "But I already lived like this in the U.K."

"Maybe," Terri said, "but did you have so much fun and such good company?"

He chuckled. "What do you think, Mary Alice? Remove the chips and trust us?"

Mary Alice checked with the Minsky who'd been sitting quietly in a corner listening. He bobbled his head back and forth for a moment then raised his hands as if tossing something in the air. Whatever that meant.

Mary Alice was appalled at this turn of events. "But this is not my home. This image you see if not the real me."

"You got us into this, sweetheart," Elliot said. "You want to go back to your home and be just another wraith floating in space or do you want to be an artist of renown here on Earth?"

She considered his words. If I go home, I'll be just another citizen of Kirospato but if I remain on Earth, I'll be Bloody Mary, creator of *Malice*. Malice, avenger of all that is wrong in the world. "What—how—how would this work?"

Elliot rubbed his hands together. "I'll be your manager. Ababou would love to be on your security team with the Minsky. Terri makes a great assistant. She can do all the scut work."

"What is scut work?"

"You know, fetch and carry. Whatever needs doing. Trust me, a lot will need doing, especially in the beginning as we get organized. I think either Raheem or Mariam might be able to handle creating your webpages and podcasts. They are both well versed in computer sciences. Once we get up and running, we'll be able to monetize *Malice* endlessly."

"Is that what we're going to do?" She thought about The Boss and his plans for Earthworld on Kirospato. Surely, her five humans wouldn't make all that much difference if she kept them for herself. She nodded as if he could see her and then said, "Let's go for it."

Through the next weeks, her comic strip morphed into a popular show streaming on televisions around the world in twenty-seven different languages. People loved the blood and guts basics. *Malice* never let anyone get away with anything.

Neither did Mary Alice.

She went on with her work and in the years that followed as her wealth grew, so did her isolation from the mass of humanity so many of whom wanted a part of her. Raheem and Ababou took great pride in promoting and protecting "their" artist. Terri went on to study law and accounting. She partnered with Elliot to ensure the group's financial security. Mariam's strength lay in her computer wizardry. As time went by and she had to hire assistants, she grew more comfortable in the world with men as her underlings.

Mapimiran had never notified The Boss about her sudden acquittal and continued to string him along. He contacted her frequently about her legal status and she always replied that she wasn't finished with her probation and would get back to him when she was free to leave Earth.

THE BOSS WATCHED as Mapimiran evolved predictably into the human behavior he'd learned about from his Earthworld project.

He nodded sadly as one night, when her part of the Earth slept, he pulled the plug on his project and left them to their own devices. He would seek out another planet to study.

AUTHOR'S NOTES - VERONICA H. HART

WHEN THE IDEA OF "LIGHT FANTASTIC" came up for this year's Alvarium Experiment Volume, I was all gung-ho. After all, hadn't I written the humorous story, "Recovery" for the Return to Earth volume?

Then I started three different stories before the idea of Mary Alice aka Malice blossomed. And struggled. It began, subtle as a blunt instrument, mocking today's political atmosphere then morphed into an alien life form capturing humans for exhibition on their planet. Following a severe tongue-lashing by my politically astute and talented writer grandson, I found motivation for Mary Alice and the entry evolved into a tongue-in-cheek story.

~VHH

THE THIRTEENTH FLOOR

SCOTT MICHAEL POWERS

"For 13 to be unlucky would require there to be some kind of cosmic intelligence that counts things that humans count and that also makes certain things happen on certain dates or in certain places."
—*Douglas Hofstadter*

RUFUS DUNCAN never understood the source of the anxiety and frustration he suffered over the past ninety-five years. He didn't used to be so tense. It came down to this though: it's hard to shed old ways, hard to overcome old lines of authority and responsibility, and hard to resolve old grievances after you're dead.

Even with nothing left to lose or gain, Rufus still took it. Had to.

Rufus was tired of it.

Sixteen, forever going on seventeen, Rufus Duncan, the elevator attendant, stood at attention, as he always did when in the presence of the Gauners. On this occasion, it was Stella Gauner. She stood in a group behind him on the thirteenth-floor landing of The Hotel Stella, waiting for the elevator. With her were the World War II soldier Sgt. Ryan, the congressional staff lawyer Parnell Himmel, and the rock 'n' roll groupie, Starflower.

They weren't there to board the elevator and leave.

They were there to see who might join them on this rare night. Halloween night. Not just any Halloween, but one with a full moon. The one occasion when the thirteenth-floor call button actually worked, at least since that fateful night of October 31, 1925, when the slaughter took place in the hotel's first month of operation.

After that night, the elevator did not stop there again until the night of October 31, 1944. It came again on October 31, 1955, and on October 31, 1974.

It was Rufus' duty to beckon the newcomers into their company. He hated doing it. He knew what it meant. But it's what Mrs. Gauner wanted. And, well, Rufus did what he was told.

Behind him, their newest companion, Starflower, waited for her first time to see the elevator bring someone new. She felt the deep rumble vibrate through the mildewed walls as the elevator ascended. Above the thirteenth-floor doors, a tarnished brass arrow arced upward at last, now between III and IV.

"Huh," she gasped, her right forefinger curled over her teeth.

She was dressed in a Native American woman's costume, black wig, beaded headband with a single feather, buckskin dress, beads, but four-inch rawhide heels instead of moccasins. In 1974, on the night she intended to sneak into a Halloween party, the outfit was labeled "Sexy Indian Squaw," and not widely offensive in 1974, but generations had changed that. She had read that Rod—*Rod Stewart*—had a thing for Indian squaws. So, that's what she dressed as, hoping to get into the penthouse where she understood Stewart would be partying that night. Unfortunately, when the elevator door opened in 1974, Rufus had enticed her to the wrong floor.

Worst mistake she ever made, stepping out of the car.

"Dearie, be a good little Indian and step aside," Stella Gauner said.

"Kiss off, Stella."

The two locked in a stare.

Stella had been dressed as Cleopatra for the past ninety-five years, also with a black wig, held by a golden headband. She wore heavy makeup, powder lightening her cheeks and mascara darkening her already-dark eyes. Her merlot-red, thin-lipped smile projected, "Mess with me and you'll regret it forever."

"Girls, girls, girls," Himmel, the lawyer dressed as a vampire, said. "You don't want to scare away our guest before he gets off. Let's make nice for just a few minutes, shall we?"

"Don't you patronize me," Stella said in a voice slow and calm.

"Don't get so high and mighty with me. You're no lady. You're a murderer," Himmel replied.

"So are you," Starflower said.

"Oh, are you taking her side now?"

"You killed me!" Starflower complained.

"Mercy killing," Himmel offered.

"You electrocuted me," Starflower snapped. "That really hurt."

"Did you a favor. Trust me."

"Except now the rest of us are stuck with her," Stella interjected.

Starflower raised a middle finger to Stella. Himmel shook his head and rolled his eyes.

Sgt. Ryan, wearing his Army dress uniform of 1944, his real one, not a costume, straightened the knot on his tie and stiffened to attention.

Behind them, the wall was lined with lamps made of etched glass in brass frames, but most were not working. The few that were threw triangles of light and shadows. In one spot the wall sagged outward from a long-long-ago unattended water leak. Faded gold-colored wallpaper curled away from the wallboard, dropping from near the ceiling, and along the edges of each sheet.

To their left, a corridor turned a corner. To their right spread a large landing foyer furnished with stout, scalloped chairs and inlaid wooden coffee tables. Some buckled from decades of unchecked humidity. A light snowstorm's worth of dust covered all, though there were no footprints.

Beyond the sitting area was the security office door.

The security office, Starflower knew, was where Stella's husband, Adam "Bigsey" Gauner, and his mistress, Molly Pecorelli, would be waiting. There was a one-way window there, so they could watch without being seen.

INSIDE THE ELEVATOR, Dr. Daniel Margolis, the lone occupant, checked his phone. No signal.

"Shoot," he muttered.

Tonight, Margolis was on his way to a Halloween party in the penthouse, at first as an invited guest but now as a psychotherapist making a house call, with some urgency. Grady Rodriguez had texted a plea for help and followed with several more. *When are U coming? How far out are you? ETA? U still coming?* There'd been no further texting since the valet took Margolis' car, so he worried. Grady was bipolar. He earned way too much money for a twenty-something and knew nothing about how to live rich. This intensified both Grady's manic recklessness and his destructive self-loathing. Grady was, by billings, one of Margolis' most important patients.

Margolis dressed as Dr. Sigmund Freud, complete with a big, fat, Dominican in his breast pocket. Looking like Freud was easy. He already had the hair loss, the tight-cropped beard, and a nagging gut.

The brass arrow above the door stopped between **XII** and **XIV** and shuddered. The car lurched to a stop. The door rumbled across, revealing a dimly lit landing.

Margolis faced a young, black hotel attendant dressed in maroon and gold, complete with a fez, a period costume from—Margolis wasn't quite sure—maybe the Depression.   Behind the attendant stood a woman dressed as Cleopatra, another as a native American, a man in a vintage Army uniform, and a man dressed as a vampire.

"Welcome, kind sir," the attendant said, stepping aside, hand outstretched.

"Oh, do come this way," the lady dressed as Cleopatra bid, reaching out her slim right hand.

Margolis stepped out. He looked left and right. There was no sign of a party. No music. No chatter. The air was attic-like, thick, musty, acrid. He turned back just as the elevator door closed.

To his side, beyond a sitting area, a naked man in his fifties and a much-younger naked woman rushed through a door and toward them.

"Get away! All of you! Beat it! You hear me?" the naked man yelled, flicking his hand at the gathering. He pointed at Margolis with a shaky finger. "You! I need to talk to you. Come on, damn you all, get out of here." He stopped and fluttered his hands at the others. "Come on, now! I said get out of here! Scoot! Now!"

Even in dim light and from thirty or forty feet away, the naked man and his female companion repulsed Margolis. The man's face was terribly mutilated, torn and bloody, as if he were missing a chunk of his head. Another bloody pulp of flesh hung from his groin, swinging as he walked, like genitals on a rope. The woman bore similarly grotesque and bloody wounds on her left breast and her right thigh. Their costumery or makeup, or whatever it was, seemed remarkable and lifelike enough to be deeply disturbing. Way beyond necessary. They were troubled. Margolis made a mental note to give them each his card before he left.

When he looked back, Margolis saw everyone else was gone, except the soldier. Where did they go?

"Follow me!" the soldier commanded. He broke for the corridor in the other direction.

Margolis followed, assuming the party was this way. When they rounded the corner, they came across a figure sprawled on the floor. It was the hotel attendant. No, it wasn't. It was a skeleton dressed as the attendant lying in a dark stain on the carpet. Margolis slowed to look closely and catch his breath. This one spooked him.

The soldier led Margolis into a banquet room. Most of its tables and chairs stacked in the back. The woman dressed as Cleopatra sat on a table, her legs crossed and dangling, swinging a bit. The vampire, attendant, and woman dressed as an Indian milled behind her. No one else. No party.

"They won't come in here," the woman dressed as Cleopatra said. "They're very embarrassed about being naked. Or at least Bigsey is. Molly probably loves it. The slut."

"What is going on? Where is everyone else? I'm here to see Grady Rodriguez," Margolis said.

"Oh, I'm sure there's no one here by that name. This is my place. Let me introduce you to Sgt. Ryan, Mr. Himmel, Rufus, and lastly, Starflower." She said the final name with a wriggling nose and a squeaky voice, mocking her. "My name is Mrs. Gauner. You may call me Stella." She stretched out her arms. "That's right. As in The Hotel Stella? This is my hotel."

Margolis knew the hotel's historic name, The Hotel Stella, but that had been replaced decades ago. The hotel had been rebranded at least a couple of times.

He followed her gaze around the room. The place looked as if it hadn't been used or even maintained in decades. Three chandeliers —following the same etched glass on brass design as the hallway lamps—hung from chains. But like the hallway lamps, most of the bulbs were dead. The far chandelier hung sideways. Behind Stella and the others, a stack of rusty chairs had fallen over.

Most concerning, there still was no sign of a party.

"I'm sorry. There must have been a mistake. Is this not the penthouse? Did I get off on the wrong floor?" Margolis asked Stella. "I have to go."

"You're not going anywhere!" the vampire shouted. "You're going to die here, just like us."

Margolis was accustomed to dealing with melodrama. Push through it.

"Please stop. I'm really not in the mood," Margolis said, calmly. "This really could be a case of life and death. You see, I have this patient and… "

"Oh, you're a doctor?" Stella asked. "Tell me. What should I do about this?"

She lifted her costume's top to reveal a large wound in her belly. It looked real. The blood looked fresh.

"It goes all the way through from the other side," Stella said. "Doctor, do I need surgery?"

She shrieked a laugh that made her head bob.

"This is too much. Seriously. You guys are nuts. And I'm a psychoanalyst so I rarely call anyone nuts. But you? It's been, um, fun, and, well, goodbye." Margolis turned to leave.

"Rufus, stop him." Stella said, flatly, a minor command.

And there—where the hell did he come from?—stood the attendant, blocking the door. Rufus was just a kid, but athletic in a wiry way.

"Please move out of the way," Margolis tried.

Rufus expanded his chest and raised his head, a sort of pre-fight cocking. His raised chin revealed that Rufus, too, had a horrific wound. A slice ran across his throat. Blood soaked his neck and shirt.

Margolis pivoted back, and gasped.

Only Stella remained. She blew on her nails.

Margolis looked right, left. There were other doors at the ends of the banquet room, but not close. The room was windowless. Where did the others go? He turned back towards the main door. The attendant now was gone too.

"What is going on?" Margolis said, his voice edgy with alarm.

"You should take a chair to hear this, Doctor."

"I need to be going. It's very important that I check on my patient."

"*Sit.* You'll want to sit for what I have to tell you. I didn't catch your name."

Margolis stared a moment at the chair she'd directed him toward. It was the only one pulled from the stacks. He nodded, gathered his dignity, strolled over, and sat facing her.

"Your name?" she asked, smiling hostess-like.

"Dr. Margolis. Daniel."

"Well, Dr. Danny, you have had the unfortunate luck of getting off on the thirteenth floor of my hotel."

"Thirteenth floor?"

"My husband had it secretly installed when he built my hotel. The architect was very clever in designing the building. So, there is no evidence of its existence." She paused, rolled her eyes upward, and raised her voice almost to a whistle. "It doesn't show up on any of the plans submitted to the city inspector. The only people who ever knew about there being a thirteenth floor all have been dead a very long time. It is our little secret." She put her finger to her lips and nodded. "Shhhh. Our little secret hideaway."

"That's all very nice. But you don't understand. I must get to the fourteenth floor. I have a patient that I must… "

"Patient? Fourteenth floor? Oh, you can't leave."

"I beg your pardon?"

"You really can't. There's no way out. The only elevator that stops here only works every, I don't know, I suppose every ten or twenty years. Mr. Himmel, that nasty little man, figured out the timetable. It won't be back for a very, very long time. Anyway, that's bad news for anyone who's alive. I'm told the water is now so brown it's undrinkable. Though, I must say, we do have some of the best spirits in the city. We have no food though. You'll probably be dead in a few days. Maybe quicker if Himmel gets to you. He thinks he's morally superior to everyone, so you better watch your back around him. You know, he killed Starflower. He said he did it so he wouldn't have to watch her suffer long. What's the fun in that?"

She splayed her hands, palms up.

"I told him not to; but he doesn't listen to me."

"Ma'am."

"Stella."

"Stella. This is a fabulous, um, kooky little party. Best spooky effects I've ever … You have my compliments. But seriously, I must insist. I have to leave. If you'll excuse me."

Margolis got up and turned to the door. The attendant was back, standing in his way with his arms folded.

"Oh, come on!" Margolis exclaimed, dropping his shoulders and swinging back to Stella in exasperation. "What's going on?"

Stella laughed, and her screeching howl annoyed and then creeped Margolis out. She waved her hands at him and then used them to hide her face until she controlled her outburst. She cleared her throat.

"Don't be so dense, darling," she said. "We're ghosts, Dr. Danny! We've all been here a very long time and we'll be here forever, I expect. The only real fun we have is when we welcome a new person into our fold, when we get the chance."

She batted her eyes. She was vamping, enjoying it.

"I'm a man of science. I don't believe in ghosts."

"Well, then, I must not be here at all!"

She shrieked that laugh again, and then she and the sound vanished. The kid was gone again too.

Margolis fished his phone from his coat pocket. Still no signal. He fiddled with the settings, trying for WiFi. Nothing.

THE DOCTOR RETURNED to the elevator landing and pushed the call button. Once. twice. The third time he pounded on it with a fist. He took out his phone and checked it again, and then put it back into his pocket. He looked up at the arrow, willing it to move.

He pushed the button again, and held it in. The arrow wasn't going to move.

"It won't come, sir," Rufus called out. He stood among the chairs and tables over in the reception area.

"Why not?"

"I dunno, sir. It only comes once."

Margolis wedged fingertips into the door's edge and pulled. He cracked a nail and pulled out his hand quickly. The fingertip stung. The fingernail bled. This place was so dusty and mildewy, Margolis almost could feel infection seeping in. He drew a handkerchief from his breast pocket, a handy prop as part of the Freudian costume. He wrapped his aching finger, tucking the cloth between fingers. He winced.

"It won't budge," Rufus said. "Mr. Gauner made sure of that."

Lost between the sting of his fingertip and the growing anxiety of being maybe, really, truly trapped, Margolis squeezed his finger, squeezed his eyes closed a moment, and sought to recompose himself.

"When Sgt. Ryan first arrived, he tried all sorts of things to pull or pry that door open. And he's strong. No offense, sir," Rufus said. "I promise you, sir, you won't get it to open."

"Well then how the… " the doctor shouted. He stopped. He collected himself. "How do I get out of here?"

"You can't sir."

The doctor looked around as if there might be a better answer apparent in the surroundings. Nothing offered any help. He walked toward Rufus and then stopped by a pair of chairs.

"Come here. Join me for a moment."

They sat and the doctor turned his chair so they faced each other.

"Rufus, is that right?"

"Yes, sir."

"How do I get out of here?"

"You can't sir. I told you. You're stuck here like the rest of us. You're going to die here."

"You're a ghost?"

Rufus nodded. His neck wound flopped.

"I'm not supposed to believe in ghosts, but you and your friends have put on quite a convincing show. So, let's go with that for the sake of argument. But first, tell me about yourself, Do you have family somewhere?"

"I don't think so. Mr. Himmel says they all should be dead by now."

"Is that supposed to be you in the hall, around the corner?"

"Yes sir. That's me. I was trying to get away but Mr. Briscola caught me. He cut my throat."

"Mr. Briscola?"

"Yes sir. He was Mr. Gauner's *cappa*. He shot Mrs. Gauner and then he tried to shoot me, but the gun didn't work. It was out of bullets or something. So, he chased me. That's where he caught me. He got me down on the floor and then he took out his knife and cut me. See?"

Rufus rolled his head back and the wound separated across his throat.

"Did he also kill the others?"

"No sir. Mrs. Gauner did. I mean. I guess. She caught Mr. Gauner and Miss Molly together in bed. And she shot them both. Mr. Briscola took the gun from her, I think, and then shot her. I was out in the hall, so I didn't see nothin'. But I heard him say, 'Give me that gun, Stella.' And then I heard him shoot her. I heard her scream. She has a nasty scream."

"Back up. Tell me how this started."

Rufus smoothed wrinkles in his pants.

"I brought Mr. Gauner and Miss Molly here, okay? Then, when I went back up to the penthouse and the elevator door opened, Mrs. Gauner and Mr. Briscola were shouting at each other. She was calling Mr. Gauner all sorts of things. And Mr. Briscola said they should go down and check. So, I took them there. Mrs. Gauner found them and shot them. Then I guess Mr. Briscola shot her."

"Why did he do that?"

"So that there'd be no witnesses, I guess. That's what Mr. Gauner says. You see, if they never found Mr. Gauner's body, then Mr. Briscola could take over the operation. And no one ever found us. Mr. Gauner says he's a lying, cheating, conniving, back-stabbing *stronzino*. So, I guess that's what happened. And Mr. Briscola kept everything hidden. I guess."

"And he killed you, too?"

"No witnesses."

"When did this happen?"

"It was Halloween night. We'd just opened a few weeks earlier. There was a big party upstairs. 1925. Ever since then, when a full moon appears on Halloween night, we keep adding guests."

"What do you mean, 'keep adding guests'?"

"Sgt. Ryan showed up in the elevator a few years later, 1944, he says. He tried for weeks to get out of here. He finally got sick and died. He's in the back corridor. Mr. Himmel came in, um, 1955. He got into Mr. Gauner's hooch and drank his self to death in the kitchen. Miss Starflower came in 1974. She died in the kitchen too. Mr. Himmel set it up so she got shocked when she tried to turn on the radio."

Rufus's eyes were wide. So were Margolis's. The doctor was aware of his symptoms. He could feel the cool sizzle of adrenaline racing through his arteries and veins. His heart pounded. His face felt clammy. His palms sweated. He was feeling the panic of unreasonable fear. His senses also were heightened. The air smelled more acrid. He could taste dust.

"Boo!"

Margolis leapt from his chair, over-rotated, and fell face first, catching himself on his knees and hands. When he looked up, Stella was standing about five feet away, wagging a finger at him and laughing.

"Ha!" she shrieked. "Got you! Oh! That kills me. Every time. Just kills me. Oh, Dr. Danny, you should have seen your face!"

And then she vanished.

Margolis dusted his palms and pants legs with the handkerchief, but there was too much dust. He took a deep breath and sat again holding up both hands, asking Rufus for a moment. He filled his lungs and cleared his head. He had to accept. They say they're ghosts. They seem like ghosts. Other explanations weren't coming. The matter at hand now was, what to do about it. The process started with resetting his assumptions, something he'd practiced many times when patients challenged his initial expectations. He gave Rufus a cool look. The young man's eyes were wide with wonder.

"Well. So. You're all ghosts?"

Rufus nodded.

"And you have been here nearly a century."

Another nod.

"And you're stuck here on the Thirteenth Floor?"

Nod.

"And you never see anyone else, except the others in here?"

"Most of the time, I don't even like to see them. I mean all anyone wants to do is harp. Mrs. Gauner is still mad at Mr. Gauner and Miss Molly. And they're mad at her. All Mr. Himmel wants to do is complain about politics. Miss Starflower, I never know what she's talking about. Sgt. Ryan scares me. So, I just try to blend in, you know? If they want me, they know how to find me. I do my job."

"After all of this. After you, you died. You died right? You still feel obligated to do your job, to be everyone's errand boy?"

Rufus didn't like that. There was a flicker of anger in his eyes. For Margolis, it was like seeing a light down a hallway. *This way.*

"What about you? What do you want Rufus?"

Rufus blinked and turned away in contemplation. Or frustration. Margolis wondered if he was the first person in ninety-five years to ask Rufus what he wanted. Maybe ever. The fact that he was taking a long time to answer, rather than offer another "I dunno" told Margolis there was something there.

"Go ahead. You can tell me, Rufus. Maybe I can help you. What do you want?"

When Rufus turned back there was life in his eyes.

"I want to be someone," Rufus said.

"Go on."

"I want the others to look at me and see someone. You see? I want them to say, 'Hi, Rufus. Thank you, Rufus. You do your job well, Rufus. How are you today, Rufus?' I don't mind doing stuff, but I don't want to be everyone's toady and just ignored, like I don't matter. You know? Even Miss Starflower treats me that way."

"We'll work on that. And what do you suppose they want?"

"I dunno. You'd have to ask them, I guess."

The doctor watched him closely. Rufus looked spirited, as if he had just contributed, and he smiled, sort of, with full lips pulling a little taut. His head came forward so that his eyes rode out over his nose. Margolis was certain they glowed a bit.

"Why don't we do that, Rufus? I think I see a way out. Maybe not out of here, but out of the doldrums of ninety-five years. Can you do me a favor? I don't want to be like the others and tell you what to do. But I really could use your help. You can talk to any of them, right? You seem to be the one everyone accepts. Acceptance is a kind of trust. Trust leads to respect, you know. Let's see what we can do. Maybe we can get that for you. Can you do me a favor? Please?"

"Sure. I'll try."

"Great. Gather the others. Tell them to meet me in the banquet room, in about a half an hour."

"I guess. I don't know if they'll all come. Mr. Gauner and Miss Molly, they don't like to come to anything."

"Tell them it is my request that they honor me with their presence. Say it like that. Make it sound like it's about me. I think they'll all want to come."

Rufus nodded, and his neck wound flapped.

IN THE BANQUET ROOM, Margolis arranged seven chairs in an arc, facing his chair. Assigned seats were a must. Bigsey Gauner was the Big Fish here, so he'd sit in the middle. He'd insist on having his mistress Molly next to him, so that was fine. Molly would sit to his right. Margolis assumed that Bigsey saw himself as a ladies' man, so Starflower would sit to his left. On the far end past Molly, Stella. On the other end, where he might be of some assistance to Margolis, Rufus. The solder, Sgt. Ryan would sit between Stella and Molly, just in case. Himmel would sit between Starflower and Rufus, a position Margolis suspected Himmel would find uncomfortable. That was fine too.

The sergeant was the first to arrive and Margolis directed him to his assigned chair. Himmel and Starflower followed.

"I can't sit next to him," Starflower complained.

"Oh, take your seat, Pocahontas," Himmel replied. "Maybe you'll learn some manners."

"No name calling," Margolis said. "Please." He directed Starflower to her appointed chair.

She lowered herself as if onto a throne and crossed her legs.

Stella made her entrance with arms spread.

"Oh darlings," she called out. "It's been so long since we've all been together. I'm so glad you've come. Dr. Danny has agreed to try to help us. I want you all to give the good Doctor your full attention. Best behavior. This should be fun."

As she stepped forward, Rufus appeared behind her. "Mr. Gauner and Miss Molly are on their way," he said.

As Margolis told them where to sit, Bigsey called out from the doorway. "Well, well, well. What have we here?" His voice was deep and firm with condescension, like a high school football coach finding a pack of cigarettes in a gym locker.

Still completely nude, Bigsey had his fists on his hips, his arms bowing around a large roll of belly. The mutilated flesh hung from his face and from his groin. "No comments about the emperor's clothes, okay? If we're going to air things out, then we're going to air things out."

Molly slipped in beside him, taller than him, also still nude, also with shredded flesh. She had her arms crossed over her breasts covering that wound, except for blood that still looked fresh running down her belly. Her leg wound looked as if it should take that leg out from under her stance. "Everybody's here. Good times are about to roll," she said, her nose up.

"Sit down, bitch," Stella said.

"Stella! We are going to be civil," Margolis scolded.

Bigsey and Molly limped across the room and took the proper seats.

There they were, assembled in all their ghastly glory: Cleopatra with a hole in her gut, a soldier, a naked woman with tattered wounds in her leg and chest, a naked man missing part of his face and with his genitals hanging by a fleshy cord, a Native American woman, a vampire, and a hotel attendant with a slit throat. The psychiatrist eased into his own chair

"I thought we'd begin with... "

"Oh, you thought we'd begin?" Bigsey blared. "You thought? Lemme tell you something, buddy."

"Boopsy, let the man speak," Molly said.

"No, no, we got to get some things straight, first. He comes in here and... "

"Boopsy?" Stella cried. "You call him Boopsy?" She shrieked her laugh.

"He comes in here and… " Bigsey continued.

Stella laughed harder, as if to make sure she got to him. "*Boop-sy?*"

"Hey, you," Bigsey said.

"Stella," Margolis admonished. "Civil."

"Sorry," she said, zipping her lips. Then she blew a giggle through her nose.

"Please, continue, Mr. Gauner," Margolis said.

"Yeah, well, as I was saying, you can't come in here and call the shots. This is my place. This is my hotel. This is my home."

"Mrs. Gauner told me it was hers."

"Pfft," went Molly.

"At any rate, I don't know what claim you have to it anymore," Margolis said. "As I recall, Hyatt bought this place a few years ago. It even has the Hyatt sign on the front now."

"Okay, okay. Let me explain," Bigsey said. "When I built this place, I wanted it to be the best. Right? And it was. I could show you the write ups. But it's much more than just a great hotel, right? I had this secret floor designed and built so I could run my, ah, off-the-books operations here without having to worry about the cops and G-men. Are you following? Everything about this place, I planned down to the last detail, okay? The last detail. I did. Me. I thought of everything. Where to keep the product. The revenue. How to keep the damned bathrooms working and the lights on. How to make sure no one can get up here. What happens if cops do anyway. Everything. I thought of everything, and this hotel is it. There's nothing like it, anywhere. And that's me. So, you need to understand who's in charge. Who's always gonna be in charge."

"Fair enough. With your permission, Mr. Gauner, let's move on. What I want to know is, why are you here?"

"Why am I here?" Bigsey replied, flailing a wave at Stella. "Because she shot me!"

"I didn't ask why you're dead," Margolis said. He sighed. "Most people who die don't haunt hotels. I don't know where they go for sure. But they don't just hang around. There's something holding all of you here. Does anyone have any idea why you're still here?"

"Well, we all came here on Halloween. And there was a full moon," Starflower offered, dragging out the last two words with wonder: *fuuuull moooon*.

"So? Lots of people go places on Halloween. Just about everyone," Margolis challenged.

"This is the thirteenth floor! And it's a crime scene. Murder! And, and betrayal. And jealousy. And anger, and, and greed! That's a lot of bad mojo all rolled into one," Starflower said, in a voice Margolis found annoyingly overdramatic, as if she were a bad actress. Yet her eyes lit up. She believed. "Don't you get it? All the negative forces of the universe were concentrated here. And it won't let us out. It wants to hold us here. It's like our metaphysical prison. That can't be broken. For whatever reason, we can't leave."

"And no one ever found our bodies," Sgt. Ryan added. "We've not had any proper send-off."

"Still not buying it."

"Well, what do you think, Mr. Hot-Shot Psychiatrist?" asked Stella.

"Hey, I'm the new guy here. I figure you've all have had plenty of time to think about this. I want to know. What do you think?"

"I think it's some sort of communist plot!" Himmel said.

"And there he goes," said Sgt. Ryan. "Our resident fascist conspiracist seeing commies behind everything."

"And there he goes, our resident Red!"

"Hey! I fought for this country! Uncle Sam called my name, I came running. He gave me a gun and told me to kill people. So I killed people."

"I did too!" Stella said with her shriek-y laugh.

The group looked at her for a second, then turned their heads away, like she was the first at the party to get really drunk and no one wanted to condone it.

"I fought for this country too," Himmel said. "I've always fought for this country. Only I've done it in a courtroom, and in the halls of Congress. I do it with reason. And the Constitution. And the law.

We're always in a kind of war, ladies and gentlemen. The enemy is always right here among us, trying to destroy our freedom, our liberty, our democracy, our very way of life."

"How does a communist plot trap people here after they die?"

"How the hell should I know?" Himmel replied. "Maybe some sort of Russian invention. Or, like the girl said, maybe some sort of voodoo. Some Satanic, un-Christian power. Don't think for a moment the Russians haven't been researching that crap. You know they'd use it against us if they figure out how."

This was getting nowhere. They were clueless. All of them. Margolis had hoped one might have some sort of insight, some sort of understanding, or just a simple explanation. If so, no one fessed. He decided to change direction and get to the question that got through to Rufus.

"What do you want?" he asked. His eyes moved from face to face.

"Want?" Molly replied.

"Sure. Maybe you're still here because you still need something. From each other."

"I want a drink," Stella said.

"I could use a smoke," said Himmel.

"I want that weaselly Johnny Briscola's head on a platter, so I can pluck his eyes out and eat them," said Bigsey.

"Right," Margolis said. "You can't have those. Any of them. Sorry. You're ghosts! Remember? What about something not material? Something said or done? Is there anything anyone here would like from anyone else here?"

If there were a clock on the wall, they could have heard it ticking. Margolis let the silence linger.

"I want the truth."

It was Molly, very softly, looking at her feet. And then she turned to Bigsey.

"That night," she said, as if she were talking only to him, though everyone could hear. "We were talking, remember? I asked you, I asked you why you hadn't told Stella about us yet. Why you hadn't left her yet like you'd promised. And then."

"Oh, this is hogwash!" Bigsey said. He got up and took a step toward Margolis. "Why the hell are you doing this?"

"This is what I do. If I were a plumber, I'd be trying to get your water fixed. I think we should let her finish. Please. Sit down."

"Yeah! I want to hear this," said Starflower.

"Sit down, Gauner," said the sergeant.

Bigsey Gauner looked around. Without Molly on his side, no one backed him.

"Please continue," Margolis said.

Molly's expression hardened. Her voice dropped and became coarse. "And then she came in and saw us sitting there on the bed, and she shot you. And then she shot me. So. So, I never got my answer. I want my answer. I still want my answer. Would you have ever left her, like you said you would? Or were you just lying to me?"

She leaned into Bigsey.

"You know," he said, softly.

"No, I don't know. Say it."

He sighed.

"Okay. You want the truth? No. I wasn't going to leave Stella. Hell, most of the organization was in her name. The hotel corporation? It was in her name. That's why it's called The Hotel Stella. I couldn't leave her, and she knew it. And that's the truth."

"I'm just, I'm just... "

"You're just his latest slut, dearie," Stella said. "And I was sick of it. He made promises to me too. And the way you two left the party? Holy Mother Mary. Don't you know anything about being discreet? How in the world did you avoid cops all those years? That's what got me. I was humiliated. Humiliated! In my hotel. At my own party!"

"It's my party," sang Starflower. "and I'll kill if I want to. Kill if I want to, Ki..."

Molly rocked back and forth, holding the seat with both hands, as if she were trying to keep herself from lunging. The session went silent. Anger thickened the air. Finally, Molly stopped. Her eyes softened, though not for tears. She looked relieved. Her body slacked. She turned to Margolis.

"That's all I wanted. That's all I ever wanted. The truth. I feel, I feel, ready to get the hell out of here. I feel like I can leave. Bye, bye to you."

Molly's form crackled with thousands of blazing sparks. Smoke swirled from each spark and engulfed her. The last Margolis saw of Molly was her eyes, looking upward. With peace. The smoke cleared quickly, and she was gone. All that remained was the stench of ozone.

Margolis stood up, pushing his chair back. His jaw dropped. He'd come to accept these phantoms' disappearing acts, but this was different. Not just showy, but conclusive. He felt like he'd just watched someone die.

"Well, well, well. She's really gone now, I can tell," Stella said. "There's nothing left of her here."

"Oh! Oh! Oh! My turn!" said Starflower, pushing her arm high into the air. "I want to go next!"

Margolis gave her a nod and sat again.

"I want people to hear me sing. I'm really good."

She looked around. No one objected. No one encouraged her either.

"You never let me sing. You people always would go away whenever I did. Now I have a captive audience. I want to perform. I was born to perform."

"Go ahead," Margolis said.

"Can I?" On those high heels, she strutted over to a small stage at the end of the room. She stepped up. She looked around at her audience. She beamed.

"This is what I was going to sing for Rod that night. She bowed her head, closed her eyes, and mouthed the words, "One, two …"

And then she sang "Maggie May."

Her voice wasn't bad, a little rough, two octaves higher than Stewart's classic, but just as harsh. Bluesy. Everyone watched and listened as she worked the stage, holding an air microphone. Margolis realized he was the only one in the room who'd ever heard the song. He wondered what the others might think of rock 'n' roll. At least she picked a good song. They all sat raptly.

Starflower finished and bowed.

"That was really good," Sgt. Ryan said. He stood and clapped. The others, even Bigsey, gave polite applause on top.

Starflower beamed. She had a nice smile, Margolis realized. She looked fresh and sincere, but in command of her stage.

"Applause," Starflower gushed. "That's what I wanted. I think I can go now."

As she curtsied, she grew brighter as if a spotlight were turned on her. She dazzled, until her colors ran together into blinding white, and Margolis could no longer see her. Silently, the light withdrew. Starflower was gone.

Sgt. Ryan stood, looking angry.

"All I want is to get away from all of you. To get away from all of the bull!"

Margolis had a few patients struggling with Post Traumatic Stress Disorder, and he sensed Ryan was in need of more than he could offer in a few minutes.

"Sergeant, in my time, people are taught to thank soldiers for their service. I'm not going to do that. I'm afraid that only comes across as dismissive and condescending. Where did you fight?"

"France, sir. Third Army."

"The breakout, hmm. Sergeant, none of us here can relate to what you've been through, what you've done, what you had to do. We didn't want to know about it when you were going through it, and I don't think anyone's going to understand if you told us about it now. But know this. You did what we sent you there to do."

"Sir?"

"No, you did. Nothing more, nothing less. America sent you to do whatever you could, within the limits of the human body and soul, to drive the Nazis out. You did that. Hell? I'm sure. How you did it, we didn't care. And neither should you. You did what you had to do. That's okay. Whatever, it's okay. You know that already. Right? It's okay. By the way, we won. Thanks to you, for that."

Ryan saluted.

Standing at attention, with his hand pressed against his scalp, the old soldier just faded away.

Himmel cleared his throat. Still seated, he waved his hands at the others and complained about how no one ever took his warnings seriously. He lectured that freedom, liberty, capitalism, democracy were what allowed every one of them to have the ability do whatever they do. The war was more complicated now because the enemy had turned Americans against America. They needed to be cut away, like cancers.

Rufus responded.

"I get it," he said. "We all need to do our parts to protect our way of life. It's not just Sgt. Ryan going off to war. It's all of us remembering what he was fighting for. Keeping that. Be on guard. Be ready. Come forward when you have to. Alert people like you when we see people who might want to destroy our way of life."

Himmel pointed at him, shaking with joy. "Yes! Yes! That's exactly it. If I can just get that through to one of you!"

"I get it," Rufus repeated.

"Well, then, young man. Well, then. Perhaps all is not lost."

Himmel's image in the chair turned translucent and wavy, as if projected onto smoke. Then all that he was swirled together toward his heart, as if sucked to that point and then away by an invisible vacuum cleaner hose.

"What a blowhard," Rufus said.

"You? You didn't buy what he was saying?" Margolis said.

"Nah, I heard the same garbage from my Uncle Horace. That's what my ma used to say about him."

Margolis stopped himself from admonishing Rufus. He didn't condone deceit in his sessions, but this was something of a breakthrough for Rufus. He had exercised individual initiative. He'd emerged from self-imposed subjugation. Margolis stopped himself from smiling.

"Okay, who is next?" he asked.

Stella bounced out of her chair and got nose-to-nose with her husband.

"By my math, we've been married a hundred years now, a hundred years, last July 10. I want a divorce!" she demanded.

"You got it."

"Just like that?"

"Just like that, sweetheart. If it's what you want. It's what I want. As far as I'm concerned, we are no longer married. Till death do us part, and all that, remember? Lord knows, I don't want to spend eternity with you."

"Uh, huh," Stella said. "I never expected you to give me up that easy. But now that I think about it, Pappa can't come after you now, can he?"

"Your father was never a problem. You were the problem."

Stella bit her lip.

"We'll never see each other again?"

"God, I hope not."

Stella turned to Margolis.

"You know, I wouldn't mind still haunting this hotel, provided I could do it on my own. I'm going to miss this place," she said. She looked into Bigsey's face and added, "Not the company."

"I don't think I can help you with that. You'll have to take your chances," Margolis said.

"Very well, then. Goodbye."

The sound of "Goodbye" barely escaped before she simply vanished.

"Good riddance!" Bigsey yelled after her.

Then he turned to Margolis. He rubbed his chin. He rubbed his hands together. He nodded his head. He stood, and Margolis had to force himself to not be nauseated by the wounds.

"Well, I, ah, you know, I was really something, back in my day. Sure. This hotel? It was only part of it, you know. I had an empire! I owned this whole damned city. Yeah. You wanted a drink? You bought it from me. And I had the best booze, the best beer, the best wine, for a hundred miles. You know, in the storage rooms back there, there's probably thirty, forty casks of wine, a hundred crates of whiskey. I don't even know how many kegs. Brandy? Cognac? Scotch? It's all there. You have any idea what that's worth? Over in my vault? There's enough cash to buy Cleveland! Women? A game? I ran those. Sure, I did. You needed something from City Hall? I was the guy to talk to first. You had problems with some punks? I was the one who could take care of you. That's right. You had problems with the cops or some judge? Hello? You come to me.

"People needed me. Yeah. People feared me, too. Sure. And they should have. I didn't let no one cross me. There'd be a price to pay. There's always a price to pay for everything, right? But people also knew that if they needed something, if I could help them in any way, I would. Yeah. Yeah. I loved that I had that power. I loved that if someone had a problem, he'd come to me. Me. I'd fix it. Me. I helped people. I could help anyone. I liked that most of all. That was what a big man does, okay?"

He paced.

"You think I wanna give all that up?"

"Haven't you already?" Margolis asked.

"Yeah. I suppose I have, sure. I mean, look at me. I can't do nothing for no one no more. By the way, it's all still there. That *stronzino* Johnny Briscola closed off the stairs and the service elevator, but he couldn't move nothing out without drawing too much attention to this place. It's all still there."

"So, what do you want now?"

"Let me ask you something, Doc. What do you want? What can Bigsey Gauner do for you?"

"I want to get out of here."

"And if I give that to you, what can you do for me?"

"Maybe you'll feel the satisfaction you crave, by showing how powerful you are, one more time."

He nodded. And then he said, "Thirty-six, twelve, forty-two."

Margolis repeated the numbers.

"That's the combination to my vault. I told you I thought of everything, didn't I? I'm pretty smart, you know. I had to be. There's always been an escape hatch out of here. Sure. When I had this hotel built, I needed some last-chance route, just in case cops found this place and blasted their way in. It's through the vault. The way out. No one can give that to you but me. Right? Just me. There. Take it, Doctor. It's all yours. Okay? But you'll remember who gave it to you, right?"

"Of course. Thank you."

The lights went out. They pitched into total darkness.

"It must be midnight," Rufus said. "The lights only work until midnight on October 31."

"Mr. Gauner?" Margolis called out. "Mr. Gauner? Bigsey?"

There was no answer.

"He's gone," Rufus said.

Margolis checked his phone. It was, indeed, midnight. He turned on the phone's flashlight app and did a search. The banquet room was nearly empty now. Just Rufus and six empty chairs remained.

"Where is this vault?"

"In his office," Rufus replied.

The attendant led the way out of the banquet room. Margolis followed, down the corridor around to the back of the hotel floor. They passed another skeleton. The soldier, Sgt. Ryan, curled to a fetal position. Around another corner they came to a room with its door ajar. Margolis pushed the door open and shined his phone inside to reveal a suite. A skeleton dressed as Cleopatra lay crumpled in the middle of the room. A naked skeleton lay on the floor beside the bed. Another naked skeleton was on the bed. This room, more so than anywhere else, smelled of thick, musty, putrid decay. Rufus pointed beyond the bed to an interior door. Margolis opened it and entered an office. On the far wall was another door. Margolis pulled that one open to reveal a vault door.

He tried the dial. It spun coarsely, but it turned. Thirty-six, twelve, forty-two, the numbers Bigsey gave him. He grasped the lever bar and tugged. The lever held. Oh, God, Margolis thought. This better be the right combination. This better work. He leaned into it and gave the handle his best shove. The bar broke free from the century of grime and rust that held it in place. As he levered it downward, Margolis heard and felt a satisfying click at the bottom.

Margolis pulled and the vault door swung outwards with a groan. He shined his phone. The vault was about four feet deep, four feet wide, floor to ceiling. Shelves began about chest high, stacked with bundled cash, notebooks, and small boxes. Beneath the shelving, the vault was empty, except for a sledgehammer.

Margolis lifted the heavy hammer and set it outside the vault. The vault's floor was steel, yet Margolis' light revealed hinges and a latch. He pushed back the latch and pulled up. The steel-plate floor lifted with a screaming creak. Beneath, concrete floor had been chiseled to a thin layer. Margolis figured a couple of taps with the sledgehammer should bust through to the twelfth floor below.

He turned to Rufus.

"Finally, you, my friend. Now, tell me. What do you want?"

"I miss my mother," Rufus said.

"I miss mine too," Margolis said. "That's a good thing."

"Do you think I'll see her again? You know, wherever?"

"I'm afraid I have no insight that can help you with that. Who knows? I know one thing for sure, though. You won't see her again if you stick around with me. Now, what is it that you want?"

"I told you."

"You're a remarkable young man, Rufus. All these other clowns, none of them could ever have gotten what they wanted without you. And what you did to Mr. Himmel. That was when you freed yourself. I think you're already ready to go."

Margolis lifted the hammer and smashed it on the floor beneath the vault. Concrete and ceiling tile tumbled away. A woman below screamed. A man yelled "What the hell!"

Margolis got down and stuck his head into the hole. A man and a woman huddled on a bed with expressions of panic. They sat against the headboard, with covers pulled up around themselves.

Margolis looked up to Rufus.

"Thank you, my friend. Now, go be Rufus, the man. Not someone's servant. You're ready."

Rufus grinned. An oval of white light, the size of a full-length mirror, blazed next to him, wavering. Rufus looked at it, and then back to Margolis.

"Go on."

Rufus stepped into it. He disappeared as the light went out.

Margolis turned to the terrified couple below.

"Well, you don't see that every day, do you?"

He put his legs through the hole. He dropped down. He bounced off the foot of their bed, and then rolled onto the floor.

He stood and wiped concrete dust from his clothes.

"Pardon me," he begged the couple. "Please don't get up. I'll just let myself out." He pointed to the hole in the ceiling. "You should complain to hotel management about that."

They said nothing as Margolis left. He strode the corridors quickly, making his way to the elevators without looking back. Along the way, he checked his phone. He had a signal. He called 911. He said he found some bodies, maybe murder victims, and asked for police to meet him in the lobby. He was uncertain what story he'd provide to the police, but he'd have to come up with something. People don't just drop out of hotel room ceilings. After someone takes a look, there would be an investigation regardless. He might as well own it.

Margolis checked his messages. Grady had texted several more times. Thankfully, the texts had evolved from urgent and disturbing to excited and teasing. He advised Margolis that he was missing one hell of a party, and too bad. Grady had cycled.

Grady promised he'd tell Margolis all about it on Tuesday, during his next session.

The twelfth floor had two elevators, not just one. The call button worked. An elevator's arrow moved. The car came. The door opened, revealing an empty carriage. Margolis got in. The door closed. Finally, as the elevator lurched downward, Margolis felt a rush of cool relief. He removed the cigar from his pocket and gave it a sniff. He shoved it between his teeth. He took a deep, comforting breath and held it. He closed his eyes. He exhaled slowly. The elevator's rattling descent soothed him.

"*Boo!*"

"Argh!" Margolis screamed. He jumped, crashing his shoulder into the elevator wall, and dropping the cigar. There, behind him, crouched Stella, hands on her knees, laughing. She raised a finger and wagged it at him.

"Ohhhh, Dr. Danny!" she shrieked. "I got you again. I got you good! I just live for that."

"Stella… "

"You called the cops."

"I did. Someone had to. About time, don't you think?"

Stella straightened, feet spread, hands on hips—Cleopatra claiming all her regal authority—and smiled triumphantly.

"It's going to be sooo much fun. Don't forget, this is *my* hotel. *Mine*."

AUTHOR'S NOTES - SCOTT MICHAEL POWERS

I FIGURE it's hard to be a ghost, especially if you're metaphysically stuck in some physical location, as so many ghosts appear to be. Sure, haunting's probably satisfying, when you get that chance. What else 'ya got? What's more, we're led to believe that a great many ghosts have serious psychological issues. Anger. Obsession. Delusions. Unfulfilled desires. A need to be heard. Love-life complications. Unhealthy self-esteem. Probably no wonder. So, every now and then, it might be a good idea to get a little counseling.

~SMP

BAKING COOKIES FOR THE END OF THE WORLD

KRISTIN DURFEE

"In 5-billion years the Sun will expand & engulf our orbit as the charred ember that was once Earth vaporizes. Have a nice day."
—Neil Degrasse Tyson

"ESTER, turn off the news and come help me," my dad calls from the kitchen.

I groan. The anchors are only regurgitating the same information anyway, but I've still been glued to it all morning watching the ticker counting down our impending doom.

I groan again and turn off the TV and open and close Snapchat on my phone for the millionth time, but my feed doesn't load. It's been hours since I connected with my friends and my palms itch from not getting any updates from them.

My dad calls to me again and I walk into the kitchen and see bags of flour and sugar, a carton of eggs, bowls, butter, and my father in the middle of the mess. He's eating a handful of chocolate chips.

"You've got to be kidding me," I say, though I know I shouldn't be surprised.

I reflexively try my phone again only to be disappointed for the millionth time. I try a few other apps, but still can't get them up to update.

My dad turns, a small bit of melted brown goo at the right corner of his lips. He tosses the rest of the handful in his mouth. "What?" he mumbles.

"Now, literally *now*?"

"Why not?"

"You want to make cookies. Now?"

He shrugs. "We said we would. I told your mother——"

"Mom isn't here."

He opens his arms. "Well, obviously, but..."

I wipe a tear from my eye, a swatch of black coming off on my finger. My mom finally relented on my last birthday and bought me some mascara. Probably should have asked for waterproof. Probably should have anticipated at thirteen I'd cry a time or two.

"Ess, don't do that, we'll find her," he says and moves forward to hug me. I shrug him off, close Instagram before he can see, and get the tea-colored recipe book down from the shelf over the counter.

I try not to obsess over his words and flip to the dog-eared page of the only recipe Mom used from the book. I graze my finger over her neat cursive handwriting in the margins, reading the notes she made as she tweaked the recipe over the years.

Seeing her writing makes me feel close to her, but also makes me realize how far away she is. Two-thousand miles to be exact. Grounded. Stuck in an airport with strangers. Knowing Mom, she's figuring out how to get a car to drive back to us. Last we heard all the rentals were booked, so maybe she's trying to catch a ride with a stranger and risk dying even earlier when she's killed by some psycho. I know she won't give up. She'll keep trying. Something. Anything to make it back to us before we run out of time.

But it won't happen. Both dad and I know that. Driving is impossible. Cars and trucks abandoned and blocking the roads. Gas stations closed and out of fuel. Wherever someone is at this moment, that's where they'll be at the end. I just hope she doesn't drive herself too crazy in her efforts. So, we need to get to her first, right? Leave this second and start running.

And yet.

And yet we are about to bake cookies.

My dad leans over my shoulder and moves his finger down the page, reading the list of ingredients.

"Oh no," he says.

My gut clenches and my attention darts to the window fearing the worst. Fearing the estimates were off and we have even less time.

But there is nothing remarkable outside. The sun still shines. The birds still sing. Nature laughs at us, moving along as it always has. Indifferent. Because it could care less about us. Good riddance.

"What?" I ask, recovering from the initial shock.

"I forgot to get walnuts."

"We could scrap the whole plan," I suggest.

He shakes his head. "Cookies first. Trust me, we're gonna need them. But the nuts…"

I wrinkle my nose, forcing myself to focus. To trust him. "It's okay. We leave them out."

"But it says—"

"No nuts. It's okay, Dad. Really."

Pozzo comes waltzing into the room, his tail, more otter than Labrador, thumps against the kitchen island.

"Hey, bud!" my dad yells at an ear-shattering decibel level since our old dog is nearly deaf. But Dad's unaware I've just jumped ten feet in the air from his outburst. I roll my eyes, but he doesn't seem to notice that, either. "Wanna treat, dude?" he asks.

He pours out a small handful of chocolate chips and holds it out toward the dog. Pozzo's tail thumps even harder as he scarfs up the sweet treat and licks my dad's chocolate-streaked palm.

"Dad!" I scream, unable to help the reaction.

"Not like it's gonna kill him," my dad says. "Let him live a little."

"I mean, it *could* kill him," I say. "Or make him sick."

My dad looks at me then our dog. "You're right, I'm sorry." He gives Pozzo a loving scratch behind his floppy ears. "No more

chocolate, buddy, but follow me." He takes a few steps to the cabinet, removes the dog treats and proceeds to fill Pozzo's bowl with
them. "Everyone gets cookies today," my dad pronounces. "But I *do*
think ours will taste better than this…" he trails off and turns the
box over, wrinkling his nose as he reads the side. "I think it's basi-
cally just chicken feet and pig lips."

I can't help but laugh. "That's gross."

He hands the box to me. "See for yourself."

"Stop it, Mom would never." I stop, the pain in my chest like a
needle to my heart.

He shakes his head. "Nope, none of that. We bake, we pack, we
find her," he assures.

I nod my head as my dad washes and dries his hands. Once he
turns his back, I whip out my phone to take a short video of Pozzo,
tail wagging his whole body as he gobbles up the treats. I laugh at
the sight, thankful for the distraction, and try to record a video on
Snapchat. Then Tik Tok. Neither will pull up. Then remember even
if I took a video, there's nothing I can do with it. Nothing's connecting. My throat tightens and I have to swallow hard against the
building panic.

"Can I turn on the TV in here?" I ask. Maybe this will make my
palms stop itching from the stress of being away from any potential
updates. To know if we need to scrap this plan and just pack and
leave, cookies in hand or not.

"Nope. We're baking."

I sigh. "We really don't have to do this. There's no point."

"It'll help, trust me. Plus, I promised," he says, as if that's all the
explanation I need.

"It might not even matter. She might not even know." I pause a
moment, considering if I'm going to say the next line. Screw it.
"Dad, it's not going to matter. It won't change anything."

"I'm sure it will."

"You can't know that," I say.

"My psychology degree and twenty years of practice may beg to
differ." He winks at me.

"Even if we found her, it's not going to change her mind."

"Maybe if we present her with the *best* cookies. Maybe then," he says.

"You've never baked in your life," I remind him.

"You just see, they're gonna be good."

"There is no point." I hold up the bright green flyer announcing the 8th grade PTA fundraiser scheduled for tomorrow. The tomorrow that won't happen. "There's no bake sale, Dad. I get you want to do something, anything," I tell him. "But instead of baking cookies, let's just start walking now. Then we'll make it a certain distance and Mom will make it a certain distance and we'll find each other. Baking feels like giving up."

"I promised," he says with finality.

I wait a beat before plucking the vanilla extract from the pantry.

THE POWER FLICKERS OFF for just a moment, causing the clock on the stove to flash and stopping the standing mixer in mid-whirl. The blade slows, scraping against the stainless-steel bowl before the house blinks and beeps back to life. I look at my dad who avoids eye contact with me.

"I think it'll be okay," he says with a smile that's supposed to reassure me.

"The news?" I whisper.

He shakes his head. "The cookies."

He removes an egg from the carton. The crack is a satisfying noise and I fight the urge to walk over and take the empty shell from him to crunch it further.

"One at a time," I say before he can add the second one to the bowl.

He looks down at the cookbook then back at me. "The recipe calls for two."

"Yes, but one at a time. That's what Mom always said."

"Well then, the boss has spoken, and we need to listen to her."

He flicks the mixer back on, the whoosh of the blade through the batter spreads a delicious aroma of sugar and butter into the air.

Once everything is added, I help him tilt the mixer head back and remove the bowl.

"How many cookies does this make again?" he asks, glancing at the recipe.

I chew my inner lip, trying to remember. "At least two dozen, I think. Plus some extra."

"Extra? Like for the people we meet along the way that we'll barter safe passage for with these incredible cookies!"

I roll my eyes. "For eating," I say, dumping more than the recommended amount of chocolate chips in the batter and fold it in with a spatula.

"And the rest of these aren't for eating?" he asks, eyebrows cocked in confusion.

I huff my frustration at him. "Like with a spoon, Dad."

"But the eggs…" he says.

I lean forward, dipping the spatula back into the batter. "Doesn't matter now."

I laugh, but the noise catches as a lump forms at the back of my throat. I swallow to rid myself of it before I can properly taste the cookie dough.

It's perfect.

But, of course, I don't say anything to him. Not yet at least.

He stands next to me, shaking his head when I offer him the spoon. I guess it's okay to almost kill the dog with chocolate, but he won't risk salmonella in his final hours. Clearly, he's distracted because he forgoes the typical dissection of personal motivations that usually accompanies me making a different choice than him and instead rummages through the drawers.

"Whatcha looking for?" I mumble around the spatula in my mouth.

The crashing of utensils brings me to his side and Pozzo struggles to his feet to join us.

"Don't we have one of those scoopy things for measuring the cookies?"

"Probably, but we never used it, just take the tablespoon we used to measure the vanilla. Less dishes to wash."

"Oh, kiddo, we aren't ever doing dishes again, so don't you worry about that."

I know it's supposed to be a joke, but the words threaten to pop the little bubble in my mind that's convinced somehow this is all going to work out. I shake my head, pressing back against him, and move to wash the mixing blade before the cookie dough can dry on it.

He holds a metal object up like it's a trophy. "Ah-ha! Got it!"

"A tablespoon really works fine," I remind him. "Plus, Mom will appreciate not having a sink full of dishes to come home to."

"A tablespoon may be *fine*, but this will make them *perfect*," he reminds me. "She'll appreciate that more."

We've just gotten the first batch portioned out and slid into the oven when there's a knock at the door. All three of us freeze, even Pozzo who normally loses his mind when someone's at the door.

I smash down the building hope in my heart.

She has a key, she wouldn't knock.

My dad holds up a hand. "You stay here."

There's an edge to his voice that takes me a moment to place.

Worry.

Which is sort of ridiculous because we're all going to die in like a day anyway. The absurdity of the whole moment crashes into me like one of those waves which seems itty bitty, but somehow takes you down at the knee. We're baking cookies for a sale that's never going to happen or to barter with people we're never going to meet. A laugh escapes me and Pozzo barks at the sudden noise, making me jump despite myself.

I shush him and strain to hear the muffled voices from the front door. I consider defying my dad and going to the door anyway. My fingers lace through Pozzo's collar, holding him beside me, and I consider letting him go. He may be old, but he's still like eighty pounds and will probably scare someone, even if in reality he'll probably just lick and greet the culprit. I'm still grappling with the decision when I hear the door close and my dad returns.

"Have you found your Lord and Savior?" Dad asks me.

"Like, in the kitchen?"

A smile breaks out on his face. "Two men in suits on our doorstep, asking about my relationship with Jesus. That was definitely not on my apocalypse bingo card."

"Oh, I'll have to check mine," I reply. "I think that completes my four corners."

He chuckles and fills two glasses with water and ice. I fish out a small piece of ice from my glass and chew it. The hard crunch helps balance the nervous energy I feel.

"Well at least we don't have to worry about solicitors anymore," he says.

"I haven't gotten a call about my non-existent car's expiring warranty all day."

"To the bright side," he says and clinks my sweating glass with his.

WE GO OUTSIDE to wait for the cookies to finish baking. Pozzo pushing through behind us, and my dad and I sit on the uncomfortable bistro chairs my mom salvaged from a neighbor's trash last year. She'd sanded and spray painted them the most obnoxious yellow color that never quite seems dry so anytime you shift in the seat, it pulls your clothes a bit. Sending a jolt thinking you might have ruined your shorts, but it never does.

My dad stretches his long legs in front of him and leans back with his hands resting on the back of his head. "Do you remember when we brought Pozzo home, and we were still so sad from losing Abby?"

"Oh god…"

My dad laughs. "And Poz immediately started trying to dig her up in the backyard?"

"Oh my god, why are telling this story and why are you laughing? It was horrible. Mom was so mad."

The image plays in my head. Dirt flying in the backyard, my mom screaming, my dad dragging the wiggling puppy away.

"It was months before we could let him outside alone," he continues.

"That's a terrible story."

"No, no, it's just that," he pauses. "Here we were, so sad, and this new creature comes into our lives, knows nothing about what happened, and just makes himself at home. Just starts exploring."

As if to remind us, at the far end of the yard Pozzo's walking some sort of patterned lap like he's on a mission. The smell of cookies begins to waft onto the porch and despite my initial reservations, my stomach growls in anticipation.

"Do you think that's what's going to happen to us in the end?" I ask.

He shrugs. "I don't know. Maybe. I just wonder if there'll be anyone left to set whoever 'them' is right. To shoo them off like your mother used to do until Pozzo lost interest. Someone to defend us, for whatever it's worth."

"I can't believe it's all ending."

"Think of all the books I didn't finish."

"Oh please," I say.

"What?"

"Dad, you didn't finish them because you don't read."

"Fair enough point."

"You should feel bad for me. Think of all the things I didn't learn."

"You're setting yourself up there, kiddo," he says.

I groan. "Seriously."

"Okay, okay, not disregarding your feelings. So, like what things?"

"I'll never learn to drive."

"Overrated. Frankly, like most of adulthood, you're being spared. But I'm sure we'll come across some cars as we're walking. I promise to teach you how to drive. Plus, not like it'll be a big deal if you crash. No insurance claims."

"Dad—"

"Taxes," he cuts me off. "Bills. Oh, the bills."

"I'm being serious," I say.

"Lord, kiddo, me, too."

We sit in silence for a little while longer, the sun and moon making their daily pass of one another. I try not to focus on the fact it will be the last time I'll see it.

"I bet I'd be a great adult," I say.

He sits up straighter and pretends to straighten a non-existent tie. "Well, you certainly learned from the best."

"Oh, yeah, because you are the model citizen."

"What is that supposed to mean?" he asks.

"You eat cereal for dinner and watch cartoons."

He put his hand to his throat in mock-shock. "I am a *doctor.*"

"I guess, it's not like you perform surgery," I say and wait a beat before winking.

I know how hard he worked for his doctorate. How many people he helps, but it's still fun to tease him.

"Mental health *is* health," he says, unable to resist the bait.

"Well, you do still watch cartoons."

"*The Simpsons* is hardly a cartoon…" he says.

"An animated show? What else would you call it?"

"*The Simpsons* is a cultural institution."

I laugh. "I'd still be a good adult."

"The best." He pats my back. "We should probably check on the cookies. Maybe if we leave some outside, we'll be spared."

"Like a bribe for some kind of cosmic Santa Claus?"

He shrugs. "You've believed in crazier things."

I decide to play along. "They've gotta be really good cookies."

"I already told you, they're going to be."

"I hope you're right," I say.

He scoffs in mock offense. "I always am."

Neither of us moves.

"I miss Mom."

"Me, too, kiddo."

I take out my phone and try to call again even though no bars show up and the Wi-Fi has no signal.

Obviously, it doesn't work.

"I know we're not going," I say.

"What are you talking about? We're gonna finish making the

cookies, then pack, I'll grab the beach wagon from the attic, and we'll just pull Pozzo along."

"I just wish Mom were *here*," I repeat again, not feeling like playing along anymore.

"She would be here if she could," my dad says. "I'm sure it's killing her she can't be here."

I sniff. "I'm sure there's a joke in that," I say, wiping my nose.

"Ha," he barks. "The student becomes the teacher."

"You're the worst."

"I do not disagree."

The oven chimes and we turn in unison.

"We should get up," he says.

"Don't want them to burn," I agree.

"It would be unacceptable. After all this work."

Neither of us moves.

Pozzo lumbers over and sits in front of us, dropping a stick at our feet. A soft whine builds in the back of his throat.

"Do you think he knows?" I ask.

"That the cookies are done?"

"Ugh, dad."

"No. I think he just wants the stick thrown. And probably a cookie while we're at it." He taps my leg. "Come on."

We enter the kitchen to the loud buzzing from the stove. Pozzo begins to howl along with it and we're both turning to yell at him when the sound cuts off. The noise of a humming, living home winds down to silence. I stiffen and feel my dad do the same thing.

I shut my eyes, not wanting to confirm the suspicion tightening in my stomach.

I hear the metallic creak of the oven door and squint through slitted eyes. It's hard to see through the darkening kitchen, the only light coming from the fading rays of what is likely the last sunset.

"At least they look done," my dad says and shrugs.

Tears pour down my face before I even know they are there. Like they've been poised, waiting until I wasn't paying attention.

My dad puts one arm around me while awkwardly balancing

the cookie tray in his other hand, managing to only squeeze part of my face with his chin. But his heart is in the right place I guess.

"Oh, sweetie," he says. "Don't cry, it's okay."

"Is it?" I bury my head into his shoulder.

I hear a shout outside and Pozzo barks again. The quiet of the house amplifies everything around us, including Pozzo's nails on the tile as he approaches us in the kitchen.

"Poz," my dad warns. "Here, come on."

He pulls me toward the island and sets the baking sheet back on the stove. Pozzo dances around our feet as my dad carefully transfers the cookies to the cooling rack. With an electric buzz, the lights come back on.

"Great!" he says. "I'm going to get this second batch going then!"

"Forget about the cookies, dad," I say, nearly shouting in my attempt to get him to listen to me.

I need him to stop. To be a realistic parent right now and freak out with me and maybe join me in breaking a few plates to fight against the injustice of it all.

He looks up, head tilted to one side.

"Why? The power is on, the oven still hot, and we have enough batter for one more batch even with all we ate."

"There. Is. No. Point," I say, enunciating each word.

He shakes his head before turning to scoop more rounded mounds of dough on the cookie sheets. "Was there ever?"

I throw my hands in the air, sending Pozzo skittering out of the kitchen. "What is that supposed to mean?"

He opens his arms wide. "This, all of it. What did it ever matter? Not like that stopped us before, not sure why it would now. Come on and help me."

"Dad…" I say.

"I'm right," he says. "It's okay to admit that. I just dropped some mind-blowing psychology truth on you, and you don't want to admit it. Look kiddo, the world was going to end some day anyway. Sure, we didn't think we'd get a front-row seat to it, but at some point, this world was going to move on without us."

"But so soon?" I squeak. "And without Mom?"

He raises and lowers his shoulders. "We still have time. We can get in one more round."

"One more round of what?"

"Baking cookies before our trip. What else?"

WHEN THE POWER goes out the second time, it's gotten so late, the house plunges into complete darkness. I stay still until Dad finishes lighting the few candles we have left. The kitchen is filled with an odd smell of Christmas holly, lemons, something called *Summer Outside*, and fresh-baked cookies.

"We're lucky," he says. "They only had one minute left anyway and I bet the oven is warm enough to get the job done."

Through the flickering light I can just make out him moving the cooled cookies into an oversized zip-lock bag and starting to place the ones from the oven over to the ventilated metal rack, but instead of waiting the ten minutes my mom always insists on, he walks out carrying the rack with him.

"Where are you going?" I ask, struggling to see him in the darkened room.

"It's a beautiful night. I want to see the stars. Coming? We can pack the rest of our stuff when we come back in."

We walk out to the small part of the deck that's outside the kitchen. Pozzo scampers on tip-toes next to us. My dad puts the cooling rack on the plastic table and then sits down on the three steps leading to the back yard.

It's only been about a half hour since the last time we were outside, but it's like the whole world has transformed. I knew there were stars in the sky, obviously, but not *this many*.

"Wow," I whisper, unable to help myself.

"Guess you don't realize how much light pollution there is until it's gone."

Pozzo, giving up on the cookies, saunters down the steps and is quickly swallowed up by the darkness of the backyard. I can hear the faint movement of paws on grass, the only indication he's still out there. That he hasn't somehow disappeared before the rest of us.

"I wish my star app worked," I say, patting my pockets for my phone but realizing I'd left it somewhere inside.

"No need for Google when you have Greg-le."

"Did you seriously make that joke?" I ask him.

He laughs. "Funny 'til the end. But really, I know a thing or two about stars. That one is Orion."

He points into the void and I'm not sure exactly which one he's talking about.

"And that little group," he gestures at another seemingly random place. "Is Pleiades. The seven sisters. They are your mom's favorite constellation."

"I didn't know Mom had a favorite constellation. *Has*," I rush to correct, feeling the ping in my heart again.

"You know, it's funny, when we first started dating, we would look up at the stars and wonder about different worlds spread across the cosmos. Wondering if they were looking up at us too. The stars we see are really the past. I wonder how the universe actually looks at this moment. How many are really there. What anyone looking at Earth sees in the future."

"Deep thoughts. I just like how they twinkle."

A shooting star skips like a pebble across the sky. I fight the urge to make a wish.

"It's beautiful," I whisper.

"I'm glad we get to see it."

I pause for a moment, contemplating the myriad of emotions running through me before settling on one. "Me, too."

He leans back and I hear rustling behind me, but I can't make out what he's doing. A warm disk placed in my hand jolts my senses for a moment before I remember what it is.

As if we're doing a TikTok routine, we both take a deep breath before simultaneously biting down. The warm buttery taste mixes perfectly with the sweet chocolate. I can sense more than see the smears of melted chocolate on my palm. I lick my hand, getting every last delicious remnant.

"They're really good cookies," I say. "We would have sold out at the bake sale."

"Once we found your mom, I'd have won her back, too."

"Totally."

We pause for a second more and I decide just to say it. Why hold back? "I'm glad we made the cookies." I take a deep breath. "Even if we're the only ones who will eat them."

"Well, let it be known, at the end—"

A half laugh, half sob escapes my lips, "Dad, please don't…"

"That I was right," he finishes.

I nod. There's no point in pretenses anymore. "You were right. The best cookies ever made for the end of the world."

Recipe for End of the World Cookies
2 sticks unsalted butter (soft, not melted)
1 cup white sugar
1 cup brown sugar
2 large eggs
1 tsp baking soda
1 tsp salt
1 tsp corn starch
1 tsp vanilla
3 cups/16 oz flour
1 bag/11.5 oz chocolate chips
Chopped walnuts (optional)

In a large mixing bowl, combine butter and all sugars. Mix until uniform then add 2 eggs (one at a time), baking soda, salt, corn starch, and vanilla. Mix until uniform then add flour. Mix until firm but not sticky then fold in bag of chocolate chips and nuts.
Bake at 350 degrees for 8-10 minutes.

AUTHOR'S NOTES - KRISTIN DURFEE

AS ALWAYS, I'm so excited to be a part of this anthology. The group of author-bees who make up the Alvarium hive are gifted, imaginative, and supportive, a perfect combination of human if you ask me.

There are many different types of comedy in writing, and when the idea was kicked round for tackling humor for this installment, I had two distinct images pop into my head: *Waiting for Gadot* and *Gilmore Girls*. Possibly not the most reasonable mash-up, but the idea of quick dialogue, a story bordering on the absurd, and dry humor fits my idea of comedy to a T. I hope you agree.

~KAD

ABOUT THE AUTHORS

BRIA BURTON
PARKER FRANCIS
CHARLES A CORNELL
KEN PELHAM
DACO S. AUFFENORDE
JOHN HOPE
SCOTT MICHAEL POWERS
VERONICA H. HART
KRISTIN DURFEE

BRIA BURTON

Bria Burton lives in sunny St. Pete with her husband and son. She's an extrovert who regularly contemplates the irony that her two life passions (writing and running) are better suited for introverts. Her short fiction has appeared in over a twenty anthologies and magazines. *Little Angel Helper* and *Her Midnight Ride* earned Royal Palm Literary Awards.

NOVELLAS
The Running Girls
Little Angel Helper

STORY COLLECTION
Lance & Ringo Tails
SHORT STORY PUBLICATIONS
"The Eyes of Mona Lisa" – *The Masters Reimagined Vol. 2*
"The Bloodiest Sword is King" – *Havok*
"Journey Into the Dying Light of Stars" – *Journey Into...*
"Her Midnight Ride" – *The Prometheus Saga Vol. 2*
"The Count of the Alician Apocalypse" – *The Masters Reimagined*
"AOB" – *Return to Earth*
"Maribel's Day of Death – *About Time*
"A Dream Within A Dream" – *Journey Into…, In Shadows Written*
"The Mute Girl" – *Youth Imagination*
"Tight Pants" – *Page & Spine*
"Ticket to Heaven" – *Faith, Hope, & Fiction*
"The Wheels Must Turn" – *Broken Worlds*
"On Both Sides" – *The Prometheus Saga*
"In Line at the DMYV" – *Welcome to the Future*
"The Darkness Below" – *The Colored Lens*
"Switching" – *The Dunesteef Audio Fiction Magazine*
"Ligeia" – *Journey Into…podcast*
"This is Hollywood" – *FICTION on the WEB*

www.briaburton.com

PARKER FRANCIS

Parker Francis is the pen name of award-winning author Victor DiGenti. Together, they've written and published six novels, a collection of short stories, and six works of nonfiction. DiGenti's novels include the Windrusher trilogy of adventure-fantasies featuring a four-legged feline protagonist. Writing as Parker Francis, he penned the Quint Mitchell Mystery series, beginning with Matanzas Bay, which won the top prize in the Royal Palm Literary Awards competition. This was followed by Bring Down the Furies, a Florida Authors & Publishers Book Awards Gold Medal winner, and Hurricane Island.

His award-winning short story, The Strange Case of Lord Byron's Lover, was included in The Prometheus Saga, a collection of speculative fiction.

As a biographer and ghostwriter, Vic's also written six personal biographies and a family history for clients. These include We Were Amateur Soldiers and Music is My Ticket: The Musical Journey of Bill Prince.

Working as a writing coach and publisher (Windrusher Hall Press), Vic has also helped others bring their creations to the reading public, as he did most recently with Dr. Norman Plovnick's AIYOBI: Act in Your Own Best Interest.

www.parkerfrancis.com

CHARLES A. CORNELL

Charles A Cornell writes speculative fiction ranging from the mysterious to the macabre; blending science fiction, fantasy, alternative history and horror. He is a regular contributor to podcasts, seminars and conferences, and conducts webinars and workshops on his specialty, retro-punk fiction (Steampunk, Dieselpunk).

Charles lives in a rural English village in Lincolnshire with his wife and ginger tabby. His first published novel, *Tiger Paw*, won the 2012 Royal Palm Literary Award for Best Thriller from the Florida Writers Association.

His dieselpunk work, *DragonFly* is a retro-futuristic collision of science fiction and fantasy with a generous dash of alternative history. *DragonFly* won a 2014 Royal Palm Literary Award Bronze Medal in Science Fiction, received two prestigious Reader's Favorite Five Star Reviews, and won the 2018 Reader's Favorite Silver Medal in the Young Adult - Action category.

Charles's short stories and novellas have appeared in the anthologies, *The Prometheus Saga*, *Return To Earth*, *The Masters Reimagined Vol 2*, and *In Shadows Written*. His Prometheus Saga science fiction stories "Crystal Night" and "The Orchid Man" have both won FWA Royal Palm Literary Award Gold Medals (2016, 2018).

Visit him at CharlesACornell.com for news on his latest publications, writing projects, author signings, promotions, and giveaways; and for musings on dieselpunk and retrofuturism. Also check out his world of Steampunk at SteampunkNovels.com and the DragonFly series at DragonFly-Novels.com featuring galleries of retrofuturistic aircraft and other illustrations from DragonFly.

www.CharlesACornell.Com

KEN PELHAM

Ken Pelham's nonfiction book, Gumshoes, Fangs, Rockets, & Spies: How Literary Genres Evolve and Change Our World, won the 2021 Gold Award for history. Ken's Out of Sight, Out of Mind: A Writer's Guide to Mastering Viewpoint was named the Florida Writers Association's 2015 Published Book of the Year. His novels, Brigands Key and Place of Fear, both won 1st-place Royal Palm Literary Awards. His short stories, "The Wreck of the Edinburgh Kate," "When the Hurly Burly's Done," and "The Medusa Jump," all have won Royal Palms.

Ken lives with his wife, Laura, in Maitland, Florida. He is the leader of Maitland Writers Group, and a member of *International* Thriller Writers and the Florida Writers Association.

NOVELS
Brigands Key
Place of Fear
NONFICTION BOOKS
Gumshoes, Fangs, Rockets, & Spies: How Literary Genres Evolve and Change Our World
(2021 Royal Palm Literary Award, Gold, for History)
Out of Sight, Out of Mind: A Writer's Guide to Mastering Viewpoint
(2015 Florida Writers Association Published Book of the Year)
Great Danger: A Writer's Guide to Building Suspense
SHORT STORY COLLECTIONS
Treacherous Bastards: Stories of Suspense, Deceit, and Skullduggery
A Double Shot of Fright: Two Tales of Terror
Tales of Old Brigands Key

www.kenpelham.com

DACO S. AUFFENORDE

Born at the Naval hospital in Bethesda, Maryland and raised in Huntsville "Rocket City", Alabama, Daco holds a B.A. and M.A.S. from The University of Alabama in Huntsville and a J.D. from the Cumberland School of Law. She is a member of the International Thriller Writers, Mystery Writers of America, Romance Writers of America, Author's Guild, Society of Childrens Writers and Illustrators, and the Alabama State Bar.

NOVELS
Cover Your Tracks
Electromancer

SHORT STORIES

The Pisces Affair
The Virgo Affair
The Alexandrite Necklace
The Adventures of Electromancer:
Mayor Bobby Baumgartner is Spitting Mad
The Adventures of Electromancer:
Charged Up at the Kensington County Fair
The Adventures of Electromancer:
The Reddies are Coming! The Reddies are Coming!:
The Light Fantastic

www.authordaco.com

JOHN HOPE

John Hope is an award-winning short story, children's book, middle grade, young adult, and nonfiction writer. His work appears in paperback, hardback, audiobook, and multiple short story collections. He gives informational and inspirational presentations to schools, conferences, and is a board member of the Florida Writers Association. John loves to travel and play games with his wife, Jaime, and two rambunctious kids.

CHILDREN'S PICTURE BOOKS
*Frozen Floppies**— Story of Unlikely Friendships
Floppyopolis—Story of Taking Pride in the Community
Watch the Butterfly—Story of Learning Patience
The Band Aid—Story of Understanding/Dealing with Grief

MIDDLE GRADE / YOUNG ADULT
Silencing Sharks*—*Fantasy/Adventure Story of Heroism*
No Good*—*Historical Fiction Story of Acceptance*
Pankyland*—*Adventure Story of Friendship*
Pankyland 2: The Movie—*Adventure Story of Sibling Rivalry*

BOOKS FOR ADULTS
Colby in the Crosshairs*—*Poignant Story of Child Abuse*
John's Shorts Vol 1* & 2*—*Collections of Short Stories*
Lake Mary, Images of America—*History of a Small Town*
* Indicates winner of one or more awards

www.johnhopewriting.com

SCOTT MICHAEL POWERS

Scott is a national award-winning journalist based in Orlando, Florida, who, in the demise of the newspaper industry, has turned to his first dream, writing fiction. His first novel, The Roswell Swatch, was published in late 2016, receiving rave reader reviews. His second, The Murder Plague, is undergoing pre-publication editing. His third, under the working title The Space Coast Out-Of-This-World News & Herald Tribune, is nearly completed.

Scott's work uses minor elements of science fiction and speculative fiction to power contemporary action-adventure dramas. One review called The Roswell Swatch a "white-knuckle thriller with a splash of science fiction," while another observed, "Sometimes sci-fi books can get way out there...this book kept everything within the realm of believability," and another touted its "very creative plot with characters that jumped off the page."

Scott and his wife Connie happily live in a quiet Orlando neighborhood that has lots of big trees, and cops for neighbors. His midlife crisis didn't result in a muscle car (though he's still keeping a delusional eye out for a '71 Plymouth Roadrunner to show up in the driveway). Yet it did cause him to go back to his rock 'n' roll roots and start wearing hats again, as he did back when Billy Jack was as cool a look as it got.

He can be reached at scottmichaelpowers@yahoo.com, or on Facebook, at **www.facebook.com/ScottMichaelPowers/**

VERONICA H. HART

Veronica lives with her retired veterinarian/author husband, Robert, in Ormond Beach, Florida. They settled there after spending the major part of their lives traveling, living, and working in various areas of the world. Between them, they have six daughters and eleven grandchildren who keep their minds active trying to remember birthdays and anniversaries.

NOVELS

Boy Comes Home *
The Prince of Keegan Bay *– Blenders Book I
The Swimming Corpse – Blenders Book II
Safari Stew – Blenders Book III
Midnight in Mongolia – Blenders Book IV
Silent Autumn *
Escape from Iran *
Elena – the Girl with the Piano *
The Reluctant Daughters

SHORT STORY PUBLICATIONS
Alvarium Experiment Anthology Publications:
Storey's Orphans
Annie Karenina
Recovery
* Winner of one or more awards

www.veronicahhart.com

KRISTIN DURFEE

Kristin Durfee is the author of MASS (Orange Blossom Publishing), The Four Corners Trilogy (Black Opal Books), and short stories appearing in several Thriller, Speculative, and Contemporary. Anthologies for adults.

She lives in Central Florida and when not enjoying the sun with her husband, son, and two quirky dogs, you can usually find her on a run, horseback ride, or wandering around a theme park.

She is a member of the Florida Writers Association.

www.kristindurfee.com

THE ALVARIUM EXPERIMENT
ANTHOLOGIES

THE LIGHT FANTASTIC

RETURN TO EARTH

THE MASTERS REIMAGINED

THE MASTERS REIMAGINED 2

THE PROMETHEUS SAGA

THE PROMETHEUS SAGA 2

www.ingramcontent.com/pod-product-compliance
Lightning Source LLC
Chambersburg PA
CBHW020235260626
47156CB00002B/689